THE
RESCUED

Center Point
Large Print

Also by Marta Perry and available from Center Point Large Print:

Pleasant Valley Novels
Naomi's Christmas

The Lost Sisters of Pleasant Valley Novels
Lydia's Hope

Watcher in the Dark Novels
Home by Dark
Search the Dark
Abandon the Dark

Keepers of the Promise Novels
The Forgiven

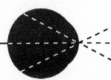

**This Large Print Book carries the
Seal of Approval of N.A.V.H.**

THE RESCUED

Keepers of the Promise
—Book Two—

MARTA PERRY

CENTER POINT LARGE PRINT
THORNDIKE, MAINE

This Center Point Large Print edition is published in the year 2015 by arrangement with The Berkley Publishing Group, an imprint of Penguin Publishing Group, a division of Penguin Random House LLC.

The text of this Large Print edition is unabridged. In other aspects, this book may vary from the original edition. Printed in the United States of America on permanent paper. Set in 16-point Times New Roman type.

ISBN: 978-1-62899-624-1

Library of Congress Cataloging-in-Publication Data

Perry, Marta.
The rescued / Marta Perry. — Center Point Large Print edition.
pages cm
Summary: "As an Amish wife and mother struggles to hold her family together, a story from the past teaches her how to face her daily challenges with strength and love"—Provided by publisher.
ISBN 978-1-62899-624-1 (library binding : alk. paper)
1. Large type books. I. Title.
PS3616.E7933R47 2015b
813'.6—dc23
                                        2015011750

This story is dedicated to my grandson, Tyler.
And, as always, to Brian.

LIST OF CHARACTERS

Present Day:
Judith Wegler, wife of Isaac Wegler; their children: Levi, 8, Paul, 6, and Noah, 3
Joseph Wegler, Isaac's brother, 14
Simon Wegler, Isaac's uncle; Emma, his deceased wife
Rebecca Lapp Fisher, Judith's cousin; her children: Katie, 7, and Joshua, 5
Matthew Byler, engaged to Rebecca
Elizabeth Lapp, Judith's grandmother
Barbara "Barbie" Lapp, Judith's cousin

Lancaster County, 1953:
Mattie Lapp, widow of Benjamin Lapp; their children: Rachel, 14, Nathaniel, 9, Toby, 7, and Anna, 5
Adam Lapp, cousin of Benjamin, widower
Becky Lapp, Mattie's mother-in-law
Jonah Lapp, Mattie's father-in-law
Bishop Thomas Beiler, bishop of the church district

GLOSSARY OF PENNSYLVANIA DUTCH WORDS AND PHRASES

ach. oh; used as an exclamation

agasinish. stubborn; self-willed

ain't so. A phrase commonly used at the end of a sentence to invite agreement.

alter. old man

anymore. Used as a substitute for "nowadays."

Ausbund. Amish hymnal. Used in the worship services, it contains traditional hymns, words only, to be sung without accompaniment. Many of the hymns date from the sixteenth century.

befuddled. mixed up

blabbermaul. talkative one

blaid. bashful

boppli. baby

bruder. brother

bu. boy

buwe. boys

daadi. daddy

Da Herr sei mit du. The Lord be with you.

denke. thanks (or *danki*)

Englischer. one who is not Plain

ferhoodled. upset; distracted

ferleicht. perhaps

frau. wife

fress. eat

gross. big

grossdaadi. grandfather

grossdaadi haus. An addition to the farmhouse, built for the grandparents to live in once they've "retired" from actively running the farm.

grossmutter. grandmother

gut. good

hatt. hard; difficult

haus. house

hinnersich. backward

ich. I

ja. yes

kapp. Prayer covering, worn in obedience to the Biblical injunction that women should pray with their heads covered. Kapps are made of Swiss organdy and are white. (In some Amish communities, unmarried girls thirteen and older wear black kapps during worship service.)

kinder. kids (or *kinner*)

komm. come

komm schnell. come quick

Leit. the people; the Amish

lippy. sassy

maidal. old maid; spinster

mamm. mother

middaagesse. lunch

mind. remember

onkel. uncle

Ordnung. The agreed-upon rules by which the Amish community lives. When new practices become an issue, they are discussed at length among the leadership. The decision for or against innovation is generally made on the basis of maintaining the home and family as separate from the world. For instance, a telephone might be necessary in a shop in order to conduct business but would be banned from the home because it would intrude on family time.

Pennsylvania Dutch. The language is actually German in origin and is primarily a spoken language. Most Amish write in English, which results in many variations in spelling when the dialect is put into writing! The language probably originated in the south of Germany but is common also among the Swiss Mennonite and French Huguenot immigrants to Pennsylvania. The language was brought to America prior to the Revolution and is still in use today. High German is used for Scripture and church documents, while English is the language of commerce.

rumspringa. Running-around time. The late teen years when Amish youth taste some aspects of the outside world before deciding to be baptized into the church.

schnickelfritz. mischievous child
ser gut. very good (or *sehr gut*)
tastes like more. delicious
Was ist letz? What's the matter?
Wie bist du heit. How are you; said in greeting
wilkom. welcome
Wo bist du? Where are you?

THE
RESCUED

CHAPTER ONE

Judith Wegler suspected that, once again, she'd be acting as a buffer between her husband and his young brother. From the back porch of the farmhouse, where she was polishing the oak study table that was her gift from Grossmammi Lapp, she could hear Isaac calling Joseph's name. Since there was no answer, almost-fourteen-year-old Joseph must have slipped away again.

Isaac appeared around the corner of the corn-crib, and Judith rose when he strode toward her. At thirty, Isaac was as sturdy and strong as he'd been when she'd tumbled into love with him so many years ago. His corn-silk hair had darkened to a deep honey color, and the beard he'd grown when they married made him look mature, but his eyes were as bright a blue as ever under the brim of his summer straw hat.

She ought to enjoy the sight of him, instead of feeling the familiar tightening of the stomach she always experienced at the prospect of intervening on behalf of the boy she'd raised as her own since she and Isaac married when his little brother was only five. The sixteen years between the two brothers sometimes seemed an insurmountable barrier.

Not that it was unusual for an Amish family to be spread out over that many years. It was unusual, though, for only the youngest and oldest to have survived. The siblings who'd come in between them had perished with Isaac's parents in the tragic fire Isaac never mentioned.

"Have you seen Joseph?" Isaac's voice was tart with the irritation that was too often there lately when he spoke of his brother.

"Not since after lunch. He went out to the barn to fix that broken board in Rosie's stall." The buggy horse had a talent for finding a loose rail and leaning against it until it broke. "Did you check there?"

"It wouldn't take him this long to fix a board."

Frowning, Isaac stepped up to the porch, using it as a vantage point to survey the pastures and cornfields of the dairy farm, still lush and green in the August sunshine thanks to a recent rain. The fields stretched along the valley, and the ground rose gently to encompass the orchard and, beyond it, the wooded ridge.

"Ach, the boy's becoming less responsible the older he gets. What's the matter with him these days?"

Isaac clearly didn't expect an answer, but she gave him one anyway. "Joseph is growing up. My brothers all went through a ferhoodled spell when they were his age." She didn't bother to compare Joseph to Isaac, since everyone knew

Isaac seemed to have been born responsible.

"It'll be time for milking before long. If he's not back by then—"

"He'll show up soon." She spoke quickly and prayed she was right. When Isaac and Joseph butted heads, as they did too often lately, everyone in the family became upset. "See how nice this study table is looking. You were right. All it needed was a good cleaning and a few coats of furniture wax."

That distracted him, as she'd hoped it might. Isaac ran his hand around the smooth edges of the rectangular table, large enough for four or even six young scholars to sit and do homework on a winter's evening.

"It's a good, sturdy oak piece, that's certain-sure. Did your grossmammi say who it came from?"

"She didn't seem to remember, but she said she'd look it up for me. It was thoughtful of her to give it to us."

Thoughtful and a bit more, Judith thought. She and two of her cousins had helped to clear out their grandmother's house this spring when she'd moved in with her son. Long recognized as the historian of the Lapp family, Grossmammi had been eager to pass on the family stories to them, and part of that passing on had included choosing a piece of furniture for each of them to cherish.

Grossmammi believed that the piece of family

heritage each one received had something to give them in return. That had certainly been true for Judith's cousin Rebecca. The dower chest given to Rebecca had contained a diary from a young Amish girl who'd lived during the Second World War, and Rebecca often said how much she'd learned from that story. It had given her the strength and courage she'd needed for a new future, and that had been a wonderful fine gift.

"The person who crafted this piece made it to last." Isaac pulled on the shallow drawers under the tabletop. Two of them slid out easily, but the third wouldn't open.

"I wanted to ask you about that drawer," Judith said. "I can't tell if it's locked or stuck."

A glance over Isaac's shoulder told her that the cows had started toward the gate, crossing the field in a long, straggly line, their udders full and swaying. They knew when it was time to be milked, even if Joseph had forgotten. There was still no sign of him.

Isaac stooped to look underneath the table, giving it the same careful attention he granted to everything he did. "Locked, I'd say. Better ask your grossmammi about a key. I wouldn't want to damage it by forcing it open." He rose as he spoke, and she could almost feel his attention shifting back to the job at hand.

But at last she spied Joseph, flying down the

lane on the scooter he used the way she'd seen Englisch boys use their skateboards, with what seemed a reckless disregard for anything that might send them head over heels. Sometimes she wished their community allowed bicycles, the way some Amish out in Ohio did. But probably, boys being boys, Joseph would still find a way to court danger on it.

"Here comes Joseph," she said quickly. "And your onkel is walking over. I'll call Levi and Paul—"

"No need," Isaac said, nodding toward the orchard, the apple trees bending with fruit that would be ready to pick soon. "Here they come now. Levi would never miss a milking time, that's certain-sure."

If there was a tiny bit of pride in Isaac's voice, she couldn't blame him. At eight, their Levi seemed a natural-born farmer, having followed his daadi around since he could toddle. Paul, six, just wanted to do whatever his brother did. Even now, she spotted him running, trying to keep up with Levi's longer legs as they raced down the slope from the orchard.

Isaac took the porch steps in one long stride, glancing without speaking toward his brother as Joseph jumped from the scooter and let it topple over into the grass. *Please, don't scold him,* Judith said silently. *He's here, isn't he?*

And if Isaac took Joseph to task, the rest of

them would be subjected to their glares at each other over the supper table.

"You're here. Let's get the cows in." There was an edge to Isaac's voice, and she prayed Joseph wouldn't flare up in response.

Thankfully, Joseph just nodded and sprinted off toward the pasture gate. She could see Levi put on a burst of speed at the sight of him and smiled. Paul might want to be like Levi, but in turn, Levi tended to copy Joseph. A good thing, as long as he didn't copy everything Joseph did.

Thinking of Joseph, she remembered something she had to ask her husband. "Is Saturday all right for Joseph's fourteenth birthday celebration? I want to be sure your cousins and onkel know."

Isaac seemed to freeze for an instant. And then he was moving. "Do what you want about it." He slung the words over his shoulder and strode off without looking back.

Judith tried not to let the hurt take over at his response. How could Isaac act as if Joseph's birthday was no concern of his? Naturally they would have a family party for the boy, as they did every year, for everyone's birthday. The relatives would find it wonderful strange if they didn't.

From the house behind her, Judith heard the thud of small feet on the stairs. At three, their Noah still needed a nap some days, and this had been one of them. She'd found him nearly asleep in his wagon and had carried him off to his bed, cherishing those moments when he'd clung to her like a little monkey. Sometimes she wished she could turn back the clock to a simpler time in their lives, when Noah was still a baby and Joseph was Isaac's good right hand, looking up to him as the big brother he adored.

Things had begun to change over the past year or two, so slowly at first that she had hardly noticed it happening, until she woke up to see that Isaac and Joseph were at odds most of the time, and more and more often she was the buffer between them, hurt by this estrangement separating those she loved.

If only Isaac would talk to her about it—but he didn't. He tightened his lips, put on a stoic face, and closed her off entirely from his inner feelings.

When she'd dreamed of their married life, this isolation hadn't been part of it. Surely married couples were supposed to share their feelings, their hurts, and their joys. Wasn't that what two being made one meant?

Isaac was a good man. They had a fine life on the family dairy farm, and they'd been blessed with Joseph and three healthy kinder of their own. Maybe that should be enough for her. Maybe she shouldn't be longing for a closeness Isaac wasn't willing to give.

Noah came running, bursting through the screen door, already chattering away, as always.

She lifted him in a quick hug, knowing he'd wiggle to be down and busy in an instant.

She was blessed, she repeated to herself, hugging the warm, wriggly little body. But at times like this she began to wonder if the gossip had been right—the things folks said when Isaac married her so abruptly before she had even turned twenty.

They'd said Isaac had needed to find a sensible, mature wife in a hurry when the aunt who'd taken care of Joseph had died. That he'd done what was expected of him and found a suitable girl to marry. That, as she'd heard his uncle say, he had settled down with Judith instead of chasing after romance and moonshine.

Perhaps she was as guilty as Isaac was of keeping her inner life hidden, because that was the one thing she could never, never tell him.

She stroked the surface of the study table again. Maybe the story of the woman who'd once owned it would have something to teach her. Could the stories of the past really reach out and touch her life today, or was that merely superstition on Grossmammi's part? If it was true, she longed for the lesson that would assure her of Isaac's love, but she couldn't imagine how that might come.

On a dairy farm, milking time took plenty of hands. Isaac strode toward the tie-stall barn, catching up with Onkel Simon, who had cut across the field from his place next door. These days his uncle farmed only vegetables for the local produce auction, but he seemed to enjoy working with the dairy cows. Reminded him of when he was growing up, he always said.

"Young Paul is getting to be a big help." His uncle's lean face creased in a smile as the boy hurried after the last of the black-and-white Holsteins.

"His mamm doesn't like him taking on too much yet." Isaac couldn't help smiling as well, liking the way his boys seemed to share his love for the big, placid animals. "But he's following in Levi's footsteps, that's certain-sure."

The Holsteins knew, as well as they did, what the barn was for. They stood patiently at their usual ties to be cleaned and attached to the milking machines, and with the four of them working, it didn't take long. Paul hovered on the sidelines, obviously eager to plunge right in, but Judith was right. His hands were still too small to handle the job.

Isaac darted a glance toward Joseph, but the boy was doing his work deftly, even if his thoughts were elsewhere. He mulled over what Judith had said about her brothers at that age. Hard to believe, now that they were all grown men, but he supposed they'd gotten into plenty of foolishness when they were in their teens. He hadn't had that luxury, and he hadn't wanted it.

His gaze caught his uncle leaning against Daisy, the oldest of the Holsteins. "Was ist letz? Is anything wrong, Onkel Simon?"

"Ach, no." Simon straightened. "Just having a word or two with old Daisy here. How is she treating the newcomers?"

"She showed them who was boss right away, didn't you, Daisy?" Isaac smiled, but his mind scurried after the decision he'd made to enlarge the herd. Forty cows was a fairly good size for an Amish dairy operation, but he'd decided to go to forty-five this year, thinking it would up the milk production so he'd be sure of fulfilling the new contract with the milk company.

"Gut, gut." His uncle patted the animal, and he gave Isaac an inquiring look. "Not worried about the contract, are you?"

"No, not at all." Isaac figured Simon knew that wasn't entirely true, but he'd go along with it. "Everything's going fine."

It was, wasn't it? He could hear the milk hissing into the steel milk tank and the soft swish as the blade turned evenly, stirring it.

Onkel Simon would also know how much money Isaac had sunk into the dairy farm over the years. It wasn't easy to make an operation like this one successful, but Isaac had done what his daad would have wanted. And eventually the dairy farm would pass into Joseph's hands, also as Daad had wanted.

The comfortable sound of the blade in the milk tank halted, and Isaac froze, his breath catching. Before he could speak the blade had started again, the movement steady. Just a little glitch, maybe in the power from the diesel generator. Nothing to worry about.

"You boys have it easier than we did when I was young." Onkel Simon loved to reminisce, and Isaac thought it was good for the young ones to hear him.

"You didn't have milk machines, right, Onkel Simon?" Levi picked up the hint, responding quickly. "Or the big milk tank, either?"

"That's so, Levi. Many's the morning I'd be leaning against the cow's side trying to get my hands warm enough to do the milking."

"What did you do with the milk?" Paul asked. "Was it in buckets?"

"Buckets, that's right." Onkel Simon smiled at him, pleased with their interest even though they'd no doubt heard the story before. "It's a good sound, hearing the milk pour into the buckets, seeing it steam in the cold air on a winter morning."

"Tell about the dog," Levi begged, as if his great-uncle's tale were a favorite storybook.

"Shep would sit right next to the cow with his eyes on me. He knew every once in a while I'd squirt the milk into his mouth. He didn't want to be caught by surprise and have it hit his nose."

The boys giggled, as they were intended to. Not hearing anything from Joseph, Isaac glanced his way to find the boy leaning against a post, gaze fixed on space.

"Joseph! There's work to be done instead of daydreaming." His voice was sharp, and Joseph jerked upright, giving his brother a look filled with resentment. He turned away to begin detaching the cows that were done.

"Ach, Isaac, there's no need to be so sharp with the boy," his uncle said quietly. "All teenage boys are dreamers at that age."

"I wasn't." He clamped his lips together, regretting the words and the tone. Onkel Simon didn't speak, but he had to be thinking, as Isaac was, of a farmhouse blazing up like a torch against the dark sky, of the pain . . .

Isaac shut the image away. He couldn't think about it, couldn't talk about it.

His uncle respected the silence for a long moment, and when he spoke, his voice was soft. "Are you so sure it's the right thing, training Joseph to take over the dairy farm?"

"It was what my father wanted." That ended the discussion as far as Isaac was concerned.

"He wanted what he thought was going to be best at the time," Onkel Simon said. "He thought he'd have you established on a farm of your own, and that when he was ready to retire to the grossdaadi haus he would build next to the farmhouse, Joseph would be old enough to take over this place. If he'd lived—"

"He didn't." The words were harsh in Isaac's throat. Daad didn't, and Mamm didn't, and the girls didn't. Only he and Joseph were left, and he had to carry out what had been his father's wishes. "I have to do what Daad would have done."

Onkel Simon looked as if he were about to say more, but instead he closed his mouth and shook his head slowly.

Much as Isaac loved and respected his uncle, he had to decide this for himself. Joseph was his responsibility, just as Judith and the boys were. He had failed to save his family, but he wouldn't —he couldn't—fail at fulfilling his father's dreams.

"With school starting in a couple of weeks, your kinder must be getting as excited as mine are, ain't so?" Rebecca Fisher, Judith's widowed cousin, set a warm pan of apple crisp on the table between Judith and their grandmother in her tidy kitchen.

"Always a happy time for the kinder. And for their mamm's, too, I sometimes think." Gross-mammi smiled and began to dish up the apple crisp while Rebecca poured coffee.

"Paul especially," Judith said, thinking of her middle son's excitement. "He's been marking off

27

the days on the calendar, trying to make school come faster." She had brought Paul and Noah with her on this afternoon visit to her cousin, but Levi had wanted to stay home and help with some new fencing. Her kinder were outside now, engrossed in some game with Rebecca's two.

Judith had been delighted to find Grossmammi here when she arrived. Since Elizabeth Lapp had moved in with her son, Rebecca's daad, on the farm next door to Rebecca's place, they were seeing much more of her. And their grandmother seemed happier, too. Much as she'd hated to leave the house where she had spent all of her married life, it had become too much for her to care for, and Rebecca's parents had been wonderful glad to have her with them.

"Fall is a time of new beginnings, just like spring is." Grossmammi put cream into her coffee and then poured a bit over her apple crisp. "Especially for Rebecca and Matthew." She sent a twinkling glance toward Rebecca.

"For sure?" Happiness bubbled up in Judith. "Have you and Matt set a date?"

Rebecca nodded, her normally serene oval face glowing with happiness. "Don't tell anyone," she cautioned. "But we're planning on the last Thursday in October for the wedding."

"Ach, that's wonderful gut news." Judith rounded the table to hug her cousin. Along with their cousin Barbie, they were the only women in their generation of the Lapp family, and that made them as close as sisters in some ways. "See how wrong you were to think you'd never love again?"

"I knew you'd tease me about that," Rebecca said, returning the hug with a strong clasp. "At least you're not as bad as Barbie. If she's not teasing me, she's kidding Matt, threatening to spill the beans to everyone."

"Everyone will know anyway," Judith said. Sometimes she thought people in their close-knit Amish community knew too much about each other, but that was a part of being Amish. "Even though we'll all pretend not to have noticed anything about the two of you right up to the Sunday the wedding is published in church."

The announcement of forthcoming weddings in worship was a high point in the Amish year, coming as it did after the fall communion. All the couples who were being married would be absent from church on publishing Sunday, staying home to have a quiet meal together. It was another of the many traditions that bound them as a community, like a coverlet tightly woven of many strands to make it warm and strong.

"At least by then the farm-stay visitors will be slowing down," Rebecca said. "Once the weather turns, not many people will want to come. We'll have plenty of time for our wedding visits."

Rebecca had reopened the house to Englisch visitors this summer, with help from Barbie and the rest of the family. It hadn't been easy to do it without her husband, but Rebecca had surprised a lot of people by her strength. And now she would have a new husband to help her, too, come October.

It was the custom for the newly married couple to spend the weekends after the wedding visiting family and friends together. The fact that Rebecca had been married before and had two kinder wouldn't alter that tradition. Matt must be introduced to her family and friends as her spouse.

"If you need me to watch the children for you, or help with the wedding arrangements, or anything at all . . ."

"Ach, I know that." Rebecca leaned across the table to clasp Judith's hands, her green eyes filled with laughter. "Who else would I call on but my dear cousins? I don't want Mamm and Daad to do too much, especially with Daad still recovering from his heart attack. But I knew I could count on you. And I certain-sure want you to be the sidesitters for my wedding, you and Barbie."

Judith blinked back a tear or two. "I would be so happy. And Barbie, too, I'm sure."

Knowing their younger cousin as she did, she suspected she'd have to keep a close eye on Barbie to be certain she wasn't planning any jokes. Pert, lively, and a bit of a rebel, Barbie delighted in introducing something different into the traditional. Judith would probably need to remind Barbie several times that the newehocker, or side-sitter, was there to support the bride, not to unnerve her.

"We've decided that Matthew will move in here," Rebecca went on, her mind obviously on her intended, not on her cousins. "He's not needed as much at his aunt and uncle's now that his cousin has come home, and since his furniture business is here, that makes the most sense."

It had been the defection of Matt's cousin to the Englisch world that had brought Matthew home to Brook Hill, Pennsylvania, from his life out west. In turn, Matt had gone after Isaiah and brought him back to those who loved him. And through Matt's return, Rebecca had found a second chance to love and be loved. God did work in mysterious ways.

Judith glanced at her grandmother to find her faded blue eyes reflecting back the shared happiness. Grossmammi, with her plump little figure and her face wrinkled like one of last season's apples, always seemed to know what people were thinking.

"Ach, where is my mind?" Grossmammi exclaimed. "I brought something for you, Judith. And I don't remember—"

"Is this it?" Rebecca reached into the basket on

the table and pulled out a small key, suspended from a faded cord.

"That's it." The worry on Grossmammi's face smoothed out. "Here is the key to the drawers on the desk I gave you. Once I remembered whose desk it had been, I knew I had the key somewhere."

Judith took the small, tarnished key, and a little wave of anticipation moved through her. "Denke. Who did the study table belong to? Someone I know?"

Grossmammi shook her head. "I don't think so. Her name was Mattie Lapp, and that was back when the family hadn't left Lancaster County yet. Her kinder would have done their schoolwork around that table."

Mattie Lapp. Judith turned the name over in her mind, trying to remember any story Grossmammi had told them about someone named Mattie. But nothing came to mind.

"Do you remember her?" she asked.

"A little," Grossmammi said. "She was enough older than me that we didn't meet often, and she was in a different church district." Grossmammi's forehead creased in a frown. "Those were difficult days for the Amish with children because of all the changes in the schools—that I do remember."

Judith's thoughts slipped immediately to Joseph. "Sometimes I think all days are difficult when the kinder hit their teen years."

"Boys especially reach an age when they're likely to cause problems." Grossmammi's wise gaze rested on Judith's face. "Like Joseph, ain't so?"

As serious as it was, Judith couldn't help but smile. "Is there anything you don't know?"

"Ach, I can see the worry on your face no matter how you try to hide it. Since it's not the younger boys, it must be Joseph."

"You can tell us." Rebecca's green eyes clouded with concern. "He's almost fourteen, isn't he? I remember how my brothers were at that age. Always doing something foolish, and turning my mother's hair gray."

"My brothers were just as bad," Judith said, relieved to get her worries out in the open. "I told Isaac that, but he doesn't seem to understand."

"No, he wouldn't." Remembered sorrow touched their grandmother's face. "He was a bit older than Joseph is now when his parents and sisters died. Ach, that was a terrible night. No wonder it turned Isaac so serious."

Rebecca nodded. "I remember about the fire, that's certain-sure, but I guess I never thought about how it would affect Isaac after so long. Still, Joseph always seems like a good boy. He can't be up to anything all that bad."

"I know." Judith turned her spoon over and over in her fingers. "But he's taken to going off and not telling us where he is, and that upsets Isaac.

He keeps saying the boy is out of school now, and it's time he took on more responsibility for the dairy farm."

"Where do you think Joseph is going?" Grossmammi put the question softly, seeming sure Judith would be able to figure it out.

But she couldn't. She frowned. "It's just guessing, but I'm thinking he likes to get off on his own. He loves the boys like brothers, but you know how noisy they can be, and they're always after him to do something with them. Joseph is quieter by nature, I think."

She'd expended as much love and time in trying to figure out Joseph as she had on her own boys. After all, he was her son, too, in every way that counted.

Rebecca nodded. "My boy is like that, as well. Sometimes I think Katie just wears him out with all her talking. It's funny that siblings can be so different from one another."

"All I can do is try to understand, and try to explain it to Isaac." Tears stung Judith's eyes, and she blinked them back. Goodness, if she started crying, they'd think something serious was wrong. She managed a smile. "Isaac and Joseph remind me of two rams butting heads. I'm always trying to keep them from exploding at each other."

"Of course you are," Rebecca said warmly. "You love them both."

"And you have always been the peacemaker."
Grossmammi patted her hand. "From the time
you could walk, you've been trying to keep
everyone happy."

Grossmammi almost made it sound like a
fault.

"It's natural to want your family to be happy
and at peace with one another." She suspected
she sounded defensive.

Grossmammi gave her a fond look, shaking her
head a little. "Ach, Judith, you must know that
happiness is the one thing you can't give anyone
else, no matter how much you love them. We
each must find it for ourselves, and usually we do
so when we're not looking for it."

Rebecca seemed to be considering the words,
maybe filing them away in her heart. But Judith
recognized an instant of denial in herself. Surely,
when you loved enough, you could bring others
happiness.

"It can't be wrong to try and keep peace
between Isaac and Joseph. If only I can stop them
from saying hurtful things to each other . . ." She
let that trail off, because her grandmother was
shaking her head again.

"You want to be a buffer between them. I
understand." Grossmammi patted her hand. "The
trouble with being a buffer is that you can end
up being hurt by both sides."

Judith wanted to deny it. Wanted to say that it

wasn't so, that Isaac and Joseph would never willingly cause her pain.

But she couldn't, because she feared her grandmother was right. And if she was, Judith didn't know what to do.

CHAPTER TWO

Judith cut into the peach pie she'd made for dessert that evening with a certain amount of relief. Isaac and Joseph had been silent during supper, but at least they hadn't been quarreling. Some days that was all she could hope for.

Besides, the three boys made enough noise among them that the silence hadn't been noticeable. Levi, from his vast experience of having completed two grades in school, had been giving Paul advice about what to do and what not to do in first grade.

"Remember to take something for Teacher Sally on the first day of school," he said, "or she won't like you."

"Levi!" Judith gave him a stern frown. "It's not nice to try and scare your brother with such stories."

"But, Mammi, you always send something for the teacher on the first day," he protested. "Remember, I took oatmeal cookies last year, because that was Teacher Sally's favorite."

"Teacher Sally will like you whether you bring her something or not." She spoke firmly and fought to suppress a smile at Levi's expression. "It's just nice to take something on the first day to show the teacher you appreciate her."

Paul's eyes went wide. "But if Levi already took oatmeal cookies, there's nothing left for me to take."

"Ach, don't be so silly, the pair of you." She glanced at Isaac, inviting him to share her amusement, but he was staring down into his cup as if he'd never seen coffee before, not heeding their conversation at all. "I happen to know that Teacher Sally loves apples, so you can take her a nice apple. You can even rub it with a dish towel to make it bright and shiny."

"That sounds wonderful gut, Mammi." Paul, his worries forgotten, dug his fork into his peach pie. "Yum. I love pie."

"I like cake even better," Levi said. "But this is sehr gut." He demolished a large bite.

"You'll have cake on Saturday for Joseph's birthday, remember? We're having a party for him, and I'll make a cake. And Cousin Barbie said she'd bring some of those doughnuts you like."

"What kind of cake? Chocolate?" Levi asked hopefully.

"Whatever kind Joseph wants," she said. "It's his birthday, after all."

"Please say chocolate," Levi pleaded, while Paul and Noah nodded.

Joseph came out of his distraction to smile at them. "Maybe yellow cake this year," he teased. "What do you think?"

"No, chocolate, chocolate," Levi chanted.

"Ja, all right." Joseph gave in, as they'd known he would. "Chocolate, please, Judith."

"There now, are you happy?" she said. She rose to gather up dessert plates. "Who wants to help me bake the cake?"

Silence greeted that suggestion, as she'd anticipated. The boys were happy to help make Christmas cookies every year, but in the summer, the last thing they wanted was to be stuck in the kitchen.

"We should have a girl in the family," Paul said finally. "If Noah had been a girl baby, he would have helped."

"Dummy," Levi said. "If Noah had been a girl, he'd be a she."

"Don't call your brother names," she said automatically, wondering how many times she'd say that before the boys were grown.

"I'm not a girl baby," Noah wailed. "I'm not."

"Of course you're not. Levi is being silly." Judith smoothed her hand over his silky blond curls. Noah was the only one of the boys to have inherited her curly hair. At least he wouldn't have the struggle of trying to make it stay smooth under a kapp.

"Stop the silliness, all of you," Isaac ordered. His tone was so sharp that all of them stared at him. He shoved his chair back, his face reddening. "That's enough about Joseph's birthday."

Joseph shot up from his chair, the quarrel rising so suddenly that Judith had no chance to divert it. "Why don't you tell them the truth?" he snapped. "You don't want me to have a birthday at all because it reminds you of what happened on yours."

Isaac's face went from red to white in an instant. Judith saw a question in Levi's face and put her hand over his lips before he had a chance to blurt it out, even as her mind whirled.

Isaac shoved back his chair so hard that it clattered against the counter. He stumbled toward the door almost blindly, it seemed.

"Isaac . . ." she began, but it was too late. He'd already slammed his way out of the house.

"I'm s . . . sorry." Joseph was nearly as pale as Isaac had been, and he stammered the words. "I shouldn't have said it. I'm sorry." And in his turn he rushed out of the house.

Thoughts tumbled in Judith's mind like pebbles tossed in a rushing stream. What happened on Isaac's birthday . . . That could only mean one thing, because only one thing could make Isaac react in such a way. The fire that killed the rest of his family must have actually occurred on Isaac's birthday.

She should have known. But how could she, if no one told her and Isaac refused to talk about it? Her chest was so tight that she could barely take a breath. What was she to do now to heal her family?

"Mammi?" Even Levi sounded subdued. "What happened? What's wrong?"

Judith managed to suck in a breath. "Nothing for you to worry about. It's a sad memory for Daadi and for Onkel Joseph, that's all. So you must not ask them anything about it, because that would make them even sadder. Do you understand?"

"Yes, Mammi," Levi said, and Paul echoed him. Even Noah nodded.

"Gut. Now go and do your chores. It will soon be time to get ready for bed."

Judith hung on to her smile until they'd all vanished out the back door. No one would come back in for a time, knowing that when they did, it would be bedtime. So she could safely cry, and even if salty tears dripped into the dishwater, no one would know.

By the time Judith had listened to their prayers and tucked the younger boys into bed, neither Isaac nor Joseph had reappeared in the house. She had no doubt that they were avoiding each other. Joseph was embarrassed that he'd blurted

40

out something so painful in front of the family, and no doubt Isaac was upset that it had come out in such a way.

Returning to the kitchen, she peered out the windows but didn't catch a glimpse of either of them. There was nothing to do but wait. Maybe now that the subject had come up so openly, Isaac would be willing to talk to her about the pain of his family's death. Maybe. But knowing Isaac, she feared this would make him close himself up even more securely.

Pacing the kitchen didn't seem to help. Usually this room didn't fail to cheer her up. Isaac had taken such pains over planning it when they'd built the house. He'd wanted to be sure she had everything she wanted in a kitchen.

She loved the house, but sometimes she thought maybe it hadn't been such a good idea to build it on the site of the farmhouse that had burned. It had been sensible, of course, to use the existing foundation, and the spot next to the lane was meant to have the house on it. But still, how much did it remind Isaac of the house where he'd grown up? Would things be better for him if they lived elsewhere?

There was no point in thinking about it, since it was far too late to make any changes now. Their children were growing up here, and this was home for them as well as for Joseph. He wouldn't remember that other house, or have its ghostly image in his mind. He'd been just a baby, less than a year old, when the house burned.

She'd best do something that would keep her thoughts occupied. Fetching the key her grandmother had given her, she pulled a chair over to the study table, which had been newly installed in a corner of the roomy kitchen. She'd be able to supervise the boys doing their homework while she cooked supper, and she wondered if the previous owner had used it in the same way.

The drawer, once unlocked, opened with a protesting squeal. She'd have to rub the edges with soap to make it run more smoothly.

She'd half-expected the drawer to be empty, but it wasn't. It was crammed with children's notebooks, still looking fresh after their years of being locked away in the drawer. Pulling them out, she began to leaf through them, smiling at lists of spelling words and pages of addition and subtraction problems. Each notebook bore a child's name, and by shuffling through them she was able to come up with the names and put them in order. Rachel Lapp was clearly the eldest, based on the reports she had written. Judith puzzled over the contents of one page before realizing that these books must date from a time when Amish and Englisch children went to their little country schools together, instead of the Amish children having their own schools.

Rachel Lapp had printed her address inside the

cover of one of her notebooks: Box 42, RFD 3, Lancaster County. Her brothers had apparently been Nathaniel, whose notebook was enlivened with carefully drawn pictures of cows; and Toby, who'd evidently had trouble with spelling, based on the many erasures dotting his pages. There was even a small notebook filled with crayon drawings of stick figures and a name: Anna Lapp, age 5. Judith smiled, thinking of the little sister, too young for school, begging to sit at the study table and do work just like her siblings.

Judith set the books aside. She'd show them to her boys, so they'd know that previous generations of young Amish scholars had sat here to do their schoolwork.

In the back of the drawer there was a thick packet of letters. Judith pulled them out and studied them for a few minutes before realizing what she held. They were Round Robin letters, still a common mode of keeping in touch among the Amish. Each person wrote a bit and then sent it on to the next, who added his or her part.

A little more searching told her that the letters had been circulated among three cousins, one of whom had been Mattie Lapp, the former owner of the study table.

Judith unfolded the letters with gentle fingers, somehow moved at the thought of these three female cousins staying so close despite whatever distance lay between them. Like her and Rebecca and Barbie, she thought, though they lived near enough to see each other often and had no need to resort to letters to keep in touch.

She opened the topmost letter to the page written by Mattie Lapp and began to read the words, faded a little now but still legible.

August 15, 1953. Dear Cousins, If the Englisch have their way, the bishop fears it could mean the end of our way of life in this generation . . .

Lancaster County, August 15, 1953

Mattie Lapp rested her hands on the circle letter that would go to her cousins. What did she want to say to them about the crisis that had fallen upon her small Amish community in Lancaster County? Would they soon face the same problems in their own church districts? Was it better to warn them, or was it kinder not to worry them?

The scripture had things to say about worrying. *Consider the lilies of the field; they toil not, neither do they spin, but even Solomon in all his glory was not arrayed like one of these.*

It wasn't so easy to keep from worrying, not when you were trying to live Amish in an Englisch world. Usually she was able to take comfort in the fact that their way was to be true to the Bible's teaching as they understood it. But that was before the intervention of the Englisch

44

world threatened her own daughter's happiness.

From outside, Mattie heard the voice of Nathaniel, her nine-year-old, raised in greeting, and a glance out the window showed her both Nate and little Toby racing to meet her husband's cousin, Adam, as he walked across the field from the neighboring farm. Most days they could count on Adam to appear at this time of the afternoon, ready to help with the two milk cows and to bring the buggy horse into her stall for the night.

Adam had started doing that soon after Ben's death, appearing and taking care of things without asking what was needed, just as the family had taken over raising and harvesting the crops. It had been so comforting at a time when she'd had trouble deciding to put one foot in front of the other. In the past two years, she and the children had all come to depend on Adam in ways she couldn't have imagined.

She hurried out the back door, leaving the letter lying on the study table. She was retreating from the problem, she supposed, much as she feared she'd retreated from every decision that had to be made in the past two years.

"Adam, wilkom. Don't let those boys climb all over you, now."

Grinning, Adam lifted Toby from his shoulder and detached Nate from his pant leg. "Ach, it's no trouble. Boys need someone to roughhouse with, ain't so?" He tapped the brim of Toby's straw hat so that it tipped down on his corn-silk-colored hair.

Rachel hurried toward them from the chicken coop, holding little Anna by the hand. At just fourteen, her Rachel was turning into a young woman before her eyes, and Mattie still had trouble adjusting to the changes in her oldest.

Rachel looked much as Mattie had at that age, with her thick brown hair and the hazel eyes that seemed to turn from green to blue depending on what she was wearing. But where Mattie had been shy and retiring, Rachel was calm and confident, with an air of maturity that had seemed to grow since her daadi's death.

"You're early today, Cousin Adam." Rachel let go of five-year-old Anna's hand so the child could hurl herself at Adam's legs. "It's a gut half hour yet 'til milking time."

"Ja, well, I hoped to have a quiet word with your mamm. But it's rare for sure to find any quiet around here," he added with a grin for the boys, who were clamoring for him to stay long enough to play ball after chores were done.

Surprised at Adam's request, Mattie nodded. "Of course. Let's get rid of these noisy kinder for a few minutes."

"Komm, schnell," Rachel said, shooing her brothers and sister toward the door. "Time for an oatmeal cookie and some lemonade, ja?"

Mattie found her gaze lingering on Rachel as

she took the younger ones inside. How was she to protect her precious girl from the changes that threatened their way of life?

"You're worried, ain't so?" Lines formed between Adam's straight eyebrows as he studied her face. "I heard Bishop Thomas had a meeting with some parents yesterday."

"That's true." Mattie moved a few steps farther away from the house to be certain sure the kinder couldn't hear. She leaned on the rail fence that surrounded the pasture, and Adam joined her. "All the boys and girls who are turning fourteen had both their parents there for the meeting. Except Rachel." Her fingers tightened on the rail.

"I'm sure you did fine." Adam's voice was warm. "Just as Ben would have wanted."

She shook her head, thinking that with Adam, at least, she never needed to be anything but honest. "Shy little Mattie who couldn't say boo to a goose? That's what my mamm always said of me. I was tongue-tied the whole meeting."

"No doubt there were plenty who talked, ain't so? The world needs some listeners."

Mattie had to smile, even though the smile trembled a bit on her lips. "We should have been prepared for this trouble, I suppose. We knew the Englisch were talking about building a new high school way over near Jefferson and busing the scholars to it."

"Ja, we should have." Adam's usually merry face sobered, making him look more like the mature widower she knew he was and less like the little boy she remembered. "I guess we just thought it wouldn't affect the Amish. We figured our young ones would still go to the four-room school down the road and still finish at eight grades."

"Now they say they won't let us." The words burst from Mattie.

Adam nodded. "It seems the law says that our kinder have to go to school until they're fifteen. Nobody paid any attention to that before. We just kept doing what we'd always done."

"It wouldn't be so bad if they could still go to the Rock Creek School. At least there, the Englisch kinder are more like ours—farm kids who have always lived around the Amish." Mattie shivered, despite the heat of the August day. "But now the new school board is sending them off to that big consolidated high school. There will be so many Englisch teens there—kids who don't know anything about us. The bishop says our young ones will be taught all kinds of things about the Englisch world. I've never seen Bishop Thomas so upset."

"He probably thinks he should have seen it coming and been able to prevent it, so I've heard," Adam said. "But I don't know that anyone could have done anything. There's been talk of forcing our children into Englisch high schools for years. Maybe the Englisch think that will cause us to leave our path and become more like them."

"That's what Bishop Thomas said." Her voice trembled despite her attempt to keep it steady. "He thinks it could be the end of us as a people if our teenagers are pushed into adopting Englisch ways."

"And you're worried about your Rachel," Adam said.

Mattie nodded, not entirely trusting herself to say the words. Sweet, gentle Rachel—what if the other students made fun of her? What if they teased her for wearing plain dress and speaking different? Mattie could feel Adam's gaze on her face. Did he understand what she was feeling, or did it take a mother to feel this way about a daughter?

"I know. You thought she'd be staying home this year with you, learning how to run a house and take care of kinder."

"That's the way it's always been." Mattie could hear the yearning in her voice. "And Rachel's so clever with a needle that Ada Busch said maybe she would teach her to work with her as a seamstress."

"Is that what Rachel wants?" Adam had a way of going right to the heart of the matter.

"She says so. She likes the idea of having a job.

You know how serious and mature she is. The idea of making some money to help support the family appeals to her. And she gets along so well with Ada."

"She's a gut person, our Rachel. Her daadi would be proud of her." Adam's voice had roughened a little, either because he spoke of Ben or perhaps because Rachel made him think of his own little daughter, lost at birth along with his young wife.

"Ja. I fear Ben would not be proud of me, though. I couldn't think of a thing to say when all the rest of the parents were talking about what we should do." She tried not to let herself feel afraid, remembering the loud voices that had made her tremble inside. "Some folks think we should take the school board to court, but Bishop Thomas could not agree to that idea."

"We always try to avoid being entangled with the law." Adam sounded as if he were thinking it through, slow and careful as always. "But in the war it was a gut thing that the other peace churches were willing to get involved to keep our boys from being sent to fight."

It hadn't been that long ago that young Amish men had faced the fear of being drafted and forced into the army to fight the war in Europe or the Pacific. At least they'd found a compromise that considered the Amish belief in nonviolence.

"That was different. That affected all of the

peace churches. This is just our little school district."

"Like David and Goliath, ja?"

Adam was trying to get her to smile, but she couldn't. She could only stare out across the land, thinking how dear this place was to her, as it had been to Ben. Some folks were even thinking of leaving for another settlement to escape the law, but she couldn't possibly leave the place that had been home to her and Ben.

"The bishop is going to talk to some of the school board members to try and get them to see our point of view. If not—well, if not, he says we parents must each decide. And if we keep our kinder home when the law says they must go, then we'll have to face the penalty."

She could feel herself grow cold inside. What would that penalty be? A fine? Jail? Would they try to take her kinder away from her?

Adam put his hand firmly over hers where it rested on the railing. "You are imagining the worst, ain't so? But this isn't the time of the martyrs any longer, Mattie. Surely people of good will can come to a decision that is right for all."

Something about the strength of his grasp and the confidence in his voice heartened her. Adam was right. There wasn't a problem that couldn't be solved if folks tried hard enough.

"You always make me feel better, Adam." This

time she didn't have to force a smile. "Just like you always made me laugh when you were tagging along behind Ben and trying to do what your big cousin did."

For a moment, Adam didn't respond. Then he smiled, shaking his head. "I'm not that little cousin any longer, Mattie." He took a step away, his gaze steady. "But I will always be here to help you in any way I can."

"Are you asleep on your feet, Judith? I've asked you three times for the salt."

Judith blinked, pulling her thoughts away from her worries about Isaac. "Sorry." She put down the wooden spoon she'd been using to stir the pork barbecue and handed the salt shaker to her cousin Barbie, who was mixing up a mammoth bowl of potato salad. "I guess I was daydreaming."

Barbie's eyebrows lifted. "They aren't very happy daydreams, by the look of you. You're not worried about the food, are you? With all the stuff the aunts and cousins are bringing for the birthday supper, there'll be more than enough."

"There always is, ain't so?" She gave the barbecue another stir and turned the gas flame all the way down. "I'm fine, and wonderful glad you came early to help."

"No trouble at all. I was done work early at the bakery, and with visitors slowing down at the farm-stay, Rebecca and I haven't been so busy there, either."

Barbie, younger by several years than Rebecca and Judith, was still not married, or even courting, as far as anyone could tell. With her pert, lively face and her fondness for pushing the boundaries, Barbie had caused her elders more than a little concern, but she was certain-sure a hard worker. Besides working part-time at the bakery in town, she'd taken on a big responsibility in helping Rebecca run the farm-stay this summer, and Rebecca declared Barbie was better at it than she was.

"You're sure there isn't anything wrong?" Barbie seemed to have grown more sensitive to other people's feelings in the past year, which was a fine thing, except not right at this moment.

"Nothing at all." Judith pinned a smile to her face. "It isn't every day a boy turns fourteen, so maybe I'm doing a little looking back. Wondering where the little boy has gone that I used to tuck into bed at night."

Barbie deserted the potato salad to give Judith a quick hug. "You've been a fine mother to Joseph." Her eyes sparkled suddenly. "I wonder how long it will be before Rebecca adds another boppli to the family."

"It's too soon to talk about the possibility of another baby," Judith chided, but she couldn't help thinking about it, too.

"Matthew's already acting as a father to Rebecca's two," Barbie said. "For sure they're going to want more children."

Barbie was probably right, but they shouldn't be speculating about it. "We need to be starting to get things lined up for the wedding, not wondering about babies. Lots of couples will have started their planning a year ago, most likely, and every Tuesday and Thursday after fall communion will be jammed with weddings."

"I'm making lists," Barbie said, adding some fresh parsley to the top of the bowl to brighten up the potato salad. "Folks are so happy for them that they're lining up to help. Maybe one afternoon next week we should get together with Rebecca to talk."

"Good idea. Rebecca will have ideas of her own, especially since it's a second wedding." Judith glanced out the kitchen window. The boys were tossing a ball around with Joseph, with even little Noah grabbing for it, missing, and then running after it as fast as his legs could carry him. The boys obviously wanted to be outside to see the first guests arrive—the little ones more excited about it than Joseph, even. But Isaac was nowhere to be seen.

Her heart gave a lurch. Isaac had to be there to greet the family. It would look so odd if he wasn't. She bit her lip. Poor Isaac. She was trying to understand his feelings, but it was hard when he wouldn't talk about them. She had tried twice since Joseph had blurted out the truth of when the farmhouse burned, and all she'd gotten in return was a stony, forbidding expression.

Joseph had known, and Isaac's own wife hadn't. Did Isaac even realize how strange that was?

Barbie slid the potato salad into the gas refrigerator. "By the way, what vocational class is Joseph taking? I was going to ask him, but I didn't get a chance."

"Vocational class?" Judith echoed the words, turning to stare at Barbie. "What makes you think Joseph is taking a vocational class?"

"Isn't he?" Barbie tilted her head to the side. "Really? You know we have a bulletin board at the bakery with all those workshops and courses listed, and Joseph was in the other day, studying it as if it was the most important thing he'd ever seen. I noticed he took one of the folders away with him, so I just assumed he was taking something. Lots of the young ones do, once they're finished with eighth grade."

Barbie spoke of the "young ones" as if she were decades older than they were instead of eight or nine years.

"I don't think he's mentioned anything about it. Anyway, why would he be wanting to take a class? He knows the farm will be his one day. Isaac is already teaching him what he needs to know to run a dairy operation." Somehow, even as she said the words, doubt crept in.

Barbie shrugged. "Sometimes kids have ideas of their own. I surely did when I was that age." She grinned. "Maybe I still do, come to think of it."

Judith suppressed the urge to say that Joseph couldn't. Of course he could. Just because he didn't talk about it, that didn't mean he wasn't thinking about it.

"He was probably getting the folder for a friend of his, that's all," she said.

She tried to believe what she was saying. Isaac was already irritated enough over Joseph's daydreaming and inattention to his work. If he thought Joseph wanted to take a class at the vocational school just when he'd started learning about the dairy operation, she could imagine his reaction.

"Could be. I'll ask him when I get a chance—" Barbie began.

"No!" The word came out far more emphatically than Judith intended, but somehow she had to stop Barbie from saying something that might cause a quarrel today of all days. "I mean, please don't say anything to him."

"Why not? And don't tell me nothing's wrong again, because I just don't believe it. If you don't want me to put my foot into the trouble, you'd better tell me what's going on." Barbie's persistence was legendary. When she wanted something, she'd never let go.

"Please, Barbie." Judith clasped her hands, trying to convey her urgency. "I'd rather not talk about it, at least not now." She'd have to say something more, she knew. She'd just whetted Barbie's curiosity. "It's just that Isaac is so set on Joseph getting serious about the dairy farm, and I . . . well, I'd like to speak to Joseph about it myself, quietly, before anyone else hears."

Barbie studied her face, her blue eyes intent. Then she nodded. "Okay. Don't worry." Her dimple appeared briefly. "I know you think I'm a terrible chatterbox, but I can keep my mouth shut when I want. I won't say anything."

"Denke, Barbie." Judith felt as if she could breathe again. "Let's just get through the birthday first. Then I'll figure it all out." She would, wouldn't she?

"I hear a buggy," Barbie exclaimed, turning to look out the window. "It's Isaac's cousins, here first to celebrate."

Isaac's cousins. They would know the significance of this day, even though she hadn't. If Isaac wasn't there to welcome them—

But he was. He came walking over from the generator shed just as they were pulling up. Isaac was putting up a good front, but Judith knew him too well to be fooled. He was hating every second of this party before it had even begun.

Her glance shifted to Joseph, and her breath caught in her throat. Joseph knew Isaac well, too. And Joseph knew exactly what his brother was feeling. Hurt and anger mingled in the boy's face before he could manage to hide them.

Judith realized she was holding her hand against her heart, as if she could keep it from bursting with pain. Surely, if she loved Isaac and Joseph enough, she could heal this rift between them. She needed to believe that, but every day it became less and less likely that she could.

CHAPTER THREE

Joseph's birthday party was drawing to an end, and as far as Isaac was concerned, that end couldn't come soon enough. Still, he had to admit that it hadn't been as painful as he'd thought it might be.

Judith probably deserved the credit for that. He knew she'd been keeping him busy, pulling him into one task or another, or insisting that he chat with each person there. He felt a tiny edge of resentment at being managed as if he were one of the kinder, but it had worked, so who was he to argue with it?

He'd done a good thing in marrying Judith—a very good thing. No man could ask for a better wife and mother. She'd taken on the responsibility of raising Joseph without a backward glance, something not every nineteen-year-old girl would do, that was certain-sure.

His gaze rested on her as she moved from one group to another seated in the backyard under the shade of the oak trees, making sure everyone had had plenty to eat and refilling lemonade glasses. She still looked much as she had that day he'd taken her hand, standing in front of the ministers and the entire church district to make their promises. Her figure might be a tad curvier, but that was all to the good. Her thick brown hair, smoothed neatly back, would be filled with waves when she let it down at night, and her oval face was as serene as if she hadn't a thing in the world to worry about.

Isaac's train of thought stumbled. Why would she worry? But he knew she did, about Joseph, about the boys, about him, most likely. She wanted everyone to be happy, and sometimes that must seem like an impossible task.

"A fine meal, Isaac." Onkel Simon clapped him on the back. He was followed by his oldest boy, Lige, a few years older than Isaac himself. He and Lige were nearly as close as brothers, as much time as they'd spent together growing up.

"You'd best tell Judith that," he said. "I didn't do much except see that the boys set up chairs. She always makes a fuss over birthdays."

"All women do, ain't so?" Lige said. "You should have heard the fuss about it when our James turned sixteen. You'd think no one had ever had a rumspringa before."

"Rumspringa means letting go of the reins a bit," Onkel Simon pointed out. "No mammi ever thinks it's time for letting her chicks out of her sight."

Isaac's throat clenched. His mother hadn't been there to see what happened after he turned sixteen, because that was the night she died.

"Mammi might have been right at that." Lige leaned against the fence post, tilting his hat to shield his eyes from the setting sun. Lige had his father's lean face and blue eyes, but his reddish brown hair came from his mother. "That boy hasn't given us a moment's peace lately. If it's not one thing, it's another."

"Like you didn't do any such thing when you were his age," Isaac said. "Seems to me I remember a boy who about drove his mamm crazy because his haircut wasn't as stylish as he wanted it to be."

Lige grinned. "I guess. But at least I wasn't asking for a cell phone."

"Only because they didn't have them back then," Isaac retorted.

"Ach, it's natural enough for a teenage boy," Onkel Simon said. "Seems to me every teenager I see is talking away on one of those things."

"That's exactly why I don't want him to have one. Of course he says that every single kid in his rumspringa gang has one except him." Lige sounded as if his son was giving him as hard a time as he'd once given Onkel Simon.

"He'll settle down when he's ready to join the church." Isaac wasn't sure how comforting that was, with five or six years, most likely, before young James came to that point. "We all did."

"You just wait until Joseph is ready to start his rumspringa," Lige warned. "He's fourteen already, and the years fly by fast. One minute they're sitting on your knee and the next you have to look up to talk to them. Remember how you felt at that age—"

Lige stopped abruptly, as if realizing a moment too late that he was on rocky territory.

Isaac felt his face freeze as he sought for words. "I should go help—"

Onkel Simon put a firm hand on his arm. "Lige didn't mean anything."

"I know." He made as if to pull his arm away, but his uncle didn't seem to be finished yet.

"You have a new home now." Onkel Simon nodded toward the farmhouse. "A happy home, and it was built on the foundation of the home that used to be there. That's a wonderful gut way to use the past, Isaac. Not to forget, not to cling to. But to make a foundation for what's to come."

Onkel Simon meant well. Isaac knew it. But he

also knew he couldn't talk about it, especially not today of all days.

"Denke." He pulled free without looking at his uncle's weathered face. "I must say good-bye to Judith's grandmother. I see they're almost ready to leave."

He walked away steadily, trying not to let his face show his feelings. All that remained was to say all the good-byes and do the cleanup. Then this long day would be over. After a good night's sleep, tomorrow would be better.

As always, that job was easier to say than to do. People lingered, chatting, while the young ones chased each other around the yard. Only when the sun had nearly reached the ridge did folks start getting ready to leave in earnest. No one wanted to be driving a buggy home after dark if they could help it.

And then there was all the cleaning up to do. Despite the fact that folks helped, it took an eternity, it seemed, until the last dish had been put away.

Finally the family was alone in the house. While Judith put the boys to bed, Isaac finished up in the kitchen, feeling as if he'd been trampled by a runaway horse.

Judith returned quietly, and she gave him what he thought was an apprehensive glance. "Everyone's settled for the night. I just hope Levi isn't up with a bellyache after all he ate."

"He'll be fine." Isaac tried to sound normal. "I think I'll get to bed soon, too. We'll be up extra early to get the cows milked before it's time to leave for worship tomorrow."

She nodded, her gaze still on his face. "Are you . . . are you all right?"

Isaac's jaw clenched. Like Onkel Simon, Judith meant well. They just didn't understand that he was handling the painful memories the only way he could.

"Fine," he snapped, and then was sorry when he saw the hurt in her eyes. "I'm going up," he added, trying to soften his tone, but it seemed to him that the hurt look followed him all the way upstairs.

Later, lying next to Judith in the double bed, he had to try deliberately to relax his muscles so that he could sleep. The windows were open to let in the night breeze, and the monotonous chirping of the crickets was soothing—almost as soothing as Judith's warm body lying next to him.

He turned his head silently to look at her. She lay on her side, as she always did, and a thick braid crossed her shoulder to shield the delicate curve of her breast. Her hand was partially curved in sleep, and her breathing was slow and even. Listening to it, he slid into sleep.

The next thing he knew, Judith was shaking him, calling his name. He jerked out of the dream, feeling the sweat on his face chill in the night air. He unclenched his fists, half fearing what Judith had seen and heard.

The nightmare was familiar even though he hadn't had it in years—of struggling through the smoke and flames, the floor hot under his bare feet, following the sound of the baby crying almost by instinct. He twisted against Judith's restraining arms, shaking his head from side to side, sure he smelled the smoke again. The house—

"Isaac, it was a nightmare. Nothing but a nightmare. It's over now. You're safe. We're all safe." Judith's hands clutched him as if she'd pull him bodily away from the dream.

"Ja," he muttered. He drove his fingers through his hair. "Ja. Not real. Not now."

"No, of course not now." She ran her hands along his arms. "It was over long ago."

Her words seemed to jangle in his ears, and he shook his head. "No. No. It's not over. Not for me."

"Isaac, don't." She sounded on the verge of tears. "What happened was terrible, but you must accept it."

"I went for Joseph. He was crying, so I went for him." The words felt as if they were ripped from his heart.

"You saved your little brother. He's alive because of you."

She didn't understand. How could she?

"If I'd gone for Daad first, maybe we could have gotten everyone out."

He felt Judith stiffen as she absorbed the words. "Don't, Isaac. Don't think of it that way. You don't know—"

He jerked away from her, rolling out of bed, his bare feet hitting the hooked rug next to it. Cool, not hot, but still, he couldn't pull free of the dream.

"Need some air."

If he didn't get out in the fresh air, he'd choke. He bolted from the room, past the doors of the children's rooms. Grabbed the railing and stumbled down the stairs. Was it now, or was it years ago?

Across the kitchen, bumping into the table. Finally he reached the door. He burst through it and out onto the porch, sucking in a long breath of the night-scented air, telling himself it was over. There was nothing wrong, not now.

It didn't help. He could still taste the acrid tang of fire.

No matter how far he ran, it wouldn't be far enough. He couldn't escape it. He never would.

Judith sat on the backless bench in the Shuman family's barn the next morning, holding Noah against her and keeping her back straight through long practice. Rebecca was next to her in the row of young mothers, and there was comfort in having her cousin so near. Her thoughts should be on the main sermon, but instead they kept wandering to Isaac.

He was sitting opposite her in the men's section, with Levi and Paul on either side of him. Levi sat up straight, eager to prove that soon he'd be capable of sitting with the other boys instead of with his parents. Six-year-old Paul was drooping a bit, his head resting on Isaac's sleeve.

Judith's heart clenched, looking at Isaac's solemn face. She'd tried to stay awake until he came back to bed last night, but she'd nodded off after an hour or so, and she'd been berating herself for that since she woke.

Still, she couldn't convince herself that he'd have said anything more even if she had been awake. The little Isaac had said seemed to have been torn from him, probably by the fierce reminder of what had happened on his sixteenth birthday. No wonder he'd had a nightmare. Her heart actually ached, so that she longed to press her hand against it to ease the pain.

There had been no opportunity to speak to him alone this morning, not in the rush to get all the chores done before they headed down the road for worship services. The kinder had been with them in the buggy, of course, and when they'd arrived they'd separated, she to go and join the women, greeting each one, while he did the same with the men.

She glanced at Joseph, in the front row with the other boys under the eyes of the entire congregation. He'd been proud when he'd been deemed old enough to sit away from the family. Like most mothers of boys in that group, she prayed he'd behave properly and not embarrass them.

Noah stirred restlessly at her side, and she patted him. It was hard for anyone to sit for three hours, and even adults had been known to doze off on a hot summer day. Noah had been playing with a piece of yarn and a handkerchief, but now he let the yarn drop to the floor.

Rebecca's daughter, Katie, bent to pick it up. With a quick smile at Noah, she began to weave the yarn into a cat's cradle. He stopped wiggling to watch, fascinated, and then grabbed for the yarn, clearly wanting to do it, too. With the patience of a big sister, Katie wound the yarn on his hand, guiding his small fingers in the movements. Above their heads, Judith exchanged smiles with Rebecca.

What would her cousin say, she wondered, if Judith told her about what had happened with Isaac last night? She wouldn't, of course. That was private between husband and wife. But if she did, somehow Judith knew what Rebecca's advice would be. The same advice she'd get from her mother or from Grossmammi. She could hear their voices in her head.

Geh lessa. Let it go. Let it be. Accept.

Judith sighed. *Gelassenheit* was at the root of most things Amish, it seemed. To be yielded, to be surrendered, and to accept whatever happened as God's will.

She looked again at Isaac. It was ironic, in a way. Isaac obviously had never truly accepted the fire that had claimed his family. And she couldn't accept the barriers that had been placed between them.

And between him and Joseph? She groped her way to understanding, going over and over the few words Isaac had spoken as he'd come out of the dream. He blamed himself, thinking he should have gone for his father first instead of following the sound of crying. Probably that made him doubly determined to do what he thought his father would have wanted.

As for Joseph—what did he want? She'd had no chance yet to question him about the vocational course information Barbie had seen him take. She had to do that, and soon, before it came out in another family explosion.

The minister began the closing prayer. Judith slid down to kneel facing the bench, trying not to wake Noah, who'd fallen asleep with the yarn still wrapped around his fingers. But he stirred and muttered something and then seemed to realize where he was. Unprompted, he slid to his knees, bringing his hands together on the bench.

The simple gesture warmed her heart. Why could she not just relax and trust in God, reflecting on how many blessings He had brought into her life?

But as they stood for the final hymn, her thoughts were already racing ahead. She had to find out what Joseph was up to. Knowing that she was failing in acceptance by trying to manage the situation herself, she ought to be asking forgiveness. Still, it was hardly being honest with God to ask forgiveness when she planned to do it anyway.

Sometimes it was hard to be Amish. Judith thought of the letter she'd read that had been written over sixty years ago. It had sounded as if Mattie had struggled with how to live Amish in her time as well.

Lancaster County, August 1953

Adam clucked to the mare as they neared the lane to the farm he ran with his daad. She'd turn automatically if he didn't let her know they were headed on to Mattie's place.

His errand could probably have waited until later, when he came to help with the afternoon milking, but what he'd heard in the village had troubled him, and the concern he felt over the school situation was building. Too bad that Mattie's Rachel was the only child in the family just turned fourteen. It might have been easier on both Mattie and Rachel if some of the cousins were affected as well. Of course, it would affect all of the Leit eventually.

Be patient. Be humble. Live separate. All the standards by which the Amish lived didn't seem to offer enough guidance in this situation.

He heard a car approaching from behind him, the engine roaring as it neared. Betsy flapped one ear, as if hearing it, too, and kept on with a steady trot. The car zoomed past, sending up a cloud of dust, and the driver beeped with what seemed a note of scorn.

It was one of those newer models, he noticed, with lots of shiny chrome, and painted a bright red. Made to draw attention, Adam supposed, just as the black and gray Amish buggies of Lancaster County were meant to be indistinguishable from one another.

There were more cars on the road every year since the war ended, even on a back country road like this one. The world around them was changing, but their command remained the same. *Live separate. Be not conformed to the standards of this world.* Sometimes he thought that grew harder all the time.

Betsy turned into Mattie's lane, seeming to know where he was headed. That was a comment in itself as to the amount of time he spent here. Still, it was up to the family to help Mattie and her kinder since Ben's death, and he was freer than most, since he had neither wife nor child. Five years he'd been alone now, and folks kept hinting it was time he was marrying again.

But not Mattie, who was unable to think of him as anything but Ben's little cousin.

He drew up at the back porch of the farmhouse and the boys came running.

"It's not milking time," Toby said. "We just had lunch."

"You've been to town." Nate patted the mare, knowing Adam wouldn't have hitched her up to come here. "What did you do?"

"Went to the hardware store is all." He jumped down in time to scoop little Anna up as she hurtled toward him. "You boys want to give Betsy a drink?"

"Ja, right away." Toby raced for the bucket while Nate held the mare's harness.

"Is Mammi in the house?" He headed for the porch, carrying Anna.

"I'm right here." Mattie opened the screen door and stepped toward him with a smile of welcome. "What takes you out and about?"

"Trip to town." He set Anna down and held out the small brown paper bag he'd been hiding.

"Penny candy," Anna crowed, knowing immediately what it was. "Denke, Cousin Adam."

"Share with your brothers and sister now," he said as she ran off.

"You spoil her," Mattie chided.

"Ach, a bag of penny candy is nothing." His little Sarah would have been Anna's age, if she hadn't been gone before she'd had a chance to take a breath.

Maybe Mattie knew what was in his mind, because she said no more about it.

"Is Rachel around?" he asked.

Mattie shook her head. "She's over to Mary Ann's, helping her with the canning. Did you need to see her?"

"Just wanted to be sure she didn't overhear what I have to say." The words brought a shadow to Mattie's eyes, but it was better if he told her about the talk before she heard it from someone else. "Let's sit a minute."

Face grave, Mattie seated herself on the porch swing. He had helped Ben hang it so many years ago, laughing at Ben's insistence that a house wasn't a home unless it had a porch swing. Adam took the place next to Mattie, trying not to think that it was where Ben used to sit.

"Tell me, whatever it is." She seemed to brace herself.

"It's not too bad," he said quickly. He hadn't meant to alarm her. "It's just that I heard a bit of talk while I was at the hardware store this morning." He frowned, trying to think of the best way to tell her. "There were some Englisch there, hanging out in the store."

There always were, picking up the latest news, he guessed. He sometimes thought men were worse than women for gossip.

Mattie's hands clasped each other tightly, and he felt an urge to take them in his. But he didn't.

"Talking about us? About this business of the school and us not wanting to send our children?"

"Ja. One of them was a bit of a loudmouth. The others tried to hush him when I came in, but he wasn't having it. He seemed to think I was a dumb Dutchman who couldn't even understand them."

"Most Englischers aren't like him," she said quickly.

"No. But I'm worried that too many might share his opinions about this school business." He frowned. He wasn't doing this right. "That was the whole gist of what he was saying, that we were dumb and didn't know enough to take proper care of our own kinder. And it worried me that nobody spoke up against him, not even Mr. Matthews, and he knows the Amish as well as anyone, running the hardware store like he does."

"What? Why would any of them think we can't take care of our children? Nobody could possibly love my little ones more than I do." Mattie's lips trembled for an instant, but then she pressed them together as if to defy anyone to argue the point with her.

Adam had been trying to figure that out all the

way here from the hardware store. "It's this whole idea of progress, I think. Since the war ended, Englisch folks seem like they're all caught up in this notion of everything being bigger and better. Faster and shinier." He remembered the car that had passed him. "They seem to think if a school is bigger, it has to be better."

"Well, fine. Let them have their bigger schools then, if that's what they want. Just leave us alone."

"That's the trouble, Mattie." Again he felt the urge to take her straining hands in his. "They won't leave us alone. They—some of them, any-way—think it would be a really good idea if our kids were sent off to a big school where they'd learn about modern Englisch ways of doing things. Then they wouldn't be backward, like us."

"Why is it backward to want to live as Jesus commanded?" Mattie's rare temper flashed. "We don't try to tell other folks how to live."

"We're outnumbered." He couldn't help smiling a little at her indignation. "I know what you mean, and I agree with you. But I'm not sure we should pin too much hope on this meeting the bishop has set up for him and the ministers to explain our point of view to the school board president."

Mattie looked honestly surprised at his pessimism. "But the board president is an educated man. He's not like one of those lazy loafers in the hardware store. Surely he'll listen to Thomas Beiler's words. Everyone respects Bishop Thomas, even the Englisch."

"Maybe not everyone. It's apparently common knowledge that the bishop asked for a meeting with the school board president." He frowned. "I don't know the man, so I can't say that the folks I heard had it right. But according to what they were saying, this Walter Graham is all for the new school plan, and he's not likely to be swayed by Bishop Thomas or anyone else."

"Walter Graham." Mattie repeated the name, frowning. "There's a Mrs. Graham who comes out about every week to buy produce from me, but I don't know that she's any kin to him."

"Probably not. It doesn't sound as if he'd have any truck with the Amish."

"Maybe those men were wrong. Maybe Bishop Thomas will convince him that our ways are right for us." Mattie sounded as if she were clutching at any straw she could find, and Adam wished he could say he agreed with her.

"Maybe," he said, knowing how doubtful he sounded. "I didn't want to upset you, Mattie. I'd never want to do that, but I thought you ought to be ready in case it's bad news coming out of the meeting."

"I know." Mattie reached over to clasp his hand, startling him when he felt her skin soft against his. "I'm grateful that we have you to depend on now that Ben is gone."

Her hand felt small and warm, and he enveloped it in what he hoped was a comforting grasp. But the truth was that comforting wasn't all he was feeling. When he looked into Mattie's clear blue eyes, he seemed to be falling right into them, unable to look away, unable even to think clearly. She was so dear, so sweet—

Stoppe! This wouldn't do. He couldn't be having these feelings for Mattie, of all people. Mattie was Ben's wife, and even though Ben was gone, it still didn't seem right. He'd always wanted to be like his big cousin, but that didn't mean he could want to take Ben's place with Mattie.

Adam shot to his feet, setting the swing rocking. "I . . . I have to get going. Daad's waiting for the things I picked up at the hardware store."

Mattie was staring at him, confusion written on her face. "You'd best go, then. I'm glad you came and told me, Adam. It's right for me to be prepared." She tried to smile but wasn't completely successful.

He couldn't keep looking at her. He had to get away and sort out his feelings, because if he didn't, he might do or say something that would change everything between them. With a quick nod, he bolted off the porch, praying the kinder were too occupied with their candy to notice that anything was wrong with him.

CHAPTER FOUR

Joseph had slipped away again this afternoon. Judith wasn't sure how he'd managed it, when she'd been alert for an opportunity to get him alone to talk. He was becoming entirely too good at this vanishing act of his.

Still, there was no use beating herself up for not keeping closer track of him. He wasn't a child any longer, and at fourteen, he'd resent it if he thought she was babying him.

At least Isaac wasn't home to notice his absence. Isaac had gone over to his uncle's place after lunch to help with some deer fencing around the truck patch, taking the two older boys with him. If she knew Onkel Simon, they'd be working and talking most of the afternoon. Surely Joseph would be back before Isaac was.

Judith moved to the next row of tomato plants in the garden, brushing aside the thick leaves to pick only the ripest ones. They'd been fortunate in the amount of rain they'd had this summer, and it looked to be a bumper crop of tomatoes. They'd been so sweet that even little Noah ate them like a piece of fruit. Unless something happened to have a bad effect on the plants, she'd probably be canning well into September.

Straightening to stretch her back, she shaded her eyes and looked over toward Onkel Simon's, but the hedgerow cut off any view of the spot where the men would be working today. Maybe Isaac would open up to his uncle about his nightmare. They were close—nearly as close as father and son. Isaac would talk to him if he'd talk to anyone.

Isaac's temper had been uncertain since Saturday, and it didn't seem to be improving much. He'd speak sharply to the kinder about some little thing, and then the next moment he'd not even seem to notice something that would ordinarily earn a rebuke. Judith suspected he hated having told her anything about the fire, and she was afraid to make matters worse by bringing it up.

Was that cowardly on her part? Maybe so. Certainly in her position, her cousin Barbie would be outspoken, as she was about everything. But Barbie didn't yet know what it was to love a man with all her heart. She might find herself becoming more cautious when she fell in love.

A flicker of movement caught the corner of Judith's eye, and she realized Isaac had walked into her field of view. Her heart gave a little jump. Was he coming home already, and Joseph not back yet?

The sound of wheels on gravel announced Joseph's arrival, and he came shooting past the house on his scooter to the spot where she'd stacked some peck baskets. Without a backward glance, he picked up a basket and joined her in the garden, stepping easily over the plants with his long legs. If Isaac looked over now, he'd see his brother suitably busy helping her with the tomatoes.

The sense of being manipulated into a part in his deception made her voice a little sharper than usual. "Joseph, where have you been?"

He looked up, startled, and perhaps wary, as well, and brushed a strand of golden brown hair from his eyes. "Nowhere. Just around."

She bit back a retort at the typical teenage response. "That's not an answer. I know you probably want to get away from the little boys once in a while, but—"

"Where are they?" he asked quickly. "They usually love to help pick the tomatoes."

"Over at Onkel Simon's with their daad. Except Noah, and he's napping." He'd distracted her, which was probably his intention. But while they had this rare private moment, she was determined to get some straight answers from him. "I don't mind if you want to get off by yourself sometimes, but I'd appreciate it if you'd let me or Isaac know when you're going."

There was silence for a moment as he picked another bright red tomato and put it in the basket, making her think he was considering his answer.

"I love the boys. You know I do." He gave her

a rueful smile. "But sometimes I do like to get away by myself. I built a little lean-to out in the woods, and nobody knows it's there. I just like to be private and think. That's okay, isn't it?"

His explanation sounded plausible, but she wasn't satisfied. "Maybe you'd better tell me where it is. I won't say anything about it to your brother or the boys, but someone should know where you are in case of an emergency."

Joseph's jaw clenched for an instant, and she thought he was going to snap at her. But then he seemed to relax, and he shrugged. "You know where the log drag crosses the old railroad bed up in the woods?"

"Ja, I do."

Joseph looked surprised. "I was certain sure you'd say no. I didn't think you ever went that far, even when you're picking berries."

"I know it's hard to believe, but I was young once myself. I did some exploring in the woods when I was here with . . ." She hesitated, realizing she'd never spoken to Joseph of her friendship with his sister. "Your sister Deborah and I were friends," she said simply.

"I didn't know." His face tightened. "I wish I remembered my sisters. And Mamm and Daad, too. They're just names to me, like they're not real."

She'd never realized—never even thought, for that matter—that Joseph would feel that way.

He'd been only ten months old when the family tragedy happened, and everyone assumed he wouldn't think much about it.

"I'm sorry." She had to say more. Surely she could give him some memory to cherish. Even as she thought it, a memory popped into her head of Deborah, eyes sparkling, leading her in to see the new baby.

"Deborah was wonderful happy when you were born." Her voice was gentle with remembered happiness and sorrow mixed together. "Another brother after having two younger sisters—she kept saying you were the most beautiful baby she'd ever seen. She was so proud when your mammi let her hold you. I can see her now, looking down into your face and smiling. Deborah had the prettiest smile."

It was getting hard to talk over the lump in her throat. Because it pained Isaac so much to remember, they never talked about the lost siblings, but she'd grieved for Deborah, her friend, and she knew that she'd missed talking about her.

Joseph blinked rapidly, and Judith suspected he didn't want her to see him cry. She bent, busying herself with a sprawling tomato plant.

"Denke, Judith," he said finally.

She nodded, studying his face for a moment, the features so like Isaac's but caught in that place between boy and man. He hadn't really answered her question, she knew. She had no doubt that he did sometimes sneak off to his lean-to in the woods, but he hadn't been coming from that direction today. He'd come along the road.

If she pressed him on that, she might never get an answer to the question she'd intended to ask. Maybe it was best to get that in while they were still in harmony with each other and no one else was around.

"When my cousin Barbie was here for your birthday, she mentioned something to me." She tried to sound casual.

"What about?" Joseph had that wary look again.

"She noticed that you were interested in the bulletin board they have at the bakery with the information about vocational classes. In fact, she says you took one of the—"

"She was spying on me?" Joseph's face reddened. "It's none of her business what I do."

Judith straightened. "Joseph Wegler, I will not have you speaking that way. No one is spying on you, and I'm ashamed of how I raised you if you can think so."

His head dropped, and he seemed to be studying his feet. "I'm sorry," he mumbled.

"You should be." Judith took a breath. She was getting nowhere by scolding him. "Ours is a small community, Joseph. Whatever you do, someone always sees, not because they are spying but because we all care for one another.

Barbie just wondered what class you were interested in. And so do I."

"I just . . . I was looking at the class they have on engine repair, that's all. I've always been interested in it."

She nodded. That was true enough. Joseph had been taking things apart to see how they worked since he was a small boy. But . . .

"You have a full-time job now, learning how to run a dairy farm, ain't so? I don't think Isaac would want to spare you to go back to school."

"It's only one class," he said, looking sulky. "It's not like I'd be gone all day. And anyway, there are always things to fix around here, ain't so? Seems to me it would be gut for someone to know how to repair them."

Joseph's words made a certain amount of sense, and she longed to find a compromise that would please everyone. Unfortunately, she didn't think Isaac would agree.

"I know what you're going to say. That Isaac won't think so. That I have to do what Isaac says because he's my big brother." He flung the words at her.

"Not exactly," she said mildly. "How soon would you have to sign up to take the class?"

Hope flared in Joseph's eyes. "There's another two weeks before the cutoff date. You mean you'll help me?"

"I'll try," she said cautiously. "Give me a little

time to think how best to approach it with Isaac." And give Isaac time to recover from the events of Saturday, as well.

"Denke, Judith. Denke." Joseph's face lit with happiness, making her realize how long it had been since she'd seen him look that way.

She'd be happy, too, if she had any idea how she was to get Isaac to agree to Joseph's plan. And if she didn't have the feeling that Joseph hadn't yet told her everything.

Lancaster County, August 1953

Mattie tried to concentrate on the hot tomato juice she was pouring into canning jars. Instead, she found her thoughts straying again to how oddly Adam had behaved yesterday. She'd have said she knew Ben's young cousin as well as she knew her own kinder, but at the moment she had no idea what was in his mind.

"Watch out, Mammi." Rachel grasped the kettle and steadied it as she poured, probably preventing a splash of hot juice on her fingers.

"Denke. I was daydreaming a little, I think," she said quickly, hoping neither Rachel nor her mother-in-law had noticed that she had something on her mind.

"Best not to daydream when you're bottling tomato juice," Mamm Becky said, wiping her forehead with the back of her arm. "I'm just as glad this is the last batch, that's certain-sure." She looked with satisfaction at the rows of filled jars ready for the canning shelves. "We did a fine big batch today."

"It goes fast when you have people to work with, ain't so?" Mattie took a step back to allow Rachel to wipe the jars and fasten the tops. "Rachel or the boys can bring your half over in the pony cart after the jars have cooled."

"Now, don't be foolish, Mattie. You have a family to feed, and they were mostly your tomatoes anyway. I'll chust take a few jars."

Mattie exchanged smiles with Rachel at hearing the familiar wrangle begin. Ben's mother always tried to get them to take the lion's share when they did the canning together.

"You have the bigger eaters at your house," she pointed out. "My little ones will go for the apple juice instead of the tomato most of the time, so you should take more, ain't so?"

"Ach, well, I guess half and half then," Mamm Becky said. "But next time—"

"Next time you two will say the same things again," Rachel said, her eyes twinkling. "Now why don't you go outside and cool off in the shade while I finish up this last batch?"

"I'm not leaving you with all the work," Mattie began, but Rachel shook her head. With a pang, she realized that her little Rachel was almost more woman than child.

"It doesn't take three of us to start this last batch in the canner. There's some lemonade cooling in the spring house, and you can have a nice gossip." Rachel shooed them through the door and onto the porch. "Nate!" she called. "Bring the lemonade for Mammi and Grossmammi."

Nate waved to show he'd heard and then darted off toward the spring house, and Rachel went back inside.

"Our Rachel is getting to be so grown up," Mamm Becky said, settling herself next to Mattie on the swing. "I wish Ben could see what a fine young woman she is."

Mattie nodded, her throat tightening. "Ja. I wish it, too."

Mamm Becky grasped her hand. "I didn't mean to make you feel sad. I've chust been thinking about Ben lately. It wonders me to know how he would have handled this business with the school."

"I know. I think of that as well." Mattie hesitated, glancing around, but Rachel was busy in the house and Nate hadn't reappeared from the spring house yet. "You've heard that the bishop was disappointed by his meeting with the school board president?"

Mamm Becky nodded, her forehead wrinkling. With a pang, Mattie realized that the brown hair pulled back from a widening part was more than half gray now, and the lines in her mother-in-law's face seemed a reminder of the sorrow she'd dealt with in her life.

"I've prayed and prayed. We all have, ain't so? But Bishop Thomas said the man didn't even seem to be interested in what they had to say. He'd already made up his mind before they even started to talk."

"Gossip has it that some of the other board members aren't so set on forcing us into the new school." Mattie repeated the only hopeful news she'd heard recently. "Maybe the bishop should talk to them. Maybe they could sway the president." She had a feeling she was grasping at straws, trying to find a way to escape what she feared.

"Maybe." Mamm Becky sounded doubtful. "You know the whole family stands with you in this, ja? Adam says we should be sure you know that, so you won't feel you're alone. He's more worried than I've ever seen him, I think."

"That might be why he's acting so strange lately," Mattie murmured, thinking aloud.

"Strange?" Her mother-in-law picked up on the word right away. "How is he acting strange?"

When forced to explain, Mattie couldn't seem to find the words. "I . . . I'm not sure. He just seems different. Like yesterday. One minute we were sitting here talking and the next he dashed off like he'd been stung by a bee."

Mamm Becky eyed her for a moment, as if Mattie were the one being strange. Then she shrugged. "Maybe Adam is finally ready to think of marrying again." She paused for what seemed a long moment. "You know," she said gently, "maybe you should be thinking that way, too."

Mattie blinked, her mind stuttering to understand what her mother-in-law had said. Marry again? "But—it's only been two years since Ben . . ."

"Nearer three years, Mattie." Mamm Becky patted her hand. "I don't mean to upset you. But I want you to know that Ben's family thinks it's a gut idea for you to marry. We all mourn Ben's loss, but you are a young woman still, with kinder who need a daadi."

Her instinctive reaction was to protest. "The kinder have plenty of men in their lives. Their grossdaadi, their cousins, Adam . . ."

"That's so," Mamm Becky said. "But not someone to call Daadi." Her faded blue eyes filled with tears, and Mattie realized how hard the words were for her to say. "And you need someone, especially now. It's not right that you should be dealing with this struggle alone."

Was her mother-in-law assuming that Mattie couldn't do it? Well, it wasn't anything she hadn't thought herself, but still, she didn't like hearing it from someone else. A tiny flicker of anger sparked.

"I won't marry someone just because these are difficult times. That wouldn't be right for anyone. And I couldn't feel about anyone else the way I felt about Ben."

Mamm Becky seemed to sigh. "Mattie, first love is a wonderful thing, but there are other reasons to marry. Family is more important than one person, just as the church is more important than one. Nobody is saying you should chust jump into marrying. But when there's someone who already cares about you and the kinder like Adam—"

"Adam!" She couldn't have been more surprised if her mother-in-law had suggested the man in the moon. "How could I think of Adam in that way? He is Ben's little cousin. He's years younger than I am." Didn't Mamm Becky see how ridiculous that was?

"Five years," Mamm Becky said. "I know. Five years is a big gap when you're a child. But five years means nothing when you're both grown. And Adam has lost his first love, just as you have lost yours."

Mattie was shaking her head, feeling as if her mind were shaking, too. This was impossible. How Adam would laugh if he heard it! Or would he be embarrassed instead?

One thing was certain-sure. She was going to feel awkward around him until she could manage to forget the whole idea.

This time when the blade of the milk tank stopped, it didn't start again. Isaac stared at it for a full minute, willing it to come back on again. They weren't even finished milking, and this had to happen. By then, Onkel Simon had noticed something was wrong and stepped away from his milking station, followed quickly by Joseph.

Isaac glared at the motor and drew back his leg to give it a kick.

"Don't." Joseph stepped in front of him. "You might break something."

"It's already broken." Isaac's temper rose, but behind the temper was a sharp edge of fear. A crucial piece of machinery, the contract with the dairy—

"Let Joseph have a look." Onkel Simon touched his arm reassuringly. "The boy is wonderful gut with fixing things. Maybe he'll be able to see what's wrong."

Isaac glanced at his brother and nodded. "Ja, that's so. Take a look, Joseph."

By that time the other two boys had joined them, staring hopefully at Joseph. The cows, aware that something had gone wrong with the usual morning routine, turned their heads as well.

If it bothered Joseph to have everyone watching, he didn't show it. He squatted by the motor, checking the outside connections and then removing the cover to peer at its innards. For a few minutes he frowned, his hands moving from one thing to another. Then he made a satisfied noise and gave something a twist, and the motor rumbled back to life. The blade began its steady movement.

"Gut job, Joseph." Onkel Simon clapped the boy on the shoulder as he replaced the cover. Joseph rose, grinning as Levi and Paul tried to copy the motion.

But he wasn't looking at them. He was looking at Isaac as if he was waiting for something.

Isaac grabbed him in a one-armed hug, shaking him a little in his pleasure. "You saved the day, for sure, little brother. Gut work."

Joseph ducked his head, looking a bit embarrassed at all the attention, but his smile touched Isaac's heart. It startled him, making him realize how long it had been since he'd been in such harmony with his little brother. He should never let distance grow between them, no matter how the boy exasperated him at times. Like Onkel Simon said, it was most likely teenage growing pains.

They told the story to Judith and little Noah over breakfast, with lots of embellishments from the two boys to help it along. It was good, feeling that they were all happy with one another.

He glanced across the table at Joseph, marveling at how the boy was growing. He must have shot up six inches in as many months, and

Judith had taken to putting deep hems in his pants so she could let them down. He'd be a man almost before they knew it.

Isaac lingered over a second cup of coffee after the others had left, with Levi and Paul scurrying to get ready for school while Onkel Simon headed home and Joseph carried Noah upstairs piggyback to get dressed.

Judith, at the sink cleaning up, glanced over her shoulder at him. It almost looked as if she wanted to say something and wasn't sure she should.

Guilt tightened his chest. That was his fault, wasn't it? Small wonder if his wife was worried about saying the wrong thing to him, after the way he'd been acting lately. He'd been like a bear with a sore paw, and he knew it only too well.

It wasn't Judith's fault that Joseph's birthday had been a difficult time for him, and it wasn't her fault that he'd spoken of things he'd resolved never to say to anyone. So it wasn't right to take his mood out on her.

He moved over to the sink, setting his cup down in the dishwater that seemed to occupy her attention. The graceful curve of her neck reminded him that it was one of the first things he'd noticed about her. He put his palm on her nape, feeling the warmth of her soft skin. Judith glanced up at him, eyes widening.

"I wanted to say—" Ach, where were the words he needed? "I guess I've been sort of grouchy lately. I . . . I'm sorry. I didn't mean to make you feel bad."

She turned from the dishpan, her hands still wet and soapy. "You know that if you feel unhappy, then I do as well."

Her response seemed to clutch at his heart. He took her hands in his, soap and all, and held them close to his heart. "Denke, Judith." He bent to touch her lips with his—lightly at first, and then not so lightly.

When he drew back they both were smiling. "What would the kinder say if they came back down and saw us?" he said. He dropped a kiss on the hands he still clasped. "I'd better get busy. I told Onkel Simon I'd come and help him finish the fencing today, since he'll be off to the produce auction early tomorrow. And we need to take the wagon over to Schultz's for a load of fence posts."

She nodded. "Before you go—it was helpful, ja, Joseph knowing how to fix the motor on the milk tank?"

"More than helpful," he agreed.

"I was just wondering if it might be a gut idea for him to take one of those vocational classes the school district offers. Maybe something to help him learn more about machinery and how to take care of it. Then you wouldn't have to call the repair shop when something goes wrong."

He paused, frowning. "I don't know. I'd hate to

see anything take him away from the farmwork. Anyway, how do you know he'd even be interested in such a thing?"

"I don't think it would take all that much time." Judith's face was so earnest, as if this was something very important. "And he actually mentioned it to me after seeing those brochures they have on the bulletin boards around town. You know how he's always liked tinkering with things, ever since he was a little boy."

"Taking them apart to see how they work, and then trying to figure out how to put them back together again." He shrugged. "Let me think on it. I should get going, but maybe tonight we can talk to Joseph and decide if it's the right thing for him."

Judith flashed him a smile so brilliant it startled him. "Gut. I think Joseph will like the idea, if you say so."

He headed out the back door, a little perplexed by how the conversation had gone. Still, this suggestion of Judith's might not be such a bad idea. Machinery was an inevitable part of running a dairy operation these days, so maybe Joseph should learn a bit more about it.

CHAPTER FIVE

"What about the celery?" Judith asked, putting down her pencil for a moment to replenish the lemonade glasses in front of her two cousins. She, Rebecca, and Barbie had been sitting around the Wegler's kitchen table for the past hour, engrossed in listing the hundreds of details involved in planning an Amish wedding.

"You sound like my daad," Rebecca said. "If he's asked me once, he's asked me a half dozen times. I keep telling him people understand that he didn't know about the wedding in time to plant a garden full of celery, but he's fretting."

"Would it be so terrible if there were an Amish wedding meal that didn't include the creamed celery?" Barbie scrunched up her nose. "I'm not crazy about it."

"It's traditional," Judith reminded her. "People expect it."

Barbie's disdainful sniff spoke volumes about her opinion of tradition.

Judith ignored her, knowing that more often than not, Barbie was just trying to get a reaction from her older cousins.

"Anyway, there's the chicken and filling, too, and the cooks need celery for it. I was thinking that probably Isaac's Onkel Simon could work a deal for it at the produce auction. After all, what's important is to have the food, not who grows it." She deliberately didn't say "traditional" food, not wanting another comment from Barbie.

"That would be wonderful kind of him," Rebecca said. "Matthew and I would be just as happy to have a small wedding, but our families would be so disappointed if we did."

"Anyway, there's no such thing as a small Amish wedding," Barbie said, her lively face expressing a sense of the impossible. "Your daad wouldn't dream of not inviting the whole church."

"And folks are wonderful happy for you and Matt, so it would be a shame not to let them share the day." Judith made a note next to the celery on her list, pleased to see that they'd made significant progress on assigning the numerous tasks related to a wedding.

All in all it had been a satisfying afternoon. They'd accomplished a great deal, and thinking about Rebecca's wedding effectively kept Judith from worrying about what Isaac was going to say to Joseph.

"About our dresses—" Barbie began. "I suppose I couldn't convince you to do something other than blue?"

"No, you couldn't," Rebecca said firmly. "I don't know why you're complaining. With your blue eyes, the color is perfect for you. Now, don't let's have any argument. I want to make the dresses for both of you, and my mother and grandmother are eager to help."

"But it's so much work, and you're busy," Judith protested, knowing the amount of time that would be involved in sewing three dresses. By custom, the bride and her side-sitters wore the same dresses, usually sewn by the bride, which were exactly like the dresses they wore every other day. After the wedding they would just become another dress, probably worn for church Sundays for a time and then for daily use.

"I want to do it." Rebecca reached across the table to clasp each of them by the hand. "You two are closer than sisters to me, and it will be a labor of love. Besides, it will keep Mamm and Grossmammi happy for hours."

"Well, I won't argue," Barbie said. "Sewing has never been my favorite pastime." She rose, stretching, and glanced out the window to where Rebecca's kinder played with Judith's boys in the yard. "By the way, did you ever find out about the class Joseph was interested in?" Her color heightened, and she cast a glance at Rebecca. "Oops. I forgot it was supposed to be a secret."

"That's the trouble with trusting you," Judith teased. "You talk so much that everything spills out eventually. I don't mind if Rebecca knows, anyway."

"I know you were a little worried over Joseph, but you don't have to tell either of us anything you don't want to," Rebecca said.

"No, no, it's nothing." She didn't want to have them worrying. It was enough that she did. "Joseph wants to take a course in repairing machinery or some such thing, and he was afraid Isaac would say no." Judith felt her lips curling up in an involuntary smile. "But I mentioned it to Isaac, and he promised to discuss it with Joseph tonight. I would just like to see the two of them agreeing on something for once."

"I'm glad." Rebecca glanced at the clock and began to gather up her things. "Look at the time. The afternoon has flown by. I'd best be getting home to see about supper."

Judith walked outside with them. Both had come in their buggies, since it was too far to walk, and they'd want to get home before car traffic started getting busier.

In the bustle of collecting children and over-coming their pleas to play a little longer, Judith realized that someone was missing who should be there.

"Where is Joseph?" She directed the question at the kinder, to be met with shrugged shoulders on the part of the older ones.

Noah came running to tug on her skirt. "He's riding his scooter, Mammi."

A tiny alarm jingled in her thoughts. "Riding

where?" Her voice had become sharp enough to have them all looking at her. She glanced around at the young faces. Levi didn't meet her eyes.

She went to her oldest, bending to clasp his shoulders. "Levi, do you know where Joseph is?"

He hesitated, looking down at his bare feet. "I . . . I . . ."

"Levi, this is important." Why had Joseph picked this moment to disappear, just when she had nearly persuaded Isaac to let him do what he wanted? "If you know, you must tell me."

Levi's face puckered, making her want to hug him close and soothe him. "He went to the machine works to see Fred Yoder." His gaze met hers, and his blue eyes were swimming with tears. "It's not a bad thing, is it, Mammi?"

"No, of course it's not a bad thing."

But she was afraid that it would be in Isaac's view. For some reason, he'd never cared much for Fred, and the idea that Joseph would be spending time with Fred and his successful business instead of here on the farm with him would be . . . well, she wasn't sure how he'd react, but she did know that this was the worst possible time for Joseph to upset him.

She hugged Levi, forcing a smile, and brushed the silky hair off his forehead. "Go and say good-bye to your cousins now."

"Don't look that way, Judith." Barbie caught her arm and gave it a little shake. "It's not the end of the world when a teenager goes off someplace without telling you."

"No, but obviously Judith thinks it's serious, so we must help," Rebecca said.

Judith bit her lip, trying to think. Was she overreacting? "I just wish he hadn't picked today to go off to the machine shop, of all places. If he's not back for the milking, Isaac will be angry, just when he's thinking about letting Joseph take that class he wants."

"What can we do?" Rebecca asked, practical as always.

"Nothing." Judith shook her head, trying to make her brain work. "If only I could get Joseph back here before Isaac comes home—"

"Maybe you can." Barbie's eyes danced, causing Judith instant wariness.

"The kinder . . ." she began.

"I'll stay with the young ones," Barbie said briskly. "You take my buggy. It's all ready, and you can go get Joseph and give him a good scolding if need be. Go on, hurry."

Undecided, Judith glanced at Rebecca, who nodded.

"It does seem the best solution." Her lips quirked. "Barbie does have some bright ideas, ja?"

Judith hesitated, but what else was she to do? Stand back and see yet another quarrel between Isaac and Joseph, just when things were looking better?

"All right. Denke, Barbie. If Isaac comes home before we're back—"

"Don't worry. I'll handle him."

That was just what Judith was afraid of. With a quick good-bye to the others, she hurried to Barbie's buggy.

The road to the village seemed longer than it ever had. At least her destination was on this side of town, so she'd be less likely to run into folks who would expect her to stop and chat.

But what had taken Joseph to the machine shop? He barely knew Fred, she'd have thought. Was this a continuation of his childhood interest in how things worked?

Judith clucked to the mare, who seemed to know that Barbie was not the one holding the reins. Perhaps Joseph thought Frederick could give him some guidance on which vocational course to take. The idea made her feel a little better, although he shouldn't have done that without at least telling her. The little boy who'd told her everything had grown into a young man who was surprisingly adept at keeping secrets, and that knowledge grieved her.

Finally the cement-block building she was watching for came into view on the right side of the road ahead. It looked as if it had started life as one small shop and then kept growing as Frederick's business expanded.

More than one person in the church harbored

questions about how close to the line of being Amish Frederick came in his business as he took on contracts from Englisch companies. Still, the bishop apparently had been satisfied by Fred's explanations, and all of Fred's employees were Amish, each earning a good living from his work.

There was a new sign along the side of the building, she noticed: *MACHINE WORKS.* She guided the mare to a hitching rail under the shelter of the trees along the parking lot. As she set the brake and hopped down, her thoughts raced. What was she going to say to Frederick? And, more importantly, to Joseph? With a silent prayer for guidance, she hurried to the office entrance.

The office area might belong to any Amish business, typically furnished with a long wooden counter, two desks, a bulletin board bearing hand-lettered notices of services offered, and a large calendar. No one was behind the counter, but she heard footsteps coming from a room beyond, probably in answer to the bell on the door.

A moment later Frederick himself appeared, his ruddy face creasing in a surprised smile when he saw her. Despite the added height and maturity, to say nothing of the beard, Judith could still recognize the mischievous boy who'd delighted in raising the teacher's ire with his pranks.

"Judith! You're the last person I expected to see today. How are you?"

"Fine." She brushed past the question, intent on her errand. "Frederick, is Joseph here?"

"Joseph?" His eyebrows lifted, and Judith immediately saw that he wasn't sure how to answer.

"Don't bother looking surprised," she said tartly. "I have to speak to him."

"All right, all right." He held his hands up, palms out in surrender, but his dark eyes twinkled. "I guess I wasn't very convincing."

"I'm raising four boys, remember? I can tell when someone is evading a question."

"Ach, you always did see right through me. If Isaac hadn't snapped you up so quickly—"

"Joseph," she reminded him.

He nodded, opening a flap in the counter so that she could step through. "Come in back and we'll find him. He's around someplace, and you can see my little business."

"Not so little," she said as they emerged into a large storage area with racks bearing all sorts of metal parts whose use she couldn't imagine.

"We do all right." Frederick gestured toward a row of boxes, clearly labeled and ready for shipping. "These are parts we made for an Englisch manufacturer. They were skeptical at first that we could produce quality products, but we convinced them."

A young Amish man she vaguely recognized as a member of an adjoining church district glanced at them, nodded, and returned to his work, guiding a machine that was cutting a piece of metal in an intricate form. She gave Frederick a questioning look. "The machine is computerized, ain't so?"

He nodded. "All approved by the bishop and ministers. It's the only way to cut the precise parts, so it's necessary to the business." He grinned. "It's not as if Ben here can use it to browse the Internet."

"I wasn't questioning . . ." She felt herself flushing. "I didn't mean to sound disapproving. I'm just wondering what Joseph is doing here."

Fred stared at her for a moment, a frown gathering on his face. "He hasn't talked to you, then. I've told him he should be honest with his family."

Judith swung to face him, shaken by the implication that he knew more about the boy she'd raised than she did. "What do you mean? Talked to me about what?"

"Don't put me in the middle, Judith," Fred said quickly. "The boy should tell you himself."

"It seems to me you've already put yourself in the middle. I will deal with Joseph, but I want to know your part in this, and I want to know it now."

He shrugged. "Are you always this bossy? All right, I'll tell you. Joseph is fascinated with the work we do here, and he's talented. Very talented. He actually helped one of the men with the design for a new metal harness part that we'll be selling before long."

Judith absorbed the impact of his words. Joseph's visit today wasn't a one-time thing, then. He must have been coming regularly. And keeping it secret.

"He's always been interested in such things. But I didn't realize . . ." She let that trail off, not sure she wanted to face the implication.

"You didn't realize that this is the work he wants to learn, ain't so?" Frederick's usually jovial voice was serious for once. "I tell you the truth, I've never seen a boy of fourteen with so much aptitude. I only wish one of my own kinder had the gift he does. I'd take Joseph on as an apprentice today if you and Isaac agreed."

She closed her eyes for an instant, imagining Isaac's reaction to such an offer. "And what about the dairy farm? It's intended for Joseph. Isaac has worked so hard—" She stopped, knowing she didn't want to share her family's issues with Fred.

"Well, I guess that's for you to work out." Fred's gaze slid away from hers, as if he was embarrassed. "I think he's in here, working with Zeb Esch."

He led the way through another door to a noisy room filled with machinery and workers. They seemed to be focused on different tasks, none of which made much sense to her.

105

She saw Joseph at once. He was bending over a machine, wearing protective goggles, and he had an expression of such total absorption that she almost didn't recognize him.

"Joseph."

He jerked upright at the sound of her voice, spinning to stare at her, his blue eyes wide and distorted by the goggles.

"J . . . Judith." He stammered her name. "What are you doing here?"

She'd never thought to see the boy look frightened at the sight of her. She had to swallow the lump in her throat before she could speak, giving her an instant to think. The only thing that could make this even worse would be to embarrass him in front of the other men.

"I'm here to give you a ride home." Judith fought to sound normal, struggled to smile. "Are you ready?"

Obviously Joseph knew the question for the command it was. He stripped off the goggles, nodded to the men, and followed her without speaking back through the building.

Wait, she told herself. *Don't say anything where the others might hear.* But her mind was running on ahead of her, her thoughts tumbling like pebbles in a stream.

It wasn't until they'd started down the road toward home that she collected herself enough to speak. "I am disappointed in you, Joseph.

Running off to the machine shop without telling me where you were going—"

"I couldn't." The words burst out of him. "Judith, how could I tell you? You know what Isaac would say about my going there. He doesn't want me to be thinking about anything but the dairy farm."

Please, Lord, give me the words. "The dairy farm is your inheritance. Isaac just wants to help you get ready to run it."

"I don't want to run it!" The statement seemed to explode, rocking Joseph nearly as much as it did her. "I know Isaac thinks I should, but I don't want to. I never did."

Her thoughts reeled wildly. What on earth was the boy saying? He couldn't mean it. "But your father planned—"

Joseph seemed to shake that off before she could even get the words out. "The dairy farm was his dream. And it's Isaac's dream, and maybe Levi's, too. But not mine! Don't you see?"

She stared at the familiar road ahead, trying to make sense of it all. *Careful.* She had to be careful in what she said, or Joseph might stop talking to her altogether.

"I know you've always been fascinated by how things work. You like machinery. That's a good thing. That's what I was telling Isaac just this morning. I tried to show him that it would be a fine idea for you to take that class. Every dairy

107

farmer has to use machinery. Maybe he'll say yes, if he doesn't find out . . ."

She stopped. Was she really thinking of keeping Joseph's visits to the machine shop a secret from Isaac? She couldn't. It wouldn't be right not to be honest with her husband. But how could she tell on the boy and see his relationship with Isaac fall apart?

"I don't want the dairy farm," Joseph repeated. "What sense does it make for Isaac to give up what he loves for me when I don't want it?"

Judith wanted to have an answer for that question. But she didn't.

After a long moment, she shook her head. "I don't know, Joseph. You and Isaac are brothers. You should be able to talk together about this problem."

"We can't. You know he won't understand." Joseph drooped on the buggy seat, head averted, and Judith sensed that he was close to tears.

"If you won't talk to Isaac about it, what will you do?" She asked the sensible question, wondering if Joseph had a plan at all. She'd like to think this was just a case of teenage rebellion that he'd outgrow, but in her heart she suspected he wouldn't. Joseph just didn't have the feeling for the animals that even little Levi had.

Joseph shrugged miserably. "I don't know. Maybe . . . you said he was thinking about letting me take the class. Maybe, when he sees I do well, he'll understand that I really mean it. Maybe then he'll let me go as an apprentice to Fred."

"That's a lot of maybes," she said, her heart wrenched by his obvious pain.

"I know. But . . ." He looked at her, his eyes filled with tears he seemed determined not to shed. "You'll help me, won't you, Judith? You understand. You can convince Isaac."

Could she? Somehow she doubted she had that kind of influence over her husband.

"If we don't get home before Isaac does, all the convincing in the world won't help. If only you'd told me—"

"Well, you didn't tell me you'd talked to Isaac about the class." At her look, he flushed. "I didn't mean that you're to blame. But we're almost home. We'll be there first. And you'll help me show Isaac that my way is right." Joseph had the quick resiliency of youth—and what she felt was unjustified confidence in her ability.

But if she didn't agree to help him, what might he do? Run away? Jump the fence to the Englisch world where he could do what he pleased? If he did, it would be her fault.

And if she did try to help Joseph, and Isaac realized she'd kept Joseph's plans a secret, what would that do to their marriage?

It seemed she was in for grief no matter what she did. Judith's breath caught in her throat. What did she believe, in her own heart, was right for

Joseph? That was the question, and she seemed to see the answer in the handwriting of a woman who'd been faced with difficult decisions over sixty years ago.

All we want is the freedom to choose what's right for us.

Mattie's words echoed in her heart, and Judith confronted the answer. "All right. I'll try to help you if I can."

And she'd pray that the price of that help wouldn't be too much for her to bear.

Lancaster County, August 1953

Adam would probably be arriving soon, and Mattie's fingers fumbled on the late beans she was snapping for supper. How was she to behave normally toward him, with her mother-in-law's words still bouncing around her mind? Her hands stilled on the colander of beans in her lap, and Anna, next to her on the porch swing, grabbed a handful.

"I'll beat you, Mammi," she declared, snapping a bean almost in half in her enthusiasm.

"No, no, just the stem, remember?" Mattie guided her small daughter's fingers to the proper place on the bean. "That's right. Gut work."

Anna grinned, a dimple showing in her cheek. "I can help, ain't so?"

"You are a wonderful gut helper." Mattie dropped a kiss on the top of her head.

Movement caught her eye, and she looked down the lane to see Adam coming toward her. Rachel was walking next to him, maybe having met him at the mailbox by the road. His head was bent, and he seemed to be listening intently to what she was telling him.

Mattie's heart gave a little lurch. One thing that her mother-in-law had said rang true. Adam did care for the children, and they turned to him quite naturally for help, for advice, even for the kind of gentle teasing that a father did so well.

But how could she feel for anyone else the way she had for Ben? She couldn't, that's all.

Adam and Rachel drew closer, and she waved, but his face didn't break into its usual smile. She felt her throat tighten. "Was ist letz? What's wrong?"

Adam exchanged looks with Rachel as they mounted the stairs. He tapped Anna lightly on the nose. "You run along and find your brothers. Mammi's going to take a break from doing the beans for a few minutes."

Anna pouted a little, obviously knowing she was being gotten rid of. But Mattie gave her a look, and she scooted off.

"What is it?" she asked as soon as Anna was out of earshot.

Rachel sat down on the swing in the spot she'd vacated, while Adam leaned against the railing. Rachel's sweet oval face was drawn and serious.

She held out a long white envelope to Mattie. "This was in the mail."

Fingers suddenly awkward, Mattie turned the envelope over so she could read the return address. It was from the office of the superintendent of schools. Her breath caught in her throat. "What . . . what is it?"

"I didn't open it, Mammi. It's addressed to the parents of Rachel Lapp."

Rachel's voice seemed to shake a little on the words. Mattie understood the feeling. It was very rare to get something so official-looking in the mail. And Rachel had only one parent, not two, as the address indicated.

Steeling herself, Mattie ripped the envelope and pulled out the single sheet inside. It wasn't even a letter, just a sheet of directions.

" 'This is to inform you that Rachel Lapp, age fourteen, is assigned to the ninth-grade class at Valley Consolidated High School, Room 204,' " she read aloud. " 'School begins on September third. Your child's bus pickup schedule will be sent to you separately.' "

She broke off then. "Well, we knew it was coming." She hoped she sounded calmer than she felt.

"There's more." Rachel took the paper and read the final lines. " 'Failure to report as assigned will result in prosecution under the Pennsylvania Public School Code.' " She dropped the paper and looked from Adam to her mother, her eyes wide and suddenly frightened, so that she looked like a little girl again. "What does that mean? Will they put us in jail if I don't go?"

"Ach, no, I'm sure it doesn't mean such a thing." Mattie wasn't sure at all, but she had to take that frightened look from her child's face. "No one could do something like that. You must not worry about it."

"I heard from a couple of other people who'd gotten their letters today," Adam said. "They seem to think that's maybe just a formality, the way they phrase the letter. Or the other side of it is that the school board is trying to make us afraid, so we'll do as we're told. Anyway, it's the parents who are responsible, not the young ones." His tone was the easy, gentle one he used with the kinder, but Mattie could see past it to the deep concern in his eyes.

Rachel turned to Mattie in a quick, impetuous movement. "No. They can't punish you. What would we do then?"

"Don't fret yourself, Rachel." She held her daughter's hands in hers. "It won't come to that, you'll see. And if it does . . . well, we must do what is right in the eyes of God, not men."

"Maybe . . . maybe I should just go to the school, the way they want me to." Rachel stumbled on the words.

Mattie's grip tightened. "Do you want to go

there?" Did she know her daughter as well as she thought?

"No." Rachel blinked back the tears that filled her eyes. "I don't. I want to do what we planned for me, the way it's always been. I'm Amish. I want to live Amish, and I have enough school learning already. It's time for me to learn my job, from Ada, and how to be an Amish wife and mother, from you."

"That's what I want for you, too." Relief flooded through her. For a moment she'd half feared she'd been wrong about her daughter.

"But if it means keeping you from being hurt by the law," Rachel added, "I would go to the school, no matter what."

"Stop, now. We can't let being afraid keep us from following our ways." She looked to Adam, longing for his assurance.

"That's right," he said quickly, as if he'd recognized her wordless plea for help. "Besides, this is for the bishop and the ministers to decide. We obey God's laws, not men's laws, ain't so?"

Rachel nodded, wiping away a tear that had escaped. "What will you and Mammi do?"

Mattie's heart jolted as she heard Rachel's obvious assumption that Adam would be part of whatever they decided.

"There's a school board meeting next week." Adam's glance at Mattie seemed wary, as if he wasn't sure how she'd react to whatever it was he intended to say. "Bishop Thomas thinks he and all the fathers of school-age children should attend. Even if they don't allow us to speak, just being there will show how we feel. And maybe they will hear us." He seemed to make an effort to sound hopeful.

"So I must go." Mattie forced the words out.

"No, no, that wasn't what I meant," he said quickly. "No one expects you to attend. Others of us can represent the family for you. Onkel Jonah and I will go."

Adam was trying to give her a way out, just as Rachel had with her offer to attend the new school. One part of Mattie longed to take it—to hide from the responsibility that was being thrust upon her. But she, no one else, was Rachel's parent.

"All we want is the freedom to choose for ourselves," she said slowly. And if she truly believed that, she could not hide and let others do what she should be doing. Hadn't she just said to Rachel that they mustn't let fear keep them from doing what was right? If she expected her child to trust those words, then there wasn't any doubt about what she should do.

"Denke, Adam." She looked at him steadily. "I will be glad of your support. But I must go as well."

CHAPTER SIX

Isaac wiped his hands and face on the towel that hung next to the sink by the back door. Installing that sink had been one of the best things he'd done when they'd rebuilt the house. He had to grin. It didn't matter to him where he washed, but Judith didn't like grubby hands in her kitchen sink, and on a farm there were plenty of those.

He walked through the kitchen, which was sparkling clean but with the aroma of the fried chicken they'd had for supper still in the air. By this time in the evening, Judith would be getting Noah ready for bed.

Sure enough, she sat in the living room rocker, her voice a soft murmur as she read to Noah, who was snuggled on her lap. Isaac paused for a moment, enjoying the way her head bent over the nearly asleep child. Even back when they had been in school together, it had been obvious that gentle Judith would be a wonderful gut mother one day.

When he took another step she glanced up, smiling when she met his gaze. Noah didn't stir— too close to dreamland even to realize his daadi had come into the room. He nodded to the boy as Noah's eyelids drifted closed.

"He's asleep," he said softly.

She craned her neck to look into the face that was turned into her apron. "Ja, I think so." She slid the book onto the table next to her, where the slanting rays of the setting sun turned its cover bright with an image of farm animals. "He wears himself out trying to keep up with the older ones all day."

Isaac sat in his own chair, tilted so that it faced hers, and leaned back, feeling the pleasurable ache of muscles that had been well-exerted. "Sorry I was late for supper. Onkel Simon had too many things to do for two people. He forgets he can't power through the work like he used to."

"It was not a problem." Judith's face was serene. "Of course you should stay and help him. You're so close—like a father and son, ain't so?"

"I guess." The admission made him a little uncomfortable. "He's sehr gut to us, too."

Judith nodded, a trace of a smile lingering on her face. She and Onkel Simon always got on fine —better than Onkel Simon did with his son Lige's wife, to tell the truth. But who wouldn't get along with Judith?

Isaac's gaze lit on the packet of letters that lay on the table under the storybook she'd been reading. The three-cent stamp on the envelope told him what they were. "You were looking through those old letters again, ain't so?"

She nodded. "They're so interesting—like

117

looking right into the lives of Amish women sixty years ago. I keep trying to get through them all, but each time I start, I'm interrupted."

"It's August. Too much to do on a farm in August for extra reading. Maybe you should save them for the long winter nights."

Even as he said the joking words, he seemed to feel the cold floorboards under his feet and the warmth of Judith's body as she curled against him in the double bed. With her snuggled close, he didn't even notice the ice on the window.

"The cousins were so close, even though they lived far apart." Obviously her mind was still on the letters. "They told each other all sorts of things about their daily lives."

"Like you and Rebecca and Barbie," he suggested. "I think you're about as close as sisters."

A smile curved her lips. "Ja, we are. I'm fortunate to have them."

He nodded, though to tell the truth he'd never really understood the need women seemed to have to talk to other women about anything and everything. He was close to his cousins and his uncle, but when they talked, it was always about the job at hand. Definitely not about how they felt. Still, her cousins, as well as these letters, meant something to his wife, so he should show an interest.

"What kinds of things were happening to them back then that were so different from today?"

Judith's eyes kindled at the question, and he realized she'd been eager to talk about it. "Mattie Lapp, the woman who owned the study table, had a terrible bad time of it. The Englisch were demanding that Amish kinder go to big Englisch high schools, whether they wanted to or not. She feared that if her daughter went, it might make her long for things away from the faith."

Isaac frowned a little, trying to remember what he'd been told about this period. "This was before the Supreme Court said we could have our own schools, is that it?"

Judith nodded. "Twenty years before. It seems as if their neighbors thought the Amish were backward. Dumb Dutch. We don't have to face much of that kind of prejudice nowadays."

"Not usually. We're blessed in that way." He leaned his head against the padded back of his chair. "Still, we've got problems of our own. Being more accepted means our young people are exposed to more temptations, like cell phones and computers. And drink and drugs and greed, too, I fear."

Faces swam in his thoughts—Joseph, Levi, Paul, even little Noah. What pressures from the world would they have to overcome in order to stay Amish?

"We can't help worrying about it for our kinder," Judith said gently. "But it's better to pray and trust than to worry, ain't so?"

119

He gave a wry smile. "Better, but not easier."

Judith seemed to be gazing at something far away. "One thing Mattie said several times in her letters is stuck in my head. 'All we want is the freedom to choose for ourselves.' "

Isaac considered the words. "True enough. I think we still feel like that when the world gets too close. But is this your way to ease into talking about Joseph and this class you feel he wants to take?"

Judith's cheeks grew pinker. "It's the same thing, ja?"

"I—" His words were cut off by the thud of feet, and he heard the back screen door slam. Somehow those boys could never come in without letting it slam behind them. Water ran, and a moment later Levi and Paul scurried in, with Joseph looming behind them.

Isaac fixed his eyes on his second son. "Hands?" he inquired.

With a sigh, Paul presented his hands for inspection.

"Looks like you missed some spots. Go back and wash again, and this time use soap and water."

Paul looked a little rebellious, but he obeyed. Shaking her head, probably at the fact that this exchange was repeated almost every night, Judith stood, holding Noah close against her.

Maybe he'd best say what he had to while she

was still downstairs to hear it. "Joseph, Judith tells me there's a class about machinery you want to take at the technical school."

Joseph sent a quick glance from him to Judith. What he saw must have reassured him, because he nodded.

"Do you have the information about it to show me?" Isaac asked when the boy didn't move.

"Ja, ja, for sure." Galvanized, Joseph raced to the bureau and pulled out a paper brochure. He thrust it at his brother. "That's the one I was thinking about." He leaned over Isaac's shoulder to point. "See, this is all about how small machinery is made and how to keep it repaired. That's a useful thing to know, and I've heard from some of the guys that this fellow is a good teacher."

The enthusiasm in the boy's face took Isaac by surprise. Why did Joseph never look that way when they talked about the dairy farm? For an instant he rebelled, even though he'd already agreed with Judith.

He stifled the feeling. What harm could one class do? It was a small price to make the boy happy. This interest of Joseph's in machinery was just a passing fad, and the boy would get over it soon enough.

Judith, standing in the archway with Noah sleeping in her arms, met his gaze, and hers was almost pleading.

"Ach, well, if it's so important to you, I guess you should take the class," he said. "But mind you don't skimp on any of your farmwork because of it."

Joseph's eyes lit up in a way he hadn't seen in a long time. And Judith—Judith came across the rug, bent over his chair, and kissed him right in front of the kinder.

A small thing to agree to, he'd have thought. But it had made two people he cared about very happy, so he supposed it was worth doing, even if he did have doubts.

"I still think we should have gone to Harrisburg to one of the big malls," Barbie said, turning around from her position in the front seat next to the driver they'd hired to take them shopping. "It would have been fun."

"We're buying material for our dresses for my wedding. Isn't that fun without going to some big mall?" Rebecca's tone was a little sharper than normal, making Judith suspect that the stress of preparation was getting to her.

"Bessie and Ada Mae will have what we need," Judith reminded her. "What would be our chances of finding plain blue cotton blends at a big Englisch store?"

The three of them had hired Sam Whitney to take them on this trip to Bessie and Ada Mae's store, since the distance was too far to travel easily by buggy. Sam, a retired mail carrier, seemed to enjoy the diversion. Even now, he met her gaze in the rearview mirror and smiled. She suspected he found Barbie amusing.

"My wife always comes to Bessie and Ada Mae's for her quilting material," he said. "According to her, the mall fabric shops are full of wild animal prints and silver glittery net. Not sure what you'd use that for."

Barbie grinned, never seeming to take offense when her ideas were dismissed.

"Oh, I don't know," she said now. "I could make a tiger-print apron, and Judith would look good in silver glitter, ain't so?"

Rebecca chuckled, her usual good humor restored. "I don't think I'll see Judith in glitter any time soon. As for you—well, you might get more than you bargained for if you went around with a tiger-print apron on."

Sam slowed the car as they approached the turn into the lane. Obviously he'd been here before, probably many times. No one who hadn't would drive so easily to the store, hidden as it was in the country. The lane wound past a cornfield and a stand of trees and then emerged into a cleared space around a barn that had been converted into a fabric shop years earlier.

Bessie and Ada Mae were twin sisters, inseparable, so they claimed, who had married a pair of brothers. As soon as their kinder were grown, they'd embarked on a business that had expanded so much it supplied most of the Amish families in the county with fabric, along with a fair share of Englisch sewers as well, mainly quilters.

Sam pulled the car into the shade of a massive oak tree. "You ladies take all the time you need. I know what the wife is like when she's shopping for material. She must look at every single bolt two or three times before she decides. I brought my newspaper and a cold soda, and I'll just relax." He grinned, his heavy face lightening. "Maybe even take a nap."

"Denke, Sam." Now that they were here at last, Rebecca looked excited. "I hope we won't be that long."

Judith and Barbie followed Rebecca as she hurried to the front entrance. "I wouldn't take bets on it," Barbie murmured. "Once she starts looking, she'll want to compare every bolt of fabric in the shop."

"You wouldn't take bets on anything," Judith reminded her. "But it's only natural, ain't so? You'll be just as bad when you're planning your wedding dress."

"What's the point of looking at everything?" Barbie said. "Rebecca's so traditional that she'll pick blue, you know she will."

"There's nothing wrong with that." Judith's dress had been blue, as well, a lovely deep blue that Isaac had said reminded him of the heart of a violet. "What would you pick?"

Barbie shrugged. "Pink, or purple, or even light green. But my mamm would have a fit."

"So blue, then," Judith said, trying to hide a smile. They stepped inside, to be confronted with a vast space completely filled with row after row of racks of fabric bolts. The colors shone in the light from the long windows the sisters had added when they'd renovated the barn.

Aside from the fabric, there were racks of sewing notions and a long cutting table. Nothing extraneous. The shop was as neat and organized as an Amish kitchen.

Bessie came forward to meet them as soon as they entered the shop, greeting them as if she hadn't seen them in a year. "So gut to see you again." She beamed, her round cheeks the color of ripe apples. "Ach, and for something special, so I guess."

She gave Rebecca a look that said news of her wedding plans had percolated all the way over here, in the mysterious way everyone in the Amish community seemed to know everything.

Rebecca nodded, blushing a little. "How are you, Bessie? And your family?" She glanced around. "Isn't Ada Mae with you?"

"Ach, she's helping an Englisch lady match prints for a quilt. They've been at it a half hour already and nowhere near done yet. I'll tell her you're here. Now, what can we show you? Some solid blue cotton blends, ja?"

"That's right," Rebecca said, and Barbie gave an exaggerated sigh and raised her eyebrows at Judith. Judith ignored her as best she could as they trailed along behind Bessie to the proper aisle.

"Bessie and Ada Mae must do a lot of wedding dress business this time of year," Judith said, once the three of them were alone in a long aisle with fabric on either side. There were rows of cotton blends and more shades of blue than she'd imagined possible.

"For sure." Barbie reached up, her fingertips just touching the top rack. "This is like being in between two rows of field corn in August."

"A little more colorful than corn, ain't so?" Rebecca moved down the aisle, pulling out a bolt here or there that caught her fancy. "There will be so many weddings this year that you'll probably end up going to a couple a day sometimes."

It was often that way as their settlement had grown. With tradition dictating that weddings were usually on a Thursday after Fall Communion and before the weather turned, a lot of weddings were crammed into a short space of time. At least the harvesting and canning were finished before the wedding season started.

Rebecca pulled out a bolt of a deep blue-violet shade. "It's a joy to celebrate the beginning of a new family. Marriage is . . ." She seemed to hesitate, as if searching for the words. "I guess it's a sign that our community is continuing."

"I hope it's more than that," Barbie said tartly. "If I get married, I want it to be a true love match." She waved her hands extravagantly, as if to express the magnitude of her proposed emotion. "I want to find someone who is like the other half of me. Someone I can share everything with."

Rebecca and Judith exchanged glances. "It can be that way," Rebecca said cautiously. "But just remember a marriage is made up of two imperfect people."

Judith nodded, caught off guard by a wave of emotion. Isaac had shown real understanding last night with Joseph, hadn't he? And when they'd lain together in the wide bed, he'd stroked her hair gently, saying he was glad he'd made her happy by agreeing to let Joseph take his class. She'd felt protected and at peace in his arms.

"Judith?" Rebecca's voice sounded as if she'd said the name several times. "Barbie has gotten bored and wandered off, but there was something I wanted to ask you in private anyway."

"Of course." She brought her attention back to the task at hand. "What is it?"

"After the wedding, we'll have our family visits on weekends, and I've had a few reservations for the farm-stay then as well."

Judith nodded. "If the weather is nice, you'll get weekend visitors right into November, ja? Is it a problem?"

"Not really." Rebecca fingered the weight of a fabric, drawing it out from the bolt. "Barbie has been working with me long enough to know how things are supposed to go, so she can take over, but . . ." Rebecca gave a rueful smile. "Well, you know Barbie. I hate to leave her on her own, so I thought maybe you'd be willing to help out for a few weekends."

"Ja, of course. I'll be glad to." Surely Rebecca knew it without asking.

"Not for free," Rebecca added hastily. "It's only fair that you have part of my share for the work you do."

"Ach, I don't want—"

"This is business." Rebecca sounded firm. "All I need to do is cover my expenses. I just don't want to risk losing repeat visitors by closing too early in the season."

Judith couldn't deny that the extra money would come in handy. "We could use it," she admitted. "Isaac is worried about the state of some of the dairy equipment. He says we should be saving for a new motor on the holding tank."

"There, you see, it all works out—" Rebecca stopped as a bolt of fabric caught her eye. She pulled it from the rack and unwound a yard or so.

The lovely deep blue flowed like water down her skirt when she held it against her. "This one," she said, her tone positive. "I mean, if you and Barbie agree."

Judith chuckled. "I don't think we would dare disagree. It's perfect." She glanced around, but Barbie was nowhere in sight. "Drat the girl, where has she gone now?"

"I'll look—" Rebecca began, but Judith shook her head.

"I'll find her. You'd best take that up to the cutting table and make sure there's enough for three dresses." She hurried off before Rebecca could argue.

By walking down the center aisle, she could look along the rows on both sides. She didn't find her quarry until she peered out the front door. There was Barbie. Hands on her hips, she was looking up at a young Englischer on the back of a truck who was unloading boxes of fabric. Her head was tilted flirtatiously, and he was regarding her in obvious appreciation.

"Barbie!" The sharpness in her voice was well deserved, she decided. "Rebecca has found the piece she likes. Come and tell her you like it, too." She spoke in dialect, so there was no danger of the Englischer understanding. "Stop flirting with that Englischer."

Barbie, pouting prettily, waved good-bye and followed her back inside. "Relax, Judith. I wasn't really flirting. I was just staying in practice, sort of."

"Let's keep our minds on why we're here." Somehow Judith didn't think that working with Barbie at the farm-stay was going to be such an easy job. She'd probably earn every cent Rebecca paid her.

In a few minutes' time they were all in agreement and stood at the counter with the fabric bolt. Bessie measured it out with a practiced hand, seeming to figure automatically the amount needed for three dresses. Well, why not? It was her livelihood, after all.

It took them a few more minutes to find the thread that matched perfectly, and then Barbie decided she ought to look for some material for another new dress for herself, but they were still finished before Judith had expected.

When they were walking to the car with their packages, Barbie turned to Judith. "By the way, you never told us what happened with Joseph. Did Isaac agree to let him take the class?"

"He did. Joseph is wonderful happy. He can't wait for the class to start."

"Gut." Rebecca patted her hand. "You see? There was no reason for you to fret over it."

She smiled in response, but her heart didn't seem to cooperate. The truth was that even though Isaac knew about Joseph and the class, he didn't know everything. He wasn't aware that

Joseph didn't want the farm Isaac had worked so hard to build up for him.

How often had she wished that Isaac would open up more to her? And now she was the one keeping a secret. She looked at Rebecca—so happy with their purchases, looking forward to marriage with a man who adored her. And Barbie—still young, still dreaming impossible dreams of the man she'd marry. And here she was, hiding a secret from the man she loved more than anything, risking all their happiness because she didn't see what else she could do.

Lancaster County, August 1953

Mattie's hands clenched in her lap when the driver the bishop had hired to bring them to the school board meeting murmured that they were nearly there. Several other vehicles followed close behind them, also laden with the parents of children who would soon be forced to make this trip every day unless something changed.

No, not parents, she corrected herself. *Fathers.* In an Amish household, it was normally the father who dealt with anything relating to the Englisch law. She was the only mother in the group.

Still, at least she was not alone. Bishop Thomas sat in the front seat beside the driver, his weathered face serene, as if he was prepared to take whatever the Lord should send. She was in the middle of the rear seat, with Adam on one side and Ben's daad on the other. Even as she had the thought, Adam caught her glance and gave her a small, encouraging nod.

"There it is," Bishop Thomas said. A sprawling yellow brick building had appeared ahead on the left, looking more like a factory than like any school Mattie had ever seen. Where were the simple clapboard building, the welcoming pictures in the windows, the school bell hanging by the door? To her eyes, used as she was to a simple four-room schoolhouse, this new building was enormous. She didn't want to imagine her little Rachel finding herself lost in such a place.

The car turned at a wide blacktop drive and swept past a lighted signboard. *Welcome Back to School,* it announced. *Opening Day September 3.* Mattie's stomach seemed to turn over at the reminder. It was coming up fast. Too fast. She felt as if she were standing in the path of an oncoming train.

Their driver stopped at the entrance to the building. Five long, shallow steps, edged on either side with a flat-topped concrete wall, led up to three sets of glass doors. Mattie's imagination filled the scene with Englisch teenagers chattering on the steps and lounging on the walls at either side, the girls in their gathered skirts and ponytails, the boys with their short-cropped hair and collared shirts. What would they make of a few modestly garbed Amish scholars in their midst?

She slid out of the car in Adam's wake. The other vehicles had pulled up behind them, their occupants emerging. It almost looked like a church Sunday, with everyone in their dark clothing, their faces solemn.

Bishop Thomas exchanged a few words with the driver as he waited until the others had assembled. He didn't have to say anything to them about the meeting. They all knew why they were here, didn't they?

His gaze moved from face to face, as if assessing their readiness, and then he nodded. "We will go inside now."

They must have looked an odd group, filing through the glass doors into the huge, modern building. Mattie was grateful for Daad Jonah's presence next to her and for Adam close behind her.

Inside, the wide, tiled hallway was brightly lit and seemed to go on forever. She'd been in a hospital once when her mamm had to have an operation, and it had felt somewhat like this— footsteps echoing along hallways, apprehension building until it nearly choked her.

The bishop started down the hall, apparently knowing where the meeting was to be held. They passed glass cases filled with photographs of school groups and what she supposed were sports trophies. They must have come from the smaller schools this one would replace. The memorabilia seemed to declare the importance of being the best, of winning, as if life were a competition.

There was a sign directing people to a chemistry lab; another to a gymnasium. She peeked through a window at a classroom and saw an array of strange-looking equipment.

Bishop Thomas hesitated at an open door for just a second, closing his eyes as if he was saying a silent prayer. Then he stepped into the lighted room beyond, and they followed him. Mattie stopped on the threshold, feeling an instant of panic, until Adam's light touch on her arm moved her forward.

A long table was set up at one end of the room with nine chairs placed behind it. Men clustered behind it in groups of two or three, talking, while at the end of the table sat a woman in a flowered dress and small hat arranging a notebook and pen in front of her. A few rows of folding chairs faced the front. Only one was occupied—by a bored-looking young man with a notebook and camera.

For an instant, it seemed all sound and action in the room were suspended as everyone stared at the newcomers, and Mattie lowered her eyes at the curious gazes. *We must look like an army of ants,* she thought nervously, *filing into the room in a long, black line.*

Bishop Thomas took the end seat in the second row and the rest of them moved in after him, finding chairs. Once again Mattie found herself with Adam on one side and Daad Jonah on the other. Had they planned it that way? She thought maybe they had, wanting her to feel secure.

There was a hurried, whispered consultation in the front of the room, with a few furtive glances at them. Had the board not expected to see them? The bishop said he had notified the board president that they planned to attend.

Several people seemed to argue in urgent whispers, and then the board members took their places. Each one had a folded paper sign in front of him bearing his name, and Mattie's gaze focused on the name she'd already heard—Walter Graham, the board president.

Mr. Graham's square face and sagging jowls reminded Mattie irresistibly of a bulldog, and at the moment his face was flushed and his eyes narrowed. He looked both annoyed and perhaps a bit wary. He must have thought he'd settled the situation when he'd met with Bishop Thomas.

All in all, she thought the board members' expressions were somewhat like those of the bishop and ministers when faced with a difficult situation regarding one of the Leit. Maybe it was part of human nature to want things to run smoothly and to be made uneasy when they didn't.

Graham shot another glance at Bishop Thomas and then rapped on the table with his knuckles. "Come to order," he commanded.

Mattie's stomach tightened again. If he demanded to know what they were doing here, what would the bishop say? At least she didn't have to speak. No one expected that of her; she need only to sit here. The bishop had said that her presence would remind the board members that real people were affected by the decisions they made.

But Graham seemed to have no such intent. Without looking up from the sheaf of papers in front of him, he rattled through what she supposed were the preliminaries of the meeting. He seemed to check items off on a list as he went, paying no attention at all to his audience.

Some of his fellow board members were not so oblivious to the presence of the Amish. They slipped frequent glances toward them, and one youngish man, wearing a gray suit and a clerical collar, nodded in a welcoming way to Bishop Thomas.

Mr. Graham rattled on. Mattie began to think he would finish the entire meeting without mentioning them when an interruption occurred.

"Excuse me." It was the man with the clerical collar. Mattie craned her neck to read his name sign—*Reverend Michael Colby,* it said. "I see that we have a number of visitors with us today, and it's usual to address their concerns at this point in the agenda."

The board president's face turned an alarming shade of red, but the minister seemed to ignore him as he turned to Bishop Thomas with a friendly smile.

"It's Bishop Thomas Beiler, right? How can the school board be of help to you and your people? Do you have a question you'd like to ask?"

Bishop Thomas rose slowly to his feet. To Mattie he seemed an imposing figure with his lined face and long, graying beard. He seemed to have an unconscious authority no matter in what company he found himself. Did the Englisch see him that way, as well?

"Denke," the bishop said. "I am here tonight with the parents of those of our children who have been ordered to attend this school next month. It is against our wishes and our tradition to have our children—"

Graham cut him off. "We've been all through this! The state has mandated attendance at the public school provided by the district, to the minimum age as directed by the school code, and that ruling applies to everyone."

"Actually, it doesn't," the minister said, his tone mild. "Children who attend a private school or a church school aren't required to come here."

"That doesn't affect this situation." Graham glared at the man. "These people just want to take

137

their kids out of school at age fourteen so they can put them to work on their farms. This country is moving forward. We can't afford to have half-educated, backward citizens. The Amish need to be like everyone else."

The minister seemed to listen attentively to his words, but then his gaze shifted back to Bishop Thomas. From the corner of her eye, Mattie noticed that the young man with the notebook and camera had begun scribbling furiously.

"Will you explain to the board, Bishop Thomas, why the Amish community doesn't want advanced education for your young people?"

The bishop nodded, his face grave. "I'm glad to do so. We Amish choose to live separate from the world in obedience to the Bible. We wish our children to be taught the skills that are necessary for the lives they will live. They will be farmers and craftsmen, and they will be part of the Amish community. They don't need advanced classes for that—better they should be learning how to run a farm or raise a family."

"But what harm will going to high school do? I mean, surely it doesn't hurt anyone to be a little better educated, even if he isn't going to use the information."

The questioner was one of the other board members, who had been silent until now. To her surprise, Mattie recognized him—it was Mr. Matthews, who ran the hardware store where the Amish shopped. He probably knew the Amish community as well as anyone. Surely he didn't think they were backward.

"We fear that if our children come here to school, they will be required to study subjects which are contrary to our beliefs, or that they will be forced to question our ways."

Bishop Thomas spoke with authority, and Mattie realized he must have been doing a great deal of thinking and praying about this situation. She concentrated on the board members, praying that they would listen and understand. She felt Adam shift slightly next to her, and a quick glance at his face told her that he was praying, too.

"We are concerned that they will be laughed at because of their clothes and their habits. They would face such criticism willingly if necessary, but it's not necessary. We fear that the school will teach them that competition, not cooperation, is right, even though it's not an Amish value. We feel that our whole way of life is in danger if our children are forced into this school."

The minister nodded as if he understood, but Graham rapped on the table.

"The board has already voted on this matter. It's no longer up for discussion. Besides, it's a question of fulfilling the requirements of the state. We can't do anything for you."

Mattie watched the face of the young minister,

but he was looking at Graham, who glared at him as if daring him to say another word. A silent battle seemed to ensue between the two men. Then Reverend Colby flushed slightly. He shrugged his shoulders and looked away.

Mattie felt as if a door had been slammed in their faces. For a moment she'd thought there was a chance for them. Now it seemed there wasn't.

Her thoughts reached out in a silent prayer for guidance and strength. These trials were nothing compared to those of the martyrs who had been tortured and killed for their faith back in Europe in the early days. Still, the burden felt very heavy indeed.

CHAPTER SEVEN

Judith glanced across the room as she finished tidying the kitchen that evening. Isaac sat at the study table, frowning earnestly at the papers in front of him, for all the world like one of the kinder absorbed in his schoolwork. This was a pleasant time of day, with the boys settled and the house quiet.

Smiling a little, she hung up the dish towel and crossed the room to put her hand on Isaac's strong, solid shoulder.

"Doing your spelling words?"

He looked up and grimaced. "I wish I were. This paperwork for the dairy gets more complicated every month, it seems like. And there's more of it, too. It wonders me that we don't all drown in a sea of paper."

"I know what you mean. It seems kind of foolish, too. The cows supply the milk, you deliver it to the dairy, and they bottle and sell it. Why do they need all these rules and regulations?" It was in the back of her mind to offer her help, but she wasn't sure how Isaac would receive it.

"Simple to you and me, maybe, but not to the health department or the occupational services people or the tax collectors." He rubbed the back of his neck as if tension had set in there, and her heart moved.

"Is there something I can do? Fill in some of the forms, maybe, if you showed me how?"

"No." His response was quick and short, and in an instant she saw that he thought he'd been too brusque. "Denke, sweetheart." He captured her hand in his. "It's gut of you to offer, but I should do it myself. You could cut me another piece of that peach pie, though."

"That'll give you strength to get through it, ja?" Judith said the words lightly, not wanting him to know that his quick refusal had hurt.

She cut the wedge of pie, reminding herself that she'd expected nothing else. Plenty of Amish husbands and wives worked together on family businesses. There was no reason why she couldn't handle the dairy paperwork except that Isaac had such a strict view of the division between men's work and women's work in running a farm.

Carrying the plate and a fork, Judith went back to the study table, preserving her smile. "Some milk or coffee with it?"

"Milk would be gut." He gave the papers another frown before shoving them away to make space for the pie. "You'd probably do a neater job of filling in these forms than I do. When we were in school, you always got the job of writing things on the board because you were such a neat printer."

Her smile became more genuine. "You were just too eager to get through the work and on to recess, that's all. You were always the first one out to the school yard, holding a ball or a bat."

"Most likely so." Isaac took an eager gulp of the milk she proffered, acting so like the boys for a moment. "All I wanted was to finish school and start working the farm with Daad. If I'd known all this was involved, maybe I'd have tried harder at the schoolwork."

Mentioning his father had brought a shadow to Isaac's face, and she sought to find a means of chasing it away. "I think boys are more practical about learning than girls. Boys want to know only the things that interest them or they can use, but girls seem to enjoy finding out about all sorts of subjects. That was true for me, anyway."

He nodded. "Could be." His expression softened. "Know what I remember about you?"

Judith shook her head, hoping it was something nice.

"I remember how good and patient you were when you helped out with the little ones. Teacher Emma said you'd make a fine teacher, but when I saw it, I thought you'd make a fine mother, and I was right."

Judith tried to show suitable appreciation of the rare compliment, but her heart seemed to be turning to ice. He'd looked at her even then and thought she'd make a good mother, and when he'd realized his small brother needed a mammi, he'd turned to her. She'd been the logical answer to his problem.

Something—some need to provoke another response, maybe—urged her to speak. "Frederick Yoder told me once that you'd snapped me up before any of the other boys had a chance."

Isaac's face darkened. "He would. I think he had his eye on you all along." He looked up at her, frowning. "When were you talking to Fred?"

She shrugged, appalled that she'd let her pain push her into saying the one thing she shouldn't. "Ach, I don't know. I see him around, ja? His kinder are in school with Levi, after all."

"That Fred," he muttered. "He flirts with every

female he comes across. It wonders me that his wife lets him get away with it."

It would be nice to think Isaac was the teeniest bit jealous, but Judith couldn't convince herself of it. "It's just Fred's way. Nobody pays any attention to it. If anyone ever took him seriously, he'd run the other direction. He's a little like my cousin Barbie. She can't help flirting, it seems."

Something seemed to tickle Isaac about comparing Fred with Barbie, because his expression eased. "I'm wonderful glad you're not like your cousin. I wouldn't want you flirting. And isn't it about time Barbie picked someone and settled down?"

"She's young yet," Judith said, trying not to think of her own concerns about Barbie. "One day she'll fall in love, and that will end her flirting for good. But speaking of my cousins, Rebecca has asked me for some help."

"More wedding stuff?" He raised his eyebrows.

"Sort of. After their marriage, she and Matt want to start their weekend visits to the family, but she still has some guests scheduled for the farm-stay on a few weekends. She asked if I could help Barbie run the place." She rushed on to what she considered the best part. "And she insists on paying me my fair share, too. Won't that be nice? We can put the extra money toward the new equipment for the dairy."

Isaac didn't respond immediately, turning his

fork over in his hand. He was silent for long enough to make Judith feel chilled. "How can you find the time?" he said. "You have too much to do as it is, with all the canning and preserving and everything else. It's all right for Barbie. She's not married."

Judith stared at his bent head. If he looked at her, she might know what was in his mind, but he didn't.

"This wouldn't be until November, most likely," she pointed out. "Everything will be put up by then, and the kinder will be well into their school routine. There will just be Noah home during the day."

Isaac's fork clacked against the table as he put it down. "That's another thing. What about the boys? They won't be in school on the weekends. They still need to be watched and fed and taken care of. I can't do everything."

"No, of course not." Surely he didn't think she meant for him to take over the house. She hadn't expected this reaction, and she wasn't sure how to handle it. "Eli's wife will be glad to help, I know."

Her young brother Eli had married his Miriam last wedding season, and they were eager for a family of their own. Miriam loved any opportunity to mind the young ones. It was good practice, she always said.

"Besides, Barbie and I will split the work. I

won't have to be there all the time when there are visitors."

Since Barbie didn't have a family yet, it made sense that she would take on more of the responsibility, and after all, she was the one who'd been working with Rebecca all summer. She knew far more about it than Judith did.

"I won't neglect you and the kinder," she said softly, putting her hand on Isaac's shoulder. "Besides, the extra money will—"

"You don't have to go out and work to support us." The words came out in a harsh tone that was so unlike Isaac it startled her. His shoulder was a hard knot under her hand. "I can take care of the farm and my family."

Her heart twisted at his tone. "Ach, Isaac, I know you can. You have always taken gut care of all of us." Couldn't he understand her feelings at all? "I just thought I could help a bit, too. And Rebecca does need me."

He was stiff and silent for another second. Then he let out his breath in a sigh and rubbed his hands down his face as if to wipe something away.

"Rebecca needs you. Of course you must help her if you can." He planted his hands on the table in front of him—the good, strong hands of a man who worked hard every day. "I just . . . sometimes I wonder if my daad would be pleased with the job I'm doing if he saw the place today."

Shocked, Judith seized his shoulders and pulled

him around to look at his face. "What are you saying? You have done everything anyone could possibly do to make the dairy farm a success. And you said yourself it's a lot more complicated than it used to be. Your daad would be wonderful happy with all you've done. As I am."

Isaac didn't respond for a moment. Then his hands went around her waist, and he drew her close, turning his face against her breast. "Denke, Judith. I couldn't do it without you."

She held him close, her heart overflowing with her love for him. And with sorrow, too, because he was working so hard to give Joseph something that Joseph didn't want at all.

Two weeks later, Judith began to think life was actually returning to an even keel. The boys were both in school, so that she and little Noah spent much of the day alone together. Joseph seemed to be approaching his normal cheerfulness now that his vocational class would start soon, and she was too grateful for his changed attitude to worry unduly about future decisions. After all, he might become disenchanted with his class once he got into it and decide that the dairy farm was best for him after all.

"Mammi, I want to do homework, too." Noah tugged at her skirt, knowing his brothers would soon be seated at the study table. "Please, can I do homework?"

"That's silly." Paul, who was having an after-school snack, spoke from the lofty heights of a brand-new first-grader. "You're not in school, so you can't have homework. Homework is school-work you do at home."

Judith put a warning hand on Paul's shoulder. "We don't talk that way to each other, Paul Wegler. Your little bruder can have homework if he wants. Finish your snack now, both of you."

Chastened, he nodded, stuffing a large bite of snickerdoodle into his mouth and then attempting to talk around it. "I know what, Noah. You should practice printing your name. Teacher Sally was happy I could print my name so well."

Judith wiped up crumbs. Teaching manners to small boys was no easy task, but she'd rather her sons be kind than be neat.

"Levi, will you empty the paper trash in the burn barrel before you start your homework? Joseph will burn it later." There was no point in calling for him to do it now, since the early September day had turned a bit breezy.

Levi, following his brother's example and stuffing most of a cookie in his mouth, nodded and slid off his chair. He grabbed the wastebasket and ran out the back door. The screen door slammed, and she heard Levi's feet pound the steps as he jumped down them. She'd always thought the boys would be tired when they came home from a full day of schoolwork, but she'd been wrong. The kinder always came home from school both ravenous and bursting with energy, it seemed.

"Komm." She took Noah's hand. "You sit right up at the study table. You and Paul can start your homework."

In a few minutes the three boys were seated at the old table, three fair heads bent over the papers in front of them with varying degrees of concentration.

Levi was as conscientious about school as he was about everything he did, but she saw him glance toward the back window now and then, as if wondering what his daadi was doing. Paul, still in the early ages of excitement at being grown up enough to go to school, frowned at his paper, the tip of his tongue showing at the corner of his mouth as he concentrated. Noah seemed to have given up writing his name and become engrossed in drawing a picture of a horse.

How many other young Amish scholars had sat at this table over the years? Judith knew about Mattie's kinder, feeling close enough to her to be able to envision her bending over her young ones' work. There had probably been others, both before and after.

It gave her such a strong sense of continuity to think of those other mothers and kinder going about their lives in much the same way she and her family did. One day she must show her boys the old exercise notebooks she'd found—

A shout from outside had her head jerking around. What . . . ?

"Fire! Fire!"

The hoarse cry struck her like a lightning bolt, paralyzing her for an instant. Then she was running, praying, her breath catching . . .

Judith bolted out the back door, hearing the children scrambling behind her, their voices frightened. She stumbled and nearly fell down the porch steps in her haste. Flames shot from the top of the burn barrel, and scraps of fiery paper floated on the breeze, a danger to everything in their path.

The grass had already caught. Isaac was beating at the flames with the flat of a shovel. A bit of flaming trash landed on the shed roof, just feet from the burn barrel, and the shingles began to smolder.

Judith started to run, then wheeled around as she realized the boys were hurrying after her. She grabbed Levi by the shoulders, shocked at his white face and frightened eyes. "Run to the phone shanty. Dial nine one one, just like Daadi showed you. Tell them there's a fire, and give the address. Can you do that?"

"I will." His voice shook a little, but he seemed to straighten under her hands. He darted toward the phone shanty. Thank goodness they had practiced this very emergency. She caught Paul when he would have followed.

"Paul, go to Onkel Simon's. Tell him what's happened. Hurry now. Run!" He raced off, and she turned to her youngest. "Noah, you stand on the porch chair and ring the bell. Loud as you can, and keep ringing it."

She waited for his nod before she ran to the outside faucet and turned the water full on. The hose wasn't long enough to get to the burn barrel, because Isaac had used the extension for something a few days earlier. But maybe the spray would be strong enough to reach the flames.

Above her head, the dinner bell began its clamor, thanks to Noah's love of making a noise. Anyone within earshot would know the prolonged sound meant trouble.

Dragging the hose, Judith hurried across the yard. "Isaac, the shed. The roof."

His head turned, giving her a brief glimpse of his face, which was as white as Levi's had been. *Fire.* The word alone must be enough to bring his horrific memories surging back.

He snatched the hose from her hands, trying to concentrate the spray onto the shed roof, so Judith took over beating at the ground fire with the shovel. They could ignore the barrel at the moment, since the fire there was contained and already dying down. But the flames that had caught the grass were moving fast—too fast.

They seemed to flatten out at every strike but then spring back up again, shooting higher each time as if they enjoyed the battle with her.

"Never mind that. It's doing no good." Isaac grabbed the shovel. "Bring buckets."

For an instant her mind didn't seem to work. Feed buckets. The barn. That would be closest. She ran for the barn, the bell still clanging. Someone shouted from a distance, but she didn't dare stop long enough to look. A moment's delay could mean the difference between saving or endangering a structure.

Thank God none of the animals were inside. They'd be safe enough in the pasture, even if the flames should get this far. Grabbing the stack of rubber feed pails, she hurried back outside. *Please, God, please, God . . .* The prayer kept time with the wild beating of her heart.

Fill the buckets, carry them to Isaac, run back for more while Isaac threw the water on the flames, and all the while the fire crept stubbornly along the shed roof and down the walls. The shed, the diesel generator inside—if they lost the generator, what would they do?

Arms aching, she was filling another bucket when someone seized it from her. Onkel Simon pushed her gently away.

"We will do it. Keep the kinder safe."

She stumbled back a step, realizing that his son Lige was with him, while from the other direction the neighbors came running. Half crying, she grasped Paul and Levi and drew them toward the house.

"I can help." Levi tried to pull away, but she held him firmly.

"No. You heard what Onkel Simon said. The men will do it." She took them back to the porch where Noah still stood on his chair, his face red, pulling the bell rope as fast as his little arms could move.

Judith put her arms around him, stilling the sound. "Gut work. It's enough now. Everyone heard. They're all helping."

They were. But the flames ate into the generator shed despite their efforts. By the time the fire truck came screaming down the lane, siren wailing, the shed was little more than a heap of black, smoking rubbish.

Judith had to restrain Paul and Noah from running after the fire truck. "They've come to fight the fire. You can watch from here."

"But, Mammi, it's the real fire truck," Paul protested. "I want to see it up close."

"Ja, but the volunteers have work to do. We mustn't get in their way. Look, here comes your grossmammi." It was actually her mamm, daad, and three other relatives, and she couldn't imagine how they'd heard about the fire so quickly. The young ones' eyes were mostly for their beloved grossmammi.

Mamm climbed down from the buggy, and the two younger boys hurried to help with the containers she began unloading, while Daad, her brother, and two of her cousins ran toward the fire.

Levi seemed to linger by the porch, and Judith frowned. Normally he would be the first one to rush to his grandmother. What was wrong with the boy?

"I had a coffee cake and some shoofly pie left from my baking, so I brought them." Mamm carried a gallon jug of lemonade while the boys toted the baked goods. "We'd best get ready to feed the helpers."

The reminder galvanized Judith. She couldn't stand here staring. Fighting a fire was hot, dirty work. The least she could do was have some cold drinks ready for the men. "We can set things up on the picnic table. If we all help, I think we can move it closer to the house so it won't be in anyone's way."

With her improvised crew, she edged the heavy wooden picnic table away from the path of the fire hoses and then hurried into the house to start a pot of coffee and slice the loaves of nut bread she'd made earlier. The young ones trotted along to help, jabbering away about the fire and stopping to exclaim when the stream of water arced from the pumper's hose to put out the flames that had survived the determined assault of the men.

"The flames went so high, Grossmammi," Noah said, lifting his fingers above his head. "It was scary."

"I wasn't scared," Paul said quickly. "I ran as fast as I could to get Onkel Simon."

"Well, I rang the bell." Noah was determined to claim his grandmother's attention.

"You were all gut helpers," Judith said firmly.

"That's right," Mamm said, smiling at her grandsons. "I know you all did everything you could to help."

"Levi used the phone to call for the fire truck." Judith glanced at her oldest, feeling a little surprised that he hadn't chimed in with his own claim.

Levi was looking out the back door, hands pressed against the screen. Something about his rigid figure made Judith's heart twist.

"Levi?" She went to put her hand gently on his shoulder.

He tensed. "If the barn burns, what will we do?"

Judith tried to hug him against her, but his small body was stiff. She exchanged a worried look with her mamm. "It won't." She put all the confidence she could find into the words. "The men had the grass fire almost out even before the fire truck arrived. Look, you can see that they are wetting down the barn with the big hose now. They won't let it burn."

Levi seemed to strain against the door for

another moment, but then he nodded. "They won't let it burn," he repeated, as if it were a promise.

Was he worrying about the animals? But he knew as well as she did that they'd all been turned out to pasture already.

"Komm and help with the food," she urged. "You can carry things out to the picnic table. The men will be glad of a drink and something to eat."

Rejoining her mother, Judith took a tray from the cupboard and began putting glasses on it, keeping a wary eye on Levi. But he took the plate his grossmammi had ready and carried it carefully out the back door.

"He's worried," Judith murmured.

"Ach, it's scary for sure," Mamm said. "Fire always is. How did it start? Do you know?"

"I'm not sure." It was the first moment she'd been able to think about it, and she realized how strange it was. "I heard Isaac shout and ran out to see the burn barrel blazing. Bits of paper flew out and touched off the fire on the grass and the shed roof."

Mamm turned a disapproving glance on her. "Don't you use a screen on the barrel?"

"Ja, of course we do."

Mamm seemed about to argue, but she glanced at the kinder. "Best we don't talk about it now, ain't so? They might think . . ." She let the sentence trail off, but Judith knew where it had been going.

The young ones knew something about the fire that had destroyed their daadi's home when he was young. It was impossible to keep the story from them. But they seldom mentioned it, and she wasn't sure how much that might be a part of Levi's upset.

Luckily the cookie jar was full. Judith arranged snickerdoodles and chocolate chip cookies on a large tray and sent the boys out with it. She and her mother followed, carrying glasses and beverages.

A few trips were enough to get everything out on the table, and by then one or two of the volunteer firemen were ready for a break.

"Fire's out now." Jim Reilly, head of the local volunteers, nodded with satisfaction. "We'll wet it down a bit more, just so you won't have to worry, but it's out."

"I don't know what we'd do without you and the other firemen." Isaac was a member of the volunteer fire company, and Joseph soon would be. That was how Isaac had known exactly how to fight the blaze.

Jim shrugged, mopping his red face. "It wasn't much of a fire, but enough to give the boys a little practice. Sorry about the shed. If we'd gotten here a bit faster—"

"Don't think that," Judith said quickly. "It burned so fast no one could have done anything."

"Yeah, those old planks go up like tinder when

they catch a spark," he said. "Sorry. Anything valuable in there?" Jim, knowing the Amish, would realize they didn't have insurance on anything.

Her throat tightened. "The diesel generator was there. It's gone completely."

And without a generator, they couldn't run the automatic milking machine or the bulk milk tank. The dairy they sold their milk to would have to be told. Isaac would be terribly upset.

"Mighty sorry for the loss." Jim's bluff, hearty face expressed regret even as she sensed he'd enjoyed the small excitement of putting out the fire. "We'll make sure there's no sparks left before we take off."

"Denke." Her worried gaze sought out Isaac. When she spotted him, the breath caught in her throat. He stood glaring at Joseph, clutching him by the shoulder, fury in every line of his body.

Fairly running across the lawn, she reached him in time to hear his angry words. ". . . trust you with a simple job like burning the trash, and you can't even do that right. You realize what you did? Without the generator, we'll lose the contract with the dairy."

Onkel Simon put a restraining hand on his shoulder, but Isaac shook it off, probably not even realizing who it was. Joseph's face twisted. "I didn't. You blame me for everything, but I didn't do it."

He hadn't, she realized. He hadn't even been here. The scooter lay by the porch where he'd dropped it, but he hadn't been anywhere around when the fire must have started.

"Who else—" Isaac began.

"Isaac, stop," she said quickly, the words racing ahead of her thoughts. But there was only one way this could have happened. "Joseph didn't start the fire." She focused on Levi's small face, dreading the fact that she had to say the words. "Levi, do you want to tell Daadi something?"

Levi was white, his face strained, his fists clenched. His mouth trembled as he nodded, and he swallowed hard. "I'm sorry, Daadi. I'm sorry, Mammi. I didn't mean it. When I brought the trash out, I thought I could help. I thought I could burn the trash as well as Joseph could."

Isaac let go of his brother, his face tightening. "How did this happen?" Judith had the feeling the question was addressed to her as well as to Levi.

"I had Levi take the kitchen trash out so that Joseph could burn it later, after the wind died down. I guess Levi wanted to help."

Wanted to show what a big boy he was, she suspected. He always wanted to show his daadi that he was big enough to contribute to the farm.

Isaac stooped to his son's level. "Is that what happened, Levi?"

The boy nodded miserably, blinking back tears.

"I thought I could do it. The screen was sehr heavy. I guess I didn't get it back on far enough."

"You must never do something like that without asking first." Isaac ran his hands down Levi's arms, and Judith knew he was trying not to picture Levi with his clothes ablaze. "It is much too dangerous."

"Ach, the boy knows it now." Onkel Simon interrupted him, putting one hand on Joseph's shoulder. "There's nothing to be done but to get the cows milked by hand. We've got plenty of willing workers here, so we'd best get at it." He nudged Joseph along. "We'll start them moving to the tie-stall barn, ain't so?"

Joseph looked as if he was ready to burst out with something, but he met his uncle's gaze and nodded.

"Right." The old man and the boy moved off together. The rest of the men, knowing what was needed without asking, headed for the tie-stall barn. Their neighbors and relatives would be here to help with the milking as long as they were needed.

But judging by the bleak expression on Isaac's face, that was small comfort to a man who'd just seen a crucial part of his business go up in smoke.

Still, that was no excuse for his having jumped to the conclusion that Joseph was to blame. How could the trouble between them ever heal if Isaac lost his temper that way?

CHAPTER EIGHT

Lancaster County, August 1953

Summer was fading into autumn, and still there was no resolution to the school conflict. Adam, perched on a branch of the apple tree in Mattie's small orchard, picked another ripe apple and dropped it to Toby, waiting below.

"Me, me," Anna squealed, bouncing on bare feet under the tree. "Throw one to me, Cousin Adam."

"The next one is for you," he promised. Reaching over his head, he found an especially bright red one and tossed it gently. Anna, apparently not trusting her small hands, caught it in her apron and raced to the basket they were filling.

Adam could only thank the gut Lord that the younger kinder didn't seem to be affected by the burden that pressed on the adults. He'd felt for days as he did when a storm brewed in the western sky. There was the same sense of black clouds massing, the same weight of heavy air and rumbles of thunder. Everywhere he went, he was greeted with worried distraction by the Leit and a kind of open suspicion by the Englisch.

161

"More apples," Toby demanded. "Rachel and Nate have their basket almost full."

Adam was just as glad to be distracted from his thoughts. "Right. Here they come."

He sped up, picking faster. As Toby had said, Nate and Rachel made a quick team, with Nate in the tree picking steadily while Rachel's deft hands sorted the apples as they went into the baskets. They were working in the McIntosh tree—Mattie especially prized those apples for sauce, so any bruised ones could be used for it.

"Mind the apples don't have a bad spot before you put them into the keeping basket," he charged his helpers. "One bad one in the bottom can spoil the whole basket, ain't so?"

Toby nodded solemnly, but Anna looked up at him with her bright curiosity showing. "Why? How can it do that?"

He grinned down at her, softening as always at the sight of this child who was what his little Sarah might have become. "If one apple in the bunch isn't sound, that spoiled spot spreads to the other apples around it, making them go bad as well. Understand?"

Anna considered for a moment, then nodded as if satisfied. "I'll be careful. I'll look at every single one."

"Gut girl." He supposed, in a way, that was what they were trying to do in preventing their impressionable children from being sent off to the

162

big consolidated school. Even one Amish child who succumbed to the lure of fancy clothes or drinking or even doubting their Creator could infect those around them.

Be ye separate from the world. That was the Biblical instruction the Amish followed, but right now the Englisch seemed determined to force change on them even when they were convinced it ran counter to their faith.

He glanced at Rachel. She was laughing up at Nate, looking as sweet and wholesome as always. But he'd seen the worry and doubt in her face when she thought no one was watching her. This situation was especially hard on her.

"Are you thinking or picking, Adam Lapp?" Mattie's voice, coming from below him, startled him so that he jerked and nearly lost his balance.

"Careful," she cried, her tone sharp with worry. Not all of it was for him, he knew.

"I'm fine." He tossed an apple down to her to demonstrate, and she fielded it easily. "Gut catch."

"I'm not that out of practice," Mattie retorted. "I could probably climb that tree as well as you."

He leaned down toward her, grinning. "Dare you."

For an instant it seemed she'd take him up on it, her face laughing and as young as Rachel's. Then she glanced at the young ones and shook her head. "Better not. I have an example to set, ain't so?"

But the kinder had caught the tone of the conversation. "Do it, Mammi," Rachel said. The others joined in, making so much noise that Mattie put her hands over her ears.

"All right, all right. I'll do it just this once." Almost before Adam realized what she was about, Mattie had caught a branch, put her foot in the fork of the tree, and hoisted herself up.

"Careful." He reached out to catch her arm, holding her securely.

Mattie wrapped one arm around the trunk of the apple tree, laughing. Leaves draped over her head, and one apple hung next to her shoulder as if it had perched there. Leaf-dappled sunlight filtered through the branches to gild her fair skin with gold.

He had to say something. He couldn't just stare at her like a gawking tourist. "What will your mamm have to say to me if I let you fall?"

"Probably that a woman my age shouldn't be so foolish as to go climbing trees." Amusement touched her eyes and her gaze caught his—caught and held—and suddenly he couldn't breathe.

Mattie was as dear to him as she'd always been, but now he felt more for her, so much more. Emotion stirred between them, thickening the air and making his heartbeat thunder in his ears.

And Mattie felt it, too. It was there in the startled expression darkening her eyes and the way her lips parted. In a moment—

"Throw down an apple, Mammi!" Toby shouted. Mattie jerked back against Adam's arm, breaking the spell. He glanced down, away from her, afraid she'd read too much in his eyes.

Rachel gave Toby a slight shove, and he shot her an indignant look. "What'd you do that for?"

"You shouldn't interrupt grown-ups," she scolded.

"But they weren't talking." Toby's lower lip came out, and he looked prepared to continue the argument.

"Never mind," Mattie said hastily. "I'm coming down. We'll let Adam and Nate do the tree-climbing."

"It'll be time for milking soon." Adam was talking at random, trying to cover up his confusion. Had Rachel actually recognized what was happening between them?

"Why don't we just finish up the trees you're working on now? You've picked plenty of apples to keep me busy for a couple of days." Mattie had reached the ground, and she bent to pick up a half-filled basket that had tipped on its side.

"Right." Adam tried to focus on the apples within his reach. That seemed to be the only safe thing to think about at the moment.

By the time he slid down from the tree, both baskets were full and he'd regained his composure enough to smile normally at Mattie. "Be sure you save me some applesauce," he said.

"I will, but I can do better than that after you helped the kinder pick all these apples. How about an apple crumble pie?"

"Yum. Your mamm makes wonderful gut apple crumble pie, ain't so?" He tapped the top of Nate's straw hat and got an instant grin.

"Save some for us," Nate said. "Don't eat it all."

"You kids run and get the wagon to take the baskets down," Mattie said. "I'll make sure there's plenty of pie for everyone."

Rachel grabbed Anna's hand. "Komm. We'll race the boys."

The four of them dashed down the gentle slope toward the barn, with Rachel suiting her long stride to the small steps of her little sister.

He smiled, watching them, but then he noticed Mattie's expression. She was looking at Rachel, and the worry was back in her face.

"No news?" he asked gently.

Mattie shrugged. "You know how the pastor on the school board said something about private schools? The bishop spoke to him after the meeting, and he thinks if we start our own schools, the board might leave us alone."

He considered the idea and found it growing on him. "It might be the only answer. As long as our kinder were going to the little school down the road with other farm kids, it didn't matter so much who was Englisch and who was Amish. We all understood each other. But now it's different."

166

"I keep thinking about how bad feelings were when the war started and the Englisch thought our boys should go for soldiers." Mattie turned wide, frightened eyes on him. "Rachel isn't old enough to remember what it was like. But I remember the mean things people said and how some of the neighbors stopped buying our produce. Is it going to be that way again?"

Adam had to be honest. "I don't know. I hope not. But our promise not to use violence against any person was important enough to cling to no matter what happened."

He found he was struggling to articulate his deepest beliefs. The Amish didn't generally talk much about what they believed and why. They just lived their faith.

"Maybe this situation is similar to that one. Sending our kinder out of our community and teaching them things that are contrary to our beliefs—this might be another breaking point between us and the world."

Mattie closed her eyes for a moment, and he thought she was reaching out in prayer. Finally she looked at him and made an effort to smile. "We were brought up on the stories of the martyrs, ain't so? I just never thought we would have to be the ones to make a stand."

"I know." His voice was husky with the pain he felt. It wasn't fair—that was all he could think. Mattie had struggled through the loss of Ben and tried so hard to raise their kinder on her own. It wasn't fair that she had to face so much trouble and make such difficult choices.

More than anything else, he wanted to protect and care for Mattie and her children. But how could he ever find a balance between his loyalty to Ben and his own desires?

The acrid smell of burning lingered in the air as Judith went through the nightly routine of settling the boys in bed. Getting everyone bathed had been a chore, with soot everywhere. The soot-covered laundry could wait until tomorrow, but her sons had to be clean.

She tucked a sheet over Noah, who was asleep already after all the excitement. In the other twin bed of the room they shared, Paul was letting his eyes drift shut, even as he still tried to talk about the fire truck.

"Shh." She patted Paul gently. "Tomorrow is another day. Go to sleep and dream about being one of the fire volunteers."

He seemed to snuggle the idea close as he turned to curl up on his side. In a moment he was sound asleep.

Judith stood, stretching, tired as much from the stress of the fire as anything else, she supposed. She hadn't really had much to do once the initial flurry of trying to hold back the flames had been taken over by the men.

When she'd finally gone back into the house after the fire truck had left, she'd discovered her kitchen counters and refrigerator filled with food—the inevitable Amish answer to trouble. Word must have spread at the speed of light. More and more folks had shown up to help or to bring supper, until there had been more volunteers than there had been jobs to do.

She stopped at the window in the hallway on her way to the bedroom shared by Levi and Joseph. Most people had gone home by now, promising to be back for the morning milking, but she could still hear the low rumble of male voices from outside.

They were probably trying to figure out a way to save the milk, but she feared there wasn't a solution. Isaac had sent jugs home with everyone who could take it, but the rest would have to be dumped—such a terrible waste. The dairy couldn't take the milk unless it had been properly handled, and without the generator that was impossible.

If the dairy decided to cancel their contract . . .

She stopped her thoughts from heading in that direction and turned instead to a silent prayer of thankfulness. No one had been injured. The dairy herd was fine. What had happened was part of God's will for them, and they must accept, even when it was difficult.

Judith moved to the other bedroom and opened

the door quietly, hoping Levi had been exhausted enough to fall asleep. He hadn't, of course. He was sitting up in bed, his arms wrapped around his knees, staring at nothing. His brooding expression was so like the one Isaac sometimes wore that it shook her. *Please don't let him shut me out the way Isaac does.*

Levi looked up when she came in but then resumed his study of the footboard of his bed. Sighing a little, she squeezed onto the bed next to him, leaning against the headboard and putting her arm around his shoulders. His little body felt stiff against her for a moment, and then he seemed to relax, turning his face into her sleeve.

"It's all right, you know," she said, stroking his hair. "Everyone understands that it was just an accident."

He shook his head a little. "Daadi will think I was dumb."

"Ach, Levi, don't say such a thing. Daadi doesn't think that at all. He knows you were trying to help. He's just wonderful glad you weren't hurt by the fire, and it makes him scared. You know that, don't you?"

He hesitated and then nodded, but her mother's instinct told her there was more going on.

"Komm, now. Tell me what is troubling you. Things never seem so bad once we've shared them with someone who loves us."

"I wanted to help. I did." He pulled away

170

enough to look at her, as if there was something she must understand.

"I know. Daadi knows, too." She waited.

Levi looked down, sniffing a little as he held back tears. "I wanted Daadi to see that I'm big enough to help with the farm."

Surprise held her immobile for an instant before she gathered her wits. "But you do help, Levi. You help with the milking, and Daadi is always saying how gut you are with the animals."

He shook his head, not looking at her. "It's not enough."

Why? That was what she wanted to ask, but she held back the question.

"Levi, Daadi wants you to learn how to farm gradually. That's how a child is meant to learn. Your onkels and cousins all learned that way, taking on more and more responsibilities as they became older. You will, too."

She could still feel him holding back from her, and she struggled to understand. He was worried. She could sense it. Finally she grasped his shoulders firmly, insisting he look at her. "You aren't telling me something. What is it?"

Levi's gaze slid away from hers. "I know," he muttered finally.

"You know what?" Her heart was aching for him, but she kept her voice calm.

"I know that the farm won't be mine!" The words came out quickly now, in a high-pitched flow that startled her. "I know what Daadi says. The farm will be Joseph's. But it's not fair. I love the farm. I love every one of the cows. And Joseph doesn't even want it." He stopped, his eyes wide, and clapped his hand over his lips.

So. She should have realized. For that matter, Isaac should have realized.

"It's all right." She drew Levi close against her, holding him as if he were a baby again. "I know." How could she defend a decision she didn't even agree with? "Listen, Levi. Daadi knows how much you love farming. He will provide for each one of you boys. There will be a farm for you."

Was she right? She prayed so. But if the dairy dropped its contract with them, money would be tight. What would the future hold for any of them? The question frightened her, but right now it was more important to comfort her son than to think about trouble that might or might not come.

"You shouldn't keep something like that to yourself," she said, stroking his back and feeling the fragile bones under her hand. "You can always talk to me or Daadi about your worries. Daadi knows what a fine farmer you're becoming. You can trust him to see that you have what is right for you, ain't so?"

Levi nodded, probably as much relieved by speaking as by any reassurance she had offered.

She kissed him lightly on his forehead. "Now you must lie down and go to sleep. There will be plenty of clean-up work to do tomorrow, so you must be rested."

And she must figure out how she was going to tell Isaac about this—yet another thing that he wouldn't want to hear.

A slight movement caught her eye, and she looked toward the door. Isaac stood in the hallway, looking in through the gap where she'd left the door ajar. She held out her hand to him, wanting him to come in and reassure Levi.

But he ignored her gesture, his face bleak. He turned and disappeared from view, and all she could think was that she was glad Levi hadn't seen him.

Isaac came out of the phone shanty the next day and stood for a moment in the morning sunlight. He could still smell the ashes where the generator shed had stood, and the acrid scent turned his stomach with its reminders of the past.

Concentrate on the next step—that was all he could do. Don't let his thoughts stray in the direction of the painful past or the uncertain future.

That was easier to say than to do. He'd just spent over an hour on the telephone, trying to find a generator of the size he needed for a price he could afford to pay. No success.

If he hadn't increased the herd this spring, they'd have had enough in the bank for a new generator. He'd taken a chance, and he'd been wrong.

Isaac rubbed the back of his neck, trying to erase the tension there. He could always borrow, of course, but he hated the idea. Daad had never believed in it. If a man couldn't pay cash for what he wanted, he'd have to do without. That had been his belief, and a son should follow his father's principles, ain't so?

That led him straight to Levi, and the painful confidence he'd heard last night. Worse, he'd sensed the truth in what the boy had said. Levi did seem to care more about the dairy herd than Joseph did. He had to find a way to make things right with his son, but he was caught by his promise to his father.

If he'd rescued Daad first that night . . . He jerked away from the idea as if he'd touched a burning coal.

Judith had tried to talk to him about Levi once the boy had gone to sleep. She didn't seem to understand that he couldn't talk about it. All he could do right now was bury his feelings and cope with the current disaster.

He caught a glimpse of movement out by the tie-stall barn. Joseph? He ought to tell the boy how sorry he was for jumping to the conclusion that he'd been careless with the fire. He should have done it before this.

But Joseph wasn't alone. He spotted another figure disappearing behind the barn. Hadn't all the milking volunteers left long ago?

Striding toward the barn, Isaac realized that a wagon was pulled up at the rear door. A few more steps took him close enough to see that Joseph was helping a couple of other Amish men move a generator into the back of the barn. One man he didn't know. The other was Frederick Yoder.

"What's going on?" He tried to dampen the irritation in his voice that always seemed to appear when he talked to Fred. Foolish, not to be able to forget that Fred had nearly captured Judith's heart before he'd made up his mind that she was for him.

"I heard about the fire." Fred straightened, his always cheerful face serious for once. "Sorry we didn't get out sooner to help."

"There were plenty of folks here. We had all the help we needed." That didn't sound very gracious. "Denke," he added. He eyed the generator. It was plenty big enough to supply the power they needed, and it looked brand-new.

"That generator—" he began, trying to think of a way to say he couldn't afford it without feeling small.

"You need one to get things up and running, ain't so? This is a spare that we keep at the shop just so we have a backup in case of emergency." Fred shrugged. "No emergencies lately, thank the gut Lord. I figured we could set it up for you to use until you're able to get one."

For an instant Isaac couldn't seem to think. The

very thing he needed, and it dropped right into his lap without his doing a thing. Isaac's relief at having the problem solved for the moment, at least, battled his reluctance to be beholden to Fred Yoder. If he turned down the loan of the generator—well, the truth was that if he did, he'd probably lose his contract with the dairy. He couldn't afford that, could he?

"I can help set it up," Joseph said, giving Isaac a sidelong glance as if to ask permission. "I'd keep it in good shape as long as it's here."

"Ach, I don't doubt that," Fred said, his usual cheerful tone returning. "This boy of yours has a fine hand with a machine."

Isaac stared at him, frowning. "It's true enough, but how do you know that?"

"Ach, half the valley knows that about Joseph. Besides, I can see it just by the way he handles a machine," Fred said quickly. "Just like I suppose you can tell by the way a man approaches a dairy cow whether he knows what he's doing with animals or not."

The man was trying to do a kind act, and here he was behaving like he had no manners at all. Isaac managed a smile.

"True enough. And Joseph does keep our equipment in order. It's certain-sure a gut thing he does. If something goes wrong with a machine, all I can do is yell at it."

Fred nodded. "That's about how I am with the

animals. My own daad is ashamed of me on that front, but I remind him that the Bible says we all have different talents."

He was stalling for time, Isaac realized, when he actually had no choice in the matter. He knew it, Joseph knew it, and no doubt Fred Yoder knew it as well.

"Denke, Fred." He held his hand out to the man. "It's wonderful kind of you. I'll try to get the generator back to you quickly."

"Don't worry about it," Fred said, shaking his hand. "We'll have it up and running for you in no time at all."

No time indeed. Joseph was already helping the other man to set it up, almost before Isaac had voiced his acceptance. The boy's hands were quick and sure as he worked.

Fred leaned over to point something out on the controls, and as he talked, Joseph looked up, nodding in agreement while he listened.

Isaac's throat tightened as he watched them. Joseph was looking up at Fred Yoder the way he'd once looked at his big brother—with a mixture of admiration and devotion that had always touched him and made him aware of his responsibility to be the brother Joseph thought him.

When had Joseph stopped seeing him that way? It almost felt as if Fred were taking Joseph's allegiance away from him, and the feeling left a bad taste in his mouth.

CHAPTER NINE

❦

Lancaster County, August 1953

As Nate trundled a wagon holding a basket of apples and one of tomatoes, Mattie walked out the lane the next day to take her turn at the vegetable stand the family shared. With all Ben's family pitching in, as well as Adam's folks, who owned the farm on the other side of Daad Jonah's, they were able to have plenty to sell as well as enough helpers so that no one had to spend much time at the stand.

"Look, there's Grossmammi," Nate said, waving so vigorously that the wagon ground to a halt. "She'll be glad we came to take over."

"I'm sure she'll be wonderful glad to see you, too." Mattie pushed her worries aside to smile at him. "Do you think she might have a treat for you?" Since she knew her mother-in-law had been making whoopie pies today, it was a safe question to ask.

"Yum, I hope so." Nate's walk turned into a trot, and he and the wagon moved ahead, reaching the stand several yards ahead of her.

Mamm Becky was already counting out whoopie pies. "One for you to eat now, but the rest are for later, ja? Make sure that everybody has one, and be sure to ask your mamm before you help yourself."

"I will." Nate's voice was muffled by the huge bite of chocolate and cream he'd stuffed in his mouth.

Mattie resigned herself to the fact that he wouldn't get any work done until he'd finished. "You are spoiling them, Mamm Becky." She gave her mother-in-law a quick hug.

"That's my job, ain't so?" Mamm Becky held her at arm's length for a moment to take a long look at her face. "Are you getting enough sleep, Mattie? You look tired."

There was no point in trying to evade the question. Ben's mother was too wise for such a move.

Mattie sent a glance toward her son, but he was absorbed in what he was doing. "Worrying too much, I'm afraid." She kept her voice low. "I try to turn the burden over to the Lord, but then I find I'm picking it up again."

The nights were the worst, alone in the bed she'd shared with Ben. That was when she felt most strongly the burden of making decisions without him.

"I know." Mamm Becky patted her shoulder. "Sometimes it's hard to trust that the Lord is in control." She glanced at Nate, who had finished his whoopie pie and was busy arranging the baskets according to some plan of his own. "You didn't bring Rachel to help you today?"

"I thought she'd be better off watching the young ones." Mattie hesitated, but the need to share the burden was too great. "I heard that some of the older scholars have been called names when they were in town among the Englisch. I didn't want Rachel upset."

Her mother-in-law nodded. "I heard the story as well. You did the right thing, I think. Rachel is a sensible child, but girls that age can be easily hurt."

They both watched Nate for a moment, and Mattie wondered if her mother-in-law was thinking the same thing she was—that Nate was so like his daad, both in the way he looked and in his disposition. Patient and sturdy, he was stolid, not easily ruffled by people or things.

If it were Nate who was faced with the possibility of being sent to the big Englisch high school, she might not feel quite so apprehensive. Nate, like Ben, could present that firm, expressionless face to the world which made folks use the phrase *dumb Dutch,* even though there was nothing dumb about either of them.

Shaking her head, Mattie tried to chase off the clustering worries that were like a cloud of gnats around her head. "Have you sold much this morning?" A quick look at the stand showed her that most of the stacks of tomatoes, peppers, eggplants, and late corn seemed untouched.

"Not much. People don't seem to be buying."

Her mother-in-law didn't say anything more, but they both knew that in all probability, the Englisch weren't supporting the farm stand in part because of the school controversy. Things that pointed up the differences between Amish and Englisch often had that effect on folks.

"Ach, well, we'll have to eat it all ourselves," Mattie said, with a lightness she didn't feel. "You should go on home and have a little rest before the men come in for their lunch. Nate and I will be fine."

"I know you will. Nate is such a gut helper." Mamm Becky turned away, then turned back again. She reached out to clasp Mattie's hand in a quick grip. "Whatever you decide about Rachel and the school, you know we support you, ain't so?"

Tears stung Mattie's eyes. "I know. Denke." She watched her mother-in-law's sturdy figure walk off along the road toward her house, feeling a wave of gratitude. They wouldn't try to convince her of anything, and she appreciated it. Only sometimes, she found herself longing for someone else to make the decisions for her.

Traffic was light, and none of the few cars stopped. Mamm Becky had long since disappeared into her house before Mattie noticed a car slowing as it approached the farm stand.

"Looks like we finally have a customer," she said, distracting Nate from his search through a patch of clover, probably for a four-leaf lucky one. He scrambled to his feet and hurried back to her.

The car slowed still more, pulling onto the gravel verge. Nate moved, as if to go and greet the customers, but Mattie pulled him back, a sense of unease fluttering in her belly. Why had the car pulled off so far away? Normally people drew right up—

The car accelerated with a roar of the engine. Gravel spun out from the tires. It rocketed along the verge, seeming to head straight toward them, and all Mattie could do was wrap her arms around Nate and utter a wordless prayer.

At what seemed to her the last possible moment, the driver veered back onto the blacktop, missing a basket of apples by inches, and sped off down the road.

"Mammi, you're choking me." Nate's protest shook Mattie from her paralyzed state.

"Sorry." She let go of him, trying to smile. "That car scared me. It came too close."

"Bad driver," Nate said, with the slightly superior tone of one who had mastered the art of driving the pony cart.

"He was, wasn't he?" She didn't want her son to think that action had been deliberate.

Car doors slammed, and Mattie realized that a

second car had pulled up. A woman approached, clutching a little girl by the hand.

"That driver shouldn't be allowed on the road," the Englisch woman declared. "If I'd been closer I could have gotten his license number. I'm sorry."

The woman was small, with pleasant features and softly curling brown hair. She wore a print dress, belted at the waist. The child was very like her mother, with pigtails tied with pink ribbons. Mattie guessed her to be about seven or eight. They had been regular visitors to the farm stand this summer—Mrs. Graham, she was, and Mattie had learned that she was indeed the wife of the school board president. This must be his daughter.

Mattie felt as if she'd forgotten to breathe for a moment. "It's all right. He didn't cause any damage."

Had it been simple carelessness on the part of the driver? Somehow she didn't think so, and her arms tightened around Nate until he squirmed.

"Ouch, Mammi, you're hugging too tight again."

Nate had spoken in dialect, but Mrs. Graham seemed to gather the meaning. Her eyes met Mattie's, mother to mother, and she smiled.

A daring thought slipped into Mattie's head. The woman seemed friendly. Open, unlike her husband. Perhaps if Mattie spoke to her about the problem . . .

She couldn't. Could she?

Mrs. Graham picked up a paper bag from the shelf and began to sort through the corn. "The white corn I bought the other day was so sweet, I decided to come back for more. Alice and I might freeze some to enjoy this winter, right?" She smiled at her daughter. "Alice, why don't you pick out some nice apples for us? Maybe this young man will help you."

Nate straightened his shoulders, remembering his importance, and led the way to the basket of apples.

"His name is Nate," Mattie said. "Well, Nathaniel, but that always seemed too long for him."

"Especially when you're calling the children in for supper, I'd guess." Mrs. Graham set aside one bag of a dozen ears and started on another. "You have an older daughter who sometimes works at the stand, don't you?"

Mattie nodded, studying her warily. "That's Rachel. She's watching the little ones today."

"She's about fourteen, isn't she?" The question was carefully polite, but Mattie thought she sensed something behind it.

"Ja, fourteen." Mattie hesitated. Here was a chance to speak, if she could manage to take it. "She is one of the children who is supposed to be sent to ninth grade at the new high school."

Mrs. Graham seemed to study an ear of corn for a moment. "I'm afraid I don't quite understand why you people object to the idea. I mean, isn't it a good thing for children to have an education?"

Mattie's heart was pounding so loudly she felt sure the other woman would hear it. Here was an opportunity, handed to her when she hadn't even been able to ask for it.

"The Amish live the way we believe God wants us to live—not concerned with what the world wants or with earthly things, but simply and humbly. We want our kinder to be taught, of course, but to be taught to live an Amish life, not an Englisch one."

She wanted so much to be understood. Could the woman possibly look at it from her viewpoint?

Frowning a little, the woman finally nodded. "I'm a person of faith, too." She glanced over to where Nate was sharing a whoopie pie with her daughter. "I suppose I want my daughter educated according to my beliefs."

"You understand what we feel, then."

"Perhaps. A little." Her pleasant face was troubled, but sympathetic.

Mattie caught at her fleeing courage. "If you could speak to your husband—"

"I couldn't do that." The words were quick and definite, and Mrs. Graham took a step back. "I couldn't interfere with what he does as the school board president."

"I see." Mattie had to blink back tears of disappointment. "Of course you must do what you feel is right." *As we must.*

Mrs. Graham fumbled with her bags. Then, quite unexpectedly, she reached out to clasp Mattie's hand. "I wish you well," she said, and Mattie saw that there were tears in her eyes, as well.

In another moment she had paid what she owed, hustled her daughter into the car, and driven off.

Judith gripped the worn wooden handle of the pastry blender as she cut shortening into the flour for another pie crust. At the counter next to her, Grossmammi slid the skin deftly from the peaches she'd brought when she'd come to visit this morning.

"These Red Havens are wonderful sweet." Grossmammi popped a juicy slice into her mouth and offered one to Judith, who took it with floury fingers and bit into it. Sweetness seemed to explode in her mouth.

"Wonderful," Judith agreed, glad to be distracted from the thoughts that went round and round in her mind lately. "Has Rebecca already finished canning enough for her family?"

"All done, and still the peaches keep coming. I can't remember when we've had them for so long." Her grandmother measured the amount of peaches in the bowl with the ease of long experience and began to stir in the sugar and cornstarch mixture that she always said was the best way to thicken peach pie filling.

"You're getting ahead of me." Judith began rolling out the dough on the smooth, floured surface of the bread board her daad had made for her years ago.

"No matter." Grossmammi rinsed her hands at the sink, surveying the three pies ready to go in the oven. "This will be a nice treat for Isaac and the boys." She glanced out the kitchen window, obviously looking to the spot where the generator shed had been. "I see you have things all cleaned up since the fire."

Judith nodded. "Isaac couldn't rest until every sign of it had been wiped away." Her heart twisted a little. "It reminded him, you see."

"Poor Isaac. We can never really forget the tragedies of our lives, even when we're rejoicing in the happy memories." Grossmammi's eyes seemed to be seeing something Judith couldn't. "Anything—a sight or a smell or a sound—can bring the pain of the moment back, it seems."

Judith tried to concentrate on fitting the top crust in place, but her fingers shook so that the center design she'd cut ended up a little to one side. "He had to get rid of the burned smell. He said it was because it upset the cows, but I think it was more for himself."

"Most likely." Her grandmother held the oven door open while Judith slid the pies onto the racks. "I remember how the scent of burning seemed to hang over the whole valley the night the farmhouse went." She shook her head. "At least this time no one was hurt, and I hear the business is back to normal with the new generator."

Setting the teakettle on the stove was an automatic movement for Judith. Her grandmother never turned down a cup of tea, and this morning the air had been chilly when the boys set out for school, with a low mist hanging in the valley.

"Fred Yoder brought a generator over for us to use. It was wonderful kind of him." She paused, but the need to share her concerns was too great. "Isaac has been . . . well, kind of odd about it. He's never really liked Fred for some reason, and it bothers him to feel beholden to him."

Grossmammi tilted her head on one side and surveyed Judith, smiling a little. "Are you telling me you're the only person in the valley who doesn't know what Isaac has against Frederick Yoder? It's you, you silly goose."

Judith could only stare at her grandmother. "What are you talking about? There was never anything between us." She could feel the heat coming up in her face. "Maybe Fred paid me a little attention and took me home from a singing, but if you're saying Isaac is jealous . . ."

"That's just what I'm saying." Grossmammi shook her head, apparently at Judith's stupidity.

"I always thought it was Fred showing he was sweet on you that woke Isaac up. There's nothing like a little competition to make a man see what he wants. Isaac realized he'd best get moving if he didn't want to watch you marrying someone else."

"He wouldn't have . . . I mean . . ." Judith stumbled to a stop, knowing her cheeks were scarlet. "Isaac was always the only man for me. Fred just likes to flirt. There's never been a reason for Isaac to be jealous of him."

Until now. The words slid into her mind and lodged there. Isaac did have a reason now, but it wasn't because of her. It was because of Joseph. And how they were ever going to resolve this tangle they'd gotten into, she didn't know.

"Well, at least Isaac didn't let foolish pride keep him from accepting the generator." Grossmammi seemed to feel she'd embarrassed Judith enough.

"He couldn't do that. Without the generator we'd have lost the contract with the dairy." She still felt a little sick at the thought of how close they'd come. "Isaac's Onkel Simon would have helped, of course, but Isaac didn't want to ask him. After all, his uncle has his own sons to help."

Grossmammi looked as if a tart remark hovered on her tongue, but she held it back. Instead she accepted the mug of tea Judith held out and settled herself at the kitchen table, sniffing appreciatively as the aroma of the pies began to fill the air.

"You'll have to hold those boys off with a stick if you don't want them eating up the pies before supper," she said.

"I'll do that," Judith promised, putting a couple of wedges of shoofly pie on the table before sitting down opposite her grandmother.

Thank goodness Grossmammi had dropped the subject of Isaac's attitude toward Fred Yoder. She couldn't possibly be right about it. And it was ridiculous for Judith to feel even the smallest pleasure at the thought that Isaac might actually have been jealous.

Grossmammi nodded toward the study desk that took up the corner of the kitchen. "Have you learned anything more about Mattie Lapp since we talked about her?"

"I've been reading the letters between Mattie and her cousins." Judith's thoughts slipped back to the 1950s and the story Mattie had to tell. "It's funny that they didn't really live that far apart—just at opposite ends of the county, as far as I can tell. But they didn't see each other much, so they started the Round Robin letters to stay in touch."

Her grandmother nodded. "That sounds about right. You have to understand that the Leit didn't travel as much then as now. When I was growing up, I can think of only one time when my family hired a driver to take us someplace, and that was to a funeral."

"Do you remember anything about the school troubles? Mattie was going through such pain over that problem, but the whole issue seems so far away and strange to me now."

"That's because we've had our own schools ever since you can remember." Grossmammi stirred her tea slowly, seeming lost in thought. "I wasn't the right age to be affected myself. I do recall how worried and upset my parents were for a time. Mattie had several young ones, didn't she?"

Judith nodded, seeming to see Mattie's sloping, rounded handwriting in her mind's eye. "Her daughter Rachel was just at the age to be affected. It must have been terrible to feel as if the whole weight of Englisch law was against you. We've had it easy in comparison."

"Maybe so." Her grandmother's face was solemn. "But it seems to me that folks value things more when they have to struggle to keep them. If ever the Amish get so that they can live comfortably with the Englisch, I fear that will mean that we have adopted so much of the world that we're no longer Amish."

"Do you really think there's a danger of that happening?"

The idea sent a shiver down Judith's spine. Who would they be if they weren't Amish? And was she doing wrong for Joseph to encourage him in his plans—plans that might take him further away from his roots? Not that she was encouraging him, exactly, was she?

"You're worrying about something," Grossmammi said, her voice gentle but her gaze as shrewd as ever. "Do you want to talk about it?"

She did. She couldn't.

Finally she sighed. "It's just that Joseph wants —well, he seems to want different things for his life. And Isaac doesn't understand."

"I thought that Isaac had agreed to Joseph taking a class at the vocational school. That's what Barbie said."

"He did agree, after a lot of hasty words back and forth between them." She had to tread carefully, no matter how much she might want her grandmother's wisdom. She couldn't betray all of Joseph's dreams. "But Isaac only went along with it because he doesn't take it seriously. He thinks Joseph will get tired of the class."

Or that even if he didn't, Joseph was only doing it because the knowledge would help him run the dairy farm.

"You don't think so?"

"I . . . don't know."

If only she could share all the things that worried her with her grandmother. But she couldn't. She was caught by a promise she should never have made. But still, if she were back in that situation again, with Joseph looking at her with such pleading in his eyes, would she be able to do anything different?

"It's . . . odd." Judith stumbled over the words. They were so inadequate. "I mean, there was Mattie risking prosecution to keep her daughter from being forced into more schooling. And now Joseph is driving his brother crazy with wanting it."

Grossmammi seemed to consider for a moment, her face bearing the marks left by a lifetime of facing problems and dealing with struggle, yet still serene. "Maybe it's not so different after all," she said finally. "For the Leit, what it means to live separate from the world may change with time and circumstance. But remember why our people fled Europe for America in the first place —so that we would have the right to choose how we live."

Her grandmother was right, of course. To be Amish was to live separate, obeying God's laws. Each time they clashed with the outside world that was the decision they had to make.

But in this case it wasn't the outside world that threatened. It was the terrible chasm between what Joseph wanted and what Isaac wanted for him. And there didn't seem to be any clear-cut answer to that dilemma.

CHAPTER TEN

Lancaster County, September 3, 1953

Mattie had arisen early after a mostly sleepless night, but even so, Adam arrived at the barn before her. She saw the glow from the door and stepped outside, wrapping a sweater around herself against the chill.

When she walked in, Adam was about to finish milking the cows. He gave her a long look by the light of the lantern.

"No sleep last night?" He straightened, removing the milking stool while the cow stood patiently.

"Not much," she admitted. "Denke, Adam. I could have done the milking this morning."

"I know. And you could also get the kinder off to school today without any help. But you don't have to."

Mattie took the two cows by their halters to turn them into the pasture while Adam picked up the pails of milk. She ought to insist she could manage alone, but the truth was that she didn't want to. She was glad of his company on a critical morning like this one.

As they walked back to the house together, she

could feel his gaze on her face. Could see the question in his eyes before he asked it.

"Have you decided what you'll do when the bus comes for Rachel?"

She longed to have a definite answer. If only her mind would stop its eternal dithering and settle on the right response. She shook her head.

"I wanted to talk it over with Rachel last night, but I couldn't seem to get the words out. And she didn't ask, either. So we ended up just hugging each other."

"Maybe that was what you both needed, ain't so?"

"Maybe." But Mattie couldn't excuse herself so readily. "But I think my own fear strangled me when I tried to bring it up."

Adam shook his head gravely. "You are being too hard on yourself, Mattie. Whatever you decide, it will be right for you and for Rachel. And we are all standing beside you, no matter what."

The kinder came rushing to greet Adam just then, sparing her the difficulty of finding a response. Nate and Toby were jumping up and down with the excitement of starting back to school, but little Anna was pouting a bit, most likely because she didn't get to attend.

As usual, Adam seemed to understand what everyone felt. He calmed the boys and then picked up Anna. "So, while the boys are in

195

school, you get to have Mammi all to yourself. What are you going to do?"

She clung to the pout a second longer and then grinned. "Mammi says I can help her bake cookies. And lick the spoon all by myself."

"That sounds like a very gut day, ain't so?" He glanced around. "I think breakfast is on the table. Is there enough oatmeal for me?"

"Always," Mattie said. "I'll get it."

"No need." He took the wooden spoon from her hand. "Rachel not down yet?"

Her tension mounted. "She was here a minute ago. I'd best check on her." She still wasn't sure whether Rachel would get on the bus.

As Mattie walked into the living room, she spotted Rachel standing on the front porch, hands grasping the railing. Her head was bowed. Was she praying?

Mattie's breath caught in her throat, and she went quickly to the door, opened it, and stepped outside. For a moment Rachel didn't move. Then she turned to face her mother, seeming to force a smile she probably didn't feel.

"Mammi, I'm ready to go to the new school. I can do it. It just means putting off my dreams for another year. It will be all right." Rachel had an air of gravity that made her seem older than her years, but her voice trembled on the last few words.

What was the right thing to say? Mattie sent up

a silent prayer for guidance. *Give me the words, Lord. Please.*

"I don't think you mean that, my Rachel." She drew closer, longing to ease the pain she knew her child felt.

"Ja, ja, I do." Rachel blinked rapidly, but she couldn't keep the tears from forming in her eyes.

"My sweet girl." Mattie cradled Rachel's cheek with her hand. "I can see you don't want to go."

Rachel met her gaze for another moment, and then her lashes swept down. A single tear found its way onto her cheek. "No. But I don't want you to be in trouble with the law, either."

"What has happened is not your fault," Mattie said, finding the strength to speak calmly. "If we are in this situation, it must be because God wants us to be here."

"But why?" Rachel cried. "What could God want us to do?"

Mattie sucked in a breath, praying she was saying what she should. "What do you think God wants of us?"

Behind her, she could hear the door open quietly, could hear Adam's footsteps as he came up to her.

Her daughter's smooth forehead wrinkled in thought. "Daadi always said that our family came to America so we could be free to live as God wants."

So in this time of trial, Rachel was turning to

what she'd learned from her father. The thought touched her heart.

Rachel gave a short nod, as if she'd decided. "I think if that freedom is threatened, God would want us to stand up for it."

Mattie's throat tightened. Her daughter was holding a mirror up to her, making her see herself clearly. The time was long past when she could let others make decisions for her. Now it was up to her.

Rachel turned, staring toward the road. In another instant, Mattie heard the sound as well. The bus was coming. The moment was here, and she felt confidence flooding through her, washing over the fear. Mattie put her arm around Rachel's waist, holding her close.

"It's all right. We are together."

The yellow bus lumbered into view. It stopped at the end of the lane, and the door opened. Mattie held Rachel firmly, and they stood watching it. Adam moved to her side, and his hand found hers in the fold of her skirt, his grip comforting.

The bus waited, and she could see the driver peering down the lane. No one moved.

Finally the door closed. The bus moved off down the road.

It was done. Maybe she'd known all along that there wouldn't really be a choice when the moment came. To be Amish was to obey God's law, not men's. The stories of the martyrs flickered through her mind. To be Amish was also to take the consequences, whatever they might be.

Judith stirred, swimming upward from the depths of sleep. Something wasn't as it should be. She knew that before she came entirely awake as a loud rumble of thunder sounded, followed by the rattle of rain against the bedroom window.

She scrambled out of bed, hurrying to close the window before the rain drenched the floor. Storms always came from the west, with the wind driving the rain against the windows on this side of the house.

The window balked a bit, long enough for her to shiver from the chill breeze, and to recognize the musty, acrid scent the falling rain drew from the ashes that were all that remained of the shed. She yanked, and the window banged shut louder than she'd intended. It would have waked Isaac—

But when she turned to the bed, a flicker of lightning showed her that Isaac wasn't there. The covers had been flung back on his side, and there was no sign of him.

Judith took a step toward the door just as it opened. Isaac came in, closed the door quietly, and leaned against it. Something in the stillness of his figure sent a shiver of alarm through her.

"Isaac? Where were you?"

He jerked at the sound of her voice and then

moved away from the door. "Checking on the kinder." His words seemed muffled. "They're all sleeping right through the thunder."

"I think it would take more than a little thunder to keep those boys awake." She crossed to the bed and slid under the sheet and lightweight blanket, shivering a little. "Aren't you coming back to bed?"

Thunder rumbled again, louder. Isaac didn't move. "I'm not sleepy." He half turned. "I'll go out so you can rest."

"Don't be so ferhoodled. If you're awake, I'm awake." She plumped the pillows against the maple headboard. "Komm. We'll sit here awhile and warm up."

He didn't move.

"Do you want me to make you some hot cocoa?" She started to get up again.

"No, no," he said quickly. He slid into his side of the bed, sitting back against the headboard, his gaze on the window. The locust tree, whipped by the wind, made black shadows that seemed to struggle against the storm.

Judith shivered and moved closer to Isaac. "It'll be cool in the morning when the boys leave for school. Still, the garden can use the rain."

Isaac murmured something, and she knew her words hadn't registered with him. He stared at the window as if mesmerized by the storm. Lightning flashed, seeming right on top of them, lighting up the room and, with it, Isaac's face—pain-ravaged, grief-stricken.

Stupid, so stupid. Why hadn't she realized? It had been lightning, coming with a sudden summer storm, that had set the farmhouse on fire that long-ago night. And now Isaac stared out at the storm as if by watching he could keep it away from them now.

She ached with the need to touch him, but she was afraid he'd jerk away if she did. She had to do something, say something. What kind of a wife was she if she couldn't comfort him now?

"I'm sorry." Her voice was hardly more than a whisper. "The storm has made you remember."

Soft though it had been, her voice seemed to sting him. He jerked, then moved as if to get out of bed.

Judith reached out to stop him. "Please," she murmured. "Please don't go." If he shut her out again, she feared they would never bridge the gap between them.

His struggle was a silent one, but real none-theless. Finally he sat back against the headboard. "Sorry." His voice had roughened. "I'm being stupid. I'm a grown man, not a child to be scared of a little lightning."

The bitterness in his tone frightened her. "You're not stupid. The fire in the shed, and now a storm right on top of it—of course it would bring your memories back." She paused, but he didn't respond. "There was a storm that night."

She said the words, praying he would speak. If only he'd open up and let her in . . .

"Ja." He was rigid, every muscle in his body tense. "Maybe it was the storm that woke me, maybe it was Joseph's crying." He stopped, making her plead with God to force him to go on. "I didn't understand, not at first. The smoke must have already been affecting me. I couldn't seem to get my brain to work. Just kept thinking the baby was crying and I had to go to him."

Lightning flashed again, illuminating the room momentarily, and his muscles jerked.

"Mamm had moved him into the little room across the hall just that day. Maybe I thought she didn't hear. I got up—" Another lightning flash revealed his eyes, staring at something that wasn't there. "The floor was hot under my feet. I opened the door. The smoke rushed at me. I was choking, couldn't think. I must have yelled for Daad. I felt my way to the baby's room."

He was back in that time, she sensed, feeling his way through the smoke, drawn by the crying.

"Seemed like his room was a little protected from the smoke. He still had breath to cry. I grabbed him up. Yelled for Daad again."

He stopped, sucking in a ragged breath, his chest moving with the effort.

"The flames—I ran down the steps. Tried to shield Joseph with a blanket. Onkel Simon, the others—they came running as I got outside. Tried to get the others out." Isaac shook his head, rolling it from side to side as if to escape the images in his mind. "They couldn't. I couldn't."

"It wasn't your fault." How many people must have said that to Isaac? It hadn't worked. It hadn't taken his guilt away. "You saved Joseph. Don't you think that was what your mamm and daad would have wanted?"

Isaac just shook his head. He moved, and she was sure he was going to pull away from her. Lightning flashed, the boom of thunder following almost immediately. She was going to lose him—

He turned toward her, grabbed her, holding on as if to a lifeline. He buried his face in her neck, clutching her.

Judith wrapped her arms around him, holding him tightly, and waited for the storm to be over.

In the usual morning rush to get the boys out the door for school on time, Judith still managed to find a moment to think tenderly about Isaac. He'd opened up to her in a way he never had in all the years they'd been married. Even though her heart still felt bruised and battered by his pain, she couldn't help but be hopeful, as well. Surely this was the beginning of a new closeness for them—of the kind of marriage she'd longed for with Isaac.

"Mammi, I can't find my homework." Levi's voice rose to near-panic level. Always so conscientious, he never seemed to lose things like his brother did.

"Levi, it has to be here someplace. I know you did it. Let's look in the drawers of the study desk." She and Levi began scouring the area of the study desk, hindered a little by Noah's decision to help until Joseph lifted him firmly out of the way.

"It's not here!" Levi was close to tears, despite the fact that his teacher would certain-sure believe him when he said he'd done it. "I can't go without it."

"Let's just have another look." Isaac gripped his shoulder in mute reassurance. "Maybe it got mixed in with your brother's things."

As soon as Isaac said it, Judith realized how likely that was. Paul had scooped his things up hurriedly last night when she'd said that supper was nearly ready.

"I didn't take it." Paul was indignant, and it was almost comical to see his expression change when Joseph pulled the missing homework from the scrambled mass of his papers. "I'm sorry, Levi. I'm sorry, Mammi." Now it was his turn to be near tears. "I didn't do it on purpose. I'm really, really sorry."

Levi smoothed out the pages carefully. Then he grinned. "Okay. I know."

Judith put an arm around each of them to walk

them to the door, followed by Joseph, who always walked far enough to watch them reach the schoolhouse door safely. Both boys had acted exactly the way she'd expected, Paul with his quick, sincere repentance and Levi with his forgiveness. This was one of those moments when she thought that perhaps she was doing something right with them.

But even as she waved good-bye to the three of them, she realized that Joseph was the exception. He hadn't been behaving at all as she'd expected, and it disturbed her. She'd thought he'd come home from his first vocational class bubbling over with his excitement at being allowed to do what he said he wanted more than anything. Instead, he'd barely spoken about it.

Odd. Wouldn't it be strange if Isaac had been right all along, and Joseph was losing his passion for mechanics now that he was into his studies? Well, she'd have to find an opportunity to talk to him about it.

More importantly, she had to find a chance to talk with Isaac, and preferably not when Noah was tugging on her apron and needing attention.

"Mammi, Mammi, Mammi!" He was always so urgent when he wanted something.

She detached his fingers from the apron carefully. One of the lessons he had to learn was that a person didn't get everything he wanted right away.

"I'll help you work on your letters after I've finished cleaning up the kitchen," she said. "Just now, you can go upstairs, make your bed, and brush your teeth. Then you'll be ready for the day." Noah's version of making his bed was sometimes rather messy, but it was important that he take the responsibility.

Daily routine was crucial in an Amish home. It kept everything running smoothly with a large family to tend to. Noah pouted just a little, but he trudged off, leaving her alone in the kitchen with Isaac.

Her heart fluttered, but she knew she had to speak. How could she justify keeping a secret from him after what had happened between them last night? He had trusted her with the most painful event of his life. There must be no more secrets between them.

But she quailed at the thought of Isaac's probable reaction to a blunt statement that Joseph had no intention of running the dairy farm. She must choose her words carefully. Surely, even if Isaac didn't want to hear this news, they could agree on a way to handle the situation without alienating Joseph completely. Isaac must know that result was not what his father would have wanted.

Judith took a breath, feeling as if her heart was beating more loudly than it should. "Isaac, there's something I want to talk to you about. Do you have time to sit down with me for another cup of coffee?"

His expression wasn't encouraging. He was frowning and preoccupied by something she couldn't guess. "Can it wait until later? I've heard about a used generator that might be just right for us. I want to follow up on it this morning, so I can get Fred Yoder's back to him."

As usual, there was a slight difference in his voice when Isaac mentioned Fred's name, and her grandmother's opinion as to the cause slipped into Judith's thoughts. "I thought Fred said there was no hurry in getting it back to him."

That must have been the wrong thing to say, because Isaac's frown deepened. "It's not right for me to be using it and not paying him, but Fred refused to take any money. I don't want to feel like I owe him."

"I'm sure he'd do the same for any in the church who needed it."

Isaac shrugged. "Maybe so, but it's as well to get it taken care of. We can talk later, ain't so?" He didn't wait for an answer, but before he left he came and kissed her, his lips lingering on hers for a moment. "Later," he said softly, and then he was gone.

Judith looked after him, touching her lips with her fingertips as if she could hold the warmth of his kiss there. *Later*—so she'd have to get her courage together again.

Still, maybe she'd be able to talk to Joseph about his vocational school experience first. That might be just as well, especially if the boy was losing his initial enthusiasm.

But it wasn't until afternoon that the opportunity to talk to Joseph arose. He came in from the barn where he and Isaac had been working since Isaac had returned, disappointed, from looking at the generator he'd heard of; the machine had proved to be unsuitable. Joseph stopped to wipe his feet before coming into the kitchen.

"Quiet in here," he said. "Is Noah asleep?" He crossed to the sink and filled a glass with water.

"Shh. He thinks he's 'reading' a storybook, but his eyes are so heavy he'll be out in a minute or two."

"I'm not surprised." Joseph leaned against the counter. "He was chasing that pesky rooster around most of the morning. It got out of the pen again."

Judith just shook her head. They both knew the old rooster spent more time out of the pen than in. "You haven't said much about your first class," she commented, trying to keep her tone casual. "Was it a disappointment?"

"No!" The vehemence of Joseph's response startled her, and when she looked at him, it was like seeing him come alive right in front of her. "It was everything I hoped it would be. More, even. You wouldn't believe how much I learned in just one session."

"That's good, ain't so? So why haven't you been talking about it? If you showed Isaac how much you enjoyed it—"

"It wouldn't do any good." All the joy washed out of Joseph's face as if it had never been there.

"Joseph, I don't think you're being fair to your bruder. If you just explain calmly how much it means to you, I'm certain-sure he will listen."

At least, she hoped and prayed that he would. It was so hard to stand them, loving them so much and seeing them constantly misunderstand each other.

Joseph was already shaking his head, his face set in stubborn lines. "I know just how it would be. Isaac will never agree. He's going to try and keep me stuck here on the farm forever, doing something I hate."

"Don't talk that way." Honestly, a teenage boy could try the patience of a saint. "You know you don't really hate the farm."

He had the grace to look a bit ashamed. "Well, maybe not hate. But I certain-sure don't want to be a dairy farmer for the rest of my life. Why should I when I can be happy doing something I'm really good at?"

"You think that now, but—" She knew that was the wrong thing to say as soon as the words came out of her mouth.

"I won't change my mind! And I am good at working with machines. Everyone says so. Even Isaac admits it. You know. Didn't Fred tell you that he'd take me on as an apprentice in a minute if only Isaac would agree?" Joseph's impassioned look demanded an answer from her.

"He did say that, and I'm sure he meant it. Fred won't change his mind about giving you the opportunity, but if you can just be patient, maybe in time Isaac will agree."

"He'll never agree. Isn't that just what I've been telling you? Isaac will never agree."

A step sounded, and both of them swung toward the door. Isaac stood there, and clearly he had heard. His face was white and set in lines as hard as stone.

"I will never agree to you throwing your life away." His voice was harsh. Final. "Never."

His gaze went from his brother to her, and Judith felt as if he'd struck her.

Isaac would never do such a thing, of course. But at the moment, she thought it might be preferable. He stood there looking at her as if she were a stranger.

As always, she had tried her best to keep everyone happy, and somehow she'd managed to disappoint them all, including herself. The beautiful dreams she'd had such a short time ago fell to lie shattered at her feet.

CHAPTER ELEVEN

Isaac felt as if he were frozen to the spot, staring at his wife and his brother. He wasn't sure how he'd even gotten the words out.

"You see?" Joseph's voice rose, breaking a little. "I was right. I told you he wouldn't listen."

"Don't, Joseph." Judith stepped between them, her eyes pleading with him. "Isaac, just listen."

Listen. Anger, hot and fierce, chased the ice away. How could he listen when it was so plain that they had been keeping secrets from him? Betraying him.

Judith looked from him to Joseph, her face taut with pain. "Isaac just wants what's best for you. If only the two of you would talk—"

"There's nothing to talk about." He ground out the words, fighting to keep his anger under control. He glared at his brother. "Our father wanted you to have the farm. I have sacrificed to keep it going for you."

"I don't want it! Can't you understand?" Joseph's fists clenched, and the muscles in his neck stood out like cords. "I don't want this life."

Isaac shook his head, dismissing the words. "You don't know. You're only fourteen."

"You knew when you were only a little older than me," Joseph flared out at him.

The words flicked like a blow on a fresh burn. "I knew because I had to. Because I had to grow up then, didn't I? Grow up and try to be the man my father expected me to be."

Joseph's face twisted. "You expect me to sacrifice everything I want to make you feel better."

"You are—"

"Isaac, don't." Judith stood between them, holding a hand out to each of them, tears filling her eyes. "Anger isn't the way."

Isaac stopped. Took a grip on himself. He was angry, all right, but wasn't it justified? "Don't you know how many boys would love to be in your position, with a thriving business to take over?"

"Sure, lots of boys would. Levi would. But not me!"

Fresh pain assaulted Isaac. Levi, his Levi, who wanted the thing Joseph was so eager to throw away. He had to do something for Levi, too. The pressure built from every side, pressing on him.

Right now he had to deal with Joseph. He had to concentrate on him, had to end this foolishness before it got any worse.

"Just put these ideas out of your head. Whatever Fred Yoder has been promising you is nonsense." A separate little flare of anger lit at the thought of Fred.

"I can't forget it. It's not nonsense. Fred appreciates what I can do even if you don't."

Isaac's jaw hardened until he thought it would shatter. "Fred is interfering in what doesn't concern him."

"Why don't you tell the truth?" Joseph's face went from flushed to white. "You wish you hadn't saved me that night. You wish I had died and the others had lived."

He ran for the door, slamming it behind him, leaving stunned silence in the kitchen.

Tears spilled onto Judith's cheeks. "Isaac, go after him. Tell him it's not so. That's a terrible thing for a boy to believe. Tell him."

"Is Joseph all you care about?" Isaac held on to his anger, because he didn't know what would happen if he let it go. Joseph, Judith, Fred Yoder—all plotting against him. "Never mind. I know."

"That's not true. You know it's not." Her voice was choked with tears. "I'm just trying to keep you and Joseph from hurting each other any worse."

He'd trusted her. He'd told her things he'd never said to a soul. And now she was siding with his own brother against him. A pulse beat in his head so loudly it seemed it would deafen him. He couldn't handle any more.

He turned away, searching almost blindly for the door.

"Isaac, wait. We have to talk." Judith touched his arm, and he jerked away as if her hand were a hot coal.

"Not now." Maybe not ever; not about this. Focusing on moving as intently as if he were drunk, he walked away.

Lancaster County, September 10, 1953

Adam approached Mattie's house, having timed his visit to arrive when he thought she and the kinder would have finished supper. Sure enough, he could see her standing at the sink, turning her face away from the window to say something to Rachel. She looked strained, as if the waiting and wondering were tugging her down.

A surge of very non-Amish anger swept through him. It wasn't fair that Mattie should be caught up in such turmoil. She'd been through enough. Still, he had to confess he'd felt another non-Amish emotion, pride, when he'd seen her stand with Rachel and watch the school bus pull away.

A week had passed since then, and the whole community seemed to be holding its breath, waiting for the repercussions which would surely come. Not one Amish child from their church district had gone to the consolidated high school. From what he'd heard, the Leit in nearby congregations who were affected had done the same. What would the school district do?

He mounted the familiar steps to the back porch and tapped lightly on the door, hearing the scurrying of the kinder and then Rachel approaching. She opened the door, the faint apprehension on her face fading at the sight of him.

"Adam. I was afraid it was the bishop and the other parents arriving for our meeting already."

He stepped inside, greeting Rachel and the two boys. Nate and Toby tumbled off their seats at the study table, both eager to show him their homework, and for a moment it was too noisy in the kitchen for Mattie to hear him if he spoke. Smiling at her over the children's heads, he looked at the papers and made suitable comments.

"Enough now," Rachel said finally. "Give Cousin Adam a chance to breathe. Mamm, do you want me to take them upstairs to get ready for bed?"

The boys looked inclined to protest, but they subsided at a look from Mattie. "Denke, Rachel." Mattie glanced at the clock. "I must prepare for the bishop and the other parents."

Bishop Thomas had arranged to gather with the parents to discuss the situation tonight, and he'd been thoughtful to set it up at Mattie's house so she didn't have to go out in the evening. The meeting was the reason for Adam's visit, as well.

Mattie would have his support, whether she needed it or not.

Before Rachel could get the boys moving, Anna came rushing downstairs, barefoot and in her little white nightgown, her hair hanging in braids.

"I heard you, Cousin Adam. I wasn't asleep yet." She ran to him, and he scooped her up to plant a kiss on her chubby cheek.

"I'm sehr glad I get to say good night to you, then. Are you sure you weren't asleep already? Maybe you're dreaming," he teased.

"I am not." She patted his face as if to be sure. "Do I have to go to bed, Mammi? I'm not a bit sleepy." The words were interrupted by a yawn, making everyone else smile.

"You'll be sleepy by the time you're upstairs in bed," Rachel said. Adam set the little girl down, watching as she caught Rachel's hand and went off, followed by the boys.

He was still smiling when he looked at Mattie. "Rachel is wonderful gut with the younger ones."

"She is. She'll be a fine mammi herself one day." But there was a slight shadow in Mattie's clear eyes as she looked after her daughter.

"Is she bothered by the school business?" He took the dishcloth from her hand and finished wiping the table, not surprised when she started setting out a stack of small plates and forks. Mattie wouldn't have folks meeting at her house without feeling she should feed them.

"I don't think so." Mattie paused, balancing a cake on one hand and a plate of cookies on the other. "She doesn't even look out when the school bus stops every morning."

He set the cake and cookies on the table. "And what about you?"

Mattie made a face. "I still start feeling my stomach turn upside down when I see it. But that's silly. They can't force the children to go, can they?"

Adam shrugged, not at all sure that was true. "I guess we'll find out what's happening from the bishop tonight."

"Is that why you came?"

"We're in this together, remember? Ben's daad will be here, too. I just thought I'd come a little early in case you needed any help getting ready."

"I think I can get coffee and dessert ready myself," she said, but she was smiling. "But we were all happy to see you anyway. I knew as soon as she heard your voice, Anna would be back down again."

"She's a sweet girl. Not so serious as Rachel was at that age, I think."

Mattie seemed to be pondering something other than his comment. She studied his face, seeming to hesitate on the verge of saying something.

He grinned. "Just say it, Mattie. You know you can say anything to me."

"You know me too well," she said lightly, but

her eyes were serious. "I just thought . . . I wondered, really, if it ever troubles you, seeing Anna and thinking of your little Sarah."

He took his time answering, sensing that this might be important. "Because they were born about the same time, you mean. Maybe at first, when I'd see Anna such a pretty, plump, healthy baby. But you see, Sarah never seemed like a real person to me. She was . . ." He struggled for the right words. "She looked like a little china doll, gone before she could even take a breath."

"I know. I remember." Mattie's eyes filled with tears at the memory of his little girl and her mammi, gone too soon.

He needed to make her understand, for reasons that weren't entirely clear to him. "After a while, seeing Anna grow and change . . . it helped me. It gave me back my Sarah, in a way, because I could imagine her doing all those things that Anna did. She wasn't just a little doll any longer. She was a real person. I love all the kinder, but I'll always be especially thankful for Anna."

One tear had overflowed onto Mattie's cheek, and Adam reached out to blot it away with fingers that weren't quite steady. Her breath caught, and their gazes met and held.

And then they heard the rattle of harnesses and the clop of horses' hooves, and knew the others were coming. Mattie turned away quickly, busying herself with the coffeepot, and he began lining up forks and spoons on the table, as if putting them in a straight row were crucial.

There was an initial flurry as people arrived, one buggy after another. Adam stayed in the background, helping unobtrusively where he was needed. He was relieved when Onkel Jonah arrived. As Ben's father, he had more right to be here than Adam, not that that fact would convince Adam to depart.

Bishop Thomas finally had everyone assembled in the living room, settled in a semicircle on the extra chairs Adam had brought in from the kitchen. He cleared his throat as a signal that he was ready to begin.

"I know we all want to thank Mattie for hosting us for this meeting," he said, looking at her.

Mattie ducked her head, seeming embarrassed to be the center of attention even for a moment.

"You all probably know that we have made a start on getting our own Amish school. Matthew Esch has donated the land, and it's a fine central location all the kinder in the church district will be able to walk to."

Matthew nodded, probably glad to know that his own seven children would have the school so close. Adam had seen the spot, and he'd already offered to help with the building, as everyone here had done, most likely. But putting the building up would be the easy part.

"There are some difficulties about starting a

school." Bishop Thomas seemed to echo his thoughts. "Lots of forms to be filled in, and most likely some disagreement about who is qualified to teach our kinder."

"The education department won't help us, I'd guess," John Stoltzfus muttered, and several of the others nodded. Most folks had had run-ins with regulations of one sort or another.

"Pastor Colby has offered to help us," the bishop said. "It surprised me, for sure, but I've come to believe he is sincere in what he says. The other ministers and I will talk with him, and I'm hopeful that with his help, we'll be able to work things out." He looked around, as if for approval, and seemed relieved at the silent nods.

Mattie was twisting her fingers together in her lap. She'd be glad to know her younger ones would go to an Amish school. But still, that didn't help with the trouble Rachel faced right now.

"Pastor Colby also suggested making up a petition to the school board, asking them to reconsider. He says that a number of Englisch people from his church would sign, and he thinks he could get some of the other Englisch pastors to sign as well, and talk to their folks about it. He thinks that sign of support for unser Leit might sway the board more than just hearing from us."

"If it's the state law, what can the board do?" Samuel Fisher leaned forward in his seat, his face troubled. His oldest boy, young Sam, was in the group of fourteen-year-olds.

"True, the law comes from Harrisburg," Bishop Thomas said. "But every school board isn't taking the action our local board has. Seems as if it's up to each board how they enforce the rules, so it may be that we can sway them to find some solution that satisfies us and them."

Most of the people here had been to the board meeting, so they'd seen the local board in action. There hadn't been a lot of room for hope, and Adam suspected everyone was thinking the same.

Mattie cleared her throat, then flushed when everyone looked at her.

"You have an idea, Mattie?" Bishop Thomas nodded in encouragement.

"I just thought that maybe, if we all talked to any Englisch people we know about why we feel as we do, it might help." Her voice faltered toward the end.

"Ja, it might help," Adam agreed, deciding a little reinforcement was a good idea. "Make folks understand that we're not just being stubborn or backward."

Some people nodded, but John Stoltzfus leaned forward in his chair, slapping a paper against his knee. "That's fine for you to say, Adam. You're not in danger of being arrested."

The word seemed to echo in the quiet room,

and Adam felt the tension drawing close around them like a fence wire.

"Who is talking about arrest?" Bishop Thomas's voice was grave.

John gestured with the paper. "I am. I was harnessing the buggy horse to come here when a police car pulled in my lane. The officer gave me this." He handed it to the bishop. "It orders me to send my boy to school tomorrow or they'll arrest me."

A murmur of dismay spread through the room. Mattie's hands clenched each other so tightly her knuckles turned white. Adam longed to reach out and take those straining hands in his, but he couldn't, not here where everyone would see.

Bishop Thomas read his way unhurriedly through to the bottom of the page, his face grave. Finally he looked around the circle. "It's true. Our brother John is facing arrest."

The murmurs grew louder. Those closest to John touched his shoulder in mute sympathy.

"We must decide how to combat this threat." He shook his head. "I blame myself. Pastor Colby feared it might come to this, but I didn't dream they would go so far. He offered to seek legal advice for us, but I held back."

They all knew why. The Amish didn't go to the courts for relief of wrongs. If trouble came, it was because God had allowed it.

"How do we know this man isn't trying to trick

us?" Behind John's usual bluster, Adam could hear the fear. So must their ancestors in Europe have felt. Who could be trusted?

"I have talked with the pastor several times," Bishop Thomas said. "He may be sincere and still not able to influence what happens." He looked slowly around the circle of faces. "I feel it isn't right for the church to make this decision for all of you. Each parent is in a different situation, so each one must decide for himself. Or herself. No one must be held to blame for the choice."

Adam hitched his chair a little closer to Mattie's and exchanged glances with his onkel on the other side of her. Mattie's face was so white it seemed there was no blood left in her at all. She wasn't going to pass out, was she?

"Denke." John's voice was heavy. "I have decided. I will not send my son to the school. If I must go to jail, I will."

Adam had never admired the man more. John might be bossy and abrasive, but, like the martyrs, he was ready to sacrifice himself for what was right.

Bishop Thomas nodded. "We will make sure that there is plenty of help at your place for however long this takes. And I think we must accept Pastor Colby's offer to get legal advice for us. If we are to stand up against the Englisch law, we must know what to expect."

There was a murmur of agreement. Adam

hadn't expected anything else. For the most part, when it came to real trouble, people relied on Bishop Thomas's wisdom.

A few more people asked questions, but the group seemed to fall silent quickly. Each one of them probably anticipated a visit from the police. Each one questioned what he or she would do in that case.

Adam looked at Mattie, and his thoughts were filled with such confusion that he barely heard the bishop's final remarks or his prayer. Mattie must be protected. What was happening to John Stoltzfus must not happen to her.

"I'm sorry to take you away from your own chores on a Friday morning." Rebecca whipped a sheet across the bed in one of her guest bedrooms, and Judith caught the edge and pulled it straight. "But with Barbie working all day at the bakery and last-minute guests coming—"

"Ach, forget about it. My mamm is happy to have Noah all to herself for a few hours, and I was glad to come. It's more fun to do someone else's chores than our own, ain't so?"

Besides, Judith had her own reasons for wanting to be away from home for a bit. Maybe here she could stop going over and over what had happened with Isaac and Joseph. She might be able to keep herself from weeping in pain and frustration.

"Barbie doesn't usually work all day at the bakery, does she?"

Rebecca shook her head, smoothing the double wedding ring quilt down the length of the bed. "One of the sisters is down with a bad cold, so Barbie is helping out longer. They're usually busy over these nice fall weekends."

"Like you." Judith plumped the pillow on her side and looked around to see if anything else needed to be done.

"I'm wonderful glad to get these extra bookings now that summer is over. It's unexpected money coming in. But with the wedding only a month away . . ."

"I know." Judith struggled to suppress her own sorrows and show the joy that Rebecca surely deserved. "Can you believe that you and Matthew will be married so soon?"

Rebecca stopped what she was doing to stand still, smiling, a stack of clean towels hugged to her chest. "I really thought I'd never find love again, but God had a surprise in store when he sent Matthew to me." She seemed to chuckle at her own enthusiasm. "Ach, listen to me, sounding like an eighteen-year-old. But love makes you feel that way, ain't so?"

The smile felt frozen on Judith's face. Somehow she managed to mumble an agreement, but she was relieved when Rebecca went out of the room to put the towels in the bathroom.

She let the smile slide away and tried to swallow the lump in her throat. Dear Rebecca. She was as close as a sister. If only Judith could tell her what had happened.

But she couldn't. It wasn't fair to disrupt her cousin's happiness with her own pain and disappointment. Besides, telling anyone seemed disloyal to Isaac.

A knife seemed to stab at her heart. Isaac was already convinced that she'd been disloyal to him, and she'd begun to think nothing could ever change his feelings.

Twice she'd tried to talk to him about Joseph— once after the kinder were in bed and again this morning. Both times he'd walked away before she could get two words out.

She'd hoped that in the privacy of their bedroom last night they might be able to talk, but when Isaac had come in, his face had been so stony she hadn't had the courage to speak. He'd gotten into bed, turned his back to her, and gone to sleep. Or at least pretended to do so.

And Judith had lain awake much of the night, trying to pray, trying to allow only silent tears to escape.

"I think that's everything up here," Rebecca said, reappearing in the doorway. "Now for the baking."

"That's even more fun." Judith forced a smile. "What are we making?"

"I thought shoofly pie and walnut streusel coffee cake for breakfasts." Rebecca started down the stairs. "And I like to have plenty of bars and cookies on hand for snacks. At least these folks didn't sign up to do suppers here, so I don't have to worry about that meal."

Rebecca served big breakfasts to all her overnight guests, and she would provide other meals if they wanted them. It meant more money, but Judith guessed it probably got a little tiring, as well. She followed Rebecca into the kitchen, where mixing bowls and pans were already out on the counter.

"At least the family eats whatever we put in front of them." Without asking, Judith began chopping walnuts for the coffee cake. "I suppose your guests might be a little fussier."

"Barbie says as long as we call something by a Pennsylvania Dutch name, the visitors will eat it."

"That sounds like Barbie." Their younger cousin seemed to have a frivolous attitude toward just about everything.

Rebecca smiled, shaking her head. "Ach, she's not so bad. She has a kind heart under her manner. Grossmammi thinks it's high time she was getting married, but Barbie claims she's having too much fun." Her expression grew tender. "She doesn't know what she's missing, does she? Sharing a life with someone you love with all your heart . . ." She stopped, staring at Judith. "Judith, what is it? Was ist letz?"

She couldn't help it. The tears she'd been so determined not to shed spurted out, and her body shook. She dropped the knife she was holding and put her hands over her face, ashamed but unable to stop.

Rebecca's arm went around her as she guided her to a chair and sat down next to her, patting her gently and murmuring the soft nonsense words they might use to one of the kinder. But this was far worse than a scraped knee, and neither Rebecca nor Judith would know how to fix it.

Finally the tears slowed. Rebecca moved to the sink and returned with a cool wet cloth. Judith took it gratefully, pressing it against swollen eyes.

"I'm sorry," she muttered. "I didn't mean to . . ."

"Don't be foolish," Rebecca chided. "You've seen me cry often enough. Tell me, but only if you want to."

Judith took a breath, trying to ease the tightness in her chest. "The trouble between Isaac and Joseph—" She stopped, shook her head. "I didn't know what to do. All Isaac can think is that the farm should be Joseph's, because that's what his father had planned. And Joseph isn't interested in the farm at all. He's mad for working with machines."

"But Isaac did let him take that class he wanted, ain't so?" Rebecca set a glass of water in front of her, and she drained it quickly.

"Ja, but only because he thought it would be useful on the farm. He's just . . . It's like Isaac is blind on that subject. Everyone else can see what Joseph wants except him. I was just trying to keep the peace. Telling Joseph to wait, to let Isaac understand gradually that running the dairy farm isn't right for him."

Rebecca patted her shoulder. "That's gut advice, but I suppose like most boys, he was too impatient to take it."

Judith buried her face in her hands, wishing she could live yesterday over again. "It's worse than that. Joseph was sounding off to me about it and Isaac heard. Now he blames Joseph for not wanting to do what their father wanted, and he blames me for not telling him." She pressed her fingers against her temples. "I just . . . I love them both. I don't want them to hurt each other. If Isaac can't change, I fear he'll lose his brother entirely."

"Oh, my dear, I'm sorry. So sorry. I wish I could help." Rebecca's voice was filled with sympathy.

"I know."

Rebecca couldn't help her. No one could. She'd thought she could deal with the problem, and look at the result. More pain for everyone, and no end in sight. If Isaac couldn't forgive her . . .

"I'll pray," Rebecca said. "God can change people's hearts, ain't so?"

Judith nodded, trying hard to believe it would happen. "If only I could find some way to get them to talk calmly about it. If I'd been wiser in how I handled it, maybe this wouldn't have happened."

"And it might have turned out just the same," Rebecca said firmly. "You aren't to blame. Perhaps it's time you stopped trying to handle things between them and let them work it out themselves."

Everything in her rebelled at the thought. How could she stand back and see two people she loved hurt each other so badly?

But what could she do? She'd already tried, and she'd failed. The cost of that failure was tearing her heart in two.

CHAPTER TWELVE

Lancaster County, Late September 1953

Mattie glanced at Rachel as her daughter turned the buggy horse into the lane at Mary Ann Miller's house. The morning was chilly, and she'd been glad of the warmth of her cape on the ride over.

Fall was in the air, and the sumacs in the hedgerows already wore their autumn colors, their tops like so many blazing torches.

With all the worries of the past weeks, Mattie hadn't really felt much like a quilting frolic, but Mary Ann would be disappointed if they didn't come. Besides, Rachel could probably use the distraction. Ever since word had come of John Stoltzfus's arrest, they had both tensed each time they heard a vehicle coming down the road. No doubt Rachel wondered, as she did, if this time the police were coming to deliver a demand to her.

So far it hadn't happened. John had been sentenced to five days in the county jail, with the rest of the community taking over the work at his farm. He'd come out sobered, but apparently none the worse for the ordeal, and still he kept his boy home, despite the threat of a longer jail term if they arrested him again.

What were the officials waiting for? Mattie had begun almost to feel that it would be better to face the situation rather than to bear this uncertainty. But perhaps that was part of their plan. If they wanted parents to be sick with apprehension, they'd succeeded with her.

"Are you all right, Mammi?" Rachel drew up to the house.

Mattie forced herself to answer normally. "Fine. Let's take care of the horse and get inside. It looks as if several folks are here before us."

But Mary Ann's oldest boy was already running toward them, looking pleased with himself since he'd obviously been given the chore of taking care of the horses and buggies. Greeting him, they slid down from the buggy, collected the sewing basket, and headed inside.

"Those who live the closest are always the last to get here," Mary Ann teased as she welcomed them into the kitchen. "Komm. Have coffee and greet everyone. We'll start in a few minutes."

It was more than a few minutes, of course. A quilting frolic was as much about visiting with the other women as it was about the sewing. Mary Ann's two married sisters were there, as well as her sixteen-year-old niece, Ella, who immediately pulled Rachel to her side and embarked on a conversation that was mostly whispers and giggles.

"Anna!" Mattie hurried to exchange hugs with Anna Lapp, who was married to one of Ben's many cousins. "I didn't know you were going to be here. It's wonderful gut to see you."

Anna and Jacob Lapp didn't live all that far away, but it was a long enough trip that it took a special effort for her to come.

"I didn't know either until yesterday." Anna's face glowed with pleasure. "But Jacob had to get a driver to take him over to New Holland for some equipment, so he said they might as well bring me on the way. And Jacob's mamm was eager to watch the kinder, so here I am."

Anna and Jacob had married soon after his return from the conscientious objector camp at the end of the war, and they already had four little ones and another on the way, Mattie's experienced eye told her. After the two of them had been forced apart for so long, everyone had rejoiced when they'd finally been able to pick up the lives that had been interrupted by the war.

"Ben's mamm is at my house, and just as eager to have her grandchildren to herself, I'd guess," Mattie said. They smiled, each knowing how much grossmammis enjoyed special times with the young ones on their own.

"Komm, now." Mary Ann eventually decided it was time to interrupt the eating and chatting. "You can talk around the quilting frame, ain't so? Let's get started. There's chicken soup on the stove for our lunch after we get some serious sewing done."

"You mean we have to work for our lunch," one of her sisters teased, but no one minded Mary Ann being a little bossy. It was just her way, and they all knew her well enough to see the kindness behind it.

They all trailed into the living room, where some of the furniture had been moved out to accommodate the quilting frame, on which Mary Ann's newest creation was stretched. Chairs had been placed around the frame, and folks chose seats and began pulling needles and thimbles from their baskets. Mary Ann would provide everything that was needed, but most women wanted their own thimbles, at least.

Mattie slipped her grandmother's thimble onto her finger, as always having an image of Grossmammi's work-worn hands creating a quilt or sewing a heavy pair of men's pants. It never seemed to matter what she'd worked on, as long as her fingers were busy.

"That's a nice pattern, Mary Ann." Anna settled into the chair next to Mattie. "A broken star log cabin combination this time, ain't so?"

Mary Ann loved quilting, and unlike those who stuck to the traditional patterns, she seemed to enjoy combining them in different ways. This time the log cabin blocks were interspersed with the angles of stars.

"It is." Mary Ann sent a smiling glance toward Rachel. "And the colors are thanks to our Rachel. She was helping me the day I started it."

There was a murmur of approval around the frame, and Rachel's cheeks grew pink as she ducked her head.

"Your Rachel has a wonderful eye for color," Anna said quietly, her words just for Mattie. For the most part, the Leit didn't praise their sons and daughters to others, not wanting to sound prideful, but Mattie had to admit that she liked hearing it.

She nodded. "Rachel loves to sew. Sometimes I'm tempted to turn all the family sewing over to her. I think she'd like to set up in business as a seamstress when she's a little older."

Unless Rachel's life changed in ways Mattie couldn't imagine. If the school board had its way and Rachel was eventually forced to attend the consolidated high school, would she lose her pleasure in such simple tasks? Would she be persuaded that it was better to do something the outside world considered important?

When needles were threaded and ready, Mary Ann looked around the quilting frame and nodded. "Let's begin."

Needles swooped, the thread diving down through layers of quilt top, batting, and backing and then sweeping back up again, like so many hummingbirds darting quickly from one flower to the next. Everyone knew who the fastest needles were in the group, just as everyone knew that the quilt would not be advanced on its frame until each person finished the area in front of her. There was no point in hurrying or trying to be first. It was far more important that the quilting stitches were straight and tiny and nearly invisible.

Mary Ann smiled in satisfaction as she glanced around the frame, and Mattie understood her feeling. With so much they couldn't control happening in their lives right now, it was satisfying to work on something they could.

Just the thought was enough to take a little of the pleasure out of the moment, and she shouldn't let that happen. As long as they were living as God planned for them, nothing should be able to take away their joy.

Of course it was too much to hope that the trouble on everyone's mind wouldn't surface soon. The break came in the form of a question from Mary Ann's sister Barbara.

"Anna, is your church district having trouble with your school board over trying to force the scholars to stay in school longer?"

Anna shook her head, a frown disturbing the peace of her expression. "Not yet, but I fear it is coming. The Englisch are planning for a new high school, like the one your district has." She looked around at their faces. "So we are watching you, I guess. Maybe we can learn from you how to handle it when it comes."

Mattie glanced at Rachel, finding her calm undisturbed. She would rather the subject hadn't come up in front of her, but it was inevitable, with every Amish parent worrying about it.

"I don't see why the Englisch can't just leave us alone." Mary Ann stabbed her needle through the quilt with unnecessary force. "It's begun to feel like it was during the war, with everyone choosing sides and mistrusting each other."

"We got through that, and we can get through

this." Anna's expression was tranquil at the reference.

Her peace must surely be hard-won, Mattie thought, remembering when Ben had told her of how Anna's own brother had left the family and joined the army, only to die somewhere out in the Pacific. And her beloved Jacob had been sent away to the camps for five long years.

"We don't have any choice," Mattie surprised herself by saying. "We must live as God wants."

"Seems like the Englisch think that freedom is just for them and not for anyone else." Mary Ann's voice was tart. "As far as I can tell, they're all set against us."

Despite the murmurs of agreement, Mattie shook her head. "Not all. Never that. There's that young minister who has been helping us. And the man from the hardware store—I think he would listen to our side."

And even Mrs. Graham. She didn't want to mention the woman's name, but she had seemed sympathetic and understanding, even if she hadn't been willing or able to help.

An awkward silence fell, and Mattie realized it was because she was the one who'd spoken up, and it was her child who was threatened.

"Mamm is right," Rachel said, her young voice firm. "Some of the Englisch understand, even if they don't have the power to do anything. And if we don't go on loving them, how can we say we are doing God's will?"

A smile trembled on Mattie's lips, even as tears filled her eyes. Her Rachel had done a lot of maturing in recent weeks. As her mamm, Mattie didn't dare to falter.

"That's well said, Rachel." Anna's voice broke the momentary silence. "If we love only those who love us, we are not deserving of God's grace. Forgiveness comes with a heavy price sometimes, but as Mattie said, we don't have a choice."

Mary Ann seemed to take a deep breath and then let it out in a lengthy sigh. "If Mattie and Rachel can say so, knowing they might be next, I guess you're right." She shook her head. "Now, can we please get back to our quilting? Otherwise we'll never be done, and you'll all have to come back tomorrow."

Everyone chuckled at that comment, as she'd probably intended, and the tension in the room eased. Mattie swallowed, trying to relax the tight muscles in her throat. She'd meant what she said, but it didn't seem to keep her from being afraid.

Tomorrow. The word echoed in her mind. If they came for her tomorrow, would she be able to count on her faith being strong enough? She just didn't know.

Isaac walked across the field toward Onkel Simon's place, well aware that his steps were dragging. He had no enthusiasm at all for the task ahead of him, but he couldn't come up with an alternative.

At least Judith had gone off to Rebecca's to help prepare for her weekend guests. If she were here, she'd wonder why he was going to see Onkel Simon when he'd just been here to help with the milking. And she'd want to talk. She'd try to explain why she had kept a secret from him. The fact that his stomach began to churn at the very thought told him he wasn't ready to talk.

Somehow he couldn't get past the fact that she had apparently shared something with Fred Yoder, of all people, that she hadn't shared with him. He was Joseph's brother. His guardian. The person responsible for him. Certainly Fred wasn't. Judith wasn't, either.

He felt a tiny pinprick from his conscience at that thought. Judith had been the boy's mother since he was five. She was as devoted to him as to their own kinder. But that didn't give her the right to act without consulting him, did it?

Every time he tried to think through the situation, his mind ended up in a tight coil. But one thing stood out clearly: He couldn't go on accepting Fred Yoder's charity in the matter of the generator.

He'd placed the order for a new generator, so there was no turning back now. He had to either borrow from Onkel Simon or borrow from the bank, and both options left a bad taste in his mouth.

Onkel Simon, pushing a wheelbarrow toward the field planted in winter squash, stopped and waited for Isaac. Now or never—he had to decide. Daad had never believed in borrowing, but Isaac felt certain-sure that he'd have accepted help from a relative rather than go to an Englisch bank.

"I wasn't meaning I needed help when I told you I was picking some winter squash this morning." Onkel Simon grinned. "Not that I won't accept it."

A flicker of shame went through him. He'd been so preoccupied with his own troubles this morning that he barely remembered hearing his uncle mention the squash. Still, the words about accepting help seemed aimed right at his current problem.

"I'm glad to give you a hand." Isaac took the wheelbarrow handles and trundled it toward the field. "It's a bit early, ain't so?"

Onkel Simon gave him a questioning glance. "Thought I mentioned the trouble I'm having with a pesky groundhog. Dratted creature takes a nip out of one, then goes to chomp on another. I wouldn't mind so much if he'd just eat a whole one while he's at it."

"Sorry. I guess I missed some of what you said earlier. Do you want me to bring the twenty-two over to try and get him?"

"If I don't get him this evening, you and Joseph can give it a try." He gestured toward a thick row of squash plants, weighed down by the acorn squash that were beginning to turn green. "I figured some of the ones he's bitten can be used instead of pitching them on the compost. Judith said she'd take some, and I'll send a few over to Lige and his wife."

Isaac stepped into the row between the plants and bent to examine a squash, turning it carefully to avoid pulling it free of the stem. "I see what you mean. There's a bite gone from the bottom of this one. It'll go bad if it's not used." He twisted it free of the stem, hefting the heavy squash in his hand and putting it in the wheelbarrow.

"Dratted things," Onkel Simon muttered. "Creeping along in silence and ruining things."

Isaac shrugged, searching carefully through the plants and finding three more that would have to go. "I suppose he's just following his nature. Still, you can't let him ruin your whole crop." He passed the squash to his uncle and moved on down the row.

"Judith can make that squash casserole she does with the raisins in it. Tell her to save some for me."

Isaac didn't comment, and he could feel his uncle's gaze on him. Weighing him, much as he'd weighed the squash in his hand. It sometimes seemed Onkel Simon knew him even better than his own father had.

They worked their way past several more plants in silence, but it wasn't the comfortable one Isaac was used to. He had to speak, but he couldn't figure out how to begin.

"I noticed you and Joseph didn't have much to say to each other this morning." His uncle said the words without emphasis, maybe leaving open the chance for Isaac to respond or not.

"No." He didn't have to talk about it, but he suspected his uncle would read his silence anyway. "We had a . . . a disagreement yesterday."

"Ja?" Onkel Simon looked at him, waiting.

Isaac straightened, clutching a squash in each hand, and felt the words pressing against his lips, wanting to come out. "I thought Joseph was just . . . well, at a difficult age. That's what everyone says, anyway. But it turns out—" The effort seemed to be choking him. "He doesn't want the dairy farm. Can you believe it? Here he has a chance most Amish boys would give anything for, and all he can think of is to run off and play with machines."

"Play with machines?" Again Onkel Simon waited. It was a habit of his that never failed to get his kinder talking.

"That's not fair, I guess," Isaac muttered. "He says he wants to work with machinery, not with dairy cows. But he's fourteen. How can he really know what he wants?"

Onkel Simon shrugged. "He's always seemed a levelheaded lad to me. We all know how gut he is at fixing things."

"Being able to fix things is a long way from giving up a decent dairy farm to try and make a living at it." Isaac clenched his teeth together for a moment. "It sounds like Fred Yoder's been encouraging him, too."

"Fred runs a fine business, so I've heard." His uncle's tone was mild. "He provides jobs for a number of unser Leit."

Unser Leit. Our people. Isaac admitted, grudgingly, that Fred hired only Amish to work at the machine shop, and he did always seem to have plenty of customers. But that didn't mean working there ought to be the first choice for an Amish boy.

"Amish should farm. Working with the land is working close to God." Isaac repeated the words that had become a litany to him over the years.

"That's what your father used to say. And our father, before him." Onkel Simon paused, glancing over fields showing the faint golden tinge of autumn. "But times have changed. Not every Amish person can farm. A man can work at another job and still serve God."

"I know." Isaac did. He certain-sure wouldn't look down on someone who did other honest work that honored God. "But Joseph." He stopped, trying to find the right way to say what he felt. "I'm responsible for Joseph, just as if I were his daad instead of his brother. I've always known Daad intended the dairy farm for him, and that's what I planned, too, from the day I took over. I've never thought of it as mine, just as Joseph's."

"Seems to me it's Levi who has the gift for working with the animals," his uncle said mildly. "I see it get stronger every year."

"I'll make sure he has a place of his own." Somehow. He had to. But the generator, the dairy contract—it all buzzed around in Isaac's thoughts, confusing him.

Onkel Simon's face was troubled, making Isaac think he wanted to argue the point. But that wasn't his way. "What does Judith think of this whole thing?"

Isaac felt himself stiffen still more, if that were possible. "We haven't talked about it."

"Not talked about it?" Onkel Simon's eyebrows lifted as if in disbelief, his lean face shocked. "Judith is as gut as a mother to that boy. And she is your wife. Don't you think you should talk about it with her?"

Isaac didn't have an answer—or at least not an answer he could put into words he wanted to say out loud to anyone. His response was so tangled up with grief and guilt that he didn't know which was which any longer. But he couldn't go on meeting the challenge of his uncle's gaze.

He took a deep breath and tried to relax his taut muscles. "Maybe so." Maybe. Once he got over feeling betrayed by her silence each time he looked at her.

Onkel Simon ruffled his gray beard and moved his hand down the back of his neck, as if trying to let go of some tension of his own.

"Do that," he said gently. He grasped Isaac's shoulder with a firm, warm hand that was still strong from a lifetime of work. "I know you're one to keep your troubles to yourself, but a man's wife is part of him. She needs to understand, and you need it, as well."

"It's hard." The words were inadequate to the way he felt.

"Ja, I know." Onkel Simon seemed to look past him for a moment, his faded blue eyes focused on something Isaac didn't see. "Your aunt has been gone nearly nine years now, and I still find myself wanting to tell her things. But in the beginning, I had to make myself speak."

Isaac didn't know what to say. "Aunt Emma was a gut woman."

"Ja. She was. Always trying to make folks happy. And your Judith is another such."

Was she? He supposed she was, though he'd never thought that much about it, not being one to analyze how he felt about others.

"Well, now." His uncle cleared his throat. "Since you didn't really come over to help me with the squash, how about telling me why you did?"

The question surprised him into a feeble smile. "You always did seem to read our minds when we were kids. Lige used to complain that he could never get away with anything, because you knew what it was before he even did it."

"Lige wasn't so difficult." Manlike, Onkel Simon seemed relieved to be onto a safer subject. "He talked too much; that was what gave him away. Still does, in fact. So what's the trouble?"

Isaac might as well plunge right in. Stepping over the plants, he put a couple more squash in the wheelbarrow. "The thing is, I'm going to have to buy a new generator."

Times like this he might almost envy the Englisch, with their insurance. The Amish preferred to trust in God and the generosity of their people.

"I thought Fred Yoder wasn't in any hurry to have his back." Understanding dawned in his uncle's eyes. "But you don't want to keep something that's his, ain't so?"

Isaac shrugged, feeling as if he were about sixteen and trying to explain something that wasn't quite reasonable. "I can't go on using it forever, and I haven't been able to find a used one."

"You're better off to have a new one anyway. No sense in taking on someone else's trouble." His uncle seemed to understand the rest of it without the need for explanation. Of course he knew that it had strained Isaac financially to add to the herd. "You need some help with paying for it, ain't so?"

"I can go to the bank—" Isaac began, but his uncle cut him off with a gesture.

"Nothing wrong with that, but it's not needed. I can put up the money." His gaze lingered on Isaac's face. "But you're not holding a grudge against Fred, I hope. If he encouraged Joseph, it would be because Joseph went to him."

"I know." Knowing didn't make it any easier. Joseph had gone to a stranger instead of to his own brother. Well, not a stranger, but someone he barely knew.

Onkel Simon nodded, seeming satisfied with his answer. "Come back to the house, and I'll get a check for you. And a bag to carry some squash home to Judith, too."

"Denke, Onkel Simon." His voice roughened. "I'll pay you back as soon as I can."

"Ach, I know you will, Isaac. There's no hurry between us. And things will work out with Joseph, you'll see."

He headed for the house, Isaac following with the barrow full of squash. Things would work out. That was a comforting thing to hear, except

247

that he wasn't sure exactly how Onkel Simon meant it. Did he mean that Joseph would come to his senses? Or was he thinking that Isaac would accept his brother's rebellion?

If he asked his uncle, he suspected he knew what the answer would be. He would say that things would work out according to God's plan. That was the answer of faith . . . to give the problem to God and accept what God sent. But he hadn't found that an easy thing to do for a long time now.

CHAPTER THIRTEEN

By Saturday, Judith couldn't stand avoiding the subject with Isaac any longer. He had been polite but distant with her, and, as far as she could tell, he and Joseph weren't talking at all. Was that better than shouting at each other? She'd reached the point that she didn't know.

She stared down at the bowl of late green beans in her lap. She'd come out to the back porch to snap them so she could keep an eye on the young ones. Levi and Paul were weeding the rhubarb patch, with Noah "helping" them. Judith knew she could trust Levi not to let him pull out any of the plants or chew on the leaves, but she still felt a bit better when she was within earshot.

If she didn't have so many worries crowding her mind, she could enjoy the early fall afternoon, with the bushes along the hedgerow and at the edge of the woods showing the first colors of fall and the slant of sunlight that proclaimed the time of year as surely as any calendar.

Fingering a mushy bean, Judith tossed it into the basket at her feet. It may as well go straight to compost. Her hands stilled on the bowl as she looked toward the barn and its surrounding outbuildings. Isaac would be there now. It was a chance for a quiet word with him.

Rebecca's comments about trying to intercede between Isaac and Joseph slipped into her mind, troubling her. But Rebecca didn't know what it was like to watch two people you loved being at such odds with each other. Surely God didn't expect her to stand back and not even try to make things better.

With sudden conviction, she set the bowl aside and rose. She'd try to catch Isaac alone. Maybe by now he'd be willing to listen to her.

Standing, she had a view of the back of the barn. Startled, she stared, frowning. A truck was pulled up behind the barn where the generator was. It must have come in by the farther lane the milk trucks used, since it hadn't driven past the house.

What was going on? Isaac hadn't mentioned any deliveries coming today, had he? She walked quickly toward the barn, waving at the boys as she passed the rhubarb patch.

The truck was painted with the logo of the local farm supply store. It was backed up to the rear door of the barn, its ramp lowered. Even as she approached, she realized the workmen were sliding what looked like a brand-new generator into place. The generator Fred had supplied sat near the truck ramp, already disconnected.

"It's a good location for the generator, all right," one of the men was saying. "Sheltered but with plenty of ventilation. You won't need to worry about any fumes getting into the main part of the barn."

"Gut." Isaac leaned over, watching the process.

A quick glance told her Joseph was nowhere to be seen, and her heart sank. Why was Isaac having a new generator put in without Joseph, who would inevitably have the responsibility of taking care of it? And, more to the point, how could they afford it?

A chill went through her. Surely Isaac hadn't taken out a mortgage on the farm. That was one option they'd always been determined to avoid.

"Isaac?"

He turned at the sound of her voice, looking for a moment like one of the boys caught sneaking a snack before dinner. Then his expression firmed.

"Not now, Judith. We can talk after the men are finished." He spoke in dialect, knowing the

250

Englisch workmen wouldn't understand, although they glanced at her with curiosity, and the one who had spoken to Isaac nodded.

She returned the nod, managing a smile, and then looked at Isaac again. "Please. We have to talk."

She'd intended to speak to him about Joseph—to try and mend what had been broken between them. But the delivery of a generator they couldn't possibly afford only served to show her how upset Isaac still was. Clearly he didn't want to be beholden to Fred Yoder for a second longer than he had to.

For a moment she didn't think Isaac would respond. Then, with a word to the men, he walked over to where she waited.

"You have bought a new generator." Even though the Englisch wouldn't understand the rest of the sentence, they'd know the word *generator,* since there was no equivalent for it in the Pennsylvania Dutch dialect.

"As you see." His face was stony. "I should get back to them." He gestured toward the men.

"I know you're upset with Fred for encouraging Joseph," she said quickly, before he could move away. "But if you're returning his generator for that reason—"

"It would have to go back sometime. That's all."

Frustration nipped at her. They both knew that wasn't all. "You are angry with Fred Yoder." She said it flatly, daring him to deny it as her own temper, always so controlled, slipped a little.

"All right. I don't want to be beholden to him. Leave it alone, Judith." His blue eyes narrowed as if to warn her.

"How can I? We can't afford a new generator. Why didn't you talk to me about it?" They always discussed any purchase before they made it. After all, that was only common sense. But this time . . .

His jaw hardened. "You kept secrets from me, ain't so?"

It was like a blow to the heart, said as it was in a furious undertone. But somehow she had to go on.

"I found out by accident. I wanted to tell you, but it seemed more important to get Joseph to tell you his feelings himself. And to get you to listen to him, at least."

Maybe it was the unaccustomed tartness in her voice. Isaac actually seemed to listen. For an instant he didn't move. Then he gave a curt nod.

"Onkel Simon has lent us the money for the generator." Isaac didn't meet her eyes, and she knew how hard it was for him to admit he needed help.

Relief swept through her. He would have to be paid back, of course, but at least there was no danger they'd lose the property. "Onkel Simon is wonderful kind to us."

"Ja. He is." Isaac seemed to struggle for a moment with his emotions before he turned away. "It had to be done, Judith. That's all there is to it."

Before she could find something to say, Isaac had turned away and was giving instructions to the driver about returning the borrowed generator to the machine shop. She expected to hear him sending a message of thanks to Fred, but he didn't.

She studied his closed-in face, feeling a touch of despair. Isaac was obviously still upset, still unwilling to listen to any viewpoint but his own. How were they ever going to get back to normal?

Lancaster County, Late September 1953

Mattie was reaching for a large pumpkin to heft it into the pony cart when Adam, hurrying to the farm stand, seized it from her. He lifted it into the back of the cart while Rachel held Dolly's head. Not that Dolly, their black-and-white pony, wasn't well trained, but they knew too well that Dolly could be unpredictable at times. She'd made a spirited effort to kick the cart to pieces one day when a blaring horn startled her.

"Denke, Adam." Mattie smiled, realizing he must have come to help as soon as the milking was finished. "I could have managed."

"You could, but you don't have to." He reached for the basket of squash at her feet. "This goes, too?"

She nodded. "We'll take it all back to the house today."

"It looks as if either you had a wonderful big load of produce today or not much sold." He eyed the stack of fall vegetables on the counter.

"A little of each." She was being evasive, she feared, but she didn't want to talk about her lack of business in front of Rachel and Anna, who had come to the stand to help her pack up. Well, Rachel was helping. Anna was attempting to roll a pumpkin that was far too big for her.

"Take this one next, Cousin Adam." She patted it. "It's my favorite."

"It's bigger than you are," he declared, lifting first Anna, then the pumpkin. Looking at the laughter in Adam's face as he teased her daughter, Mattie remembered what he'd said about Anna giving him the gift of remembering his little Sarah. That was a gut thing, for sure.

Working together, they quickly had everything packed up and ready to go. Adam lifted his eyebrows. "Don't you usually leave a few things out with a jar for money?"

Instead of answering, she nodded to Rachel and helped Anna up to the seat of the pony cart. Once Rachel had started down the lane, she met Adam's gaze and shrugged. "Usually. But not any longer, I'm afraid."

"Why? What's wrong?" Instant concern filled his face.

She moved slowly down the lane with Adam beside her, trying to think how to frame her answer without upsetting him. "It was my turn to close yesterday, and I'd left a few pumpkins and squash out, like we usually do. Sometime in the night I was wakened by noises out at the farm stand."

Trying to be calm wasn't working. Her voice had trembled, and Adam, always so quick, would hear it. Even as she thought that, his hand closed over hers. "Who was it?"

"I don't know. Englisch teenagers, I think. I could hear them shouting and laughing. They were throwing the pumpkins on the road, breaking them."

"You didn't go out!" His grip tightened.

"No, no, I'm not so ferhoodled as that. I waited until morning, and then I got Ben's daad to help me clean it up before the others saw. I'm surprised he didn't say anything to you."

"We didn't have much chance to talk today." Adam's straight eyebrows were drawn down, and his usually merry face looked suddenly older.

"I'm thinking it might have been just some early Halloween mischief, ain't so? The Englisch kids get wilder every year with their pranks. I'm glad we don't celebrate such a holiday."

"Maybe," Adam said, sending a frowning glance at her. "But it could be that the kids were showing off their ill will toward the Amish."

"And my family in particular, you mean, because of Rachel."

She'd struggled with that thought through most of the night. Fear was infectious, it seemed, and she'd certainly felt its power when she'd lain awake, listening for any sound.

"It's not safe." Adam stopped in the shelter of the massive willow tree that overhung the lane, turning her to face him with his hands on her wrists. "You being here at night alone with just the kinder. I'll bring some blankets over and sleep in the barn until this trouble is over."

"No, Adam." As tempting as it was to be able to sleep knowing he was near, she couldn't let him. "That wouldn't be right. Besides, what could you do?"

"I don't know." He was as angry as she'd ever seen him. His blue eyes flashed, and even his beard seemed to bristle with it. "But I'd be here. I wouldn't let anyone hurt you."

His emotions touched her own, and she fought to tamp them down. In the shadow of the tree they were as alone as if they were shut away in a room somewhere. "If we are persecuted, it is because God allows it."

"Those who commit evil can't escape the responsibility of their actions so easily."

"It's not up to us to punish them." She put her hand on his arm, feeling the muscles so taut that they trembled. "Just leave it alone. We will be fine."

He caught her by the shoulders, startling her so

that her gaze widened. "You and the kinder mean too much to me to let you go unprotected. Don't you know that? Don't you feel it each time we're together?"

Mattie could only stare at him, trying to understand the feeling that surged through his voice—that radiated from his very touch, so that it flowed through her as well. Her breath caught.

Adam's lips found hers. For an instant Mattie's mind rejected the idea, but then emotion swamped her reason and she was responding, returning the kiss, holding him closer—

With a gasp she pulled back, feeling heat flood her face. She put her palms to her cheeks. How could she? She had no right—

"Mattie." His voice deepened on her name. "Don't. Don't be embarrassed. You must know how I feel about you. I've tried to deny it to myself, but I can't. Don't you see? Ben is gone. We both loved him, but he's gone, and it can't be wrong for us to be happy."

She shook her head. "Don't. It's not that." In the confusion of her mind she realized that perhaps it should be, but that wasn't what her immediate thought had been. "You're too young. Don't you see that? You should marry again, but someone young. You're ready to start a new family, not take over a half-grown one. You are so kind, so loving, Adam. That's what you deserve."

Adam studied her face, seeming to find something there that made him smile just a little. "But that's not what I want. I want you. And the kinder. And any others we might have together."

Mattie put her palms to her cheeks again, hoping she could hide the blush she knew was there. "You—you're confusing affection and responsibility with love." She drew in a breath, trying for calm. "You'll see that when you've had a chance to think."

"I don't think so." His voice was as calm and cheerful as always.

"You will." Mattie was regaining her poise, thank the good Lord. She pinned a smile on her face and turned toward the house. "We won't speak of this . . . of what happened just now. We'll forget it."

Again Adam fell into step beside her. "I might be able to keep from talking about kissing you, Mattie. But I know I can't forget it."

She judged it better not to comment on that, since she didn't think she'd be forgetting it very soon, either. But Adam mustn't know it.

They'd reached the back porch before he spoke again. "Somehow I'd almost forgotten the thing I came to tell you." His lips curved slightly. "Something must have distracted me."

Mattie chose to ignore his comment. "What did you want to tell me?"

Adam's smile disappeared, and concern filled

his eyes. "I heard the news just a bit ago. Two more from our district—Thomas Beiler and Josiah Kile—received their warnings today. They must send their children tomorrow or face arrest."

She rubbed her arms, feeling suddenly chilled. "It's coming closer."

"You—" Adam stopped, as if he'd changed his mind about what he was going to say. "Try not to worry too much. The bishop and Pastor Colby are talking to each of the board members. Surely someone will listen to reason."

"I know." If anyone could make a difference, it must be those two. *Please, Lord.* "I'll be all right."

Maybe not all right, she thought as Adam moved away reluctantly. But at least Adam's unexpected kiss had given her something to worry over besides the current trouble.

Here was one thing that had probably not changed since the days Mattie Lapp wrote about in her letters. Judith glanced around the backyard at the Byler farm, where the after-worship lunch was about finished. They still had worship services every other Sunday, lasting for three hours, followed by a lunch provided by the host family for that particular day.

Change didn't come quickly if you were Amish, and some fundamentals didn't change at all. It was only the particular challenges to being

Amish that were different from one generation to the next. Even the lunch served was predictable, with only a few changes in the dessert depending upon what was in season.

Apples, of course, this time of the year, and there had been big pans of apple crisp on the table today. Delicious, making her think of working her way through her collection of apple recipes.

The smallest children ran and played, weaving between groups of chatting older people. The little ones were just happy to be moving after sitting quietly in worship for three hours. The slightly older kinder had an organized game going.

As for the teenagers—well, they did what teens always did by ignoring the adults and focusing, no matter how they tried to hide it, on the opposite sex.

There would be a singing tonight for the rumspringa gang in the same barn where worship had been held this morning. Already some boys were setting up a volleyball net with probably a lot of unnecessary flexing of muscles. The teenage girls clustered in small groups, talking and giggling and casting frequent glances in the direction of the boys.

At least Joseph wasn't involved in that yet. They had two years before he'd be starting rumspringa, with all the worries that would entail.

"Those youngsters remind you of your rumspringa, ain't so?" Grossmammi said, startling her.

Judith sprang up to give her grandmother her chair and then pulled another one over for herself. "A little, I guess. I don't remember being that silly, that's certain-sure."

"You weren't. Not like those teenagers, and for sure not like Barbie. Neither you nor Rebecca was." Grossmammi's eyes searched the crowd for Barbie, and Judith nodded.

"She's over by the pasture fence." She pointed out her cousin. Barbie was chatting with the Esch brothers, her head tilted to one side as she flirted impartially with each of them.

Grossmammi shook her head, looking resigned. "I'd like to think she was interested in one or the other of them, but I don't."

"They wouldn't be gut for her, anyway. They're too eager to please her. Barbie needs someone who's a bit older and stronger than those two."

Judith had spoken without thinking, and then she realized that what she'd said was probably true. Lively Barbie could wrap either or both of the Esch boys around her little finger, and that wasn't a good basis for marriage.

Of course, given her current situation, she might wonder if she even knew what a good marriage was.

"Someone like Isaac, you mean?" Gross-mammi's tone was innocent, but there was no escaping the wisdom in her eyes.

Judith shrugged. "It was different for us. I was much younger than Barbie is, for one thing. She's old enough to be settling down, even if she doesn't think so."

"From what I remember about you, once Isaac showed his interest, no one else stood a chance with you, ain't so?"

Tears stung Judith's eyes, and she blinked them back furiously. She didn't want to talk about Isaac, not now, but she couldn't fail to answer when her grandmother asked her.

"I guess so. I never thought of him being interested in me. Since he was so quiet and serious himself, it seemed more likely he'd go for a lively girl."

"People don't always do what we think they would, especially when it comes to love." Grossmammi paused, but when Judith didn't respond, she went on. "There was talk of him and Becky Fisher for a while, I remember. She was certain-sure a lively one."

Becky was long since married to someone else, with a big family of her own and a comfortably spreading figure, and her flirting days were past. Judith struggled to keep back the words that wanted to be said, but she lost.

"By that time, Isaac knew how sick his aunt

was. He must have figured he needed to court a girl who could be a mother to Joseph."

Grossmammi looked at her questioningly. "That was a compliment, ain't so? He knew you would be a gut mammi, and so you are."

"A woman might want something a little more romantic as a reason for marrying." Her tone was sharper than she'd intended, and she couldn't even hope that Grossmammi had missed it.

"Was ist letz, Judith?" Her grandmother's voice was gentle. "You can talk to me, ain't so?"

Judith bit her lip, knowing she had to speak but knowing, too, that she shouldn't burden Grossmammi with her own worries.

"I think Isaac is being stubborn and wrong-headed about Joseph, insisting the boy take over the dairy farm whether he wants to or not. And Isaac thinks I am interfering when I try to help."

"It can't be interfering when you love the boy, too," Grossmammi said. "After all, you raised him."

"That's what I feel." She frowned, then tried to rub the furrows away from her forehead with her fingertips. "Ach, it's all mixed up in Isaac's mind with losing his family. But I hate being at odds with him over Joseph."

"It's not a gut thing—" Grossmammi stopped abruptly, glancing over Judith's shoulder.

Judith turned, following the direction of her grandmother's gaze. Joseph stood there, and it was obvious from his white face that he'd over-heard at least some of what they'd been saying, if not all.

"I . . . I'm sorry," he stammered. "I didn't mean to listen."

"Joseph, it's all right," she began, but Joseph had already turned. He bolted toward the barn.

Her heart twisting, Judith rose. "I have to go. I have to talk to him." She hurried after him, trying not to look as if anything was wrong. Poor Joseph. She'd had no idea he was anywhere near her, or she'd never have spoken that way.

When she reached the barn, the boy seemed to have disappeared. Judith paused in the doorway, scanning the yard and the fields beyond. There was no sign of him. He must have gone inside.

Moving quietly, Judith stepped into the barn. It retained the remnants of the worship service, even though most of the benches had been moved outside and turned into tables for the lunch since it was a nice warm day. A few remained, mute reminders of the worship that had taken place.

She walked through the space, glancing from side to side, listening. Finally she heard the sound she was waiting for—a muffled sob.

It came from the hayloft. Without pausing, Judith started up the closest ladder. When she'd climbed high enough to see across the loft, she spotted Joseph, crouched over a hay bale just a few feet from the top of the ladder. He stared at her, his face white and tearstained. He looked much more like a little boy than a man just now.

"Give me a hand up, Joseph." She kept her voice cheerful with an effort. "I'm getting a little old for climbing, I think."

Sniffling, he moved toward her, grasping her arm and helping her until she stood in the loft. When he started to turn away, she held his arm firmly and piloted him to the nearest hay bale, sitting down and drawing him down next to her. He didn't make an effort to run again, but he kept his face turned away, maybe ashamed for her to see his tears.

"Now then, we must talk, the two of us." No response. "I'm sorry that you heard what I said to my grossmammi about our troubles. But you know that she won't repeat it to anyone, ain't so?"

That got a slight nod.

Her heart twisted as she studied him. The curve of his cheek and the back of his neck were as familiar to her as Levi's or Paul's or Noah's. But the hands were different now—nearly a man's hands, which he'd have to grow into. And his shirtsleeves were already too short for him, showing bony wrists that were somehow vulnerable.

"You are thinking that it is your fault that Isaac and I are disagreeing." In a way it was because of Joseph, but it went far deeper than that, and it was important that Joseph not blame himself.

Again she got a nod, and his head seemed to sink between his arms.

"Married couples disagree sometimes. It's part of marriage. If we always agreed with each other, we wouldn't be normal. Men and women sometimes see things differently, that's all."

She tried to keep her voice light, hard though it was. But the words made her realize how seldom she had expressed disagreement with Isaac, even when she felt it. She had always been willing to let her desire go in order to keep the peace, until it had come to something as important as Joseph's future and his happiness.

"Komm now." She nudged him. "You've heard Lige and his wife disagree, haven't you? Even Onkel Simon, much as he loved her, sometimes argued with Aunt Emma. You should have heard her scold him when he came into the kitchen without taking off his work shoes."

That actually got a slight smile, as everyone knew that Onkel Simon was often guilty of tracking in mud.

"You see?" Some of her tension slid away. "You can accept responsibility for things you caused, but not for everything, ain't so?"

Joseph was like Isaac in that trait, she realized suddenly, and she felt the knowledge clutch at her heart. But Joseph, being young, still had time to

266

learn a different way to react, while Isaac . . . She wasn't sure that Isaac could ever accept that truth, and as long as he didn't, he'd never come to terms with the death of his parents.

CHAPTER FOURTEEN

Lancaster County, Late September 1953

Adam walked across the field between Mattie's place and his uncle's, his mind still caught up in the effect of that kiss. He hadn't planned it, but maybe it was the best thing he could have done. Mattie had responded, there was no doubt in his mind about that or about the fact that she cared for him, whether she knew it or not.

Mattie was unwilling to admit that her feelings for him could lead to marriage. For all the reasons she'd put up against a relationship between them, she hadn't said she didn't love him. He was in a mood to consider that a triumph.

Patience—that was what was called for now. With time and persistence, Mattie would surely come to see, as he had, that this was right. He'd said nothing but the truth when he'd pointed out that though they'd both loved Ben dearly, he was gone.

Strange, how that had clarified in his mind once

the threat to Mattie had reared up. All of his worries about what Ben would have thought seemed like so much foolishness. Ben would want Mattie and his kinder to be happy and taken care of if he couldn't be here to do it. He'd never been one to try and hold on to the past.

Onkel Jonah moved into his line of sight, carrying what looked like a burlap bag of chicken feed over his shoulder. When he spied Adam coming he thumped the bag to the ground and raised his hand. Adam obediently veered toward him.

"On your way home to supper?" he asked.

Adam nodded. "All finished at Mattie's. I helped her and the girls bring everything back from the farm stand."

He walked across Onkel Jonah's land every day at this time, on his way back to his parents' place. He'd moved back to the family farm after losing his wife and child, not having the heart to stay in the house that had been so full of their dreams.

Since his uncle knew all that perfectly well, he must have something he wanted to say.

A frown clouded Onkel Jonah's face. "You heard about the trouble at the farm stand last night, ain't so?"

"Mattie told me." His hands clenched into fists. "I wish I'd been there."

"Ja, and I wish I'd heard it. At least I could have gone over and stayed with them. Mattie said the kinder didn't wake, so at least they weren't frightened. But she was, that's certain-sure."

"No one was hurt this time." The thought that those boys could come back refused to be dismissed from Adam's mind.

Onkel Jonah rubbed the back of his neck. "If only we'd set up the stand at the end of our road, or yours. But we thought we were doing a gut thing, making it more convenient for Mattie, since she has the kinder to watch."

"It might not have made a difference," Adam said slowly, hating to voice the fear in his head. "It might have been that the vandals hit there because of knowing that's where Rachel lives." His jaw hardened until it was difficult to speak. "If so, I'm afraid they might come back."

"Ach, no!" The shock in Onkel Jonah's face made it plain the idea hadn't occurred to him. "I never thought of such a thing. If you're right, we have to do something."

"That's what I think, too. It worries me. I said to Mattie that I'd bring blankets and sleep in the barn for a bit, but she wouldn't hear of it."

"There's no use asking her and the kinder to sleep over here with us for a time, either. I know she wouldn't." Onkel Jonah glanced toward Mattie's house. "Still, I don't see any reason why the two of us might not take some late-night walks in that direction, is there?"

Adam grinned. "That's just what I was thinking."

"That's one thing we can do, then, even if it's not as much as we'd like to do."

"No. It's bad enough that she's threatened by the school district, without having to put up with hoodlums as well."

"Ja." Onkel Jonah's expression darkened. "I hear two more of unser Leit were served with papers today."

"Thomas Beiler and Josiah Kile. I heard." Who would be next? "I keep hoping the board will take account of the fact that Mattie is a widow, with no one to share her burden. Why would they take their only parent away from those kinder, and a woman besides?"

"I would like to believe they would consider it." But his uncle's expression showed his doubt. "Still, everyone knows that Josiah's wife is in the hospital, and that didn't stop them from going after him."

"I keep trying to understand the Englisch who are doing this, but it is sehr hard." Adam kicked at a loose clod of dirt. "I have to believe those people on the board really think they're doing something good, otherwise I'm not sure I can forgive." Adam shrugged, trying to relax the tension in his shoulders. "At least they have some reason for what they're doing, even if we don't agree with it. Not like those boys who broke up the pumpkins."

"The Lord says we have to forgive, but He

doesn't say it is easy." Onkel Jonah looked as if he was struggling with that forgiveness as well.

"No. The most important thing now is to rescue Mattie from this threat, but I don't know how it's to be done." His fists clenched again, and again he forced them to relax. Anger was a sin, just as not forgiving those who wronged you was. It would be easier, he thought, to forgive a wrong done to himself rather than one done to Mattie.

"If Mattie were married, her husband would be the one the law went after, even if he were the stepfather, ain't so?" Onkel Jonah dropped the question and seemed to look at it, as if wondering whether he should have said it.

Adam studied his face. "Are you saying what I think you are?"

Onkel Jonah met his gaze without wavering. "We all still miss Ben, but it's time to move on. It's what he would want." He was echoing Adam's thoughts. "You're my own brother's boy, and you've grown into a gut man. You're already attached to Mattie and her kinder, ain't so? We've been thinking for some time it would be a gut match."

Adam hesitated for a moment, but he may as well speak, since Ben's own father had brought it up. "I have been thinking it, too. But Mattie doesn't see it that way." His lips quirked a little. "Still, I think she might change her mind, given some time."

Relief washed over his uncle's face. "I'm wonderful glad to hear you say so. I wouldn't be matchmaking if it weren't for the way things are right now."

"Once Mattie gets used to the idea—" he began.

His uncle was shaking his head. "That's the trouble. If we are to save Mattie from jail, there might not be time for waiting and thinking. They could come for her any day now, and then what will we do?"

The words sent a chill down Adam's spine. He would go to jail every day of the week to spare Mattie, but the only way he could do that was as her husband, and he didn't think she would agree to it, at least not yet.

All the way home from worship that Sunday morning, Judith had been pondering her conversation with Joseph. Her heart hurt when she thought of his efforts to keep from crying in front of her. Once, he'd have buried his face in her apron and wept out his sorrows, but he considered himself a man now. He'd try to keep his suffering to himself, no matter what the cost.

Like Isaac. She stole a glance across the buggy seat at her husband. His face was set in firm lines, his expression unreadable under the shadow cast by his black hat. The two brothers were more alike than they realized.

Somehow, there must be a reconciliation

272

between Isaac and Joseph. Even if Isaac refused to change his mind about Joseph's future, even if Joseph walked away from the dairy farm when he was old enough, surely they could find some common ground for Isaac to show the boy he still loved him. Joseph needed that reassurance. And Joseph wasn't the only one.

She had to talk to Isaac. She was the only one who could. Even though her heart shrank from confronting him, she had to do it.

The opportunity to talk to Isaac alone didn't arise until after she'd settled the boys for the night. She'd barely reached the bottom of the stairs before she heard Levi and Paul fussing at each other. She turned to go back up, but Isaac, just heading for his chair with the weekly newspaper, shook his head.

"I'll do it." He tossed the paper aside and headed up the stairs. "I don't know what's the matter with those two lately. All they do is snap at each other."

She watched him, bemused. Did he realize he'd just described another pair of brothers in the family? Apparently not.

As Judith settled into her rocker and picked up the mending basket, she could hear Isaac's voice, scolding. He sounded out of sorts. Maybe this wasn't the best time to approach him about his relationship with Joseph.

And maybe she was being a coward. There

wasn't going to be a good time, and the thought of another evening spent mainly in silence was more than she could bear.

He came back down. "Paul was out of his room, teasing his brother about something or other. And Levi was calling him names. The two of them are going to earn spankings if they don't settle down, and quickly."

She would not point out the similarity to the relationship between him and his brother. If he didn't see it, how could she make him?

Besides, she already had enough of an issue on her mind. Judith waited until he was seated with the newspaper in his hands, so that he couldn't say he was on his way to do something else. "I want to talk to you, Isaac."

The newspaper rustled. "Can it wait? I still haven't had time to read the paper."

"This is more important than the newspaper." Judith forced as much firmness as she could muster into her voice.

The newspaper lowered, and she thought Isaac looked a little surprised. Maybe he wasn't used to her speaking so firmly to him.

Now that she had his attention, she wasn't sure where to start. Best just to plunge right in.

"I think you need to be talking more to Joseph." That wasn't quite what she wanted to say, but at least it opened the subject.

"We talk." But there was a defensiveness in his

voice that declared he knew what she meant.

"Telling him to pass the salt isn't talking." Judith drew in a breath, trying to approach the subject calmly. "He became very upset today after church. I think he feels that he is coming between the two of us."

Now she'd startled him. The newspaper slid to the floor. "That's foolishness."

"Maybe so, but it's what he feels." She leaned forward, willing her husband to understand. "Isaac, Joseph is carrying a load of guilt that he shouldn't be." *Like you,* she thought, her heart aching. "He needs to talk to you about all of this and feel you've heard him."

Isaac's face tightened. "I'm not changing my mind about the farm. I have to do what I feel is best for Joseph."

Patience, she told herself. "You can talk to him without changing your mind."

"Why do women think they have to talk things to death?" Isaac muttered, but the words were said in the grudging murmur that told her he was weakening.

"Because we know it's often the best way to make things better," she said promptly. "Like now. Joseph needs to know that even if the two of you disagree about his future, you still love him."

His gaze slid away from hers in typical male embarrassment. "Joseph is getting too old for that, ain't so? Besides, he knows what I feel for him."

"How can he know when you never say so?" Her throat clenched. It was true for her as well as for Joseph. Sometimes people needed to hear the words.

"He's all that's left of my family." His voice grew tight. "He has to know what that means."

"Isaac, you never talk about them." She leaned toward him, reaching out helplessly. "I know it hurts, but sometimes we need to share our grief." Suddenly, unexpectedly, her throat clogged with tears. "I'd like to talk about Deborah once in a while. Don't you see that? She was my best friend." The tears spilled over, and she put her hands on her face.

This wasn't about her. She'd never intended to say such a thing. Men hated tears, and Isaac was no exception. He'd make some lame excuse to leave—

His chair creaked as he rose. Then he clasped her shoulders and drew her up out of the rocker, her mending falling to the floor. He put his arms around her.

"I'm sorry," she whispered, and buried her face in his shirt.

"No." He kissed the top of her head. "I'm sorry. I had forgotten. You and Deborah . . ." He held her for a long moment, motionless, his cheek against her forehead. "How could I forget?" he murmured. "The two of you running around the garden together, whispering secrets, her braids coming down and yours curling out of control." He stroked her hair.

Judith managed a smile through her tears. "I know. I think most of the secrets were plots to spy on you."

"Mischief makers," he teased softly.

"Only when I was with Deborah." Her heart swelled, remembering. "I was always shy and quiet, except with her."

He nodded, and she felt the movement against her face. "Ja. She was so lively she could bring people out."

They just stood there for a long moment, holding each other. Finally Isaac sighed. "Komm." He settled her against his side. "Let's go up to bed. Tomorrow I'll try to do better with Joseph. All right?"

Judith's heart lightened. "All right."

Much later she lay awake, listening to Isaac's steady breathing, grateful for the weight of his arm across her. Somehow, and she wasn't sure how, she'd gotten through to Isaac. At least, he'd said he'd try. She could only pray that it would be enough—that it would be a new beginning for him and Joseph.

Isaac came out of the barn the next afternoon, pausing to adjust his hat and let his eyes become accustomed to the sunshine. He automatically searched for Judith and found her over by the old generator shed.

She was kneeling on the grass, sorting through some bulbs, her head bowed as she focused on her task. Some tendrils of brown hair had, as usual, escaped her kapp to curl around her ears. He smiled, tenderness filling him at the sight of her.

Judith tried so hard to keep everyone in the family happy. She had a heart full of love for all of them. He should have remembered that when he'd been so angry with her over keeping a secret from him. She would only do such a thing out of love, and he knew it, even if he thought she'd been mistaken in what she'd done.

Right now, she had all of the boys involved in planting bulbs. Joseph was digging the bed while Levi and Paul broke up the clots of dirt. Noah, of course, was mainly getting in the way, but he had his own little shovel, and he was trying to help.

Joseph. He studied his brother as he walked toward them. The boy was growing so much that he'd stopped thinking of him as a child who needed reassurance and encouragement. But maybe a boy his age needed it even more. When Isaac had been fourteen, he'd had Daad to talk to about the things a boy wanted to ask a man.

The trouble was, he'd never been one to talk about his feelings, and Joseph would certain-sure think it odd if he started now. Still, he'd promised Judith he would try, and so he must. He could be more responsive and patient. That wouldn't be hard. If only Joseph could be satisfied with the life ahead of him instead of longing for something else . . .

"Daadi!" Noah spotted him and jumped up, nearly cracking his head on Joseph's spade. "We're planting flowers."

Isaac reached him and scooped him out of the way, lifting him in his arms. "You are helping, ain't so?"

Noah nodded vigorously. "Mammi says if we bury the bulbs in the ground now, we'll have flowers in the spring." Worry wrinkled his forehead. "But won't the winter be too cold for them?"

"They'll be fine, because you're going to put a nice blanket of dirt over top of them to keep them warm." He let Noah slide to the ground and then sat down, pulling his youngest onto his lap. He lifted an eyebrow at Judith. "You decided some flowers would hide the burned spot?"

"Ach, it will disappear by spring anyway. But this seems like a gut place for bulbs, with the lilac bushes behind them. I don't know why I never thought of it before."

A memory slid into his mind. His mother had had a flower bed in that spot, hadn't she? He'd forgotten it, but surely this was where it had been.

He seemed to see her bent over a colorful display, hand gently cupping a blossom.

He choked down a lump in his throat and pushed the memory out of his mind. Make an effort to talk to the kinder, especially to Joseph—that was what he had to do. That was what Judith wanted him to do, and he'd agreed he'd try.

"Should be a pretty sight in the spring." Luckily he sounded normal. "What are those bulbs you're planting?"

"My mamm shared them with me. She was dividing some of her clumps of flowers. The tiny ones are snowdrops." She touched them lightly with her fingers. "They bloom first, and they're small, so we'll put them in front, with daffodils interspersed and the tulips behind them. That way we'll have something blooming all spring."

Isaac nodded, trying to think of something he could say to Joseph and wondering why it should be difficult. "Joseph is doing a gut job of digging the bed for you, ain't so?" He smiled at his brother and got a startled look in reply.

"He is, for sure."

Joseph looked a little embarrassed at the attention, but he grinned. "It's easy enough digging. Almost like someone had dug it up before."

Isaac didn't respond. There was no reason why any of them needed to know that Mammi had once tended her flowers in this same spot.

"Hey! There's something here." Levi dropped

to his knees and burrowed into the dirt like a puppy uncovering a bone.

"Careful." Joseph knelt next to him, using the hand spade to help him unearth it, whatever it was.

"Probably just a rock—" Isaac began, leaning forward to look, but the words died when Levi pulled out a small wooden object and held it up triumphantly.

"Look, it's a dog. A little wooden dog."

Isaac was looking, and his heart seemed to stop as he recognized the small toy. He looked away, afraid to let Levi see his expression.

"See, Daadi?" Levi scrambled over to shove it into his hands, and Isaac had no choice but to take it.

"Ja, I see." He turned it over, handling it gently, running his fingers along the rough knife cuts. He hadn't been very good at woodcarving then. And he'd never attempted it again after the fire, he realized. He'd shut it out of his life, most likely afraid it would make him remember being with Daad in the workshop, listening to Daad's patient voice encouraging him. He'd always encouraged, Isaac realized, whatever his kinder wanted to do.

"Isaac?" Judith's voice was questioning. She knew something was wrong, whether anyone else noticed it or not.

"I . . . it belonged to my little sister. To Jessie." He fought his treacherous voice, which nearly broke on the name. "I made it for her birthday when she was five."

He saw them, suddenly. All of them around the pine table in the kitchen, lamplight glowing on smiling faces and Jessie's smile even brighter than the lamp as her big brother handed her a birthday gift. The image was so clear in his mind that he could almost reach out and touch them. He could almost feel Jessie's small hand in his.

"You made it?" Luckily, Levi focused on the fact that his father had produced such a thing, saving Isaac the embarrassment of revealing his feelings to his son.

"Ja." He cleared his throat. "We tried to make the presents we gave each other for birthdays, just like you do."

"Why don't you make anything like that now? Why, Daadi?" Levi put his hand on Isaac's knee, persistent.

"I wasn't very gut at it," he said. He managed to glance at Joseph, and his brother's expression hit him in the heart. Joseph stared at the battered little dog as if it were the most amazing treasure he'd ever seen.

"Was Jessie five when . . ." Joseph stopped, as if he couldn't manage the rest of the question.

He nodded. Short. Curt. *Let this be an end to it. Please.*

Joseph held out his hand without speaking. Isaac had to fight his reluctance. Then he put the toy dog into Joseph's hand. Amazing, that the boys weren't clamoring to hold it. Maybe they sensed without understanding that this was something too serious for fussing over.

He didn't really want to watch, but he couldn't seem to help himself. Joseph turned the toy dog over in his hands much as Isaac had done, touching it carefully. With respect.

It hit him then. Joseph had never so much as seen anything that had belonged to his family. Everything had been lost in the fire. Nothing remained to remind them of the five who died. Mamm. Daad. Deborah, nine. Mary, seven. And Jessie, just five.

The boy looked up suddenly, his face open, a startling difference from the sullen look that had been habitual recently. "What was she like?"

Isaac felt as if a vise had closed around his heart. He didn't want to talk, didn't want to remember, and he certain-sure didn't want to feel the pain again. But Joseph was looking at him with such hope, and he could sense Judith willing him to answer.

For an instant resentment flared in him that she would pressure him to do something so painful, but it died instantly, and it shamed him. He'd promised to try to talk to Joseph. He hadn't expected it to be about sweet, lost little Jessie, but so it was.

"She was happy," he said, forcing the words out

past the lump in his throat. "I never knew such a happy little girl. Every time I looked at her, she was smiling." He glanced at Judith, pleading silently for help. "Wasn't she?"

"Jessie was like sunshine," she said, lips curving a little with the memory. "Her hair was so light a yellow that it was almost white, and she had the biggest blue eyes. She had a dimple in her cheek that showed when she smiled. Right here, just like Noah does." She touched Noah's dimple, and he giggled, not quite sure what was going on.

"She always wanted to do what the older ones did," she went on. "And when I came to see Deborah, she followed us around. I remember when we taught her and Mary to jump rope. No matter how many times Jessie tripped, she'd laugh and try again."

Just when he'd thought he'd gotten his emotions under control, Isaac's eyes filled with tears. Jessie was suddenly so alive in his thoughts, her eyes dancing, squealing with joy when he gave her the little dog he'd made, throwing her arms around him in a huge hug.

Levi patted his knee as if to comfort him. "Daadi? You look like you want to cry. Does it make you feel sad to think about your little sister?"

He put his arm around his son. "A little bit." He hugged the boy close, rejoicing in the sturdy little body. "I wish . . ." *I wish you could have known her.* That's what he was thinking, and it shocked him. Whatever Levi might know about his aunt Jessie, it had come from someone else, not from him.

He was shamed, suddenly. How could it be right that Jessie and Deborah and Mary, to say nothing of Mammi and Daadi, should be unknown to Joseph and the other children, and all because of him?

"I wish I remembered them." Joseph said it in a soft voice, his eyes still on the dog. "I've always thought maybe it would be gut to have pictures, like the Englisch do, because then I could see them."

"The pictures you make in your mind are even better," Judith said. "You can see her now from the things we said about her, ain't so?"

Joseph nodded. "Ja." His voice trembled on the word, and he wiped his face with his hand, leaving a smear of dirt on his cheek. He held the wooden dog out to Isaac, not speaking.

Isaac's throat clenched. He closed his hand over his brother's, carving and all. "You should have it. To remember your sister." He glanced at Levi, who had found it, after all. "Okay, Levi?"

Levi nodded, his face solemn as if he knew he was taking part in something very important.

"Denke." Joseph's face lit up like sunshine, and for an instant he looked so much like Jessie. "Denke."

285

CHAPTER FIFTEEN

Lancaster County, Late September 1953

Mattie sat at one end of the study table in the kitchen, trying to catch up with her part of the Round Robin letter for her cousins. She wanted to sound more hopeful than she felt at the moment, even while being honest with them. If she couldn't write out her confused feelings to her dear cousins, whom *could* she tell?

Still, she didn't want them worrying overmuch about her. There were plenty of worried people around her already, and no sense in adding any more. She could only hope and pray that what happened here in their small school district would put an end to the struggle, so that other mothers wouldn't have to face what she did, but somehow she didn't think it would be that easy.

God had not promised life would be easy. He had promised that He would be with those who believed. Their part was to believe and to keep their own promises.

"Greet the cousins for me, Mammi." Rachel sat at the other end of the table with Anna on her lap, helping her little sister practice printing her name.

"Ja, I will," Mattie said, cherishing this quiet time at the end of a busy, worrisome day.

On either side of her, the boys did their homework—Nathaniel working through his steadily, while Toby circled objects on a page quickly and then had to turn back and erase when Rachel pointed out an error.

Rachel had been cutting out a new dress when Mattie told the boys it was homework time, but she'd left her work to come and supervise the younger ones' tasks. Without being asked, of course. Rachel had voluntarily decided to take over homework supervision once school started, and Mattie suspected Rachel did it even better than she did, never growing impatient and quietly recalling her brothers to their jobs when their attention wandered.

Mattie turned back to her letter and started a new paragraph.

Rachel is getting so grown up these days—far more mature than we were at fourteen, I think. Perhaps the trouble we've gone through has made her more serious than she otherwise would be, but she's such a sweet girl, and I long so much for her to have the life we've dreamed of for her.

Why shouldn't Rachel have that life? A flare of rebellion lit Mattie's thoughts. Rachel had already

287

been through the pain of losing her father. Why should she have to be the one to undergo this trial?

Mattie fought to dismiss the thought. God was with them, and nothing would happen to them that was not in accord with His will. It was just so hard sometimes to remember.

She put her pen down and moved to the sink for a glass of water, drinking it standing and looking out the window. It was getting dark already, with the days growing shorter as autumn drew in, tightening its grip. Despite the beauty of the season, with the fields turning gold in the slanting afternoon sun, she hated to see the year moving inexorably toward winter.

The kinder loved winter, of course, looking forward eagerly to the ice on the pond and the first snowfall. But it became lonely on those long winter evenings. When it was dark by suppertime, no one dropped by to visit. She'd never thought of winter evenings that way when Ben was alive, instead looking forward to those precious moments when the kinder were in bed and they were alone together, talking or reading or just sitting quietly, knowing the other was close at hand.

The memories were fading, she knew, gently but as inexorable as winter's arrival. At first, after Ben's death, those memories had been too painful, but eventually she'd welcomed them.

She'd clung to them, even when they were bittersweet. Now, it seemed they'd become removed enough to look at, remember with love, and then put away like a letter she'd read but wanted to save.

And that thought brought her inevitably to Adam. At least now she could think about him without her cheeks growing hot as if she were a sixteen-year-old. Surely by now he had gotten over his foolishness. He hadn't mentioned it again, so maybe that meant he had realized how wrong it would be to marry a woman older than he was, and with a family already.

That was what she wanted, wasn't it? For him to forget about it? So why did something in her heart long to reject the thought that he'd given up so easily?

She turned back to the room and then glanced out the window once again, half watching for someone moving along the lane or across the field. Adam had accepted her refusal to let him sleep in the barn to protect her and the children, but apparently only because he and Daad Jonah had hatched another plot between the two of them.

They seemed to think she wasn't aware that the two of them had been coming by the house to check on her throughout the evening, and on into the night, as well. The younger children hadn't realized it, but Rachel had noticed, too. It hadn't taken much explaining on Mattie's part to let her know why they were doing such a thing.

In fact, Rachel seemed to feel better because of it, as if she had been secretly uneasy when they were here alone in the night. Mattie had to admit, though she didn't think she'd tell Adam or her father-in-law, that she felt a bit safer knowing they were out there.

It was pointless to peer out the window, she chided herself. They wouldn't come by this early. She returned to her chair and her letter.

It wasn't a minute later that Mattie heard the sound of a vehicle turning into the lane. She stiffened, dropping her pen, and her gaze met Rachel's. She read there the same fear she felt herself.

The deputy serving the papers wouldn't come at this hour, would he? Each time it had happened so far, it had been during the day. She had convinced herself, once evening came, that she was safe for another night. What if the police had changed their plans, maybe thinking to avoid having other people around when they served the papers?

The sound of the car grew louder as it neared the house. It wasn't just someone using the lane to turn around in. It was someone coming to see her.

Mattie was suddenly so cold she felt as if she'd been turned to ice. Would she be able to move if she had to? Or would she shatter into pieces, like an icicle the kinder might knock down from the eaves?

"Mammi?" Fear laced Rachel's voice, and it recalled Mattie to herself. She was the mother. She had to stay calm so the kinder wouldn't be frightened.

"It's all right." They both heard the slam of a car door and footsteps mounting the porch steps. "I'll go. You stay with your brothers and sister."

Rachel nodded, her eyes wide, and the other three children watched with varying degrees of comprehension. Had she explained well enough what might happen if the police came to her? If not, it was too late now, as a knock sounded on the door.

Mattie rose, steadying herself with one hand on the study table. Then she walked to the door, ready to see a uniform through the pane.

She didn't, and for a moment she couldn't comprehend what she was seeing. Mrs. Graham stood there, on Mattie's back porch—the school board president's wife.

Smoothing down her apron, Mattie opened the door. "Mrs. Graham. Wilkom. I'm afraid the stand is closed, but if you need something . . ."

"It's not that." The woman's smile flickered unconvincingly and was gone. "I . . . I'd just like to talk with you."

"Please, komm."

She gestured, and Mrs. Graham walked into the back hallway, lined on one side with hooks for outdoor clothing, and through into the kitchen. There she paused, looking around so intently that Mattie guessed she'd never been inside an Amish home before.

"These are my children. Rachel and Anna you've probably seen at the stand. And the boys are Nate and Toby."

"I remember Nate, too. He gave my little girl half his whoopie pie." She managed a genuine smile for the children.

"We were just doing homework," Mattie explained, her mind whirling in search of a reason why the wife of the school board president would be calling on her. "I have coffee warm on the stove, and there's berry pie—"

"No, no, I can't stay," the woman said quickly. "Is there someplace we can talk privately?" She glanced at the children, making it clear that whatever she wanted to say wasn't for their ears.

"Come into the living room, please." Mattie darted a stern look toward Anna, who'd begun to slide off Rachel's lap as if she thought the invitation was for her. "Rachel, will you finish up here with the kinder?"

Don't let them come into the other room. That was what she meant, and her daughter's expression told her that Rachel understood. Rachel nodded, drawing Anna close to her.

Mattie led the way to the living room and gestured toward the sofa. Once her guest sat, she drew a rocker up closer to her, so that they might talk in lower voices. With the gas lamp on the table between them, the room was as it might have been in those memories of hers of evenings with Ben. But nothing about this visit from Mrs. Graham was likely to be comforting.

Mattie clasped her hands in her lap to keep them from shaking, and then she realized that the other woman was doing the same thing. Oddly enough, that gave her a little confidence. If Mrs. Graham needed the comfort of a hand holding hers, they were more alike than she might have feared.

"Are you sure you won't have something? A cup of tea, if you don't care for coffee?" Just the action of putting the kettle on, then of drinking or eating something together, might make this encounter less upsetting.

"That's kind of you, but no. I really can't stay. Walter thinks I'm at a women's meeting at church." The woman glanced toward the front windows as if she expected to be spotted and asked to account for her presence.

"He doesn't know you're here, then." There'd been little chance that Mrs. Graham had come at her husband's suggestion anyway. But it surprised Mattie, after what Mrs. Graham had said about never interfering in her husband's business, to find her apparently doing so. Why else could she have come, if not because of the school problem?

"No, Walter doesn't know I've come. He wouldn't be pleased." She paused, her hands clinging to each other in her lap. "This is so difficult." The woman's eyes widened, as if she feared she'd said something she shouldn't. "I don't mean that being here with you is difficult. You've always been so nice when we've talked at the stand. I felt . . . well, as if we might have been friends if not for this whole situation. This business of the school is what is so upsetting."

"Ja, it is," Mattie agreed.

More for her than for the other woman, Mattie would think, but she fought down the uncharitable reaction. Clearly the Englisch woman was upset. Not all the Englisch had turned against them in this struggle.

Mrs. Graham took a deep breath and seemed to straighten. "I want to apologize to you."

"It's not your fault." Mattie wasn't sure it was right to blame anybody for what was happening. In this matter, the Amish and the Englisch just seemed to be on a collision course.

"No, but perhaps . . ." She hesitated. "Perhaps none of us can sit back and say it's not our fault. If people had talked with each other sooner, we might have resolved the conflict."

"The bishop says that people of good will can

always come to an agreement." Mattie frowned, feeling her way, longing to express herself but afraid she couldn't. "Maybe that will still happen. I know some people are working toward a resolution."

The woman nodded. "I've heard, and I'm praying they will succeed. I'm just so . . . so very sorry that things have gotten so out of control. I'm sure this was never what anyone imagined. How could anyone want to see parents going to jail for trying to take care of their children in the way they think best?"

The words touched Mattie's fears. She closed her eyes for an instant, reaching for calm, and then tried to smile at the woman who looked so worried.

"Denke. Thank you. It's kind of you to say so." She hesitated, but it might be important to know as much as possible, and she couldn't let this opportunity slip away. "Do you think there are others in the Englisch community, besides people like Pastor Colby who have already spoken up, who feel the same as you do?"

"I'm sure there are many." A shadow crossed her face. "People like me, who stayed silent too long. But it's only fair to tell you that my husband isn't among them."

That would have been too much to hope for, Mattie supposed. "I'm sure he feels he's doing what is right."

Mrs. Graham surprised her by wrinkling her nose. "Or maybe he just can't admit he's been wrong."

Encouraged, Mattie asked, "Isn't there anyone he might listen to? The bishop, or Pastor Colby, or . . . or you?"

The woman was already shaking her head. "I have tried. It's no use." She seemed to brace herself. "That's why I'm taking the step of coming here. I shouldn't get involved, but Walter won't listen, and you've always been so kind, and I just felt . . ." She seemed to peter out.

Impulsively, Mattie reached out to clasp her hand. "I'm glad you came tonight. I was sitting here worrying, and it makes me feel better to know you understand."

Mrs. Graham's eyes suddenly filled with tears, startling her. "That's not the only reason I came. I had to tell you—" She stopped, shook her head, and started again, staring down at their clasped hands.

"When I was cleaning Walter's den, I saw some papers he'd left on his desk. I shouldn't have looked at them, I know. But I just glanced that way and saw something, and then I couldn't look away. I saw your name." She looked up again, meeting Mattie's gaze, and her eyes were filled with anguish. "I read the paper. It contained a list of names, and it had dates on it. At first I didn't understand, but then I realized. They were the dates on which each person was going to be served with the order to obey or be arrested."

She must be numb, Mattie decided, because she couldn't seem to move. She could only hold on tightly to Mrs. Graham's hand and wait.

"I'm sorry." A tear spilled over on the woman's cheek. "I truly am sorry. But you're going to be served with the papers tomorrow."

So. Mattie had known it would come, sooner or later. Now she knew when. Tomorrow. She was astonished that she felt so calm now that the blow had fallen. She had been waiting for it, and now that it had come she actually was relieved that she didn't have to wait and worry any longer.

"Thank you." Mattie articulated the words carefully. "I know it must have been hard for you to come here."

Mrs. Graham shook her head. "Not hard, no. Just . . . it seemed to be right, and I hope I haven't made things worse for you. I just thought, if I was the one, I'd want to know."

"You were right," she said quickly. "It's best to know. I'll be able to prepare the kinder . . . the children . . . better for what is going to happen now that I know."

Mrs. Graham nodded. "That's what I felt." A smile trembled on her lips, and her hand moved in an almost unconscious gesture that seemed to link them. "We're not so different. We're both mothers."

They were both mothers. Mrs. Graham was right. That made a bond stronger than anything that separated them. Even if Mrs. Graham could do nothing else to help her, she had understood a mother's feelings.

Somehow that understanding made Mattie a little less afraid of what was to come. As the bishop had said, surely people of good will could reach an understanding if they really tried. Just by coming here, Mrs. Graham had proved that was true.

One bad-tempered hen squawked furiously before flapping out of Judith's way so that she could claim an egg from the nest. It was still warm, and she cradled it in her hand for a moment before putting it in the basket. Isaac kept saying she ought to turn this chore over to the kinder, but the truth was that she enjoyed gathering the eggs.

The harmony brought on by the discovery of Jessie's carved dog had lasted nearly a day now, and Judith was beginning to breathe easier. Maybe this would be a new beginning for Isaac and Joseph. And for Isaac and her, as well.

Did he realize how thankful she was that he had managed to talk to the kinder about his little sister? She hoped so. Even though she could see that the reminder had brought its share of renewed grief to Isaac, his expression had eased, as if the telling had not only helped Joseph, but had lightened Isaac's own burden, as well.

It seemed to her that Isaac's grief, turned inward, had festered like a wound that had to be exposed in order to heal. Maybe now that he'd taken some painful first steps in bringing his pain into the open, he would find his grief easier to bear by sharing. That was what she prayed for.

Pulling her wandering thoughts to the job at hand, Judith scanned the pen, well aware that the hens could suddenly decide, for no apparent reason, to lay in an odd place. However, apparently none of them had felt adventurous today.

She started for the door, and the hens gathered around her feet, perennially hopeful that if she'd entered the pen, she'd brought mash with her. Most animals seemed to have internal clocks that told them when it was feeding time, but hens tended to be witless creatures, she had to admit, even though she was fond of them.

"Shoo, now. It's not time." She flapped her apron at them, sending them, fluttering and squawking, back far enough that she could open the pen door and slip out without inadvertently taking any chickens with her. She latched the door and headed back toward the house.

A buggy was coming up the lane. Judith paused for a moment, shielding her eyes as she tried to see who it was. Then she recognized the buggy horse, knowing it the way Englisch people might recognize a kind of car. Her visitor was her cousin Barbie.

Quickening her steps and smiling, Judith went to meet her. Whatever her faults, Barbie had a way of cheering a person up just through her presence.

"Looks like the hens are performing well for you," Barbie said, nodding to the basket as she jumped lightly down from the buggy seat, disdaining to use the step. "My mamm was just saying this morning that ours must be feeling sad that summer is over, because their production is off."

"I'll be happy to send some home with you . . ." Judith began, but Barbie was already shaking her head.

"There's still plenty for us." Barbie's eyes twinkled. "You know my mamm—if there's not anything to worry about, she'll invent it."

"Komm in." Judith gestured toward the kitchen door. "I'll make some coffee."

"Don't bother with the coffee. I can't stay. I have to get to the bakery." Barbie patted the mare's neck. "Funny. I was just thinking about the day you took my buggy and went off searching for Joseph." She stopped, eyeing Judith's face as if wondering whether or not she should have mentioned it.

"You were a lifesaver that day," Judith said warmly. "I won't forget it."

Barbie shrugged, her lips tilting upward as they did so easily. "It was nothing. Are Joseph and Isaac getting along any better now?"

Judith was almost afraid to mention it, but quickly dismissed the idea as superstition. "Ja, they are, a little. Thank the gut Lord."

Of course she still felt as if she had to be constantly on the alert, ready to tamp down any flames of annoyance or resentment between them, but that was minor compared to hearing them shout at each other.

"That's wonderful gut news." Barbie grinned. "Makes it easier to ask what I've come for."

"And what is it?" Judith couldn't imagine there was anything Barbie needed that she could provide, but she'd try.

"I've just come from Rebecca's." Barbie leaned back against the buggy frame. "She says that Matt's parents are coming in from out west this weekend for a nice visit before the wedding. They're going to stay at Matt's aunt and onkel's place."

She nodded, not sure where she fit into this scenario. "Matt will be sehr glad to see them, I'm sure."

"And Rebecca, too. The fact is, Rebecca would like to take the kinder and go to stay over there as well, so that the family can get better acquainted before the wedding. But she has guests coming this weekend."

Judith thought she knew where this was headed, and she felt a moment of panic. "Does she want us to take over?"

She couldn't, that was her initial reaction, despite the fact that she'd promised to help. Aside from the fact that she'd probably be terrible as a hostess to a bunch of Englisch, how could she leave Isaac and Joseph together? Without her to provide a buffer between them, who knew what would happen?

"Of course she does. So I told Rebecca she should go plan to go," Barbie concluded. "I knew you wouldn't mind. And I'm looking forward to actually being in charge." Her eyes sparkled. "Don't tell Rebecca I said so."

"I know we planned to take over . . ." Judith began, but Barbie was rushing on, heedless of her reaction.

"Now, don't think you need to stay the nights. I know that would be hard for you with the kinder. I can manage that all right, if you'll just be there during the day to help run things. I told Rebecca it would be perfectly all right. After all, we offered to do it, didn't we?"

Barbie had an uncanny knack of landing right on a person's weak point. They had agreed. On the other hand, this felt like a critical point in Isaac and Joseph's relationship. They had just begun to take small steps toward each other, but at any point, that peace could erupt into a pitched battle. How could she leave them alone? But how could she let Rebecca down?

"I'm so glad to have the chance to do this for Rebecca." Barbie, seeming to take Judith's acceptance for granted, was already climbing back into her buggy. "You know, for all that I worked with Rebecca all summer, this is the first time she's trusted me to run the farm-stay for a whole weekend on my own."

"Rebecca trusts you," Judith said, wanting to assure her. "She wouldn't have taken you on as a partner if she didn't, ain't so?"

Barbie settled herself on the seat and looked down at Judith, appearing unusually serious for her. "It's important, you know. That I show everyone I can handle the responsibility when Rebecca isn't there. Important to me," she added. Her smile flickered, but her face wasn't the usual, bubbly confident one she generally showed people. "This is my chance to prove to myself that I'm not as feather-witted as most folks think."

Who would think that lovely, poised Barbie could long so for reassurance? Judith reached up to clasp her hand briefly and tried to swallow her own fears.

"I know you're not a bit feather-witted," she said. "And when we run the farm-stay this weekend, everyone else will know it, too."

Barbie's brilliant smile blazed. "Denke, Judith. I certain-sure hope you're right."

Judith hoped so, too. Still, she didn't really have a choice about helping. She'd agreed. And after all, she'd be home every night. Isaac and Joseph would have plenty to do to keep them busy during the day. What could go wrong?

CHAPTER SIXTEEN

Lancaster County, Late September 1953

Adam approached Mattie's house from the field between her place and his uncle's, moving easily enough even without the aid of the flashlight he'd brought. The nearly full moon sent a silvery glow over the land, interrupted by the shadows that were trees, hedges, and outbuildings. Even if it hadn't been for the moonlight, he was accustomed enough to being out in the dark, tending to the animals without the help of a light that came on with the flick of a switch.

Folks had lots of superstitions about the full moon, it seemed to him—the idea that more babies were born then, or that the moon could make people wakeful or give them bad dreams, or even encourage some to wild behavior. He'd always taken most of that with a grain of salt, but he had to admit that the ease of seeing tonight could encourage people who were up to no good to be out and about. He and Onkel Jonah would have to make sure that none of them got away with targeting Mattie for their mischief.

He walked on, striding easily and with little noise. He'd have known it was late in September without a calendar by the aroma of the air—a compound of drying grasses, fallen apples, and a hint of smoke from someone's fire. It was cool, not cold, and a light breeze touched his face as he looked up, hearing something ahead.

For an instant Adam froze, thinking the intruders might have come back. Then he saw a doe step delicately into the open, her ears flicking in every direction, it seemed. He watched, enjoying the sleek lines of an animal who'd been created to escape its enemies by fleeing or by fading into the surroundings.

The doe took another step forward and stopped, as still as a statue save for the ears that probed for danger. He didn't move. But seeming to recognize his presence by instinct, the doe spun on the spot and bounded away toward the woods, her white tail flashing.

Smiling a little from the encounter, he moved on, coming out onto the farm lane between the outbuildings and the house. He and his uncle had worked out a route for themselves that let them circle the house without coming near enough, they'd figured, to startle Mattie and the kinder. Once he'd crossed the lane, he could see down the length of it, past the willow tree where he'd kissed Mattie, and on to the rectangular shadow that was the produce stand.

Nothing disturbed the peace of the night. Maybe the vandals had found something else to occupy them, bothering someone else instead. Strange, this business of trying to live separate in a world that changed around them almost daily.

Mattie would not think of reporting the vandals to the police, not even if she knew exactly who they were. But the police would arrest Amish parents, just because those parents didn't want to send fourteen-year-olds to the consolidated school. He'd long since stopped trying to understand it, instead reminding himself that whatever happened was God's will for them.

That practice had worked very well, right up until the time Mattie and her kinder were threatened, and he'd realized how much he loved her. He didn't doubt any longer that she could love him. Her response to his kiss had told him.

But he did fear for the amount of time it might take for her to accept her feelings. In the ordinary way of things, time wasn't an issue. He could have courted Mattie slowly, letting her get used to the idea without disturbing the balance of their friendship.

It was only the intrusion of Englisch standards into their lives that made it so difficult. If he and Mattie were married, he would be the one to pay the price for following their ways instead of Englisch ways.

Adam moved another step or two and realized that a light glowed from the kitchen window. The angle of the porch had hidden it from him until he reached this point, and now he stopped, wondering. Why was Mattie up so late? Was she sitting awake, worrying? Or was one of the children sick?

His first thought was to let her know he was there, for whatever comfort that might provide. Anytime in the past three years, tapping on her door late at night would have been perfectly natural. But what had happened between the two of them had changed things. After they had shared a kiss, a late-night call would be awkward.

Better leave it, he thought, but even as he did so he took an unwary step and knocked over a flowerpot that clattered against the one next to it, loud in the still night. A horse neighed once from the direction of the barn and then was quiet, probably recognizing his scent. He froze, hoping Mattie hadn't heard and been frightened.

The back door opened, sending a rectangle of yellow light out onto the porch, with Mattie silhouetted in it. "Adam?" Her voice was pitched just loudly enough to reach him.

"Ja, I'm here." Like the deer, it seemed she'd sensed him. "I didn't mean to alarm you. Sorry."

"It's all right. I was waiting and listening,

because I want to talk to you." She moved forward to the edge of the porch as he approached.

"You knew I would be out here?"

He had a feeling she smiled. "You or Daad Jonah, but I thought it would be you at this time of night."

"I guess we haven't been as sneaky as we thought we were." At least she didn't seem angry that they'd taken it upon themselves to watch over her.

"Not really, no." Mattie sat down on the top step and patted the place next to her. "Komm. Sit. We have to talk."

He sat, half-turned so he could see her. Her face was a pale oval in the light from the door—pale and strained, as well. She was worried, and no wonder, and yet there was something in her voice that was different. More decisive.

He was imagining it, he told himself. Enough weighed on Mattie to keep anyone awake at night.

"You should be asleep. You need your rest." His voice was gruff with the need to keep his emotion out of it.

She dismissed the idea with a short chop of her hand. "I couldn't."

"Ach, Mattie, you'll do no gut to yourself or the kinder by losing sleep over this trouble. The worry will still be there in the morning." He longed to touch her in comfort, but that might not be wise, not after what had passed between them. He might have trouble keeping it brotherly.

"It's not . . . not so simple." She seemed to have difficulty getting the words out. "Something happened tonight. I have to tell you about it. Just . . . just listen until I'm done."

The tightness in her voice alarmed him, and he fought to keep control of his feelings. If listening was what he could do for Mattie right now, then he would listen.

"Ja, all right. Tell me about it." His gaze traced the pure line of her profile, the soft curve of her cheek, and his heart swelled with the love he felt.

Her fingers closed on her apron, wrinkling the fabric. "I had a visitor this evening. After supper. I didn't expect . . . but it was Mrs. Graham." Her gaze met his, seeking understanding. "You remember. I told you she comes to the stand, and she's so kind and sympathetic. Not at all like her husband."

Adam nodded. "Ja, you told me you'd spoken to her about the trouble."

"She said before that she couldn't interfere, but tonight she came. She said her husband didn't know she was here, you understand, so we must be careful with letting folks know about it."

"Ja, of course."

Mattie drew in a breath, audible in the still night. "She saw some papers her husband had. It was a list of who was going to be arrested and when. My name was on it. I will be served with the notice. Tomorrow." Her voice cracked on the final word.

Pain ricocheted through him. He grasped her hand before he could even think of his resolve not to touch her. For an instant he thought she would pull away, but then her fingers closed around his, clinging tightly.

His first instinct seemed to be to deny it. "Are you sure she was telling you the truth? Maybe they're trying to frighten you."

"No. I could tell. She was honest. And it hurt her even to say it. She loves him, but she thinks he is wrong."

"This can't be. We must find some way—"

"Hush, Adam. There isn't any way, and now I need you to help me."

"Anything." She was right. Denying the obvious didn't help anyone.

"I need you to pass the word to the others—the family and the bishop. I'm not sure when . . . when it will happen." Her voice trembled and then steadied. "But if it's the same as with the others, probably I will be arrested the next day after tomorrow. At least it gives us time to make plans. Someone must be here for the kinder and to take care of the animals. I have to know that everything is arranged. Will you do it?"

"Whatever you say. You know I will. Everyone will help. But you must listen to me now." He captured both her hands in his, holding them firmly. "There's nothing else to do. You must marry me so I can protect you."

His mind raced, coming up with and rejecting ideas. There was no way they could be married before the police arrived, but they could do something.

"Surely if the bishop tells the police we are betrothed, even that I am guardian for the young ones, they will take me instead of you. But we don't have any time to waste. We must act now."

Mattie was already shaking her head, but he rushed on, not giving her a chance to mount an argument.

"Mattie, don't you think I want to take my time in courting you the way I should? It's my fault— I left it too long, and now we are forced by this injustice to act."

"I won't marry you just to stay out of jail. I won't." Her hands twisted in his.

"Stop, Mattie. The children—what will they think if you are arrested? It's too hard for them." He was losing her—he felt it, and desperation gave passion to his voice.

"They will think that their mother is standing up for what is right." Her voice was surprisingly strong. "Besides, you will be here for them, and the rest of those who love them. They will turn to you, like always."

His heart nearly broke to hear her say it so

calmly. "Ja, I love them. And I love you. If you're refusing me because of this foolish notion that I am too young for you, you have to forget it. I know what I want. I want you, to love and care for all the days that God gives us."

It was no use. He could feel it. Her face seemed impossibly remote, and only her hands, warm and trembling in his, assured him that she was still his Mattie.

A spasm of what might have been pain disturbed the stillness of her face. "It's not that, or at least not only that. All my life I was taken care of—my parents, my older brothers and sisters, even Ben—they all thought they had to take care of me. And now you think it, too."

"It's not wrong, to take care of each other. It's God's plan for us." *Please, make her understand.*

"Not wrong, no. But I've learned something through all this trouble. Each of us must stand alone before God and pray we've done right. I won't marry you so that you can go to jail in my place, Adam. I won't marry you because I need to be taken care of."

"That's not the only reason, and you know it. We both felt it when we kissed." He was losing. He knew it.

"Adam." She said his name gently. She touched his cheek—a featherlight caress. And then she fled into the house, closing the door and leaving him alone in the dark.

•••

Judith put the packet of decades-old letters down and glanced at the clock. Joseph would be home from his vocational class soon, and the boys returning from school as well. She'd best put the letters away for now to be safe. She wouldn't want them getting mixed up with Paul's homework.

She folded the papers carefully, mindful of how brittle they felt, and slid them into the study table drawer she had taken for her own use. The letters from Mattie's two cousins were interesting, giving a glimpse into Amish women's lives in an era when a terrible war had finally ended and change was sweeping across Englisch society at what must have seemed an alarming rate. As fast as the changes the Amish faced today, with the threat posed to their young people by drink, drugs, cell phones, and the Internet?

It had doubtlessly seemed so to them. Maybe that was destined to happen to each succeeding generation, as the Leit struggled to hold onto their values in a world that was always strange and sometimes antagonistic.

But it was Mattie's story that held her fascinated. She felt so strongly for Mattie's efforts to know what was right and have the courage to do it.

Judith closed the drawer and pushed her chair back. Maybe Mattie's story resonated with her

313

because she constantly struggled with the same questions. How did she know what was right for Isaac and Joseph? And even if she was sure, did she have the courage to stand for it?

Footsteps sounded on the back porch, and the screen door swung open.

"Joseph. You're home from your class already. How did it go today?"

"Great." Joseph grinned, looking happier than he had in a long time. Maybe the breach with Isaac had been weighing on him more than she'd thought. "The instructor let us do some work on our own this time. Judith, you wouldn't believe the equipment they have for us to practice on. I'm learning so much."

"I'm wonderful happy for you. The class is everything you hoped for, then, ja?"

She was tempted to add that he shouldn't show so much enthusiasm around Isaac, but wasn't that foolish? After all, if Isaac could begin to see how much this business meant to his brother, surely it would help him understand.

"More," Joseph said with emphasis. "I'm really loving every minute of it. If only . . ." He stopped, shaking his head a little, but she knew what that *if only* was. If only his brother would understand.

One thing was certain sure. If Isaac was still clinging to his hope that Joseph would become bored with the machinery and turn his focus back to dairy farming, obviously he'd be disappointed.

For the moment, she'd just be happy it was going well for Joseph. One problem at a time. "I'm glad. Now, don't forget that I'm going to be at Rebecca's all day tomorrow, helping with the guests. So I need to know you're here to help."

"Ja, ja, for sure," he said, impatient. Joseph hesitated, glancing toward the window as if looking to see who was in sight. "Something else happened today." He couldn't seem to keep his enthusiasm from breaking through.

She really shouldn't be regarding the boy with such wariness when he was excited, but she'd learned enough about what thrilled Joseph to be cautious. "What was it?"

"Fred stopped by the school." He glanced at her and then looked away, seeming to study the pottery pitcher on the counter.

"To see you?" She was alarmed, and a little surprised. It seemed unlike Fred to go chasing Joseph down when he knew how Isaac felt about it.

"No, not exactly." Joseph leaned against the counter, facing her. "The thing is that he's just gotten a rush order. He has an opening for an apprentice for several hours a day. He came to the school to see if they'd recommend someone."

Judith discovered that her hands were clenched into fists, and she struggled to relax them. "And did they?"

"Well, he didn't ask." Joseph resumed his study

315

of the pitcher. "You see, he was only going there because he was certain-sure Isaac wouldn't let me accept."

She searched for the right thing to say, but couldn't seem to come up with anything. "Did you tell him Isaac's attitude had changed? That he would permit it?"

Joseph shrugged. "Well, not exactly. But things have been easier with Isaac the past few days, haven't they? And maybe I did sort of hint that he'd say yes."

"Joseph." She went to him, tilting his chin so that he met her gaze. How odd it seemed, that she now had to reach up to do so. "You know you shouldn't have told Fred any such thing."

"Judith, you understand, don't you?" His blue eyes were intense with emotion. "You always understand. It's so important to me. It's the only thing I want. Isaac has to agree. He just has to!"

Her heart hurt for him. This wasn't just some passing adolescent fad with Joseph. It was real, and he felt it so. But she couldn't assure him that everything would be all right, the way she used to when he fell and hurt himself.

"I know things have been better between you and Isaac the past few days, but your brother is not one to be rushed into a decision. If he's going to agree—"

"You will help me!" Joseph clasped her hands. Unfortunately, the disastrous effects of the last time she'd tried to intervene were still fresh in her mind. She gripped his hands firmly, and the memory of herself sitting in Rebecca's kitchen and weeping flooded in on her.

What was it Rebecca had said? Something about Isaac and Joseph needing to find their own way to a solution, instead of relying on her.

"I didn't say that." Her throat was so tight she had to struggle to bring the words out. "I think the right thing is for you to talk to Isaac about it yourself."

"But he never listens to me." He jerked his hands free, turning away. "You'd do it so much better than I would."

"Maybe, but it's not really up to me, is it? This is between you and your brother." She fought to believe this course was for the best. "You said yourself that it's been better lately. Just talk to him, don't demand anything. Show him how important it is to you. He loves you, you know. He wants what's best for you."

"He thinks he knows what's best." Bitterness laced Joseph's voice.

She sent up a silent prayer for guidance. Was this the right way? She just didn't know any longer, but nothing she had done was working.

"Try, Joseph. Please. And try it remembering how close you used to be."

Joseph didn't speak for a moment. Then he blew out a long breath. "All right. I'll try."

317

He didn't sound very hopeful of success, and Judith could only pray for understanding on both sides. For peace between brothers. Surely that was God's plan for them.

Levi and Paul came storming in from school at that moment, so there was no time for more discussion. The kitchen suddenly seemed full of the boundless energy of small boys. A glance out the door told her that Noah was running toward them from the barn as fast as his little legs would carry him.

Joseph managed to smile and greet the boys, teasing them about their day at school and how much homework they had. Then he eased his way out the back door.

Would he approach Isaac cautiously on this subject? Would he bring it up in a way that would let Isaac see how important it was to him? Judith was suddenly assailed with doubts. What if the advice she'd given him was wrong?

What else could she have done? Some quiet part of her asked the question. She'd had to try something different, as hard as it was to let go when she loved them both so much. Surely this was the right path.

There was no time for Joseph to have a quiet talk with his brother now—that was certain-sure. Soon they'd start milking. The earliest it could possibly happen would be after the younger ones were in bed.

In the meantime, all she could do was tend to the boys and her own chores while keeping up a silent stream of prayers for God's guidance and help.

By the time she and Isaac went up to bed, she felt quite sure nothing had been said. The atmosphere of the house would have changed instantly if Joseph had spoken to his brother. It fretted her, knowing that Fred was probably waiting for an answer and well aware that once again she knew something that Isaac should know.

But if she told him, she'd be doing exactly what she'd decided she shouldn't do. No, she had to let Joseph handle this for once.

"Pleasant dreams." Isaac leaned across the bed to kiss her. "You deserve them."

She looked at him, startled. It was so unlike Isaac to voice anything that might be a compliment that she wondered if something was wrong. "Why? I mean, why do you think I deserve them?"

Even in the shaft of moonlight from the window, she could see his embarrassment. "It's nothing. It's just . . . you are so patient with the kinder, with Joseph, even with me. I know it isn't always easy, raising my brother as your own."

She touched his cheek, her heart flooded with love for him. "He's as precious to me as the babies I carried. You know that, don't you?"

"Ja," he said, his voice roughened. "That's what I mean."

For an instant she thought she should speak—should try to tell him about Joseph's longing and the opportunity he had. But Isaac's arm went around her, drawing her close, and she let the moment slip away.

Chapter Seventeen

Everything at home was organized as Judith prepared to leave for Rebecca's farm-stay on Saturday morning, but her nerves were still jumpy. She'd gone over the previous afternoon to help Barbie prepare for the visitors, but since the two Englisch couples hadn't planned to have supper at the farm, she'd been able to get away early.

She'd returned to find all was still harmonious between Isaac and Joseph, and she'd been grateful that there hadn't been problems while she wasn't there. But today she would be gone all day, and the thought of trouble erupting during her absence wouldn't be banished.

She loaded a pan of cinnamon walnut coffee cake into the buggy, wedging it against the plastic container of snickerdoodles and the loaves of homemade bread. Isaac, probably sensing her fears even though she didn't mention them, had kept reminding her that Barbie had run the farm-stay before and presumably knew all about handling the guests.

The trouble was, Isaac didn't realize that she was really nervous and worried because of him—him and Joseph. She'd hoped that Joseph would talk to his brother as soon as possible, but since he hadn't done it yet, she could only hope he would wait until she'd returned.

All was in harmony at the moment. Isaac had harnessed the mare to the buggy, told her not to worry, kissed her, and gone off to finish cleaning stalls in the barn with Joseph while Levi and Paul gathered eggs. Her young sister-in-law, Miriam, was settled in the house, playing Noah's favorite game of farm animals with him and seeming delighted to be there.

Judith smiled at the thought. Miriam would be a good mother, she could tell. Noah would be fine in her care, and Isaac was close at hand if there were any problem. He'd keep the older boys busy.

She'd feel secure that everything at home was taken care of, if not for the continuing worry about Joseph. The current harmony between him and Isaac was a false one. If he decided to talk to Isaac about the apprenticeship when she wasn't there—

Well, maybe that would be for the best. At least

she'd avoid the temptation to try and referee the discussion.

With one foot on the step up to the buggy seat, Judith stopped. Raised voices, coming from the barn. It didn't take much to know what was happening, and her heart started to thud in her chest. Joseph had come out with his news, and it was going badly.

The voices increased in volume. They were shouting at each other, so loud that even the mare flicked her ears back at the sound and Levi and Paul emerged from the henhouse to stare.

"It's all right, Rosie." She patted the chestnut mare. "Nothing to do with you."

But everything to do with her, she feared. Judith realized suddenly that all she wanted to do was pretend she hadn't heard, climb into the buggy, click to the mare, and drive away, leaving the trouble behind her. But it was too late for that escape.

She turned toward the barn. Isaac and Joseph seemed to explode out of it, both of them headed right for her. Isaac covered the ground in long, angry strides.

"Did you know about this nonsense?" he demanded, waving his arm toward Joseph.

"I told you he wouldn't listen to me!" Joseph's voice was shrill, and she thought there were tears of rage in his eyes. "I told you, didn't I?"

"So you knew about it. Why didn't you tell

me?" Isaac's angry tone blamed her, and she winced.

But she wouldn't take more blame than she was entitled to. "Joseph told me yesterday afternoon, and I told him he must talk to you about it." She glared right back at Isaac, frustrated with both of them for putting her in this spot. "I also told him that if he talked to you about it rationally, you would listen to him."

"I knew he wouldn't," Joseph said, before Isaac could respond. "He thinks he knows what I should do, but it's my life."

If Isaac's anger had softened a bit when she spoke about him listening to his brother, that comment hardened it again. "I will not have my brother turning his back on his inheritance to go to work for Fred Yoder, of all people. You can just forget that idea."

"I won't." The two of them glared at each other, looking very alike in their anger. "In a couple of years I'll be old enough to do what I want, and the first thing I'll do is leave here."

"When you're old enough you can run off all you want. Until then you'll stay here and do as you're told."

Judith's head was pounding from the loud voices, and her heart ached so that she pressed her hand against her chest. Didn't Isaac realize that he couldn't persuade his brother to stay with those tactics?

"Isaac, don't. Don't say that. This is always going to be Joseph's home."

"Stay out of it, Judith." Isaac looked at her as if she were a stranger. "You're not the boy's mother."

He might as well have struck her. She took a step back, away from him. Away from them. How could he have said such a thing? Only last night he'd praised her for caring for Joseph as if he were her own.

They were both talking at her, but their voices had turned into a loud blaring that made no sense. She seemed to see them from a distance.

"Enough." She must have said it more sharply than she realized, because they both looked at her in amazement. "I am not going to be a buffer between you two any longer. It hurts too much. You'll have to settle this quarrel for yourselves. I can't."

In the stunned silence that followed, she climbed into the buggy, picked up the lines, and clucked to the mare. The buggy rolled off down the lane, leaving them behind.

She couldn't do anything else. She'd tried and she'd failed, every time. She just prayed she didn't pass anyone she knew on the road to Rebecca's, because she was going to be crying the whole way.

Lancaster County, Late September 1953

To her surprise, Mattie actually slept that night, even knowing what was coming the next day. Somehow, sharing the problem with Adam had made it easier for her to let go and trust God for whatever might happen.

But she seemed to have traded one problem for another, since the entire time she was cooking and serving breakfast, she'd been thinking about Adam. Was she really considering him as a potential husband? Mattie stood still, staring absently at the egg pan in her hand, and then set it in the sink.

She couldn't be. Adam was very dear to her, but she didn't have the same feelings for him that she had had for Ben. It wasn't possible.

Guilt swept over her. She'd been relying on Adam too much. Two people couldn't marry just because they needed or were needed. Well, they could, she supposed. Families had been founded for worse reasons. But if so, they ought both to be honest with themselves and with each other.

This line of thinking wasn't leading to any conclusions. Mattie tried to dismiss it, or at least sweep it to the back of her mind, so she could concentrate on getting the boys off to school. She hadn't told any of the kinder that the police would probably come today, and looking at the boys' freshly scrubbed faces, she knew she couldn't say anything to them now.

Rachel would have to know, of course, but the little ones could wait until tonight. Then she'd have to prepare them for the fact that she would probably not be there when they came home from school tomorrow. And Anna—what about Anna?

Maybe it would be best to send Anna off for the day to her grossmammi or one of her aunts. At least then she wouldn't see her mammi being taken away by the police.

Mattie rubbed her forehead. So many plans to make. How long would she be gone? The others had been sentenced to a few days in jail. If it was the same for her, she must be sure the kinder understood and knew who would be taking care of them.

"Mammi, isn't it time for us to go?" Toby clutched his homework papers with one hand and tugged her apron with the other. "I think it is."

She glanced at the clock. "You're right, it is. Take your lunches. Are you both sure you have your homework?"

They nodded, grabbing lunch bags from the counter. "Hurry, Nate." Toby was practically bouncing with his impatience. "Let's go."

"Not until I have my hugs." She knelt to sweep them into a hug, holding them until they wiggled to be free. Then she rose, forcing herself to smile.

"All right. Mind your teacher. I'll see you after school, ain't so?"

It was what Mattie always said, and the boys nodded, as always. Her heart winced as she realized that tomorrow she wouldn't be able to say the words.

It's not fair! The rebellion startled her, coming as it did when she thought she was resigned to what she must do. But it wasn't fair. Her children had already lost their father. Why must they face this further trial?

Obey. Accept the Lord's will. That was the church's teaching. She believed it. But sometimes it was so hard.

With the boys off to school and Anna upstairs dressing, Mattie looked at Rachel, trying to find the right way to tell her.

"Mammi? Was ist letz?" Rachel's eyes widened as she caught her mother's expression.

"Komm. Sit." Mattie led her to the table, and they sat down next to each other. "You know that Mrs. Graham came to see me last night."

Rachel nodded. "She's the wife of the school board president, ain't so?"

So Rachel knew that much, which would make it easier. "She is." She paused. "She is a gut customer. And a kind woman, I think. She seems willing to listen to what we believe about the school anyway, even if she doesn't entirely agree."

Some of the apprehension faded from her

daughter's face. "I'm glad of it. I don't like feeling as if everyone is against us."

"I know." Mattie put her hand over Rachel's. "She came last night because she found out something, and she thought it was right that I be told." She couldn't help clinging a little tighter to her daughter's hand. "Mrs. Graham learned that I will be served the order today to send you to school tomorrow or be arrested."

Tears formed in Rachel's eyes. "No, Mammi." She shook her head. "I thought . . . I prayed and prayed that they wouldn't come for you."

"I'm not different from any of the others." Her voice surprised her by its calmness. "We knew that all of us would face this at some time. For me, it's come."

Rachel swallowed, as if fighting back sobs. "Aren't you afraid?"

She owed Rachel the truth, she thought. "Ja, I am afraid, a little. But we have to trust that God is with us everywhere. Even in jail. Remember how Paul and Silas praised the Lord when they were shut up in prison?"

Rachel was silent for a long moment—long enough that Mattie began to have doubts. Had she said the right things? Was she handling this badly?

Finally Rachel met her eyes, her face very serious. "God delivered Paul and Silas," she said. "We will pray that God will deliver you, too."

"Ja, that's a gut prayer, for sure." If Rachel could keep from crying, she could as well.

There was a clatter outside, and then the back door swung open, revealing Mamm Becky carrying a large basket. Beyond her, Mattie glimpsed Adam turning the cows and the buggy horse into the pasture beyond the barn, while Daad Jonah leaned on the fence.

"Here I am," Mamm Becky announced, bustling into the kitchen and surrendering her basket to Mattie. She took off the black bonnet she'd worn to come across from her house and patted her hair to be sure it was still smooth under the kapp. "I thought we could do some baking together today."

"We're wonderful happy to see you." Mattie set the basket on the table. Clearly the family had decided that she shouldn't be alone today.

Rachel, turning from hugging her grandmother, walked quickly toward the stairs. "I'll make sure Anna is dressed before she comes down. When she hears you're here, she won't bother to finish."

As soon as she was out of earshot, Mamm Becky clasped Mattie in a warm hug. "Adam told us. We wanted to be sure you aren't alone in case the officer comes to serve the papers today."

"Denke. I'm sehr glad. I think it will happen. Mrs. Graham said my name was on the list with today's date."

"Ja, Adam said." Mamm Becky eyed her. "Are you sure you can trust this woman? After all, her own husband is the one who is causing all the trouble."

"I'm sure," she said. "At least, I'm sure she believed she was telling me the truth. We understood each other, I think, the times we talked. She is a mother, too."

Her mother-in-law shrugged. "Best to be ready, anyway. Adam said you were still up when he came by last night. Did you get any sleep?" She was busy unloading things from her basket as she talked—a big bag of the apples from the McIntosh tree that were so good for pies, a tin of cinnamon, a bag of flour, and one of sugar.

"A little," she admitted. Mattie had to smile at the provisions Mamm Becky was unloading. As if she wouldn't have those basic ingredients. But her mother-in-law always liked to come prepared for anything.

"You guessed Adam's idea to check on your place at night, ain't so? He and Jonah weren't as quiet at slipping around as they thought they were."

"No, I knew all along that they were there. But it did make me feel better, and Rachel, too. Adam is always kind."

"Kind." Mamm Becky snorted. "It is what Adam would do because he cares about you. You must know it. He would gladly go to jail in your place if allowed."

It was Mattie's turn to study her mother-in-law's face. "Did he tell you that he wants

330

me to marry him so that he can take my place?"

"He didn't tell me anything, but I can see as well as anyone which way the wind is blowing. Why didn't you tell him yes?"

Mattie should have known that Mamm Becky would ask the tough question. "I can't. I can't marry him just to let him protect me. It wouldn't be right."

"Ach, Mattie, that's no reason at all."

"I won't have him spend the rest of our lives thinking we got married because I needed help."

"Adam loves you," Mamm Becky said flatly. "I see it, Jonah sees it, now even Adam sees it. Everyone but you."

Mattie shook her head, discovering that her eyes had filled with tears. Why was it so hard for others to understand her feelings? It would be different if she could be sure . . .

Wait, what was she thinking? Sure of what? Sure he loved her? Or sure she loved him?

Before she could face the questions her heart asked, she heard the thump of Anna's feet on the stairs.

"Ach, how one light little girl can make such a racket I don't know." She wiped her eyes with the back of her hand. "We won't talk about it anymore now. Rachel knows about the papers," she added quickly. "Anna doesn't. She wouldn't understand."

There wasn't time to say more about it, because

Anna hurled herself at her grandmother as if she hadn't seen her for months instead of a day.

"Grossmammi! I tied my shoes all by myself. See?"

Anna stuck out one black shoe. The laces were looped in a very lopsided bow, but they were tied.

"Gut. You're a big girl now, ain't so?" Mamm Becky hugged her. "Do you want to help us bake?"

"I do! I can bake, can't I, Rachel?" Anna appealed to her big sister.

"That's certain-sure," Rachel said quickly. "What are we making?"

"How about a big batch of apple dumplings?" their grandmother asked. "Some for now and some for later."

In the midst of Anna's noisy response, Adam and Daad Jonah appeared on the back porch. One look at Adam's face was enough to tell Mattie. It was happening now.

She swallowed, feeling as if her throat was too tight for speech. "Will you keep the girls inside, Mamm Becky?"

Her mother-in-law nodded. She reached for Anna, pulling the child against her.

"Not me," Rachel said, her young voice firm and decided. "I belong with you, Mamm."

Mattie wanted to argue, but Rachel was right. If her daughter was indeed old enough to leave school, she was old enough to join her mother in standing for what they believed.

"Ja," she said. She clasped Rachel's hand, and together they stepped out onto the porch, watching as the police car made its way down the lane.

Adam and Daad Jonah moved close so that the four of them stood together. Adam touched her arm lightly. "It's not too late," he murmured. "If I tell them . . ."

He let the words die out when she shook her head.

It wasn't too late to do something to keep from going to jail. She could agree to marry Adam for all the wrong reasons. Or she could agree to send her daughter for an education she didn't believe in.

The car came to a halt near the porch. The officer seemed to wait for a moment, as if expecting them to make a move. Then he opened the door and stepped out, settling his cap squarely on his head.

The officer was an older man. With his graying hair and lean, weathered face, he looked more like a farmer than her idea of a police officer. But the weapon in a holster on his hip would convince her if she needed convincing. This was the real thing.

He came to the bottom of the steps and stopped, unfolding a sheet of paper and consulting it. Then he looked from one face to another. "Mrs. Benjamin Lapp?" he asked, though it must be obvious that she was the person he was after.

"I am Mattie Lapp." Her voice didn't seem to be attached to her at all.

"Mrs. Lapp, I'm required by law to serve you with this summons. It requires you to send your underage daughter, Rachel Elizabeth Lapp, to the consolidated high school to which she has been assigned. If she is not there tomorrow morning when school begins, you will be in violation of the law and subject to arrest." He rattled that off in an expressionless voice. Then he stopped and looked at her, and she thought some emotion moved in his eyes. Pity, maybe. "Do you under-stand what I have said to you?"

She felt the warmth of Adam's arm brushing against hers and imagined he was trying to send her strength.

"Yes."

The officer looked embarrassed all at once, and it seemed to make him more human. "Are you sure? Maybe you have questions. If there's anything . . ."

Mattie shook her head. What was there to say?

"Okay, then." He handed the paper to her, started to turn away, and then swung back toward her. "You know, if you told me you intended to obey the order, you wouldn't have to worry about it anymore."

He was trying to be kind, she realized. "Thank you. But I can't do that."

He nodded, as if it was what he expected.

"Sorry," he muttered, and then turned and went quickly to the police car. They stood where they were, not speaking, until he'd turned the vehicle and driven back down the lane.

Mamm Becky erupted onto the porch as Rachel put her arm around her mother's waist, holding her tight.

"It's wicked," Mamm Becky said. She was scolding, probably as a way of holding back tears. "I've never heard of anything so wicked. Threatening a widow that way."

"Hush, Becky. The man was only doing his job." Daad Jonah put a hand awkwardly on Mattie's shoulder. "You did real good, Mattie."

She nodded, holding on to Rachel, trying to think calmly. But her mind seemed to be tumbling ideas around and around until she felt as if they were clanging against her temples. She appreciated their support, really she did. But she needed to think. To absorb everything that was going to happen. If only—

Her gaze touched Adam's face, and his expression pierced her heart, nearly making her gasp with the strength of it. Pain filled his eyes and tightened his face into a mask. He was suffering more than she'd imagined possible.

Mamm Becky must surely be right. Why would he look that way unless he loved her?

And what did it say about her, that she hurt so much at his pain?

CHAPTER EIGHTEEN

Adam hadn't slept at all—how could he? He could only hope Mattie had gotten some rest. On his frequent trips around her property during the night, all had been dark and quiet. Even the dog, used to his smell, hadn't made a sound, but just padded along after him. He and Onkel Jonah had passed each other several times, probably neither of them willing to stay away, even though there had been no disturbances.

Disturbances. He repeated the word bitterly in his mind. What was happening to Mattie today was a far bigger thing than a few smashed vegetables on the road.

He'd come over again at first light to milk the cows and turn them out into the pasture. No sooner had Adam finished than he spotted Onkel Jonah walking toward him, his shoulders stooped as if the weight he carried had become too much for him. Adam stayed where he was until his uncle came up to him.

"You're here early," he said, unnecessarily.

Onkel Jonah nodded. "And you. Well, what else would we do on a day like today?"

They stood in silence for a few minutes,

watching the sun make its way over the hills to the east. There wasn't much to say, just as there was little they could do. No point in saying they'd both take Mattie's place if they could. They both knew it, and that answer was impossible.

Had their opponents come after Mattie so soon deliberately? Maybe they reasoned that arresting a young widow would show the world that they were serious. Or even frighten the rest of the Leit into obedience, even though they should know better by now, he would think.

"Bishop Thomas should be along soon." His uncle gazed absently down the lane toward the blacktop road. "He's bringing the ministers with him. Your aunt and your cousin Emma are coming along behind me from the house."

"I didn't know Emma was already here." His married cousin lived far enough away that she had to bring the buggy on her frequent visits to her folks.

"Ja, she drove over yesterday before dark. Said she couldn't just sit home while all this was happening, and this way she didn't have to drive this morning before it was light. She'll take Anna home with her. We thought it was best. Until . . . well, until Mattie is back again."

Adam's heart clenched at the words. How long would it be? How long would they keep Mattie shut up in a cell for following her church's teaching?

Onkel Jonah seemed to expect a response, so Adam nodded and tried to speak normally. "Emma's kinder will keep Anna too busy to fret, ain't so?" His cousin had four younger than six, two of them lively four-year-old twins.

"Ja, I expect so. And some of Mattie's kin have a driver bringing them over from Littleton."

"Gut. Maybe it'll help Mattie to know so many are here with her."

His uncle surprised him by resting a hand on Adam's shoulder. "We would do more if we could, ain't so?"

That went without saying. The trouble was that there was little they could do. Just stand by and try to take the worries of the family off Mattie's heart.

Light appeared in the kitchen window, and Adam's heart seemed to jump. "Mattie's up," he said, not that he needed to. Jonah would see it as quickly as he did.

"You go on inside," Onkel Jonah said. "I see Becky and Emma coming. I'll wait for them."

His uncle was giving him a last opportunity to be alone with Mattie, he realized, not that it would do any good. He'd certain-sure argue with her if he thought there was a chance of changing her mind, but he knew his Mattie, through and through. She was a gentle soul, but she had decided that this was her trial to bear. She wouldn't waver now.

When Adam reached the door, he found she'd already unlocked it, obviously knowing he was there and would come in. Mattie turned from putting the coffeepot on the stove as he stepped inside. "You'll have coffee, ain't so?"

"Denke." He wiped his feet thoroughly on the mat, scanning her face. Mattie looked pale, but she seemed composed, as if ready for whatever would come. "Have you spoken to the kinder yet?"

She nodded, setting out mugs and spoons, milk and sugar. "I did. Rachel helped, and the younger ones listen to her. Anna doesn't grasp much except that Mammi will be away for a few days and she gets to stay with Aunt Emma and her cousins. She's already packed her bag."

He managed to produce the smile she seemed to expect. "And what about the boys?"

Mattie shrugged, staring at the coffeepot as if willing it to perk faster. "It's difficult for them, but I think they understand as well as they can at their age."

A wave of bitter anger nearly swamped him. "How could any child be expected to understand it? I'm a grown-up, and I certain-sure don't."

She swung around as if propelled by his tone. "Adam, you must not feel anger or bitterness. It's not right. Please, promise me."

Mattie had made her way to acceptance, he realized. Even confidence. He shouldn't act in a way that disturbed her. "I'll try," he said.

She took a deep breath and nodded. "Gut. I knew I could count on you. And anyway, maybe we don't need to understand. It is enough for unser Leit that we be content in what God sends us."

The longing to argue surprised him. He couldn't. He, like Mattie, like the rest of their people, had only to obey and trust, even when they couldn't see the way. God's word was the only light they needed for their path.

He wasn't sure what he'd have said, but he heard the sound of the kinder coming down the stairs. Anna was chattering to Rachel a mile a minute as they entered the kitchen. Rachel, like her mother, was wan but calm, even managing to laugh a little at Anna's excitement.

A look at the boys told him they weren't doing as well, especially Nate. His small face was pinched. Even as Adam started toward him, he burst out at his little sister. "Stop talking so much. Don't you know—"

Adam reached him, put a hand on each boy's shoulder, and steered them back into the living room. "Komm," he said. "It's going to be all right."

"It's not." Nate's fists clenched. "They are going to take Mammi away and put her in a jail. They—"

"Hush." Adam squatted, drawing both of the boys close. "Mammi will be home in a few days.

She's going to be fine. No one will harm her there. And you will be taken care of, you know that, don't you? You have all of us who love you and will take care of you while she's away."

Toby, pale and solemn, nodded gravely, but Nate's face twisted. "I hate it." He said the words defiantly, and then looked abashed, clearly expecting a reprimand.

Adam held Nate so that he could look into his eyes. "I hate it, too. It's right to hate injustice, so long as we don't hate the people, too, ain't so?"

Nate, surprised, nodded.

"All right then." He breathed a little easier. "All we can do now is be here to help Mammi and to do whatever we can for her."

"That's what I want," Nate said quickly. "I want to help Mammi, but Rachel says we have to go to school."

Adam considered how to respond. Being a parent was harder than it looked, it seemed.

"We can help her best by doing what she wants, not what we want," he said. "Mammi wants you to go to school. When you do as she says, you are helping her because she doesn't have to worry so much about you. See?"

Toby nodded immediately. Nate took his time, his lower lip protruding, but finally he nodded as well.

"Gut." Adam rose, patting their shoulders. "Let's go and have breakfast, so Mammi won't worry that you're not eating." He shepherded them into the kitchen.

Anna seemed to have calmed down. She eyed her brother with a tad of resentment but then went happily back to her oatmeal until she was distracted by the arrival of her grandmother and her aunt.

Under cover of the chatter, Adam made his way around to the stove, where Rachel seemed to be intent upon stirring the oatmeal.

"Some of that for me?" he asked.

She jerked, the spoon in her hand hitting the side of the pan. Her eyes were wide and frightened in her pale face. "I . . . I'll dish some up for you."

Leaning against the sink, Adam watched her. Rachel was hurting, but what could he say that would make things any better?

"It's my fault," she muttered suddenly, and then glanced toward her mother to be sure Mattie hadn't heard.

He paused long enough to assemble his thoughts. He should have realized that conscientious Rachel would find a way to blame herself.

"How is it your fault?" he asked, keeping his voice low.

"If I hadn't been ready for ninth grade, Mamm wouldn't be going through this." Rachel's blue eyes challenged him to argue with her.

"True," he said. "What could you have done about it?"

She looked startled, obviously not expecting agreement. "Well, I . . . I . . ." She stopped. Shook her head. And gave him a smile that trembled on the brink of tears. "Nothing, I guess."

"Nothing for sure." He patted her shoulder. "It's nobody's fault. It happened this year because the new school was finished and because some people on the school board are unwilling to listen to our beliefs. Not because of you. So don't let your mamm know you have such ferhoodled ideas."

Some of the tension seemed to slip out of her. "I won't. Denke, Cousin Adam."

Nodding, he turned away, stopping at the counter to add a little milk and brown sugar to his oatmeal. When he looked up, he saw that Mattie was watching him. Her expression was somehow different, and he wasn't sure what that meant.

Before he had a chance to think, his cousin Emma was elbowing him out of the way. "Go and sit down and stop standing there blocking traffic, Adam. I'm going to cut the shoofly pies, if you want any."

He grinned, used to his cousin's bossiness. "How can I resist when you ask me so nicely?"

She swatted at him with a dish towel, but he evaded it and went to sit next to the boys. He'd no more than sat down before he heard a buggy coming down the lane. Most likely the bishop and the ministers, he supposed.

Aunt Becky gave Emma a look, and she stopped what she was doing.

"We should be getting on our way, Anna. Your cousins are so excited to see you they're probably driving their daadi crazy. Are you ready?"

The bustle of getting Anna out the door and packed into Emma's buggy seemed to overcome a slight tendency toward tears on Anna's part. Adam stowed her suitcase carefully, as if it contained something precious, and Anna smiled at him, pleased that he took her trip so seriously.

"You have a gut time, now. And be nice to your cousins." He hugged her.

"I'm always nice," she said, looking surprised.

He looked at Mattie, inviting her to share his amusement, and she managed a smile.

"Well, see that you stay that way," Mattie told her, hugging her tightly. "And be a very gut girl for your aunt, okay?"

Anna's little face started to pucker as Emma released the brake and the carriage began to move. "I don't think I want to go away."

"No fussing, now," Mattie said. "It's not polite to fuss when you are getting such a treat. You'll have so much fun with your cousins that you won't want to come home again. I'll see you soon."

Anna brightened a little. With a speaking glance

at Mattie, Emma clucked to the horse, no doubt thinking it best to get moving while Anna was momentarily distracted.

They stepped back, standing together as they watched the buggy roll down the lane. Mattie waved as long as Anna was visible, seeming composed and cheerful. But Adam saw her face when she turned back again, and the pain in it twisted his heart.

By the time they returned to the kitchen, she had managed to put her smile back on. She handed the boys their lunches.

"Time for you two to get moving. Grossdaadi says he'll walk you partway to school, so get your hats."

For an instant it looked as if Nate would object. Adam caught his eye. Nate swallowed, his neck moving, and then took his lunch bag. "Good-bye, Mammi." He hugged her fiercely and then turned away quickly. "Let's go, Toby."

With the departure of the kinder and the arrival of so many black-suited men, the atmosphere of the farmhouse changed subtly. Aunt Becky bustled around, making sure everyone had coffee and a slab of coffee cake or shoofly pie, with Rachel as her quiet helper. It reminded Adam of folks gathered after a funeral, the low voices sometimes interrupted by a chuckle as people forgot for a moment why they were there.

A vehicle coming down the lane startled

everyone into strained silence, but a glance out the window assured Adam it wasn't the police car. Not yet.

He turned back, his gaze seeking the bishop. "It's that minister from the school board. Pastor Colby."

"Is it?" Bishop Thomas didn't sound surprised. He gestured to Adam and Jonah to accompany him, and they went out onto the porch as the minister emerged from his car.

The minister greeted them, glancing from one face to another. "I hope Mrs. Lapp isn't too upset this morning."

"She's doing well." The bishop naturally took over the role of spokesperson. "But the threat of jail is hard for a widow with young children."

"It's unconscionable," Pastor Colby said emphatically. "I prayed it wouldn't come to this, but . . ." He shook his head, his youthful face concerned. "Some in authority have hardened their hearts, as the scripture says. I'm not giving up, though."

"We, too, have not given up." Bishop Thomas's grave dignity contrasted with the other man's indignation. "But we will take what God sends to us."

Colby nodded. "I've come to stand with you, if you'll allow it. Also, I thought my car might be useful to take the family on to the jail and to the hearing."

"Denke. That's sehr kind of you. We'll be glad of both," Bishop Thomas said.

Adam could only chastise himself. Why hadn't he thought that they would need drivers today, of all days? He should have arranged something. The young minister, unfamiliar though his manner sometimes seemed, was proving to be a good friend to the Leit.

Another set of wheels crunched on the gravel. "The police." It took Adam a moment to realize that he had spoken. He glanced toward the house, but obviously they had heard the vehicle as well. After all, it was what they'd all been listening for this morning.

Mattie moved through the group to stand between him and her father-in-law, with Pastor Colby and the bishop just beyond. The others filed out to stand silently behind them, their faces grave.

The car stopped at the porch. There were two of them today—the chief of police himself and a young patrolman. They got out of the car and then hesitated, obviously surprised at the number of people who waited there. The patrolman, his young face paling, made a movement with his hand toward the weapon on his hip.

"Don't be any more of a fool than you can help," Chief Ferguson snapped. "That's Bishop Thomas Beiler and Pastor Colby. Obviously these folks are here to give support, not start a riot."

The patrolman, going from pale to flushed, took a step back, his hands dropping to his sides. The chief mounted the steps and stood in front of them to greet by name each person he knew.

His face grew nearly as solemn as theirs must be. "Seems to me I ought to explain to Mrs. Lapp and everyone else exactly what is going to happen. Since her daughter has not gone to school as ordered, I'll have to escort Mrs. Lapp to the county jail. When it's time, we'll go to the magistrate's court." He paused, looking from face to face. "It's not the main courtroom, you understand. It's not as formal."

Several people nodded. After all, some of them, like Bishop Thomas, had been through this already with those who had been arrested.

Apparently satisfied that they understood, he went on. "In the magistrate's hearing, Mrs. Lapp can plead guilty, in which case she agrees to send her daughter to school. She'll pay a fine and then come home. If she doesn't plead guilty . . ." He hesitated, and Adam suddenly saw how reluctant he was. "Well, then, it's up to the magistrate." He focused on Mattie, who looked very small in the midst of the men surrounding her. "Do you understand, Mrs. Lapp?"

Her composure held. "I understand." Her voice was steady. "I'm ready."

"Then if you'll come—"

"Wait a minute, Chief," Pastor Colby interrupted. "In view of the fact that Mrs. Lapp is a woman, I think someone should be allowed to accompany her in the police car. The bishop, for instance."

Adam held his breath. Certain sure they wouldn't let *him,* but if they'd allow the bishop to go . . .

"That's against the rules," the younger officer said.

The chief gave him an annoyed glance. "I have no problem with Bishop Thomas accompanying Mrs. Lapp as far as the jail, if he wishes."

"I do." The bishop seemed to send a silent thank-you to the minister. "Komm, Mattie." He touched her arm lightly, and they walked steadily down the steps and to the car. The officer nipped in ahead of them to open the back door.

Adam kept his gaze pinned to Mattie's dear face. His heart was breaking, but as long as he could see her, maybe he wouldn't fly into pieces. The door was closed, and two officers got into the front. When the car pulled away, Adam felt as if a part of him had been severed.

"I'll take as many as I can in my car," Pastor Colby said. "If you want, I have some members of my church standing by who will come and drive anyone to the hearing once we know what time it will be."

"Denke." Onkel Jonah's voice shook a little, and Adam took hold of his arm in support.

"My uncle and I would be glad to come with you," he said. "And I'm sure there are many others who would like a ride to the hearing."

"Fine. Let's go, then. As soon as we reach a phone, I'll make some calls for drivers to come here to pick people up. In the meantime, I'll get you to the jail." He hesitated. "You know they probably won't let you see her once she's checked in."

Onkel Jonah seemed to have recovered his strength after his momentary lapse. He straightened. "It makes no matter. We will be close by, and Mattie will know we're there. That's all we can do now."

All we can do for someone we love. Adam had never felt so helpless in his life.

Isaac watched Judith and the buggy disappear from sight down the road toward Rebecca's place, his insides churning as if the paddle from the milk tank were stirring them up. He made an effort to hang on to his righteous indignation. He had a right to be angry when his own wife sided against him.

Against that conviction stood an even stronger one: He should never have let those words come out of his mouth. How could he say that Judith was not Joseph's mother, when she had been just that to the boy for most of his life? Joseph didn't even remember his own mother.

Still, it wasn't right that she and Joseph conspired against him. A wife was supposed to support her husband. Joseph was his responsibility, trusted to him by Mamm and Daad as surely as if the words had been written in stone.

"See what you did?" Joseph's hands clenched into fists, and his face was red with anger.

"What I did?" The boy's words were a match touched to tinder. "I didn't do this to Judith. You did. You're the one who pressured her to help you do wrong."

"It's not wrong!" Joseph flared. "Just because it's not what you want, that doesn't make it wrong!"

"You're not old enough—"

"You were my age when you made decisions for the rest of your life. And you're the one who's pressed Judith, trying to make her support you."

"She's my wife." A small voice in his heart was telling him not to talk to the boy that way, but his anger and pain drowned it out.

"You only married her because you needed someone to be a mother to me!" Joseph threw the words at him like a rock, and, as if it had actually been one, Isaac was struck backward.

"What are you talking about? Where did you get that crazy idea?"

"Judith said so."

He grasped Joseph by the shoulders. "She

351

didn't. She couldn't have. She'd never tell you such a thing."

Joseph's gaze slid away from his. "She said it. Just not to me. But I heard her. She said it to Grossmammi. She said you married her because it was sensible. Because you needed someone to take care of me and you thought she'd be a gut mammi to me."

Isaac let go of his brother, trying to dismiss the words. "She can't believe it."

"She does." Joseph's voice cracked. "So you can blame that on me, too, just like you blame me for Daad and Mamm dying. You don't need to worry about me anymore. I'm leaving!"

Before Isaac could even focus, Joseph turned and bolted, running straight across the field. Recovering himself, Isaac started after him, only to give up before he'd gone twenty feet. The boy was as fast as a hare. He'd never catch him.

At least he was headed toward Onkel Simon's. Simon would take care of him.

Isaac turned away to discover that Levi and Paul were standing a few steps from him, looking at him with wide eyes.

"What's wrong with Joseph?" Levi said. "Why is he running like that?"

"Never mind Joseph. Have you finished with the hens?"

Levi stiffened at the sharp tone, and Paul inched back, looking frightened.

What was wrong with him? He was blundering around, hurting the people he loved, and he didn't even know why.

"I'm sorry," Isaac said quickly. He held out his arms to his sons.

They came to him slowly, as if reluctant to trust his mood, and it was like a knife in his heart. He drew them close.

"Everything will be all right." Could he really promise that? "Why don't you go in to see your aunt? I bet she has a snack for you, ain't so?"

Paul nodded and raced toward the house. Levi took a couple of steps and looked back. "Daadi? Aren't you coming?"

He tried to smile normally. "I'll be there in a few minutes. I have to finish something in the barn first. You go ahead."

Levi nodded, but still he went slowly, as if he wasn't confident that things were right.

Isaac spun and headed for the refuge of the barn. There was work to finish. There was always work to finish on a farm.

Somehow the work got him through the day. He kept Levi and Paul busy, relying on Miriam to handle Noah. Joseph didn't come back.

He's at Onkel Simon's, he told himself. *He's all right. Maybe Onkel Simon can make him see sense.*

But by early afternoon, the words had lost their

power to soothe him. Doubts crept in. Why hadn't Joseph returned? What was Judith doing? What was she thinking?

The doubts grew louder and louder until they nearly deafened Isaac. *Do something,* he told himself. *Keep busy.*

Realizing he'd never finished the stall he'd been cleaning when the trouble erupted with Joseph, he headed for the barn. If he kept moving, he wouldn't have to think.

But when he reached the stall he could only stare at the shovel that lay where he'd left it. This was what he did. This was how he handled things. He went on to the next job and did it, and sooner or later, things started to go better.

But somehow he didn't think it was working this time. He couldn't ignore what had happened and hope the trouble would disappear. Joseph. Judith. What was he going to do?

He didn't know. The emptiness inside him sent him to his knees.

Isaac wasn't sure how long he knelt there, struggling to face the truth about himself. About his life. About his love for Judith and his brother.

A board creaked, and he turned, hoping it was Joseph, hoping he could find the words to heal the trouble between them. But it was Onkel Simon, regarding him gravely.

"Isaac? Was ist letz?"

Isaac rose to his feet. "Is Joseph with you?"

"Joseph?" Simon's eyes widened. "No. I haven't seen the boy since we finished the milking this morning. Why?"

Isaac's thoughts stumbled over the words. "I thought . . . I thought sure he was coming to you." All this time, and he didn't know where Joseph was.

As always, Onkel Simon seemed to understand more than you thought possible. He put a hand on Isaac's shoulder. "Tell me what is happening."

"It's Joseph. We quarreled." Usually Joseph would run to Judith, but Judith wasn't here. Judith wouldn't stand between them any longer—that was what she'd said, and Isaac hadn't even thought about what that would mean. "I thought . . ."

But it didn't matter any longer what he'd thought. Judith was gone. Joseph was gone. And he was responsible.

He spun and ran for a horse. Onkel Simon, a few steps behind him, grasped the halter when he brought Blackie out. Isaac readied the harness for the wagon. He'd have to take it. Judith had the buggy.

It was a matter of minutes for them to back the horse between the shafts and then, working in unison, harness him. When Isaac clambered up to the seat, Onkel Simon put one hand on the lines. "Just tell me. Where are you going?"

Isaac tried to make the tight muscles in his

355

throat work. "Joseph has run away. I have to get Judith."

Onkel Simon nodded, face solemn. He stepped back. "Da Herr sei mit du," he murmured.

The Lord be with you. He was going to need it.

CHAPTER NINETEEN

❦

Lancaster County, October 1953

Mattie had been in vehicles before, when going to a wedding or a funeral at a distance, and that time when the ambulance had come for Ben. But the police car wasn't like any of the other cars. The backseat was tiny and cramped, with little room for their feet. The doors didn't have handles, and there was a heavy screen between them and the front seat.

She tried not to shiver outwardly, but inside she knew she was quaking with fear. She didn't dare to look back at the others as the vehicle drove off, because that would surely make her cry.

As they pulled onto the main road, Bishop Thomas spoke quietly in dialect. "Have courage, Mattie. The Lord is with you and will be your protection."

The patrolman shot a glance toward them. "Chief, shouldn't they have to speak English? We don't know what they're saying when they talk that way."

The bishop spoke before the chief could answer. "I am accustomed to saying prayers in my own language. If you insist, I will pray in Englisch instead for our sister Mattie to be delivered from those who persecute her."

Silence, lasting for a long moment.

The chief cleared his throat. "You go ahead and pray however you want to, Bishop Thomas. We don't have a problem with it." The glance he directed at the patrolman was irate.

"Thank you." The bishop's tone was tranquil, as if he hadn't just accused them of being persecutors. He turned to Mattie and switched back to Pennsylvania Dutch. "Don't be frightened. No one will harm you."

Mattie looked down at her hands, clasped tightly in her lap. "When I talked to Rachel about it, I said we should remember Paul and Silas in prison. She said she would pray for me to be delivered like them."

He nodded. "Rachel is growing into a young woman of strong faith."

"But I'm afraid I'm not. I don't think I would be able to praise God in an Englisch jail. I would be too frightened."

"We don't any of us know what we can do until we face a situation," he said. "We must trust that God will give you strength for what lies ahead."

Mattie nodded, hoping her faith and strength would be enough.

"Komm. We'll pray."

He launched into a familiar prayer in German, one from *Christenpflicht*, the prayer book found in every Amish home. The words were familiar and comforting, words she'd used and heard hundreds and hundreds of times, and Mattie began to say them silently in her heart, trying to make them her own petition to the Lord Jesus Christ.

The ride to the jail wasn't long enough, it seemed to her. Too soon they were on the outskirts of town, and then the vehicle pulled up in front of an imposing stone building. Mattie's heart seemed to jump into her throat at the sight of it, and for an instant her head spun.

The bishop's hand closed on her arm. "Have faith, Mattie. Only hold to your faith."

She swallowed hard, trying to cling to the words.

They could not get out until the patrolman opened the door for them. The bishop slid out first and then held out his hand to help her. As she stood, he nodded toward a car that had pulled up behind them—Pastor Colby, with Daad Jonah and Adam. A surge of warmth went through her at the sight, and then the chief had taken her arm and was escorting her toward the entrance.

A small group of people had been gathered around the door, but now they turned and rushed toward her. Several people held notebooks, and one had a camera. They began pelting her with questions, not waiting for one another, their voices turning into a jumble of noise that she was glad not to understand.

The camera appeared in front of her, and the man snapped several pictures, it seemed. She couldn't get away from the camera, not with the chief clutching her arm. She could only duck her head and pray the camera hadn't caught her face.

At a gesture from the chief, the patrolman began pushing people back away from them, and with the chief on one side and Bishop Thomas on the other, they propelled her the rest of the way to the door and through it. The door swung shut behind them, cutting off the relentless noise.

They were in a large lobby, she realized, much like the one at the hospital. Directly in front of them was a high counter with a uniformed policeman sitting behind it.

"I'm afraid you can't come any farther with us, Bishop." Chief Ferguson sounded firm but regretful, as well. Mattie realized that he had welcomed the bishop's presence. Perhaps he had been afraid she would break down if the bishop hadn't been with her.

"I will wait here for the others, then." He nodded toward a bench against the wall and then looked steadily into her eyes. "Have courage, Mattie. The Lord is with you."

She nodded, determined not to make this worse by bursting into tears. Then she turned, moving with the chief through a doorway into the labyrinth beyond the lobby, into the unknown.

Apparently being brought in by the police involved a lot of paperwork. She was asked a number of questions as an officer painstakingly filled out a form with her answers. When she'd finished, another officer appeared, carrying something that looked like a small toolbox. He opened it and put a lined card on the desk in front of her. She looked up at him questioningly.

"Fingerprints," he said loudly, as if she were hard of hearing. "I have to take your fingerprints." He reached for her hand, and she drew back instinctively.

"Enough," the chief said, his voice rasping. "No fingerprints, no photographs."

The man put on a mulish expression. "Regulations say—"

"Forget it," Chief Ferguson snapped, seeming at the end of his patience. "I've been pushed around by politicians for weeks now, and enough is enough. We don't need to trouble Mrs. Lapp with fingerprints and photos. Time enough for that once the hearing is over, if necessary."

Apparently the anger in his voice was convincing. The man who had been hovering over her slipped back, closing his little box.

"This way," the chief said, gesturing to her. He

guided her through several more doors and hallways. When he stopped, it was in front of a small cell, empty except for a narrow cot. From somewhere beyond another door, she could hear clattering noises, the sound of women's voices, a snatch of a song and a voice raised in anger.

"This is what's called a holding cell." He opened the door and gestured.

Mattie walked inside, went to the cot, and sat, folding her hands in her lap to stop their trembling. He was going to leave her here. She might never have seen an actual cell before, but she had seen the drawings in the *Martyrs Mirror*, and she knew what they looked like. At least in this one there were no chains, and a bed instead of a heap of straw.

The chief stood in front of her, frowning and ill at ease, as if he wished he were somewhere else. "You're safe here. I have to lock the door, but nobody can get in, and no one will bother you, understand?"

She nodded, clenching her hands together even tighter.

"I'll come back and get you when it's time to go to the hearing. I promise I'll come myself." He hesitated, started to turn away, and then turned back. "Look, it's not my place to advise you, but if you don't back down when you go in front of the magistrate, he'll sentence you to jail. You know that, right?"

"Ja . . . yes. You explained." Mattie used her words sparingly, afraid of losing control if she spoke too much.

"Then you'll have to be fingerprinted and photographed. You'll be searched. And I'll have to put you in with the general female population." He jerked a nod toward the door beyond which the voices came. "I'll be honest with you— I don't want to do it, but I won't have a choice."

Was he asking her forgiveness? She wasn't sure.

"I understand."

He blew out an exasperated breath. "Just give way. Nobody expects you to carry the burden of this fight. Let the men do it. Their shoulders are broad enough. Just pay the fine and go home to your children. Obey the law until it's changed."

She didn't speak. What was there to say? The Leit hadn't sought out this battle.

Finally he shrugged. He went out, and the cell door clanged shut behind him. Shut and locked, leaving her alone.

Mattie looked around at the bare stained walls, at the metal bars, at a high window in the opposite wall covered with a heavy grate. A shudder went through her.

She tried to project her thoughts back the way they'd come, back to the lobby where by this time Daad Jonah and Adam would be waiting with the bishop. She tried to feel their presence. Tried to feel the Lord's presence. But she couldn't. Like Jonah in the belly of the whale, she was alone.

One thing Judith could say for Barbie—she was never at a loss for words. She'd seemed to realize from the moment of her arrival at the farm-stay that Judith was in no mood to talk, and she had easily filled in the gap with her chatter while they worked together around the house, making the beds and putting out fresh towels. Now they washed dishes together, and she was still talking.

"I told Rebecca that I think retired couples make the easiest guests," she was saying now, referring to the current visitors. "Look at these two couples. They came down to breakfast right on time, and now they've taken off on their own to go sightseeing. All I had to do was give them a map and a few suggestions, and they were off for the day."

Some response seemed needed. Judith rubbed a plate dry with unnecessary vigor. "They seem very nice. Polite and friendly."

She hadn't had much to do with them, since, as Barbie said, they were willing to entertain themselves. And Barbie's bubbling personality made folks turn to her naturally, rather than to Judith.

"They'll be back later this afternoon," Barbie continued, up to her elbows in hot, sudsy water. "The men want to try their hand at milking.

Rebecca's brother will take care of that, so we don't have to deal with it. He's gotten wonderful gut at explaining farmwork to the Englisch."

Judith discovered that if she focused the upper level of her thoughts on Barbie's chatter, she could ignore the fear and pain that lurked beneath. "Are we supposed to do something with the wives then?"

"If they seem at loose ends. Rebecca says when they start wandering around the house like they're looking for something, it's time to suggest an idea." Barbie put another plate in the drainer and attacked a baking pan. "Rebecca is much better than she thinks she is at taking care of the guests. She was tongue-tied that first weekend, she says."

Ignoring the temptation to comment that Barbie didn't suffer from that, Judith considered the bigger problem. "What are we supposed to do with the women?"

"We could take them over to the workshop and show them Matt's furniture." Rebecca's intended ran a handcrafted furniture business in what had been intended for a stable. "We might even sell something."

Judith managed a noncommittal sound at the idea. Was she even going to get through the day? And what was she going to do when it was over and time to go home? That seemed even worse.

Judith had never felt so tired and discouraged in her life. She gripped the counter edge, willing herself not to give in to the weakness.

"That's that," Barbie said, taking the towel from Judith's hand. "Now you're going to sit down and have a mug of tea. The water's already hot, and there's nothing else needs doing right at the moment."

While she was talking, Barbie was bringing the water back to a boil and pouring it into a mug.

"Now, just sit." She gently pushed Judith into a chair and plunked the mug in front of her. "I'm going to the phone shanty to check for messages." She hesitated, frowning at Judith. "When I get back, you can tell me about whatever is wrong, if you want. If not . . . well, that's okay, too. I might not be as wise as Rebecca or Grossmammi, but I can listen."

Before Judith could find something to say, her cousin had whisked out the door.

So, she hadn't been doing as well as she'd thought in hiding her feelings. That wasn't so surprising, since she felt as if she'd been battered with a board. Propping her elbows on the table, Judith buried her face in her hands.

Where did she go from here? Somehow, she had to find the strength she needed so desperately.

One thing was certain—she couldn't keep trying to be a buffer between Joseph and Isaac. She'd spent what seemed the past year trying,

365

and she had failed. The two of them were further apart than ever, and it seemed she could do nothing about it.

Isaac would have to find his own way to deal with his brother, just as Joseph must. That disastrous scene this morning had convinced her more than any words of advice possibly could. She loved them both so dearly, but she couldn't change them. The weight of it seemed to crush her heart.

Judith blotted away a tear and took a gulp of the hot tea to ease her tight throat. There. Crying would not help. Nor would feeling sorry for herself.

The letters she'd been reading slid into her thoughts. Mattie must have had the same feelings she did. Mattie had struggled with grief and denial and the sense that she had been unfairly burdened. But she'd found the courage to do what was right when her tribulation came. Surely Judith's problems were small compared to Mattie's.

A buggy coming down the lane jerked her to attention. Quickly she patted away any trace of tears and rose, moving to the door.

It wasn't a buggy. It was a wagon, with Isaac driving. Her heart turned over. Something was wrong—Isaac would never have come unless someone needed her. The kinder—

By the time she reached the porch, Isaac was

jumping down. She flew to him, her heart pounding.

"What is it? What's wrong? Is one of the kinder hurt?"

The face he turned to her was so grave that it terrified her. "The boys are fine. It's Joseph. Judith, is Joseph here?"

"Here?" She stared at him blankly. "Of course he's not. Why would he come here?"

"I thought he would come to you." He stared at the house, as if expecting Joseph to appear.

"Isaac, you're not making sense. What has happened?"

He turned his face away from her. He wasn't going to answer. He was going to shut her out, as he did so often.

The muscles in Isaac's neck stood out like cords. His jaw clenched, but then finally he spoke. "After you left, we kept arguing. We both said things to each other, hateful things. My little brother has run away, and it's my fault."

Her heart seemed to jump against her ribs, but she had to stay calm. If steady, responsible Isaac was falling apart, it was her job to strengthen and support him.

She struggled to speak gently. "What makes you think Joseph ran away? Surely he wouldn't be so foolish . . ."

That thought died. For all his size, in some ways Joseph was still just a boy.

"He said he would leave. That I wouldn't have to think about him any longer." Isaac rubbed his palms on his face. "I thought he was going to Onkel Simon's. I thought he'd be all right. But he didn't go to Simon, and he didn't come to you. He's run away."

"He'll come back—" she began, but Isaac shook his head.

"You didn't see his face. He's gone. My parents entrusted him to my care, and I've let them down." His voice shook with emotion. "I can't even think where he might be. Would he go to Fred Yoder? I could go to the mill, ask Fred to help."

It was a measure of how desperate Isaac was that he would consider asking Fred for help, Judith knew. "It's possible, I guess, but I don't think so. He'd be bound to realize that Fred wouldn't hide him from you."

"Then where?"

It hit her, quite suddenly. That day in the garden, talking to Joseph, hearing about his secret hiding place up in the woods. She'd nearly forgotten it with everything that had happened since then.

She started to speak and then closed her lips. If she told Isaac, if he went there and found Joseph, Joseph would know she'd revealed his secret. Would Isaac handle it wrong and make matters worse? If she went herself—

The truth hit Judith like a blow. She was doing it again. She was trying to intervene, to come between them and settle their struggles for them. Hadn't she just told herself how wrong that was?

She took a deep breath, trying to calm the thudding of her heart. The choice was clear, wasn't it? She had to trust that this would turn out the way God intended if only she did what was right.

"I know where he might be." Her voice sounded strange to her. "He told me once he has a place where he goes when he needs to be alone and quiet. It's up in the woods beyond the pastures."

Isaac grabbed her hands as if he'd pull the words out of her. "Where? Where exactly is it?"

"He said he built a little lean-to out where the log drag crosses the old railroad bed. Do you know it?"

Isaac didn't bother to answer. He climbed to the wagon, picking up the lines. He'd forgotten about her entirely, it seemed, and the pain pierced her heart.

He seemed to freeze, staring down at the leather straps. Then he turned and held out his hand to her. "Come with me."

Blinking back tears, she reached for him. Stopped. "The work—the guests—"

"Go." Barbie's voice had both of them turning to stare. She had come out of the phone shanty. How long had she been standing there, and they hadn't even noticed? "Go," she called again. "I can take care of everything here. Just go."

Isaac's fingers closed on Judith's in a firm, strong grip, and he nearly lifted her up to the seat beside him. He released the brake and slapped the lines. "We'll go. Please God, we'll find him."

Judith gripped the seat as Isaac steered the horse in a rough circle over the grass to head back down the lane. *Please, God.* She repeated the words in her mind. *Please, God.*

CHAPTER TWENTY

Lancaster County, October 1953

Mattie wasn't sure how long she had been sitting on the hard cot, waiting. At some point, a woman came in with a tray containing tomato soup, soda crackers, and a glass of juice. Mattie feared the crackers would choke her, but she drank the juice thirstily and settled down to wait some more.

She focused her mind on prayers at first, reciting in her mind all those prayers she remembered from childhood on. Then she began telling herself silently the story of Paul and Silas. God had sent an angel to rescue them, but nonbelievers thought it was an earthquake. Would God send someone to rescue her?

The door rattled again, and this time it was the chief. He unlocked the door of the cell. "It's about time to head for the magistrate's office. I thought you might want to stop in the ladies' room and um, freshen up before we go."

At her nod, he led her into another long hallway, stopping at a restroom door. "I'll wait here. Take your time."

It seemed he wasn't afraid she would try to climb out the window. Mattie almost managed a smile at the thought. Luckily the room was empty. She didn't want to face any more curious gazes at the moment.

Chief Ferguson was waiting when she emerged. "Down here. Please don't stop to talk to anyone on the way."

She couldn't imagine whom he thought she would talk to, but when they came into the lobby, she saw that Daad Jonah and Adam were there, as well as several of the other Amish fathers. Meeting Adam's gaze, she struggled to smile. She couldn't quite manage it, but she nodded as she passed, watching his familiar figure as long as she could.

Once again, there were people—reporters, apparently—waiting outside. Even more of them than when she'd gone in. A second police officer joined them and led Mattie to a waiting car. The police seemed able to ignore the shouted questions, and she tried to do the same.

But one lodged in her mind and stuck there. *Why are you doing this, Mrs. Lapp?*

For an instant she longed to answer—wanted to explain their beliefs and try to make people understand. But what good would it do? Most folks seemed to have already made up their minds.

The ride was a short one to a building a few blocks away. She found she was peering out the window at the street behind them, searching for Daad Jonah and Adam. If they didn't reach the hearing—well, if they didn't, she would have to go on alone. She could do it. But she would rather know that they were there, supporting her. Loving her.

Once again the car was parked, this time at the rear of a building, making her think the police wanted to avoid any possible reporters in the front. Mattie was led by what seemed a very circuitous route through the building.

Finally they stopped in front of a door with a pane of frosted glass. A card posted next to the door identified it: *Magistrate's Court Number One. Theodore Ransom presiding.* Mattie puzzled over it for a moment before deciding that Theodore Ransom must be the magistrate who was in charge of the hearing.

The police officer tried the door, found it unlocked, and led the way inside, with Mattie and Chief Ferguson following.

Mattie wasn't sure what image had been in her

mind of the hearing room—something vast and intimidating, she supposed. This room wasn't all that large; it was more like the room where they'd met with the school board in the new school building than anything else. At one end stood a high desk, rather battered-looking but flanked by flags on either side.

"Over there." Chief Ferguson touched Mattie's elbow, directing her to a small table placed at one side of the room. There was a matching table on the opposite side. "We'll sit here." He gestured to several chairs behind the table. "The district attorney will sit at the other table."

Two rows of chairs faced the front, but as Mattie settled herself in the padded wooden chair, a man came in carrying a stack of metal folding chairs, which he began setting up behind the existing rows.

"Looks as though they expect a full house," the chief muttered. He didn't look very happy about it. "They'll start letting other people in soon."

What other people? she wanted to ask, but she decided silence was a better option. A row of high windows let shafts of afternoon sunlight into the room, and they fell in neat squares on the opposite wall. The windows were rather dirty, making her wonder whose job it was to climb up there and clean them.

The door opened, admitting several men with notebooks. One had a camera, which was promptly taken by a police officer who followed him in. "No pictures," he said firmly. "You can pick this up when you leave."

At least she wouldn't have to worry about trying to shield her face from the camera. It was nearly as bad, though, to have the reporters staring at her avidly, writing things down in their little notebooks.

Fortunately the next time the door opened, it was to admit a small group of Amish men, led by her father-in-law and Adam. They came across the room to fill in the rows behind her, with Daad Jonah and Adam directly behind.

Mattie glanced at Chief Ferguson, who was staring gloomily at the reporters. "Please . . . may I speak to my family now?"

He looked startled, as if she'd been silent for so long he'd thought she'd forgotten how to talk. "Yeah, sure. Just don't leave your seat."

"I won't." She turned until she could see those behind her, trying not to let tears form in her eyes at their dear faces.

"Are you all right?" Adam kept his voice low. "No one has bothered you?"

"I'm fine." She shot a glance toward the chief, but he wouldn't understand as long as they spoke in Pennsylvania Dutch. "The chief has been very nice and understanding. He wouldn't let them take my picture."

"People say he is a fair man." Daad Jonah gave

him a doubtful glance. "He seems not to like being here."

Maybe he didn't. Certainly he had been kinder to her than she'd expected, and impatient with the other officers. But he'd said that once she was sentenced, he wouldn't have any choice. Mattie's throat tightened, and she swallowed hard.

"Where is Bishop Thomas? I thought he was with you."

"He and Pastor Colby went off a couple of hours ago," Adam said, looking concerned. "He didn't say why, but we thought surely it had to do with the hearing. He did expect to be back by now, I know."

The room was filling up. Soon there would be no chairs left if the bishop did come. Mattie tried not to feel bereft that he wasn't there. A young man approached the table opposite them, opened a briefcase, and sat down. Almost simultaneously, Pastor Colby arrived and took the chair next to her at the table.

"You don't mind, do you, Chief? I'll act as Mrs. Lapp's advisor until her bishop arrives."

Chief Ferguson nodded. "Fine by me. But if the magistrate objects, you'll have to move."

Adam was leaning forward, his hand on the back of Mattie's chair. She could feel the brush of his fingers and the warmth of his hand, and they seemed to comfort her. "Where is the bishop? I thought he was with you."

"He was. Don't worry, he'll be here. I left early so I could join you in case you need someone to explain what's going on."

Mattie wanted to ask where they'd been, but that would probably sound officious. Obviously two busy men like the bishop and Pastor Colby had other matters to attend to besides her.

"That's interesting," the minister murmured. "The district attorney apparently isn't coming himself this time." He nodded toward the young man across from them, who was riffling through papers. "He looks like the most junior attorney in the office to me."

The magistrate arrived, waving away a reporter who tried to ask a question and hurrying to the tall desk, where he slid onto a chair and scrutinized the papers that lay in front of him.

"I thought he would wear a robe," Mattie murmured, eyeing the man's dark suit and bright red tie.

"This is much less formal than being in court." Pastor Colby sounded confident, as if he'd been in this situation often, instead of what she hoped would be once in a lifetime for her. "You don't have to be afraid. Just answer any questions he asks you."

She nodded, wondering what he would ask. Would he care why the Amish believed as they did? Probably not, if he was the one who'd sent the others to jail.

The magistrate rapped on the desk with his knuckles. The conversation died, and he glanced around as if he were irritated by the whole business. His glance lit on the young man at the opposite table.

"Well, now, it looks as if we have a substitute today. Where's our esteemed district attorney? I thought he was pursuing this cause himself. Caught a cold?"

For some reason, several people tittered at that question, and Mattie saw one reporter elbow another one.

The young man rose, his fair skin flushing as he spoke. "I don't think . . . I mean, Mr. Whittaker directed me to take today's case."

The magistrate glanced at Mattie and seemed amused. "I think I can see why. All right, let's get on with it." He shuffled through the papers again. "Mrs. Mattie Lapp?"

Pastor Colby nudged her. "You should stand while he asks questions."

She rose. "I am Mattie Lapp." Her voice quavered a little, and the reporters wrote furiously.

The man seemed to focus on her, and she thought his expression softened slightly. "Have the charges against you been explained to you, Mrs. Lapp?"

"Ja . . . yes, they have."

He frowned down at the paperwork again. "Did you receive a notice this summer, telling you when school started and what school your daughter, Rachel Lapp, was to attend?"

"Yes." She pressed her fingertips on the edge of the table in front of her, glad it was there.

"Did you keep your daughter, Rachel Lapp, at home instead of sending her to school?"

"Yes, I did."

He stopped looking at the papers and looked at her instead. "I am fining you twenty-five dollars for willful violation of the school code. If you agree to send your daughter to school as assigned from this time forward, the matter is ended. Do you so agree?"

Her heart beat so loudly that surely everyone in the room could hear it. All she had to do was agree, and then she could go home and be with her children.

She took a deep breath. "No, I do not agree."

It seemed to Mattie that everyone exhaled at the same time. The young lawyer rose. "The state requests jail time in this case of willful defiance of the law."

The magistrate stared at him with what was surely a look of distaste. But he would have no choice, would he?

"Very well. I sentence you, Mattie Lapp, to serve—"

The door into the hearing room swung open, and several people entered quickly, one after the other, as if racing to be first. Confused, Mattie stared at them. Those were people from the school board, including Mr. Graham, the president, along with the teachers from the small school her children attended. And then the bishop came in.

Bishop Thomas moved toward the group of Amish and sat down in the back row, while the other people went to the table where the attorney watched them, startled. Another person entered, sliding into a chair near the door. It was Mrs. Graham. For an instant their eyes met, and the woman nodded.

"What is happening?" Daad Jonah whispered. "What are they doing?"

"Settling things, I hope," Pastor Colby said.

Muttered conversations ensued at the attorney's table. Were they disagreeing? Mattie couldn't be sure.

Then abruptly the conversation seemed to be over. Everyone either found a chair or stood against the back wall.

"Well?" The magistrate's face had reddened. "If you're all quite ready to proceed . . ."

The attorney stood, looking flustered and uncertain. "The district attorney's office has been informed that the school board is withdrawing its request. Therefore the state is dropping all charges."

Mattie wasn't sure she'd heard what she thought she had. What did it mean?

The magistrate rapped on his desk, muttering something she couldn't hear. When silence had been restored, he spoke. "Now that you've wasted the time of the court system and the taxpayers' money, maybe someone would like to explain."

Walter Graham rose to his feet, his face flushing at the reprimand. "The board apologizes for the inconvenience. We are . . . pleased to announce that we have reached a temporary agreement with the Amish community. We will allow ninth-grade students to complete their schoolwork at home with their families under the supervision of the school district."

A babble of conversation broke out, silenced once again by the irritable rapping on the table. "Come to order, please," the magistrate barked. "Mrs. Lapp, the charges against you have been dropped. The fine is rescinded. You're free to go, and you have my apologies for the difficulty you have undergone."

Mattie felt dazed. Excited voices sounded around her, but she couldn't seem to make out what they were saying. Then Adam's hands closed on her shoulders, steadying her.

"It's all right," he murmured, his voice close to her ear. "It's over. You can go home. Mattie, do you understand?"

She nodded, looking up at him. "I know I can go home, but I don't understand how this happened. Why did they change their minds?"

"Does it matter? The important thing is that it's over. You don't have to be afraid."

Mattie looked around. Pastor Colby was openly jubilant; Bishop Thomas appeared quiet but satisfied. The school board president looked as if he wished he were somewhere else. Mrs. Graham came up and spoke to him, and he nodded.

Then the Englisch woman glanced across the room. Her gaze met Mattie's again, and a silent message seemed to pass between them.

Mattie knew. Even if they never spoke of it, she knew that somehow, Mrs. Graham had interceded on the side of peace and understanding.

Adam's hand was warm on her elbow as he turned her away from the reporters who were headed in their direction. "You won't want to talk to them, ain't so? Let's go home."

When Isaac and Judith reached home, Isaac drove straight past the house and on toward the barn and beyond it, leaving the lane behind and jolting over the field. Clinging to the seat as she rocked dangerously, Judith looked at Isaac, and the cautioning words died on her tongue. His face was so determined and so solemn that she couldn't speak.

They'd nearly reached the woods when the wheels ran into such soft earth that the horse couldn't go on. Setting the brake and looping the lines, Isaac jumped down. As she started to follow, he lifted her and swung her to the ground. He seized her hand and started up the path into the woods.

Judith hurried along, trying to keep up with his long, rapid strides. Their feet scuffed through the remnants of seasons' worth of fallen leaves, and the trees here were tall enough to form a canopy over their heads.

She was winded by the time they reached the level, cleared ground that marked the old railroad bed. She tugged on Isaac's hand.

"If he's there, hurrying isn't going to matter," she gasped. And if he wasn't . . . She didn't want to think about that possibility. They could both imagine what might happen to an Amish fourteen-year-old out in the wider world with little experience of its dangers.

"Sorry." Isaac finally looked at her as if he was seeing her. "You're right. I just—" He stopped, the tiny muscles around his eyes twitching with stress.

"I know. You want to find him. So do I." *Please, Lord Jesus, keep him safe.* "I'm all right. Let's go on."

He nodded and set off at a more reasonable pace on the level railroad bed that curved around the side of the mountain. The railroad had been abandoned years ago, the tracks removed, even the ties gradually picked up and used for other purposes. Only the level ground remained, carpeted with grass that managed to push up through the bed of cinders and gravel that marked where the rails had once been.

They'd picked blackberries here not long ago, the wild brambles seeming to like the edges of the rail bed. The boys had loved the excursion into the woods, and Joseph had promised to help them build a fort up here when they were a little older.

Joseph. Her heart clenched. He was so good with the younger ones, and they loved him so. She could only pray that some good would come out of Isaac's fear for his brother.

Their feet crunched along softly, an accompaniment to her prayers. They arrived at a spot where the ground fell away more sharply on the down-hill side, and the woods were open enough to glimpse the stream below.

"It's not far now." Isaac kept his voice soft. "Will you let me speak to him first?"

Will you, not *I will.* She was too startled to answer for a moment, and she was almost afraid to speculate as to what it meant. "Of course," she said, equally quiet.

He clasped her hand briefly, and then they went on. Another curve in the path, and she spotted the old log drag, slanting diagonally downward on the hillside above them. When the woods had been logged, the logs had been dragged down a natural crease in the hillside, deepening it with their passage. It was still visible, even though young trees had started to sprout in the soft earth.

Judith's heart thudded. They would come within sight of Joseph's lean-to at any moment. If he was there, would he run when he spotted them?

And there it was. He'd made a good job of the building, cutting thick posts to form the front. The covering logs had been lashed together to form a fine roof.

Joseph was there. An old blanket lay on the ground. He sat on it, bending forward, his face in his hands, his whole body in an attitude of abject misery.

Judith longed to rush to the boy and gather him into her arms, but she obeyed the pressure of Isaac's hand. She let him go on alone, but she felt as if he took her heart with him.

Isaac's approach was quiet, and Joseph didn't look up until he'd nearly reached him. Joseph's eyes widened and he braced himself, but Isaac sank down to sit next to him on the blanket. Elbows on his knees, Isaac appeared to focus on his hands, linked in front of him.

"You found me." Joseph's tone was so flat that Judith had no idea what he was feeling. She moved a few steps closer, as cautious as if she approached a deer in the woods.

Nodding, Isaac turned toward his brother

slowly. "I had to. I have to tell you something—something I've never told to anyone."

Clearly Joseph hadn't been expecting that from his brother. His expression lost a bit of its wariness. "What is it?"

Isaac took a deep breath and let it out. Judith couldn't see his face, but she could still sense his pain.

"Maybe I should have talked to you more about the family all this time. I guess I got in the habit of not saying anything, because it hurt too much to remember." He shook his head. "That's not a very gut excuse."

"I . . . I always wondered about them. About why you couldn't talk about them." Joseph's voice wavered a little.

"Ja." Isaac rubbed his forehead. "That last day, Mamm had had a birthday party for me. You were not even a year yet—too young to understand—but you laughed and clapped at the cake and the excitement."

Judith had never heard that either, and she clutched the image to her heart—the family laughing around the table, the birthday cake and simple gifts, Isaac's young face relaxed and beaming.

"Somebody—one of the onkels, I think—made some comment about Daad having to start looking for a farm for me before too many years passed. I guess I must have looked funny at that, maybe because I'd never pictured living any-where else."

He wouldn't have, would he? This land, the farmhouse—that would have been most of his world then.

"Anyway, after everyone had gone and Daad and I were doing the chores together, he brought it up. Explained that he wouldn't be ready to retire to a grossdaadi haus yet when I'd probably be starting a family, so he'd saved up to buy a farm for me. He wanted to be sure everyone was taken care of. The girls would marry, and he'd help with whatever they needed, and then by the time you were grown, he and Mamm would be ready to let you and your family take over the farm." Isaac paused, and Judith realized that had probably been the very last conversation he'd ever had with his father.

Her heart twisted. No wonder it had had such a profound effect on him all these years.

Joseph made an instinctive move back. "If you're saying this so—"

"Wait." Isaac put a hand on his shoulder. "I want you to understand why I've felt the way I did. All I could see was that what Daad told me on the last night of his life had to be done. I've been so intent on it that I couldn't see anything else. Not until I realized I could lose the very person I was doing it for if I didn't change." His voice was rough with emotion.

Joseph seemed to struggle, his face working as he fought to hold back tears. "I don't want to go away. I just want to do what I love."

Isaac nodded, his hand still on his brother's shoulder. "Ja. I see that you have to be free to follow your own gifts. But the farm is always here, and the farm is always your home, no matter what you do. All right?"

For an instant no one moved. Then Joseph flung himself into his brother's arms. Isaac held him tightly, his head bowed over Joseph's. Judith wiped tears from her cheeks, thankfulness filling her heart.

Without letting go of his brother, Isaac held out his hand to her. She ran to them, her heart full, dropped to her knees, and put her arms around both of them.

CHAPTER TWENTY-ONE

Lancaster County, October 1953

It was not exactly a celebration, but somehow people gathered at Mattie's house that evening, relieved and eager to hear exactly what they could expect from the school district now in the wake of that surprising agreement.

Mamm Becky and Rachel kept urging food on

Mattie, as if she had been starved for days. Knowing it was an expression of love, Mattie took their hovering as best she could. She finally deflected them by suggesting that all these people might need coffee. Recalled to her usual hospitality, Mamm Becky scurried off to start a pot and slice up the pies, cakes, and breads that had apparently been arriving all day as word had spread of her arrest.

By the time the stream of buggies slowed, the farmhouse was filled to the bursting point. People kept asking Mattie questions, but she didn't seem to have any answers. All she really understood was that she had faced imprisonment and the Lord had rescued her. Maybe it hadn't been as dramatic as the angel breaking open the cell doors for Paul and Silas, but she could see God's hand at work.

"Komm, settle, everyone." The bishop spoke in Englisch, in deference to Pastor Colby, who had come in at Bishop Thomas's insistence. "We will try to explain what has happened and how our sister Mattie came to be delivered."

Mattie was standing back against the wall with Mamm Becky and Rachel, and she could feel herself flush as every eye turned toward her. It wasn't usually the bishop's way to single anyone out, and she'd have been wonderful glad to escape it this time. After experiencing the stares of so many strangers this day, she was ready to hide even from the attention of those she knew best.

Adam, standing silently against the door, met her gaze. He gave her a reassuring smile that somehow helped her stand up to the scrutiny. He had been there throughout the ordeal, quiet and steady, thinking only of her. How did she begin to thank him for his faithfulness?

Leaning back in his chair, Bishop Thomas looked tired but pleased. Some of the lines that had marked his face in recent weeks seemed to have smoothed out, despite his fatigue. He waited until silence fell.

"I know it wonders you how we got to where we are today," he said. "We would not have such a happy resolution to our problems with the school district if it were not for the help of our Englisch friends." He nodded gravely toward Pastor Colby.

It seemed to Mattie that the young pastor, who'd been so confident in the difficult surroundings of the court, was now a bit ill at ease, perhaps feeling that here he was the outsider.

"You know that we've been trying to come up with a plan that would satisfy the school laws but still allow us to keep to our ways," Bishop Thomas said. "It seems best for the future that we have our own schools, so that families have control over what our kinder are taught. But that takes time, and a quick resolution was needed for today's problem." His face tightened. "I should have been more aware of what was coming. Then this might have been avoided."

Pastor Colby cleared his throat. "I'm not sure even that would have helped. We wanted to find common ground, but there were some who were so sure of the rightness of their cause that perhaps it took something shocking to change them."

He paused, and the bishop nodded for him to continue.

"I confess that I, as a school board member, was ignorant of the particular needs of the Amish children in our district until the struggle escalated. The night when so many of you attended the board meeting opened my eyes, and maybe the eyes of others on the board. We should have acted more quickly then, but it took some time just to rally together. I think most of us had no idea the issue would reach the point that parents were arrested for doing what they considered right for their children."

Strange, that none of them had been able to foresee it, Mattie thought. With the memory of young Amish men forced into conscientious objector camps far from home so fresh in their minds, they should have.

"In any event, once I and a few others began talking about finding a solution, we realized that part of our problem came from the fact that we were a new, consolidated board, with members who were far removed from the small, local boards it replaced. When we seemed to reach a stalemate, it occurred to me that former members of that local board might be helpful, and so they were. I believe that when they began lodging their concerns with the new board, people listened."

Several heads around the room nodded at that point. Most of them knew the members of the old board—farmers, for the most part, people like themselves who understood more of Amish ways.

"People of good will can find a common ground," Bishop Thomas said. "But it takes time and patience."

Pastor Colby nodded, seeming to regain his confidence as he spoke. "I believe Walter Graham was already beginning to have doubts about his position, but pride made it difficult to back down. Then Mrs. Lapp was arrested." He glanced toward her, and again Mattie felt like shrinking into a corner. Rachel put her arm around her mamm's waist, and the simple gesture reminded Mattie to be strong for her children.

"I'm sure this was a terrible experience for Mrs. Lapp," he went on, "but I believe it was pivotal in changing minds. The image of a young Amish widow being taken into the jail by police officers brought an outpouring of criticism from people who had remained silent until then, prompting a change of heart."

People who had remained silent until then. Pastor Colby was speaking of Mrs. Graham, even though he didn't know. And Mattie wouldn't tell him. Mrs. Graham wouldn't like it. She had acted quietly, behind the scenes, and Mattie felt sure she was content.

"And so we reached a settlement," Bishop Thomas said. "Thanks be to God."

There was a moment of respectful silence before a question was raised.

"What exactly does it mean that the fourteen-year-olds must study at home under the district's supervision?" The questioner was Josiah Kile, one of those who had served his days in jail already. "Are we going to have someone looking over our shoulders all the time?"

Bishop Thomas and Pastor Colby seemed to defer to each other for a moment, and then the Englischer answered. "I don't know exactly, but I've received a promise that the details will be worked out with the help of Bishop Thomas and the district's ministers. I think most likely the students will have to report to a teacher every week or two about what they're learning."

"My thinking is that a scholar who is learning to run a dairy farm or working with a seamstress might be expected to tell about their jobs or keep a journal," Bishop Thomas added. "That seems reasonable to me."

That seemed to satisfy Josiah, and Mattie exchanged glances with Rachel. She would be able to do what she'd always planned, then.

Pastor Colby smiled. "Someone expressed concern that the young people be educated so that they would not become a burden to the taxpayers." His smile widened. "I've learned enough in recent weeks to assure them that no Amish person, educated or not, has *ever* become a burden to the public in the history of the county. That seemed to satisfy them."

It was a truth so evident to every Amish person in the room that it was difficult to imagine others not understanding. The Amish took care of their own. That would never change, no matter how the world changed around them.

There were a few more questions, a little more talk, but finally people seemed satisfied. They began to drift away, many pausing to squeeze Mattie's hand or whisper a word of affection. She was almost too tired to respond. It had begun to seem as if this day had lasted forever.

But when everyone was gone and the kinder were safely asleep in their own beds, Mattie felt herself at loose ends. There was something yet to be said, yet to be done, and she knew very well what it was.

She stepped out onto the back porch, letting the light from the kitchen pour out onto the worn boards. Adam was there, sitting in the porch swing, waiting, as she'd known he would be. She went and sat beside him, as sure as a horse headed back to its familiar stall after a long journey.

"It's over now," he said, just as he had done in the magistrate's court. "You don't have to worry."

"I know." She closed her eyes briefly, searching for the right words to say. She had hurt Adam when she turned down his proposal of marriage, and she'd misread his feelings, just as she'd misread her own. Now she had to find the courage to make the first move.

"You have been such a gut friend through all of this trouble." It was true, but it wasn't enough. She could feel him waiting, patient as always. "I . . . I was wrong to dismiss your feelings that day when we stood beneath the willow tree."

She glanced toward the tree, unable to see it in the dark but knowing it was there, just as she always knew that Adam was there.

"My feelings are the same now as they were that day." He seemed to make an effort to speak lightly, but his voice roughened on the words. "I shouldn't have rushed things, but I was afraid for you."

Afraid. How often had she been afraid? Afraid she couldn't manage on her own, afraid to try something new because she might fail, afraid even to trust her own feelings.

She had been afraid when she'd stood in the court that day, but God had given her the strength to do what was right. Surely that courage might carry over to this moment, when it meant so much.

Mattie turned, looking up into his face, which

was clear in the light from the kitchen window and so familiar and so dear to her. "I don't want you to marry me because you think I need your help and protection." Somehow the words came out. "There must be a bigger reason."

Relief spread across his face, and his lips curved just a little. "Mattie, Mattie, don't you know yet? I love you. I don't want to marry you just to take care of you. I want us to take care of and love each other for all the years the good Lord gives us."

All her caution fled away at the look in his eyes. He loved her. She loved him. Not in exactly the way she had loved Ben, but she wasn't the same person now that she had been then. She smiled, seeing Ben's dearly loved face in her thoughts. Ben would not feel betrayed. Ben would be happy for them.

"That's gut." She reached up to touch his face, feeling the softness of his beard and the warmth of his skin under her hand. "Because love is too important to waste, and that's what I want, too."

Joy seemed to shimmer between them. Adam bent his head to kiss her—a solemn kiss that began in serious promise and surged into desire. Mattie turned more fully into his arms. She wasn't a shy teenager any longer, and she wouldn't act like one. She was a woman who had found someone to love who loved her.

The kiss ended on a soft chuckle from Adam.

He drew her against him, so that her head rested on his shoulder. "Let's hope the bishop will agree to set a date as soon as possible after Fall Communion."

Mattie put her hand on his chest, feeling the steady beating of his heart. "I think we will be able to convince him."

"He probably knows already." He kissed her temple, his lips warm and inviting. "Bishop Thomas doesn't miss much."

She snuggled closer, feeling his arms tighten around her, strong and secure. "The kinder will be happy. The way they turn to you already—that should have told me that we belonged together."

"I love them," he said simply. "I will try to be the best father I can to them. And to any more babies that come along."

He was thinking as she was, then. She'd been a little concerned, fearing that what had happened to his wife and baby might have made him afraid. They would have children together, and that would be a special joy that wouldn't lessen their joy in the children they already had.

Thinking of kinder made her think of the school situation, and she sighed.

"Regrets already?" Adam teased, catching her mood instantly.

"Never." She touched his lips lightly with hers. "I was thinking that the struggle over how we raise our young ones might not be over yet."

"No, I'm sure it's not." He laid his cheek against her head. "There will be trials ahead. It will never be easy to live Amish in an Englisch world. But whatever comes, we will face it together, ain't so?"

"Together," she said, and it was a promise.

Judith was washing the dishes, and Levi and Paul were squabbling about whose turn it was to dry. She smiled at the familiar complaints. Things were back to normal in their home if the greatest worry was who dried the dishes.

"I know, I know," she said, swatting the dish towel at them. "If you had a sister, you would not have to dry dishes, but since you don't, you will take turns helping. Paul, you know very well it is your turn."

Paul tried to pout, but it turned into a grin. "I was just fooling, Mammi."

She couldn't help returning the smile, even though she knew she should chide him. "Try not to drop anything this time," she said.

"I do try, Mammi. The plates are just so slippery." He picked one up gingerly. "Maybe we could get a girl baby the next time."

"Maybe," Isaac said, laying his newspaper on the table. "In the meantime, it's important for all of us to help Mammi, ain't so?"

Paul nodded, his small face serious under the strength of his father's gaze.

"Gut." Isaac took the dish towel from his hands and gave him a gentle shove. "You two take Noah outside and play with him for a bit before time for bed. I'll help Mammi with the dishes."

She'd been thinking she had to be a little cautious with Isaac and Joseph both after all the emotions of the day, but Isaac, at least, seemed to have his feelings well in hand. Or maybe it would be more accurate to say that he had gained a peace and acceptance she hadn't seen in him for a long time.

A plate slipped in his hand, and he grabbed it, grinning at her when her breath caught.

"Are you sure you know how to dry dishes?" she asked, remembering another day when they'd stood at the sink and she'd felt a closeness to him that had nearly been lost.

"With three sisters, you'd think I'd never have learned, but sometimes I'd help out, especially when Mammi was tired and the girls were small."

He spoke of them so naturally that it startled her. "I . . . I didn't know that about you." *About your family,* she'd nearly said.

"You wouldn't, would you?" He fell silent, staring at the soap bubbles as if they held some secret. "I thought it was safer not to talk about them. Less painful." He shook his head slightly. "I was shutting them out so completely that I'd begun to forget what they were really like. But I don't want Joseph or the other children not to know them. That would be much worse."

Judith's heart was so full of gratitude. It was as if Isaac had been suffering from a terrible illness and was finally beginning to heal. "I'm glad you can talk about them. I want to remember them, too."

He clasped her hand, getting his own covered with suds as he did. "Ach, Judith, I've made so many mistakes. I said a terrible thing to you when I said you were not Joseph's mother. I don't know why I did. I've never believed it, not even when I was saying it. You're the only mother he's ever known, and a much better wife than I deserve."

"Don't, Isaac." She turned toward him, sudsy water from their clasped hands splashing on both of them. "I've tried to be a gut wife and a gut mother, but . . ." She stopped, afraid to go on. "Don't use words like *deserve* between us."

She'd startled him; she could see it in his face.

"All right." He clasped her wet hand in both of his, and his expression grew very serious. "But you must tell me. Is it true that you thought I married you to give Joseph a mother?"

The words nearly rocked her off her feet. The thing she'd promised never, ever to tell him . . . how could he know it? "How did you . . . I mean, why would you . . ."

"Joseph. He must have overheard or misunderstood something. It doesn't matter how. What matters is if you think it."

She couldn't meet his eyes. The only time she'd ever talked about it was that day with Gross-mammi, and Joseph had heard.

"I don't . . . I don't know." She was stumbling over her words, trying to find the courage to be honest. Why couldn't she be brave, as Mattie had been?

"Tell me, Judith." Isaac's hands clasped hers tightly. "I must know."

"People talked, you know." Her voice was flat, almost as if she didn't care, when in reality she cared more than anything. "When you began courting me so suddenly after your aunt passed. You'd been paying attention to Becky Fisher before, and then everything changed."

"Becky Fisher?" He repeated the name as if he hadn't thought of her in years. "I took her home from a singing or two, that was all. She was a pretty girl, but such a blabbermaul. A man would never have a moment's peace with her around."

But he'd noticed how pretty Becky was. And when he'd suddenly switched his attention to quiet, steady Judith, she'd been so happy. But then, she'd started loving him when she was eight and running around the farm with his sister, pestering him.

"That's not all, is it?" When she didn't speak, he shook her hands gently. "Komm, don't make me guess."

She would say it, no matter how much it cost.

"The day we married, I happened to hear Onkel Simon talking to one of the other relatives. He said how responsible you were, and how you'd done right to pick a sensible, serious girl like me instead of chasing moonshine."

"And you thought that meant I had married you to get a mother for Joseph?" He was so frankly incredulous that she had no choice but to believe him. "Didn't you stop to think that I had all the moonshine I wanted in you?"

"I . . . well, maybe it sounds silly to you, but at the time—"

Isaac wrapped his arms around her so tightly that he nearly squeezed the breath out of her. "Ach, Judith, what a ferhoodled notion. I asked you to marry me because I loved you. I think I'd loved you since the days when you were running around the farm with your hair curling out of your braids." He traced a wet finger along her cheek and wrapped it round a curl that had slipped free of restraint.

"You . . . you don't need to squeeze me to death to convince me," she said, happiness bubbling up in her until she seemed filled with it.

Isaac laughed, loosening his grasp just a little, but then his eyes grew serious. "This would not have happened if I'd been open with you from the beginning. I just . . . I got so used to hiding my feelings so I didn't have to feel the pain that I did the same with you."

She leaned against him, loving the feeling of his solid body against hers, of his arms strong around her. "You don't have to chatter all the time, as long as you let me in when it counts."

"Always." He ran his hand down her back. "Always."

The back door rattled. Before they could pull apart, Levi was there, with Joseph and the other boys right behind him.

"Mammi, what—"

Joseph grabbed his shoulders and spun him around, herding them all back out the door. "One more game before bed," he said, laughter in his voice, and the door banged again behind them.

Laughter gurgled up in Judith, and in an instant she and Isaac were both laughing helplessly, clinging to each other. Finally she caught her breath enough to speak. "We shouldn't expect privacy in a house with four kinder, I guess."

"They'll all be asleep sometime," Isaac said, still chuckling. "Maybe then we can try for the little girl dishwasher the boys think we should have."

"Maybe so," Judith responded, trying to keep her tone light despite the happiness that so filled her it seemed about to lift her right off the floor.

"Ach, my Judith." Isaac dropped a kiss on her lips. "You are all the moonshine I want in my life, forever."

EPILOGUE

Laughter and joy seemed to fill the stable at Rebecca's place to the rafters as the community gathered around the tables to celebrate Matt and Rebecca's wedding at the traditional meal. Judith, seated at the Eck, the corner table that was always reserved for the wedding party, could see the happiness on the familiar faces.

"Reminds me of our wedding," Isaac whispered, leaning over from his seat next to her. "I'm glad Rebecca decided to let me sit with you, even though I'm not one of the wedding party."

"She knew I wouldn't be happy otherwise," Judith said. Matt might have a special glow on his wedding day, but as far as she was concerned, her Isaac was the handsomest man here.

Tradition had been bent a little this time, since the bride and groom were older, and one of the newehockers was married. And Rebecca would always do what was thoughtful instead of following custom blindly.

In every other way, though, the wedding had gone off as Amish weddings always did. The lengthy service this morning, with Rebecca, Judith, and Barbie sitting in straight chairs facing

Matthew and his two side-sitters, had been much the same as every other wedding that would be performed this season. The same scriptures, songs, sermons, and prayers had emphasized the gravity of the occasion when a new family was formed in their community.

When the bishop had come to the end of a part of the main sermon, he had looked gravely from Rebecca to Matthew. "Now here are two in one faith," he had said, and their faces had shown that they truly were of one faith. Judith's heart had swelled within her as Rebecca and Matthew stood and held hands before him.

They had both come through many trials before reaching this place, and that made their joy all the sweeter. Judith's thoughts flickered to Mattie, who seemed like such a close friend, even though they'd never met. Mattie and her Adam had gone through trials to come together, too, and when Judith had read of Mattie's wedding in the letters, she'd found herself crying a little—happy tears, but bittersweet because she'd never really know them. Still, they had kept their promises and found their happiness.

Isaac squeezed her hand under the table. "Look at Barbie, flirting again. It's going to catch up to her one of these days."

"She'll run into someone so determined that she'll be married before she has a chance to think twice about it," Judith said, watching as her cousin chattered away to the nearest male, who happened to be one of Matthew's cousins.

"That might be the best way where she's concerned." Isaac craned his neck to glance across the room. "I wish they'd let us help with the serving."

Rebecca, hearing him, leaned across Judith, her cheeks pink and her eyes glowing. "You and Judith did plenty of the work getting ready for the meal. Now it's your chance to sit still and enjoy it. Believe me, there will be plenty of cleanup afterward."

"We'll be ready," he said. "And thank you for asking Joseph to help, too. He's feeling very proud of his responsibilities today."

Judith glanced around the stable, searching for Joseph, and found him carrying a tray in from the wedding trailer that had been set up outside, holding all of the extra utensils needed to feed the hundreds of guests who were present. Joseph did indeed look as if he enjoyed what he was doing, actually pausing to say something, laughing a bit, to a girl who must be about his age.

Their Joseph, getting interested in girls? He was growing up.

Judith met Isaac's gaze, to find that he'd seen the same thing she had. He smiled, shaking his head. "Girls. What next? At least we'll be well broken in by the time our Levi hits his teenage years."

405

"I imagine we'll worry just as much about each one of our kinder."

And especially about the next one, should it turn out to be the little dishwasher they'd joked about. She smiled to herself. She hadn't confided her suspicions to anyone, not even Isaac. Wait until she was sure before she spoke, but if she was right, it would be time to set the cradle up again next summer.

Isaac's gaze was on her face, and his eyes seemed to grow more intent. "Judith? Is there something you should be telling me?"

She could feel the flush growing in her cheeks. She had longed for this sort of closeness with Isaac, and now that she had it, it was so much more than she'd even dreamed of. He almost managed to read her thoughts.

"I wasn't going to say anything, not until I knew for certain."

His hand squeezed hers tightly, and for an instant tears seemed to shine in his eyes. "Nothing would make me any happier than another child to love."

She leaned closer, knowing that no one would hear their words in the clamor of voices that filled the space. "Are you sure? Think about a baby disrupting your sleep, and needing all my attention, and us having to hush the boys when they're noisy."

For just an instant something seemed to startle

him. He looked as if he had seen an image he hadn't expected.

"Isaac?" Her fingers tightened on his.

"It's nothing." He squeezed her hand, his smile growing warm. "I will love every minute of it."

"You looked as if something had shaken you." Her gaze searched his face.

"Ach, I should know I can't keep anything from you, my Judith." His voice softened. "I just suddenly understood something, and I must tell Joseph about it. And you." He looked down at their clasped hands. "That night—the night when folks say I saved Joseph from the fire."

"You did save Joseph," she said quickly.

"I got him out." He paused. "But I just realized, when you spoke of the baby waking us up at night. I woke up because Joseph was crying." He looked at her, his eyes filled with wonder. "If he hadn't, I would never have wakened. I'd have gone under from the smoke, like the others. But he cried, and he woke me. Don't you see? Joseph saved *me* from the fire."

For a moment her heart was too full for speech. Then she stroked his hand gently. "You saved each other," she said. "That was how it was meant to be."

He nodded, holding her hand tightly. They'd saved each other that night. And each of those who loved went on rescuing one another throughout life, saving them from grief, or pain, or doubt, or any of the other perils of living as people of faith in the world. That was always their promise and their joy.

RECIPES

Sticky Buns

Sticky buns are a favorite treat in our area, and they're best served warm from the oven.

1 pkg. yeast, dissolved in ½ cup lukewarm water
2 cups scalded milk, lukewarm
½ cup sugar
1 teaspoon salt
6 cups flour
½ cup butter
½ cup raisins
1 cup brown sugar
extra brown sugar, about 2 cups, as needed
2 teaspoons cinnamon

Add yeast mixture to the warm scalded milk. Stir in sugar, salt, and flour. Shape into a ball and place in greased bowl, turning to grease all sides. Cover and let rise in a warm place until doubled in size, about 2 hours. Meanwhile, melt the butter and soak the raisins in warm water to soften. Prepare 3 9 x 12–inch baking pans by greasing well and sprinkling the bottoms thickly with 1 cup brown sugar.

Once the dough is raised, punch down and roll

out on a floured board to a rectangle 1½ inches thick. May be divided in half for easier handling. Spread with the melted butter, brown sugar, and cinnamon. Drain the raisins and dot over the surface of the dough. Roll up like a jelly roll and cut into 1-inch slices, making 36 to 40 pieces, depending upon the size of the slice. Lay the slices flat in the prepared pans. Sprinkle tops with brown sugar and cinnamon. Let rise until the rolls are doubled in size.

Bake 25 minutes at 375°F.

Shoofly Pie

FOR FILLING:
1½ cups boiling water
1 teaspoon baking soda
1 cup of light or dark molasses

FOR CRUMBS:
4 cups flour
2 cups brown sugar
pinch of salt
1 cup shortening

FOR PLAIN PASTRY:
make or purchase 2 9-inch pastry shells

For filling, mix together the boiling water, baking soda, and molasses.

For crumb layer, mix together flour, brown sugar, and salt. Cut in shortening until crumbs form.

Line 2 9-inch pie tins with pastry. Pour half the filling into each shell. Divide the crumbs and put half in each shell atop the filling.

Bake at 350°F for 35 minutes.

Dandelion Salad

2 quarts of dandelion greens, leaf lettuce, or
    spinach
2 eggs
½ cup sugar
½ cup water
½ cup cider vinegar
¼ pound bacon, fried crisp and broken up
sliced hard-cooked eggs or sliced mushrooms
    (optional)

Wash and drain the greens and place in serving bowl.

For dressing: Beat eggs; add sugar, water, and vinegar. Add to bacon pieces and stir over low heat in a frying pan until the dressing thickens. (Or heat in top of a double boiler, if you prefer.)

Pour the dressing over the greens and add sliced hard-cooked eggs or sliced mushrooms, if desired. Serves 6.

Dear Reader,

The Rescued is the second book in my Amish series Keepers of the Promise, in which three cousins are drawn by their grandmother into helping preserve the story of their Amish family in America. Each book combines a story from the present with one from an important point in the past of the Amish community.

In the fall of 1953, more than one hundred Amish parents were arrested for their refusal to send their fourteen-year-old children to a consolidated high school. This stark fact became the jumping-off point for my story. The writer is faced with a difficult dilemma in creating a novel around a historical event. In order to imagine Mattie's story, I have fictionalized the events, compressing the time period in which they occurred, but I hope I've succeeded in creating the feelings of real people when their beliefs run counter to those of the prevailing culture. The Amish struggle to educate their children as they saw fit took place over many years and finally culminated in a case before the Supreme Court in 1972, which affirmed their rights.

I would love to hear your thoughts on my book. If you'd care to write to me, I'd be happy to reply with a signed bookmark or bookplate and my brochure of Pennsylvania Dutch recipes. You can find me on the Web at martaperry.com, follow me on Facebook at facebook.com/MartaPerryBooks, e-mail me at marta@martaperry.com, or write to me in care of Berkley Publicity Department, Penguin Random House, 375 Hudson Street, New York, NY 10014.

Blessings,
Marta Perry

About the Author

A lifetime spent in rural Pennsylvania and her own Pennsylvania Dutch roots led **Marta Perry** to write about the Plain People who add to the rich heritage of her home state. She is the author of more than fifty inspirational romance novels and lives with her husband in a century-old farmhouse.

Visit the author online at martaperry.com and facebook.com/MartaPerryBooks.

Center Point Large Print
600 Brooks Road / PO Box 1
Thorndike, ME 04986-0001 USA

(207) 568-3717

US & Canada:
1 800 929-9108
www.centerpointlargeprint.com